A Walk In the Dark

By Carol L. Craig

© 2023 by Carol Craig
Published by Ingram Spark
1 Ingram Blvd.
La Vergne, TN, 37086

Printed in the United States of America.

Titles may be purchased in bulk for educational, business, fundraising, or sales promotional use. For more informa-tion, contact Carol Craig @ www.editinggallery.com.

Library of Congress Cataloging-in-Publication Data

Craig, Carol, 2022
    A Walk in The Dark / Carol Craig.
  p. Cm. -- Romantic suspense
    ISBN 978-1-73622227-6-8

Interior Design by Sara Rolat.
Cover design by Darrin Brenner: D. Brenner Art & Design.

Printed in the United States of America
09 10 11 12 13 RRD 7 6 5 4 3

Praise for

A Walk in the Dark

"*A Walk in the Dark* roams on fragile ground. Carol Craig paints a vivid portrayal of love, pain, and vulnerability in the midst of threats, trauma, and secrets. The strong, triumphant characters will leave you wanting more. I love the book! It's a page-turner!"

~**Carmen Peone, award-winning author of *Captured Secrets***

"Only the most ingenious author could meld together into a single plot the Grand Tetons of Wyoming and the forbidding territories of Afghanistan, but that's what Carol Craig does in this inspiring page-turner of a novel. The story is as suspenseful as it is heartwarming, and the characters, both human and canine, are as compelling as they are unforgettable!"

~**Evan Howard, author of *The Galilean Secret***

"Trouble begins in the opening paragraph of Carol Craig's *A Walk in the Dark*. The mysteries follow—a missing grandmother, a forgotten Afghani dog, and threats against the new veterinarian. If not for one good neighbor, a veteran who is trying to heal from his emotional wounds caused by his tour in Afghanistan, Tracy Barnhardt might not survive the continued disasters. This is a story that keeps us turning pages and allows us to experience the joys of community while leading to a happy ending."

~**Jane Kirkpatrick, New York Times Best-selling, Award-winning author of *Beneath the Bending Skies***

"Carol Craig creates another masterpiece as she brings to life the people who live in a remote Wyoming area. The tension and building of each character, along with moments that are riveting, moving, *and* heartwarming, only add to the spiritual elements of A Walk in the Dark. It is one of Carol Craig's best literary masterpieces to date. I couldn't turn the pages fast enough to find out what came next. Brilliant!"

~Karen Hall, author of *Hasonta: The Lost Tribe* and *Jennica's Secret*

"A Walk In The Dark, C.L. Craig's newest romantic suspense, tugs at the heart, draws chuckles and unexpected chills, then keeps the reader guessing to the very end.

This second novel in the Mending Warriors series unfolds in the shadow of Wyoming's majestic Teton Range and continues the story of a ranch dedicated to helping struggling veterans move forward with their lives. Caring for animals is a large part of that process and brings our hero together with the town's new veterinarian, a young woman determined to rehab her own life despite mounting evidence she's purchased property with a dark and dangerous history.

In Craig's signature style, she offers not only stunning imagery, well-developed characters, engaging dialogue and warm humor, but also fascinating insights into the history and geography of her setting and its inhabitants. It's clear the author has undertaken extensive research, and the reader reaps the benefit. A highly recommended read."

~Candace Calvert, best inspirational medical-romance writer of The Mercy Hospital series, The Grace Medical series, and The Crisis Team series

Other Novels by Carol Craig

From The Mending Warrior Series:

A Thousand Bits of Wonderful
A Walk in the Dark

From The Tapestry Fantasy Series:

Dancing the Loom
Threading the Loom

Southern Historical Novels:

The Vast In Between
The Great Unraveling

To all the men, women, and dogs who put their lives on

the line for the country they love.

Wishing you hope for a better future . . .

One

"No, no, no!" Tracy Barnhart pounded the steering wheel with her fist as her 1950s GMC pickup bounced along the ruts of the clearing into the open expanse that fronted the farmhouse.

She put on the brakes and sat back, stunned, as she inspected the homestead that was soon to be hers. The picture she'd seen when she'd purchased the home had clearly hailed from an earlier time, a time before the farmhouse had begun to sag, its porch and overhang having nearly caved in, the white paint dirty and peeling. Worse than that, a rusty washer sat to the right side of the building. Boxes atop it and beside it had long since caved in, their contents leaking onto the ground, the wind causing the lighter belongings to drift, becoming part of the dirt and muck. Off to the right stood a huge red barn.

At least that's still standing.

Tracy parked the old GMC and hopped out to look around, grateful that she'd had the foresight to wear boots. Not ready to face the house quite yet, she decided to first check out the red Gambrel roofed, double-pitched barn, since she would need it for her clinic. Though weathered, it would be perfect for livestock and she could store hay in the loft come wintertime.

Old chipped white paint outlined the front doors, which were rusted shut, so she meandered to a side door frozen on hinges that hadn't seen oil in decades. She pushed and shoved, until it squealed open with a final pop. As her eyes acclimated to the dark, dank interior, she took a step back. Every square inch, from floor to rafter, was filled with junk. Piles and piles of it. But as she stood there, taking it all in, she began to pick out things that made sense. An ancient tractor. Stacks of wood. Oil cans. Off to the side stood an old dresser which could prove useful if she could ever pry it out of this mess. It would take months to sift through everything, and she didn't have months. She would need a place for her large animal hospital and she would need it soon, if she planned to make a living as a veterinarian. In her head she counted up the money she'd saved and sighed. She'd saved enough money to last a year at most. To get this operation off the ground. A year to build a practice. But she hadn't counted on the house's poor condition.

She heard a creak and nearly jumped. In slunk a cat, black and lean, with a bright white diamond at the apex of its nose. It wore one white boot on its front left paw.

2

"So, I've already got one mouth to feed." She absentmindedly bent down and scratched the cat behind its ear. "Well, come on. Let's check out the rest of the damage."

She made her way toward the house, the cat close on her heels. Before stepping up onto the front porch steps, Tracy gauged the safety of the rotting wood. If she was careful, she should be able to make her way inside without falling through the aging floorboards. Steeling herself, she forged ahead. The front door of the dilapidated building opened with only slight trouble, the lock long since gone. To her surprise, the hoarding seemed to be limited to the barn and outdoors. For here, inside the house, though musty and gathering dust, the contents of the home appeared intact as though someone had left for a picnic long ago and had simply forgotten to return.

Suddenly realizing how truly alone she was, Tracy tapped her phone to see if she could receive cell service this far out. Nothing. She trekked outside to check. Still nada. She climbed up on the running boards of her pickup. "Darn." She turned the phone this way and that. The cat meowed as if in sympathy.

"Well, let's take a look at the rest of the place." Tracy tucked her phone away, then bent down to pick up the cat, more for her own sense of security than the cat's, which was clearly a male. She made a quick check of his fur, relieved when she found no fleas. One less thing to worry about.

For the next half hour, Tracy inspected the farmhouse, from the musty basement with its ancient store of preserves, to the large farmhouse kitchen with a view to the Sawtooth Mountains. Beside an antique phone hung an old linen apron with faded red apples. The refrigerator hailed from the sixties, a pale blue Frigidaire, while the white and gold linoleum was worn bare in places. And the stove was one step above the old clawfoot stoves that required sticks of wood to keep them going.

She heaved a sigh. "It'll have to do."

Next she marched up the interior stairwell, relieved to see that at least the stairs were still in good working order. On the top floor, three bedrooms lined the eastern wall of the old building. Fortunately, whoever had owned the house had kept the roof in good shape, so that although it would need patching and probable replacement, no water appeared to be leaking into the top floor of the rickety old farmhouse. Still, she would see to the roof soon.

Now, to stake out her bedroom for the night. She decided on the largest room where she would have a perfect view of the Sawtooths on one side, a view of the barn on the other. That way she could see anyone coming or going down the old dirt road. The bed appeared to be queen sized and sported a dirty old chenille bedspread, pink, her least favorite color, but in here, it actually seemed rather pretty. It brightened up the faded wallpaper, which would be the first thing to come down. A trip to the store was in order to pick up fresh paint for the entire house, inside and out. Locating a handyman would be her next order of business. Fortunately, she had thought to bring a generator with her, just in case.

"Okay, little guy, let there be light." The cat meowed as if he understood perfectly.

For the next few hours, Tracy tore into the house. First,

4

she got the electricity going. Next, she found the cistern and began pumping water. That done, she went inside and dug out her broom and vacuum cleaner, along with a plethora of cleansers and dusting sprays. She spent the rest of the day scrubbing, until she was so tired she could hardly move. But no matter how hard she scrubbed, she couldn't get the rings of rust out of the sinks and toilet from years of hard water. Maybe she could find something in town for that as well. In the meantime, she needed food. The idea of cooking felt overwhelming. Instead, she dug out some crackers and peanut butter along with a decidedly borderline looking banana and munched on it, throwing the cat little tidbits along the way.

"Well, I guess I had better give you a name."

The cat meowed.

"I suppose I could call you Boots, even though you have only one boot. Not too original, but you can't expect much from a girl after working all day, so Boots it is." She lifted the cat off the chair next to the kitchen dinette and wandered into the living room where she plopped down into a dusty rose colored recliner, the cat on her lap.

Across from her, along the far wall, hung an oval mirror. In it was a person she hardly recognized. Her wavy chestnut hair was in disarray and she had smudges of dirt on her cheek and chin. Her red-and-white flannel shirt appeared rumpled and was covered in bits of debris from all the nooks and crannies she'd cleaned. Though tired, she had to admit she was eager to put together a list of repairs, prioritizing the greatest needs first. But that would have to wait until tomorrow. For now, she was tired, her eyelids heavy with fatigue.

"Tomorrow we'll get you some kitty food and a collar," she told Boots, her eyelids fluttering. The cat yawned and stretched, then nestled deeper into her lap, warming her further.

Like the cat, she curled up in the chair and drifted to sleep.

* * *

"Mabel . . . Mabel, is that you?"

Tracy's eyes fluttered open and for one brief moment, she couldn't recall where she was or what she was doing. Above her, in relief, stood a stooped figure, an old man in overalls, a crooked mahogany cane in his hand. And on her leg lay the head of a very fluffy, very inquisitive sheltie, its head cocked slightly to the side, its sweet brown eyes peering up at her. Odd that she couldn't feel his head on her leg.

"Where have you been? We've been waiting for you."

Tracy squinted, but her eyes felt grainy, as though filled with sand, and she couldn't focus, couldn't see the man's face, only his outline.

"Who are you?" she asked, surprisingly unafraid.

"It's us . . . your boys."

And despite the fact that Tracy couldn't see the old man, she had the feeling he was kind, as though the soft golden glow of lamplight around him was an aura of the man himself. As if to confirm the old man's words, the dog whined and leaned in closer as though wishing her awake.

6

"My boys?" Tracy licked her dry lips and rubbed her eyes, but try as she might, she couldn't seem to see the man's face.

"We're here, when you're ready." He stood taller. *"Just remember that."*

Before Tracy could respond, the man turned and the sable brown-and-white dog followed with a longing look backward as though urging her to come.

"Who are you?"

Before she could say anything else, the man disappeared through the door with the dog. But in the distance she could hear the click-click-click of paws on wood and of the cane tap-tap-tapping the steps outside.

Tracy jumped to her feet, realizing too late that the cat was still on her lap. He fell to the ground with a yowl, his back hunched, his round eyes straining and his ears perked as though he too heard the sound outside. She ran to the door and peered out the frayed curtains, but the crescent moon gave off very little light, and nothing to ever insinuate that an old man and his dog were wandering the grounds. She shook her head, muttering like a crazy person as she made her way through the living room to the bedroom upstairs, the cat racing her to the second story.

At the top of the landing, she reached down and picked up the cat, relieved to have something solid in her arms.

"That was one heck of a dream. One *very* weird dream."

* * *

7

Hank heard the phone ring on his nightstand next to his bed and squinted at the digital clock glowing a faint blue in the darkness. 1:10. His wife stirred beside him. Jumping to his feet, he grabbed the phone and hurried to his office, flicking on the lightswitch. His eyes quailed at the sudden brightness. "Who could be calling at this late hour?"

The voice on the other end of the phone left no doubt.

The man growled into the phone. "This is Derrick."

Hank winced at the code name Derrick, short for oil derrick.

"We need to talk."

"Yes?" Hank had been dreading this phone call, and yet he had known it would come . . . just not this soon. He peered down the dark hallway to be certain his wife was asleep then glanced up at his calendar.

"She's there . . . at the homestead."

"Tracy? So?" Hank rubbed his forehead. He was getting too old for this . . . the mid-night calls. Always being sent to hotspots to put out fires, usually of his caller's making, or one of his caller's many cronies. He fingered the photograph on his desk. It was of him standing next to a top dignitary. As a former security officer for some of the top embassies around the world, "The Company" had thought Hank perfect for this current job. Hank was supposed to be retired, doing only small jobs scattered here and there. And now they wanted him to get rid of a veterinarian. All to keep one age-old secret. A secret that would probably never be revealed, *if* his caller would just take it easy, play it cool. He ran his fingers through his thinning gray hair and closed his eyes momentarily, before opening them.

"You don't understand." Derrick once again growled into the phone. "The missing woman's son is back. He's poking around. What if he talks to this Tracy person and tells her what happened?"

"You're jumping to conclusions." Hank spun around in his office chair. "Besides, why would the veterinarian even care about any of that? You're worrying for nothing." Hank peered up at the many citations and awards he had received over the years. And now, he'd been reduced to this. A company security job, albeit for a multinational company. "Look, give it time. I'm sure everything's going to be okay. The place is a dump. She'll take one look at it and run back home with her tail between her legs."

On the other end of the line, Derrick sighed. Through the phone, Hank could hear the man strumming his fingers on something. "You're probably right. It's just that . . ." He paused as if wanting to say more and deciding better of it. "Never mind. I have a lot on my plate. You're right. It'll all be okay. Go. Get some rest."

Gee, thanks, Hank wanted to say but didn't. He hung up, yet something about what Derrick was *not* saying gave him pause. Hank frowned, staring at his empty screen.

Two

Ryan McCauley entered the 12x12-foot stall, hay and dust a familiar smell as he reached over and felt the withers of the Morgan, brown with black mane, his hands moving downward over the bulging belly of the pregnant mare. He thrilled at the shift inside, sometimes feeling the nose or the hoof as the fetus struggled to find comfort in an ever tightening womb.

"Don't worry, girl. It won't be long now."

Yet even as he said it, he couldn't deny his worry. The current large animal vet had left–packed up for his next gig in a larger market. Ryan couldn't blame him. All the same, Cody, Wyoming, needed a large animal vet for the ranchers who couldn't easily get to town, or vice versa. And although a new veterinarian should be here soon, he had a feeling she would be in for a real culture shock, he realized as he forked hay into the hay net. First off, she had purchased the old Grayson place, which hadn't been lived in for nearly twenty years. It was nowhere close to being ready. They needed her *now*.

Ryan patted the mare's shoulder as she munched hay and snorted appreciatively, then he grabbed the comb and began grooming the tangles from her mane, his thoughts turning to Afghanistan. While there, he had carried 60 pounds of gear on his back and an assault carbine. Even now, he worked off excess energy by hiking the local hills or bench pressing 175 pounds in the gym they'd built at the ranch.

As he combed the mare down, he thought back to the first day he'd arrived at the ranch, which had become a rehab center for former veterans. He had felt lost after his return home from war. Suddenly, he was expected to put the last couple of years behind him. Forget. But he couldn't forget when it filled every waking thought, every nightmare.

The Morgan chuffed a breath of air, then laid her head on Ryan's shoulder as though understanding what humans could not. That sometimes you just needed to deal.

"Thanks, buddy." Ryan leaned gratefully against the horse's shaggy, charcoal-colored mane.

Just then, Wyatt's dog came ambling in and sniffed the Morgan. Ryan's thoughts turned back to the dog that had trailed them in Afghanistan, a short-haired mutt they'd named Hercules, Herc for short. Herc had slept in Ryan's bedroll—thought he was one of the soldiers. He'd even warned them on more than one occasion of enemy incoming. When the brass had found out, that had been the end of it. No one would cop to being the one to keep the little guy. They all had protected the dog in one way or the other, but they were ordered to take it away from camp, let it loose in the desert. Ever since that day, a giant ball of guilt hung over Ryan at the thought of Herc. He should have spoken up, said it was his dog, told of the dog's heroics. But he would have been court-martialed and the dog would have been taken away anyway. Still, it didn't sit well. With any of them.

Ryan threw his arm around the horse's neck, wishing he could cry.

"Okay, girl. I better find you a vet or we're both going to be in a world of trouble." He gave the Morgan one last pat, then shut her back in the stall where she had fresh straw for the delivery.

"Ryan!" Wyatt entered the barn where a diffused ray shone through the open doorway, giving light to the dust midair.

"Over here!" Ryan leaned out of the stall and waved.

In walked Wyatt, the veteran who had started the ranch on a wing and a prayer. Sure, he'd faced troubles along the way and almost lost the ranch after a series of events that began and ended with a troubled vet. Since then, Wyatt, a craggy-faced guy with wavy black hair and a scar that bisected his chin, had managed to do the impossible. He'd not only saved the ranch, he'd begun to bring in trainers who would teach these young men in all manner of professions, and he'd done it without spending a cent, or at least far fewer cents than he might have, had he done it on his own. No, Wyatt had offered a month-long vacation package for the trainer and his family in exchange for free training. It was a win-win, and so far, it was working smoothly, minus a few hiccups.

"What've you got for me?" Ryan closed the door to the stall and turned to face Wyatt.

"Your pups are here. Sandy, the gal from the shelter, brought over the best of the batch, along with a sheltie, courtesy of one of the neighbors. Jason will train you. He hand picked them ahead of time. They're six months old and potty trained."

Ryan couldn't think of anything more perfect. Rescued dogs turned into search and rescue animals or service dogs for disabled vets. "Let's take a look at them." He started after Wyatt, eager to see what Sandy had brought him.

"They're up at the bunkhouse." Wyatt led the way.

Kate, Wyatt's wife, was standing on the porch out front of the old homestead, where she and Wyatt lived with their cantankerous housekeeper Emajean, a half Lakota woman who they both adored.

"We're heading to the bunkhouse," Wyatt shouted. "Be back in a few."

Kate waved with the kitchen towel she held in her hand and then turned toward the screen door, used to her husband's few minutes turning into an hour when the need arose, and with a ranch this size, it arose often.

"Just wait 'til you see these pups." Wyatt marched at Ryan's side as they headed down the graveled drive toward the bunkhouse. "The boys were all over them when I left. You're going to have a hard time prying the pups away from the men."

Ryan laughed. "Truth is, I'm not. I'm going to give each of them a pup to train, and they might as well start now."

Ten minutes later, they came in sight of a towering lodge that the men had built out of downed logs and lumber. They'd dug a pond out front, added a bridge, and one of the guys who knew something about landscaping filled in the rest. Over the past several months, they'd added a bunkhouse for the men so that the lodge could go to the trainers. At first there had been a lot of grumbling, but over time, the men had come to like the bunkhouse and its Southwestern flair. In the middle of the room, Emajean had placed a tooled-leather saddle on a sawhorse with a pair of boots that sported two red roses on the sides. Then Wyatt had added a giant picture of the Duke with the words "Don't Let the Bastards Get You Down." That brought a smile to all their faces.

Next, Kate had outfitted the men with Pendleton blankets, each one unique. Soon after, the men had gone in together and bought a bright red Navajo rug to place in the middle of the floor. Lastly, one of the guys had found an old stove from a farmhouse he had been helping to renovate. The owner had given him the stove, along with other things, in exchange for labor. All in all, the place had actually brought them together because they interacted more, living in such tight quarters. And surprisingly, the guys slept better because they felt safer, as if in their unit again where they had each other's backs.

Even before they entered the barracks, Ryan heard the puppies' mewls intermingled with all sorts of sounds he'd

14

never thought he'd hear from his men. Wyatt opened the door and stood back to allow Ryan to enter first, then hurriedly closed the door behind them to keep any of the little guys from going AWOL. In a matter of minutes, his men had been turned into overgrown kids, cooing and talking baby talk to a squirming bundle of pups. Ryan knelt down and one leapt out of Bryce's hands. Within seconds, the brindle shepherd was licking Ryan's face, its body in constant motion, tail wagging. The pup smelled of sweet milk and puppy chow.

"Looks like you got your hands full." Wyatt chuckled, his pale blue eyes glistening.

"How many did we get?" Ryan took a quick head count and came up with six. Besides the brindle, two of them were a black-and-white mix, one a butter colored lab, one a kinky haired fur ball with a mixture of colors, and an all-white dog of unknown origin.

"Seven." Wyatt nodded. "Should be enough to keep you busy."

"Seven?" Ryan once again took a head count and frowned. "We're missing one."

All eyes scanned the room, searching under bunk beds, behind the wood stove. One of the men even stood and peered inside the bathroom in case one of the little guys had gone exploring. Nothing. Then Ryan saw it. The back door was slightly ajar, too narrow for a full-grown man. Too narrow for most anything, except a puppy that was used to slinking into tight spaces.

As if one, the entire group seemed to register the meaning of the open door and paused. Then one by one, their sheepish gazes turned to Ryan. He could ask who had left the door open, but he knew that whoever had was already feeling bad enough about what had happened. No use putting salt on the wound.

"Okay." Ryan commandeered the men. "Bryce, you shut the door. How long has the pup been missing? Any guesses?"

Each of them shrugged in turn, an uneasiness settling over the group, which soon transferred to the puppies who were now whimpering.

"How long have the pups been here?"

"Twenty minutes." The gravity of the situation made Wyatt's voice drop even lower than usual.

"Twenty minutes." Ryan fingered his lip. "The little tyke could be anywhere. Okay, let's split up. Bryce, James, you come with me. Bruce, Mark, and Reese, you stay here. This is my problem, Wyatt." He turned to the older man. "No use taking up your day too. We'll find the little guy."

Wyatt nodded, a mile long list of chores on his roster for the day. "I know you can handle it." He gave Ryan a parting pat on the shoulder, then quietly left, careful to shut the door behind him before there were any other escapees.

"Okay, men." Ryan gathered the two men together for the search party.

Chances are the pup would be waiting near the door, wanting back in to be with his brothers and sisters. But that vague hope soon vanished when they made their way outdoors and saw nothing in any direction. They immediately set in calling and whistling in the vain hope that the pup would come to their calls. That hope was soon dashed, however, as they searched and whistled for the next ten minutes with no response.

"Okay, guys." Ryan pointed to each of the men. "We're going to have to split up. Bryce, you go north. James, you go south. And I'll head out west, toward the new veterinarian's ranch. She's supposed to be here soon. Any luck and I'll get a chance to introduce myself and find the dog all in one fell swoop." He didn't mention the east. The Sawtooths. If the dog wandered up into the woods they would probably never find him. Better to head west. And fortunately they found what looked like small paw prints close to the wooden fence that held in the cattle. But those led into a field of shortgrass that hid most prints. Still, better to take no chances and to fan out.

"I'll check out these prints, see if any show up on the other side of the pasture. In the meantime, you two see if any can find any prints north or south of here. I've got my phone on. Call me if you find the pup. I'll do the same." And with that, they were off, hopefully to return with a puppy in tow.

Three

Tracy awoke to a dog barking. For one brief moment she recalled the dog from the night before and wondered if it had returned. Still groggy from sleep, she stumbled to her feet, grabbed her robe from the hook at the back of the child-sized closet. Then she pushed her arms inside each of the sleeves, tying on her robe as she walked to the window and peered down. She could just barely make out the corner of a gray Ford F250.

"Who could that be?" She took stock of herself in the mirror that hung on the door of the closet.

Great! She moaned.

Her auburn hair looked as if she'd been through a sandstorm, and her eyes were swollen from a night of restless sleep after spending it alone in a new place. For a farmhouse so far off the beaten path, she'd sure heard a lot of unfamiliar noises. The house creaking. An owl hooting somewhere outside her window, probably the barn. And something not tacked down had kept up a rhythmic clatter throughout the night. She would need to check on that soon, but the day might prove to be busy, she realized as she made her way down the stairs on unsteady legs, the cat darting past her.

By the time she arrived on the landing, she could see a silhouette at the door. She glanced at the clock she had plugged in last night, a Felix the Cat clock with a tail that swished. Eight a.m. Who on earth went visiting at such an early hour? She grumbled, tightening her belt as she marched through the kitchen, its gold and white linoleum appearing more dingy in the early morning light. She walked into the living room, which seemed smaller than it had the day before, and to the door, opening it with a loud creak. She would have to oil the hinges soon. One more thing to add to her ever growing list.

"May I help you?"

The lanky woman standing at the door wore heavy-duty Wranglers, a Levi's jacket, and a T-shirt that read "Cowgirls Rock." Her face was lined from years in the sun, while her newly graying hair was cut short in a bob.

She removed one of her hands from her back pocket and held it out to shake Tracy's hand. "The name's Lindsay. Lindsay Mitchell." She nodded vaguely toward the northeast. "Me and my husband, Gabe, have a farm out thataway. You the new vet?"

Tracy shook the woman's hand, surprised that word had spread so fast. "How did you know about me?"

"Everybody 'round these parts knows about you. Grady, our local veterinarian . . . packed up and headed out already. Said you were gonna be our new vet. That right?"

Tracy had to laugh. Apparently, the townsfolk knew a lot more about her than she did about them. "Do you want to come in?" She stepped aside and held the rickety screen door open for Lindsay.

"Don't mind if I do."

As someone who had spent her life in Seattle, Tracy didn't know the protocol for guests here in Wyoming, but she felt certain it involved food, none of which she had, except for some granola and beef jerky. She would need to go grocery shopping this morning and pick up some things for the farm.

Lindsay walked over to the bay window that overlooked the weathered red barn and bent over, peering out. "You sure got your work cut out for you."

Tracy released a brief sigh. She'd thought of nothing else as she lay awake, staring at the ceiling, wondering what on earth she'd gotten herself into. She knew no one in Wyoming. Plus she had purchased what could only be described as a money pit by anyone's standards. She'd had this horrible vision of returning to Seattle, her tail tucked between her legs as she asked for her old job back. The very thought of it had set her heart pounding. But then she'd done some quick visualization, a technique she'd learned from her therapist after the accident. She'd visualized the farm with a shiny new coat of paint. With a beautiful porch, two gray rocking chairs on either side of the picture window. Along with that vision, she pictured a barn, repainted red and white, and gleaming in the sunshine. The flowerbeds would be filled with peonies, roses, delphinium, and hydrangeas—a huge vegetable garden out back. And inside the barn, she'd have a practice filled with stainless steel tables for the smaller animals, and stalls for the farm animals that she would be treating when she wasn't working on site. Somewhere around two a.m. she'd finally drifted off to sleep and had slept like the dead.

"I wish I could offer you something, but I haven't been to the grocery store yet. I could boil you some tea."

Lindsay snorted. "This is coffee country." She smiled wryly.

Score one for the new girl.

"So, what brings you here?"

Lindsay scratched her forehead as if to buy time before she spoke. "You've got a lot of work to do around here, looks like."

"That's putting it mildly."

Lindsay offered one short nod. "And I suppose you could use some fence . . . for the animals you will be rehabilitating, am I right?"

Tracy offered the woman a seat, but she continued to stand.

"See, my husband, Gabe, and I have a proposition for you. It could help you, and at the same time help us."

"Oh?" Tracy yawned. "Do you mind if I make some tea? I didn't sleep very well last night."

"I bet you didn't." Lindsay absentmindedly picked up a porcelain sheltie. Just like the one from Tracy's dream. It sat on a shelf with other knick-knacks that lined the wall next to

21

the kitchen. "This place must have been quite a shock."

Tracy liked that Lindsay didn't beat around the bush. "To tell you the truth, I don't think I've totally adjusted yet."

"It will take some time, but that's why I'm here."

"Oh?" Tracy set about pouring water into an ancient kettle and putting it onto the stove. She twisted the knob to the burner and then reached into the cupboard, pulling down an old mug.

"Yeah." Lindsay appeared at the doorway and leaned against the door jamb as though she'd done it a thousand times before. "See, you need a fence, and I need a place to store my sheep for the next year or so. My husband and I could send down a couple of our guys to get your fence up and running, no charge. In exchange, maybe we could use a portion of the space to graze our sheep. We move them periodically to give the grass time to regrow."

Tracy stopped what she was doing. She stood there staring at the woman for what seemed a long time, but could have been no more than a moment. Suddenly, the kettle whistled, prying Tracy out of her stupor.

"Well?" The woman splayed her hands. "What do you think? Don't leave me hanging."

"It's a deal!" Tracy nearly danced with excitement at the proposition of free help. She had more than enough land for the two of them. For all she cared, Lindsay and her husband could keep their livestock on her property permanently. It would be nice to look out the back window and see sheep.

The woman shook Tracy's hand, this time giving it a firm handshake. "Well, I got chores to do and I'm sure you have a mountain of work ahead of you." She laughed, then headed for the door before Tracy had a chance to pour her tea.

Tracy followed her out to her truck where, from a side window, a furry face looked out at her. "Is that a sheltie?" Tracy reached up and let the female dog sniff her hand before she gave the dog a scratch behind the ear.

"Sure is. She's a grandpup of one of McDuffy's dogs."

"McDuffy?"

"McDuffy Grayson, the old guy who used to live here. He and his dog, Weber, were joined at the hip. Where you saw one, you saw the other. His dog sired my Millie's mother. This is one of her dogs."

The news that the man who lived here had a dog, a grandparent to this one, sent a chill racing through Tracy. If she had dreamt about the old man and his dog, how had she known the dog would be a sheltie? She hadn't come across any pictures in her cleaning. Except for the porcelain figurine, nothing had suggested a sheltie had lived here. Nor could she remember her friend Jan having told her about the pair when she'd suggested Tracy buy this place. Maybe she had, but Tracy had just forgotten. No, she would have recalled that, surely.

"Did the old man use a cane . . . this McDuffy fellow?" Tracy peered over the hood of the Ford.

Lindsay opened the driver side door. "Sure, those last few years. Why? Did you find one in the house?"

"No." Tracy's mind whirled over the possibility that she really *had* seen a ghost. "At any rate, thank you for offering to work on my fences."

"No problem." Lindsay climbed up onto the running board of her truck, then swung in like an old pro. "I'll send a couple of guys over later this afternoon to start work. So, if you see a couple guys hanging around, don't get spooked. They're a really good pair of young men. They do lots of work for us around the ranch." She put the key in the ignition then paused. "Come visit us sometime. If you take a walk out back, you'll see our homestead at the base of the hill. You may need your binoculars, but it's there." She laughed. And with that, she slammed the door and started up the engine. As she was backing up to leave, she swung the truck around so that she pulled up alongside Tracy. "Oh, and if you need anything, here's our number." She handed Tracy a card for the ranch with her cell number, email address, and website. "Chances are we'll be calling you before long. Between the horse, the cattle, the sheep, and the dogs, you never know when we'll be needing your service."

With that, Lindsay dipped her head and honked as she peeled out across the rugged terrain. For some minutes, Tracy stood there frowning, her thoughts still on the dog and the old man.

"I don't believe in ghosts." The cat, who she'd completely forgotten until now, meowed as if in agreement.

* * *

As Tracy rode toward Cody in her old GMC, she passed Old Trail Town, a ghost town filled with weathered storefronts and a line of old buckboards, as if someone had simply

24

parked them a hundred years ago and left for parts unknown. Tumbleweeds blew through the main street, skipping along in a zig-zag fashion only to lodge themselves against a wheel well or one of the covered walkways. The ghost town intrigued her. Maybe she could find out more about it at the store in Cody. But first, she had a laundry list of to-dos. She needed to find cell service out her way and she needed computer access so that she would feel more connected to the world at large.

But first, paint. She'd found the Big Horn Paint store on Sheridan Avenue from a directory she'd picked up in town on her way out to the old homestead. Now, if she could just locate the paint store. Fortunately, the town was small by Seattle standards. Everything about the town spoke of the Old West from the western storefronts down to the Buffalo Bill and Native American bronzes. The town even had a fire-engine red, horse-pulled trolley, the horses' hooves click-clacking against pavement, as it made its way through town for those last few stragglers who had come here to sightsee before the town closed up for the winter.

Five minutes later, she found the store with the huge ram's head on the window, pulled her truck to a stop and hopped out. She would have to estimate the number of cans she would need to paint the entire house and barn. Already, she had decided that she was doing nothing fancy with the paint, just white for the house and barn red for the outbuilding. But as she stepped into the store and looked at the number of shades of white, she threw up a flag of surrender. Eeny meeny miny moe. She chose Navajo white. Next, she perused the color for her barn, which she had

25

assumed would be barn red. No such luck. Eventually, she settled on Old Fashioned Milk Paint. She ordered the two colors of paint and then told the beefy woman behind the counter that she would be back to pick them up.

Tracy was about to turn to leave when she thought of all the work to be done around her place. Perhaps the woman behind the counter would know who did good work for a reasonable price.

"Would you happen to know where I could find a handyman or two to help around my farm? I'm the new veterinarian. I'll be replacing Grady."

"Living at the old Grayson farm?" The woman paused with a can of paint in her hand.

Tracy nodded. Did *everyone* know she was coming?

The woman set the paint can down and came around the counter, her girth wider than her apron. "That place is haunted, you know." She held out a hand that had splatters of green and red paint on it.

Tracy shook it. How did the clerk know about the ghost, and was there really a ghost? "What do you know about the old homestead? And how did you know about me?"

The woman bent her head down and peered around at the nearly empty store. "People talk. Pert near everyone around these parts has livestock. A veterinarian leaves, people notice. As to the haunting, everyone knows about that too. The old man and his dog never left. They say a person's spirit doesn't leave if there's unfinished business."

"And what unfinished business did the old man have?" Goosebumps traveled up Tracy's arms.

26

Suddenly, the woman pulled herself to her full height, whatever confidences she'd planned to share gone. "That's for you to figure out. As to the paint, it will be done in one hour. You can come back then."

It wasn't until Tracy was inside the truck and heading for her next stop that she realized the woman had never given Tracy advice on where to find good help. She sighed, wishing she had someone to talk to about this very unsettling past twenty-four hours.

The next two stops ran a bit more smoothly. She would soon have cell service and internet service, albeit a little sketchy because of her remote location. It would take a little longer to get electricity out her way, but she couldn't use the generator forever. Now, for food. She spent the next forty-five minutes gathering everything she would need for the next several weeks, then stopped at the hardware store for basic tools, in case she couldn't find them in that mound of junk in the barn. Not only that, she'd added two-by-fours to the back of her bed so that she could start on the porch. She'd like to be able to walk on it without falling through the floorboards. She had to admit she was exhausted by the time she arrived back at the paint store. Plus, she'd completely forgotten about the needed help with her farm until she was done loading the paint into the remaining space at the back of her truck and had climbed into her pickup. That's when the woman came toddling out, her hand waving in the air as Tracy keyed the ignition.

"Wait! I forgot to tell you where you could find a handyman."

"Oh?" Tracy pushed in the clutch and pumped the brake pedal.

"There's a veteran's ranch not far from your place. Five miles tops. The men there do all kinds of work around these parts as part of their rehabilitation. Get a hold of Wyatt Madison. He's in the phone book. He can send over a couple of men if you need it."

Tracy was surprised that the woman had remembered. "Thanks, I'll do that."

She backed out of the parking lot, the bed of her truck hanging lower than usual. Thoughts of all the work ahead sent her mind swirling. Before she started on anything, she would need a small siesta to make up for the loss of sleep from the night before. Then she would tackle as much as she could until sundown. But a half hour later, as she drove up the rutted driveway, careful to go slow so as not to bottom out due to the heavy contents of her truck bed, she saw a male figure in the distance and waved. *It must be one of Lindsay's young men here to work on the fence.*

Tracy journeyed the last leg of the driveway. With a squeal of the clutch, the truck lurched to a stop. She jumped out and clambered over to where the startled man stood, his blonde hair blowing in the breeze.

"Oh, thank goodness you're here. Lindsay said you would be by."

"Lindsay?" The man frowned.

"You *are* here for the fence, aren't you?"

"The fence?"

Tracy didn't know if the young man was deaf or pulling

28

her leg. Just then, she heard the faint sound of a dog howling from inside the barn.

Four

Off to the west of the old Grayson homestead, Ryan could hear a bull elk bugling. Yellowstone was just an hour and a half away, making elk, antelope, and herds of bison a regular sight, not to mention the occasional gray wolf that had been successfully reintroduced into the park in 1995. By her look of surprise, Ryan could tell that the new veterinarian had heard the elk, too. Yet Ryan had no time to ponder the sound, nor why the woman thought he'd been hired to mend her fences, because at that moment, he heard a pup whimper and paused only a moment before swinging into action. He would set her straight about why he was here once he found his pup.

"It sounds like there's a puppy inside the barn." The tall, chestnut-haired woman, her eyes a tawny green, nodded toward the dilapidated structure. "And by the way, my name's

Tracy. I'm the new veterinarian."

"I know." Ryan raced to the large red barn in three long strides, Tracy following close at his heels. "And my name is Ryan McCauley."

He rushed to the side door of the barn, Tracy in hot pursuit, and flung it partially open with a rusty squeal, but stopped short when he saw the mountain of debris. "What the—"

"I know. Isn't it something? I've got to clean all this out before I can open my clinic."

Another whimper came from beneath the piles of stuff accumulating inside the cavernous barn, about a football field away. Ryan scanned the contents of the barn—old rubber tires stacked high, a broken down riding lawn mower, an ancient looking table saw and piles of boxes spilling out in every direction. Where to begin?

"Is there another entrance?" He exited the building and peered around the side of the barn.

"I don't know. I just arrived here yesterday." Tracy's tawny eyes followed his to the back of the barn as she brushed away a tendril of stray hair.

"One way to find out." He trekked to the rear of the barn and peered down the back side where a door hung loose on its hinges. To get to it, he would have to cut back a mountain of bramble that had grown up over the past twenty years or so. "Do you have clippers?"

The veterinarian nodded, then sprinted to her truck and returned carrying a small tool chest that still had the price tag on it. From Fritz's Mercantile. Inside were a variety of tools,

31

some that came with the box, some that she had purchased and were still in their packaging. He lifted the tray, relieved to find a pair of clippers. Just then, the puppy began howling in earnest.

"We're coming. Hang on, little guy." Ryan ripped open the cardboard package with his teeth and tossed the paper aside. It would never be missed in all this debris that included engines and bicycle parts, spare signs rusted with age. A virtual treasure trove for a collector like old Grayson. To Ryan's surprise, Tracy pulled out a small Swiss Army knife and began chopping at the vines right alongside him.

"So much for the fencing." It wasn't an admonition, merely a statement.

He still didn't know what the heck she was talking about, but time was ticking away, and he needed to get to the pup before the entire mountain of junk collapsed on the poor guy. Fortunately, the door was close to the corner of the barn and they didn't have far to go to get to the door, which was now swinging as the wind picked up, slamming the door open and shut, open and shut, as though ticking off the minutes wasted trying to get to the pup.

"We're coming," Ryan cooed as the pup began a plaintive soliloquy that ran on and on.

As if feeling the pup's pain, the wind began to howl in sympathy. The Cheyenne sometimes called these winds Nonomo, seen as a giant bird, a spirit much like Winter Wind, more often the spirit of Thunder. And sometimes he felt it too. A force more powerful than mere wind. To be respected. Revered. He felt a frisson, like butterfly wings against his skin, and shivered, hoping that Tracy hadn't noticed. She hadn't been in Afghanistan, didn't know what it was like to spend days in 100 plus heat, crawling on your belly and knowing, without a shadow of doubt, that your life was in the hands of Fate. To know that God and nature had conspired, from the moment a person was born, to keep humans both grounded and afloat, tethered and set free. Only in that small window of time between birth and death did one learn the truth. A fraction of a second. That's all that stood between life and death. The great knowing. *That we are all actors in a play not of our design. Never of our design.* That's what he had learned on those thin ridges in Afghanistan, on the precipice between living and dying. He heard it now in the pup's frantic wail and felt another shiver crawl up his spine.

"I'm coming," he whispered.

For a moment Tracy stared at him, as though recognizing that he had gone somewhere inside himself. For a few split seconds he had traveled far, far away, to another world, another time. The knowledge that she had seen it, recognized it, sent fire to his cheeks. But he would deal with that later. For now, he had a dog to save.

* * *

Deja Vu. In French it meant "to see again." Goosebumps scampered up Tracy's arms, as she held the door open and peered at yet another mound of debris piled high to the ceiling. How they would ever get that pup from beneath the sheer volume of clutter, she had no idea. She saved animals that had already been rescued. She didn't rescue them. And yet, here she was, tugging at boxes and baling wire, pushing aside lamps and faucets. No rhyme or reason to the stashed possessions. All of it borne out of a Depression Era mentality. But she had no time to contemplate the past because the pup whined from some unknown spot near the far wall.

"Careful!" Ryan put a hand out to stop her from rummaging through the mass of debris. "You move the wrong box and this stuff could come crashing down on the pup. Let me handle this."

Tracy bristled at the idea that, just because he was a man, he was better suited to dealing with this situation, but she had to admit he was right. One wrong move and the pup would be buried.

"I'm trained for search and rescue." Ryan tapped his chest. "I was the team leader in Afghanistan. We did nighttime reconnaissance missions primarily."

"Oh!" Tracy lifted an eyebrow. It surprised her that Lindsay would use someone so skilled to repair fencing. She cocked her head, eying Ryan through a different lens. Now she could see it. Six feet, broad shouldered, muscular. He clearly worked out. He had a scar running across his chin. Had that been a wound he sustained in Afghanistan? And she could see that both his copper hair and his skin had been burnished by years in the sun. Already, he had crows feet at the corner of his eyes, though he could be no more than late twenties, thirty tops.

The pup began with a more persistent whine, as though reminding them they were wasting daylight. And it was true.

The sun would be down in less than an hour. The idea of working in the dark with a generator and a flashlight wasn't appealing in the least. They would need to work fast.

"How can I help?"

Ryan frowned. "Do you have any rope? And wet dog food or lunch meat that we can rub on the rope."

She bent down beside him as he tried to peer through the debris to locate the pup. There, just beyond an old treadle sewing machine and a tractor wheel, they spotted one eye and a nose peering up. Tracy's heart melted, but she quickly quelled any feelings she might have for the dog. She'd been there, done that. Loved an old man who had been like a father to her and a dog. And had lost them both. Her heart scrunched tight, emotion flooding her, her throat aching at the memory.

"I have a rope in the truck. And I don't have any dog food, but I just picked up some wet cat food. Would that work?"

"Let's try it." He reached out a hand before she could leave. "And thanks. For helping."

He pierced her with those golden brown eyes of his. For a moment, she couldn't move. But the dog's renewed whimpering ended the spell, and she took off at a run. Five minutes later, she was back with an opened can of cat food and a rope, which Ryan snatched up and turned into a lasso as though he'd done this all his life.

"If we can get him into the lasso, we can cinch it around him and pull him up." Ryan rubbed the front edge of the lasso with cat food. "Okay, here goes nothing."

He lowered the rope down. At first it caught on the spokes of an old Schwinn, red like the one she'd had as a child, only covered in dust and rust and all means of little fuzzies.

The second time through, he almost made it to where the pup peered out, its black face sporting a jagged white line up the length of his muzzle. But at the last second, the rope caught on the wheel of the sewing table with its ornate wrought iron legs.

No go.

Tracy breathed in, only now realizing that she was just as vested as Ryan in getting the puppy out, maybe more so. "C'mon, little guy," she implored in a whisper. "You can do it."

Ryan disentangled the rope from the wheel and once again tossed it toward the hole where the pup sat crouching. This time it connected, landing in the right spot. Without thinking, Tracy let out a whoop that sent the pup scurrying away from the rope and toward the dark recesses of the piled up refuse.

"Shh!" Ryan scolded.

Tracy merely nodded an apology, while inwardly berating herself.

Ryan wiggled the rope around, hoping the smell of cat food would lure the pup out. Every muscle in Tracy's body tightened as she watched the rope dance. Little by little, the pup poked his head forward, sniffing only to back up then sniff again, his hunger eventually getting the best of him. Propped up against a table, Tracy crouched beside Ryan in silence, watching the spectacle below, but the puppy would start to lean forward only to put it in reverse before Ryan could pull the rope tight around his middle.

"Hold the can of cat food out as far as you can."

Tracy did as told. Slowly, the pup inched forward until snatch! Ryan had him around the middle and began reeling him up, careful not to snag the little pup on any of the many bits of detritus that surrounded him. The pup's sable and white limbs flailed as he fought to be free of the rope, a white bib on his chest flashing an equally white underbelly. Despite her misgivings, Tracy's defenses faded away as the nurturer took over. Before Ryan had the pup all the way up, she bent down so far that her belly ached, reached underneath the pup's midsection and pulled the tiny dog the remainder of the way up to her chest. Once there, the squirming puppy assailed her with kisses of gratitude, his puppy breath smelling of milk.

"We did it!" Ryan wrapped his arms around them both and hugged them tight.

Tracy threw an arm around him and squeezed, the pup taking turns licking them both until finally the spell had worn off, and Tracy pulled away, her cheeks flushed and her heart racing. For one brief moment, the years since the tragedy seemed to have been wiped away.

"Th-thanks . . . for helping me, I mean." Her voice gave out.

"Actually, ma'am—" Ryan cocked his head. "That's *my* pup you have there."

Tracy leaned back. She couldn't have been any more

shocked than if he had said he was a Martian just in for a visit. "W-what? *Your* pup?"

"That's right. We got our first batch in. We're going to train them to be search-and-rescue dogs and service dogs for veterans." With that, he scratched behind the little dog's ears, flustering her further. "I can take him from you now, if you'd like."

"Oh, right." Reluctantly, she gave the dog one last hug then held it out to Ryan who snatched him up into his arms, cradling him.

"But since you helped rescue him, I'll let you name him." Ryan scratched the dog's ears in turn. But before she had a chance to speak, the front of Ryan's shirt grew wet and he let out a groan. "Sheesh . . . he peed on me!"

"Uh oh." Tracy couldn't help but laugh to see the dog so happy and Ryan so . . . so . . . wet. "Come inside. I can get you a pair of Old Man Grayson's jeans and a shirt, if you don't mind flannel. That must be all he ever wore except for denim work shirts and those are pretty thrashed."

"Thanks," he mumbled.

Tracy tried to contain her mirth but soon gave it up entirely as she walked him back to the house. "You can clean up inside and get changed. Then you can call it a day with the fence, if you like. Come back tomorrow."

He halted at the bottom of her stairs. "No offense, ma'am, but what the heck are you talking about? I'm not working on your fence."

Five

Tracy paused before opening the screen door, eyes widening. What did Ryan mean he wasn't working on the fence? *Then who is he?* She nearly rethought inviting him into the farmhouse, but the temperature was starting to drop, and both the pup and Ryan had begun to shiver. But first, the groceries. She ran past him and returned with two bags of groceries she'd procured from her toolbox.

"Come inside, but watch your step. The porch is rotted in parts." She sidestepped the sagging floorboards to get to the front door, both Ryan and Boots following her footsteps. "What did you mean when you said you're not working on the fence?"

"I came here looking for my pup. One of the boys left the door open back at the ranch."

So he was married. That figured. Well, that was for the

best. She didn't need any obstacles in her life. Once indoors, Tracy put the groceries away, then put on a pot of coffee. "The bathroom is upstairs, to your left. Let me get you some of Old Man Grayson's clean clothes. I did some laundry yesterday because I thought I might need something to paint in or when I'm doing repairs around the place. You wouldn't happen to know anyone who does that sort of thing . . . at a reasonable price?" She felt her face flush.

Ryan frowned, the silence a chasm between them.

"We don't need to talk about this now. Let's get you some clean clothes." She glanced at the clock, her stomach growling. "It's dinner time. Are you hungry?"

His round eyes told her that he was. The pup yipped as if in agreement.

Tracy laughed. "Well, okay then. I'll get the pup something to eat while you clean up. I could whip up an omelet, if you don't mind having breakfast for dinner."

"An omelet sounds good."

That settled, she led him upstairs and procured a towel and washcloth from the linen closet. She laid it on the counter, then went in search of old clothing left over from the previous homeowner. Ryan handed her the moist pup, which she held away from her body until she could get him cleaned off. Then he thanked her and closed the door, but not before she'd felt the awkwardness of the situation. Still, ten minutes later, she found herself whistling as she set about cooking the omelet while sipping a steaming cup of coffee from one of Old Man Grayson's mugs, one with Cody, Wyoming, written on the front and a picture of a buffalo to one side. With the

40

pup in the house, Boots was nowhere to be seen. Probably under the sofa, or hiding behind the curtains in the living room like he had the day before, believing he was out of view, despite the fact that she could see his paws. She smiled at the memory.

The sound of the running water from above, followed by a squeal of the pipes as the water was turned off, felt oddly comforting. It had been a long time since Tracy'd had a man in the house. She didn't know why she'd never committed. She'd had opportunities over the years, but if she were to be perfectly truthful, somewhere in the back of her mind she always feared she would lose the man as she had lost everyone else in her life. Part of her reason for coming here had been to take time to figure out how to overcome that fear. She'd just had that thought when she heard footsteps on the porch and a knock at her screen door. She stood, frowning.

Who can that be?

She peered through the sheer curtains and saw a man, slightly taller than Ryan and rail thin. Hesitantly, she opened the door a crack until she could get the pup out from under her feet. One escape for the day was enough. She lifted the little guy into her arms. She couldn't keep thinking of it as "the little guy." The pup would need a name . . . soon.

"Can I help you?"

"Hi, ma'am. My name's Lloyd." The young man tipped his hat to her to reveal a cascade of wavy blond hair. "We're finished out back for the day."

"Finished?" She frowned.

"With the fence. It's going to take at least another couple

41

of days, but we'll be here bright and early tomorrow."

The pup, which had been huddled in her arms, squirmed forward to get a closer look at the stranger. He reached his nose out, smelling the man's hands first, snuffling up his freckled arm to his Levi's shirt.

"You're a little nosy Parker!" He scratched the pup behind the ears.

"Parker." Tracy rolled the name around on her tongue. "I like it. That's what we'll call him."

"Ma'am?"

Just then, Lloyd looked past her. Tracy turned in time to see Ryan standing behind her, his chest still wet as he rubbed a towel behind his ear.

"Oh, hi, Ryan." Lloyd's eyebrows pinched together. "What are you doing here?"

Tracy set Parker onto the floor and shooed him in Ryan's direction. The pup easily complied, rushing toward him, scrambling on skidding paws and sliding into Ryan's shins.

"Slow down there, buddy." He set the towel down on the counter and leaned over to pick the pup up and cradle it in the crook of his arm.

Lloyd frowned. "I didn't know you two knew each oth–"

Tracy threw her hands up to stop him. "No, no, you've got it all wrong. It's not what it looks like." The aroma of the omelet wafted in. "Oh no, my omelet!"

She brushed past Ryan, relieved not to have to face either man any longer. What a way to start. Word would get around that she was a homewrecker, and she would be back in Seattle with nothing to show for the move. And she was many things, but that wasn't one of them. She quickly fried up an egg for Parker in the pan after she scooped out the omelet then divided it onto the two plates.

"Would you and your workers like to stay for dinner?" Tracy called into the living room.

"No. Me and Tom need to get back to the ranch before dark or Lindsay will have our hides." Then he turned to face Ryan. "Don't do anything I wouldn't do. And say hi to Kate for me." He followed that up with a hearty laugh, then lifted his cap and was gone.

Tracy turned to Ryan, fire burning her cheeks. "I am *s-so* sor-ry!" She nearly dropped the omelet off the plate she handed him. "I hope this doesn't get back to your wife. I would never do anything to jeopardize . . . well, you know!"

For one brief moment, Ryan stood there, omelet in hand, staring at her. Then he sputtered, as he set the plate onto the red formica table. Within seconds the sputtering had turned into an all-out belly laugh. He was bent nearly double, the towel having long since slipped to the floor, where the pup took it in tow and was parading it around the room as if it were a prize. In the meantime, Ryan's face had turned an unhealthy shade of crimson and tears were pooling in his eyes. At last, he plopped down in the metal chair with red-and-white plaid plastic for its cushions. He used the napkin she handed him to wipe his eyes.

"What's so funny?"

He took a moment to compose himself, then turned to her. "There's something you should know about Kate."

* * *

Tracy and Ryan had finished eating, Ryan having donned one of Old Man Grayson's shirts before sitting down to the meal. But every time the subject of Kate came up, he would dissolve into fits of laughter and begin pounding his leg. Tired of his continued laughter, Tracy turned to him. "When you're finished up there, I'll drive you home, if you'd like. The sun will be down soon. You can tell me about Kate then."

"I'd appreciate a ride home, ma'am." He nodded his thanks for the meal and her hospitality.

Ten minutes later, the truck bucked and rolled as it took the ruts in the dirt road, dipping into the potholes, plowing through vines that had overgrown the path, and sidestepping a whole myriad of hoarded items that McDuffy Grayson had left behind when he died. Tracy peered at the Rocky Mountains, cradling the pink-tinged clouds on the western horizon. The pup sat between them on the bench seat.

"To make a long story short–" Ryan stroked the puppy's back. "–Kate is my boss's wife. I'm not married."

Tracy couldn't say why, but a weight lifted from her chest to know that he was single. She was about to ask him what he did for a living when a shot rang out, the flash from the muzzle coming from the northern side of the road amid the deepening shadows of the sunset.

"What was that?" Her heart raced as she gunned the engine.

"Probably just some kid target shooting, or someone doing some illegal hunting." Ryan placed a hand on her arm.

"Nothing to worry about."

Sure enough, in her rear-view mirror, she could just make out the dark shape of a deer leaping across the road. "Poor deer."

Ryan snorted, and scratched at his neck. "Better not say that too loud around here. Someone will mistake you for an eco-nut."

She turned on him, nearly running off the road. Fortunately, he caught the steering wheel in time and righted the truck before they drove into the ditch.

"What did I say?" Ryan appeared truly puzzled in the light of the moon that shone on the horizon.

Tracy could just see the outline of Ryan's face, a lock of brownish blond hair concealing one eye, a three-day stubble covering his rugged jawline. "What did you *say*?" Fire burned in her belly, but she tempered it. "I guess I *am* a bit of an eco-nut. I *care* about the environment, about wildlife. What's wrong with that?"

He put up his hands in surrender. "There's nothing wrong with it. But some folks don't view hunting in the same way you do. It's no different than buying meat at the grocery store, pardon me for saying so."

She rubbed her neck to loosen the tension. "You're right."

Eager to stamp out the darkness, she turned on her lights now that the sun had gone down behind the Grand Tetons to the east. The narrow beams revealed an array of bugs and long-eared bats swooping at the edge of her vision to dine on mosquitoes and other unwanted insects. Tracy had read once that a bat could eat up to 1200 insects in an hour, all 1200, it would seem, if the "tink-tink" sounds were to be believed, hitting her windshield as she drove the washboard road, her teeth rattling along with the GMC's aging metal.

"But some people hunt for sport."

"True," Ryan agreed. "People have been known to go after coyotes and wolves for sport. But I give you a month, you get called out to a lamb or calf mauling, then you tell me what you think of the wolves. And you see a starving calf because it can't compete with the wild horses grazing federal lands, then we can talk." He must have seen her look of frustration. "Tell you what, let's change the subject for now." He held out a hand to signal a cease-fire.

Tracy rocked her head back and forth to relieve the remaining tension, the mention of horses setting her stomach churning. Still, though she and Ryan may not believe in the same things, she could at least be neighborly, give him the benefit of the doubt, especially since she was new to the area. It would do no good to prejudge, even though it was clear he had prejudged her.

"So . . ." She shook his hand in truce. "What ever happened to Grayson and his wife?"

Ryan laughed, the laughter nervous to her ear. "Grayson was a good guy. Everyone loved him. He died of old age, or maybe he just missed his wife and dog."

"What happened to them?" She sat taller in her seat, suddenly alert.

He shrugged. "His dog just got old, like him. They were inseparable right up until the dog died, six months before

46

Grayson did."

She frowned. "And his wife?"

"Don't know."

"What do you mean you don't know?"

This time when she turned, Ryan yelled. "Watch the road! Are you always this bad of a driver?" He eyed her with suspicion. "Maybe I should watch the road for you."

Despite his warning, Tracy felt as though she were cocooned within a bubble of darkness, the only light the one shining through her headlights. But what she saw made her feel . . . what? *Alive*. Through the half-open window she could smell the agricultural smells as the day cooled, bringing new scents to life . . . sagebrush, alfalfa, the earthy scent of cattle. There was something deeply satisfying about it. All of it. Her mentor had been right when he'd made her promise to stretch her wings. To test her mettle. To find out who she really was when she wasn't so worried about failing.

"I'll keep my eye on the road. Now, what happened to Grayson's wife?" She did as promised, the hum of her tires on the road replaced by loud thuds as the truck bottomed out in spots with larger than average potholes.

Ryan scratched his head and frowned. "Well, no one rightly knows. She just disappeared one day. Townsfolk thought she got into a spat with Grayson. After all, he could be a crotchety old man, at times. Thought maybe she returned to her folks, out in Illinois. But she never showed up there. People waited, thinking maybe she took time out before she got there, but she never arrived."

Tracy didn't know why she felt so vested in the story.

Maybe it was the fact that she was sleeping in the woman's bed. She just knew that it didn't seem right that the woman hadn't been found. "Did anyone go looking for her?"

"Of course!" He pointed to a fork in the road, telling her to take the left one. "The sheriff put together a team. Plus, townspeople look after their own. Got a lot of volunteers, my granddad included, to go looking for her. They searched for weeks. Finally called off the search. Plus, it was too dangerous, with that mountain of debris in the barn, to do much searching there. Course, we didn't have the technology we have nowadays."

The stars had made an appearance on the horizon. Like shiny sprinkles on a wedding cake, they winked and shimmered, the scent of pine filling the nighttime with fragrance, so different from the streets of Seattle, which had an urban smell all its own. She would take this aroma over the smell of asphalt any day.

"Did they suspect foul play?" She rolled up the window and turned on the heater as the temperature cooled.

"Maybe, at first. But the old man loved Mabel."

"Did you say Mabel?" The name sent off sparks of recognition after the nighttime visitation.

"Sure did. Everyone loved her. Who'd want to do something to someone so sweet? She used to bring the best-tasting potato salad to the Fourth of July picnics." Ryan licked his lips, as if imagining it. "The old guy was heartbroken when she disappeared. We'd see him out roaming the backroads, as if he were still searching for her. Did it the rest of his life."

Tracy thought back to her first night at the farm, recalling her dream, and yet it didn't feel like a dream. It felt real. Even Boots had behaved as though someone or something had been there, on the porch. The old man and his sheltie. Were they ghosts? Did she even believe in ghosts? She'd never given it much consideration, but there had been times in her life where she'd guessed at things to come, had felt someone close by, had dreamt things that had come to pass. She didn't know how much to tell Ryan.

"At the paint shop in town, the lady said that the old man and the dog haunt the farm."

Ryan gave a snort of laughter. "Yeah, just about everyone in town has heard that story."

"And what do you think?" Tracy eyed him tentatively. "Is there any truth to it?"

Ryan bit his lip and looked out the side mirror, his body language making it clear he didn't want to talk about it. That was one thing Tracy understood after years of working with animals. Every person or animal, no matter the species, had "a tell," the body expressing what words would not or could not say. Tracy had learned to look for those tells. To spot them when an animal was hurting or ready to strike, or simply timid or afraid.

Ryan lay his arms across his chest and scratched idly at his left shoulder. "Well, see, lots of people swear they have seen him and his dog . . . out on the road searching for something."

"Mabel?"

"Probably." He tilted his head slightly.

"And you?" She nodded toward the shadows at the side of the road.

"Me?"

"Have you ever seen the old man and his dog?"

To her amusement, he squirmed like a five year old just asked if he'd pinched the neighbor's cat. She had a feeling she was getting all she was going to get out of him, if she didn't do something to put him at ease.

"I saw them." She surprised herself at the admission. "The other night, at the farm. I thought I'd had a dream, but then I was awake and I saw them . . . walk through a closed door." Before he could tell her she was crazy, she quickly added, "The cat saw him, too. Boots yowled."

Tracy's face grew warm, prickles of humiliation running up her arms. How silly she must sound. Now she would seem like some "woo-woo" eco-nut, who saw ghosts in her spare time. She was getting a reputation already, and she wasn't even in Wyoming a full 48 hours. If she hadn't promised to watch the road, she would have buried her head in the steering wheel to hide her face.

But to her amazement, Ryan lifted his jaw and rubbed his ear, releasing a large sigh. "I saw them, too."

Forgetting her promise, she veered off the road slightly so that Ryan had to reach over the pup to correct her steering.

"Next time, I drive." He shook his head, but by the awkward grin, she could tell he wasn't mad at her.

"So, are you going to tell me . . . what happened?"

She kept one eye on the road, one eye on the wide rear-view mirror so that she could see Ryan's expression, only to

50

discover that he had paled considerably. The image returned
to her of a five-year-old child when he twisted his head back
and forth, but in the end, he spoke.

"See, it was before I went into the military. Some friends
and I went to the old Grayson place. He'd already been gone
a good ten years. His headstone is out on the property, in a
homemade cemetery. It has a white picket fence around it,
though I doubt it's still white after all these years. Probably
could stand a fresh coat of paint. Anyway, me and my friends
went down there to drink, to celebrate my last day as a
civilian before I got shipped off to bootcamp, and eventually
Afghanistan. Figured it was as good a place as any, and no
adults to shoo us off."

He seemed to have warmed to the story, but it had clearly
affected him because she noticed he'd taken to stroking the
dog over and over, as if to calm himself, his eyes glazed with a
far-off expression, as though he had indeed gone back in time.
She knew not to interrupt.

"We'd been there going on an hour, when we felt this
. . . cold air move in, like a wet fog. It was eerie. And then,
suddenly, we heard what sounded like whispers. Got to tell
you, it about freaked us all out. I was ready to dump my
booze and split. We all were. But then we saw them, next to
the old guy's headstone, it was like he was talking to the bare
earth, telling it he was sorry . . . telling *her* he was sorry. Then
the old guy's dog started to keen, and that was it. You never
saw a group of guys run so darn fast in your life. 'Bout had a
heart attack by the time I got home. My mom asked where I
had been, could smell the whiskey on me, and just shook her

head. Never said anything to my dad. I guess she figured if I was old enough to sign up for the military, I was old enough to drink. And plus, I think she knew I just needed a send-off with my bros. Know what I mean?"

Tracy had never been a parent, but she did understand. She knew it wasn't the same, pulling up stakes and coming a few states over compared to enlisting and being sent to Afghanistan. But she could understand the culture shock. The feeling of being a fish out of water. Wondering if she would make it or walk away, never proving her worth. Maybe the only one she needed to prove anything to was herself. Her mentor had faith in her. She thought of him fondly. He'd been kind, and elderly. He'd taught her to believe in herself even after the accident with her horse. It had been her fault. She'd wanted one last sendoff with her friends before she headed to college to become a vet. She'd talked her parents into letting her and her friends take Jedi, her blonde Palomino, and their horses, up on the Santiam ridge. At first her parents had said no, fearing there might still be snow at those elevations. They had finally relented, after much begging on her part and the parts of her friends, especially Jen. They agreed, but only if Jen's brother came too. Tracy's parents had given Tracy clear instructions to take the longer path, should she encounter snow, and she had promised she would. But then she had made it all the way up to the north ridge when she saw it. One patch of snow, no wider than a basketball court. Go back the way they had come and lose almost an hour of time, or two minutes over a snow field?

"I'm going back," Jen said, her brother agreeing.

"Me too." Sara turned her Morgan's head in the direction they'd come.

"Well, I'm not. You go if you want to." Tracy pressed on. "But I'm crossing. Meet you on the other side." She'd thrown her shoulders back and, despite her palomino's protests, tested the ground and was relieved when her horse found purchase. "See? It's easy."

But she'd barely got that out of her mouth when her horse took another couple of steps and slid. At first, Tracy didn't register what was happening, but then she heard the screams of her friends, followed by the panicked sound of her horse as he tipped over on his side, flinging her upwards even as his weight pulled him ever closer to the edge of the cliff. She shivered, even now, remembering that horrible day. As long as she lived, she would never forget the sound of her horse as it cascaded over the mountainside, at his almost human scream of fear as he fell.

She fought back the searing pain that edged the back of her throat, tears hovering, even now. How could she have been so careless? She'd had to crawl on her hands and knees back to her friends, to wait for the helicopter to airlift the horse's lifeless body out of the canyon. To face her parents and her friends. She had thought she'd never get out of bed again, never risk loving an animal again, never pursue her lifelong dream of becoming an animal vet. Her life was over before it had begun, and it was all her fault. Her impatience, her longing to prove herself and her abilities, had caused her to make the biggest mistake of her life, and now she would have to live with it. Forever. She'd had a hard time even looking at herself in the mirror after that.

It had taken weeks, but with the aid of her mentor, she'd finally pulled herself up out of bed, forced herself to attend classes each day, to put one step forward. To "fake it 'til you make it," as the saying went. And finally, one day nearly a year later, she could remember hearing the birds sing for the first time in ages. Appreciate the robin-blue sky. Take in the smell of freshly mown grass. From then on, she'd made it her life's mission to save large animals. To atone for the one she'd been unable to save.

"You okay?" Ryan yanked Tracy out of the nightmare of her memory. "I didn't mean to stir anything up." He lay a hand on her arm in compassion.

"Sorry." She wished she could hide the tremor in her voice. "I guess I have some ghosts of my own." She gave him a watery smile.

"It's okay. We all have 'em."

The sorrow in his words made it clear she had touched a raw nerve. If he'd been to Afghanistan, he probably had many such ghosts.

"Oh look! There's the ranch now."

Beside them stood a large corral, a dozen or more scattered cows off to her left. The moon hung low, casting a silvery glow over the setting, creating an almost surreal landscape of blue-toned mountains and a valley that rolled out like a pale brown carpet as far as the eye could see. A huge log cabin loomed in the near distance with a smaller bunkhouse beside it.

"We're easing in the back way to the ranch." Ryan

pointed to a spot in front of the bunkhouse. "You'll probably want to leave by the main road. It's a little longer, but the paved road is straighter so you'll get home faster. And it's safer. Thanks for returning me and the pup. You saved my bacon." He produced a 100-watt smile that radiated his love for the ranch. "Hey, I meant to tell you, if you need any help, me and the other vets can come over and put in some time on the farm."

Tracy stopped in front of the bunkhouse. "You live on the vet ranch?" Nothing should faze her anymore, on this day filled with surprises.

"Sure do."

"Can I take you up on that offer?" She hoped she wasn't being presumptuous. "To help me around the farmhouse."

"Call me." He lifted the pup into his arms, then hopped out of the truck and slammed the door shut. Through the partially opened window, he handed her a card from his wallet with his phone number on it.

"Thanks!" She smiled. "By the way, I named the dog."

"The dog?" He tilted his head, confused.

"You said I could name your pup."

"Oh, right!" He lifted the puppy and peered into his eyes as if to divine the name. "So what did you call him?"

"Parker . . . for nosy Parker."

Ryan laughed, but the laughter died as a glint of metal seemed to catch his attention near the front of the large log cabin. A black BMW. He frowned. "I wonder who that can be?"

Tracy shrugged and put her truck in reverse.

With a tip of his head, Ryan waved goodbye, then walked over to the cabin, Parker in tow. But before she could pull out, she saw a man come over to stand beside Ryan, heard the mumble of their voices. With a grind of gears, she put the GMC in forward. As she drove away, she watched the two grow smaller and smaller in her rear-view mirror. When she was about to round the corner past a ranch house, before heading to the main road, she saw the man jump into his BMW and start it. He revved the engine twice, before peeling out, headed her way.

Six

In Tracy's rear-view mirror, she spotted the twin set of lights from the BMW she'd seen in front of the log cabin. They appeared menacing as the car barreled down the driveway behind her at an alarming speed, slowly gaining distance until it was on her bumper as she reached the road. The driver laid on the horn. Did he want her to pull over so he could get by? All she could see was the silhouette of a man, his head bent forward. She maneuvered her GMC to the side of the road and then opened her window, waving him on. But to her surprise, he stopped his vehicle, got out and walked over to her car. She opened her glove compartment, so the .22 she carried would be within easy reach should she need it.

She rolled her window halfway down. "Can I help you?"

Through the darkness, in the neighboring field, Tracy spotted a large harvester with its headlights on to guide the farmer down furrows of what she could only guess were potatoes. She placed her hand over the horn, but would the farmer even hear her over the harvester engine?

The man bent down to speak through the partially opened window. "Are you the new veterinarian?"

At this range, she saw that he was a big man, bald, with a single silver hoop earring. "I just spoke to Ryan, and he told me I could catch you if I hurried. My name's Peter–Peter Flanagan. I work for Blake Fordham who owns a ranch farther up the valley and I have something to show you. Could you follow me?"

Tracy's mind flashed to all the slasher movies that reeled up as spam on her computer screen when she was searching for something inane, like a stethoscope.

The fear must have registered on her face because he quickly added, "If you'd like, we could take Ryan with us."

Tracy released the breath she'd been holding. For some reason, the idea of Ryan tagging along comforted her, and yet she was going to have to get used to going out on calls on her own with complete strangers. *Someday, but not today.* She nodded her head.

"Hang on then, and I'll run back and get him. You both will want to see this."

Fifteen minutes later, Ryan was tucked neatly in the truck beside her, fatigue showing in the tilt of his chin and the set of his eyes, dark circles beneath them. He hopped in without asking.

"Where's your sidekick?"

"One of the guys at the ranch is taking care of Parker."

He nodded in the direction of the bunkhouse.

The BMW pulled out onto the road, its headlights casting a long shadow across the barren stretch before them. Tracy put the GMC in gear and followed, bugs pinging off her windshield and leaving oily splatters that would take a scraper to peel off. But that was for another day. For now, she needed to get through this one.

"Just wait 'till you see this ranch," Ryan said with a note of intrigue.

"Why? What's so special about Blake's place?"

Ryan snorted. "You'll see."

They skirted the foothills of the Sawtooth Mountains as they traveled the bottomlands for miles. Tracy was just about to ask how much farther to their destination when Ryan pointed to a driveway. "Turn here."

Her tires crunched against the gravel, which was soon replaced with a recently paved road bordered by a series of cypress trees that reminded her of a road leading to a French Chateau.

"Get a load of what's coming up," Ryan said, leaning forward to get a better look.

With something akin to awe, Tracy blinked twice, certain she had entered the Twilight Zone, for situated in the vast prairie was the largest mansion she'd ever seen, complete with a lit fountain and dancing waters that changed colors along with direction. Marble nymphs cavorted in the center, their bodies glistening with water.

"The guy's a movie mogul. He's got houses all over the place, but likes to get away to Wyoming during his down time.

No paparazzi that way."

The entire mansion was lit from within, a soft golden glow casting shadows onto the pavers that flowed in a circle around a fountain large enough to rival the Trevi fountain in Italy. Yellow poplar trees with their beautiful white bark flanked the mansion on each side, making it appear larger so that it mirrored one of the finest ski chalets in Europe. Tracy's brain cast around in search of the size of a place this large.

As if reading her mind, Ryan said, "His mansion is nearly 20,000 square feet."

Tracy whistled in spite of herself. Before she could check her words she said, "Who needs that much space?"

Ryan shrugged. "Blake Fordham, apparently. He entertains some pretty famous names, from time to time. Out back, he has his own airstrip and hangar where he keeps his Lear jet and helicopter."

A heavy-set guy with a tattoo wrapping around his arm materialized out of the left portion of the house and got into Blake's BMW as Peter got out. The driver quickly put the sports car in gear to ferry it into the leftmost stall of the six-car garage that was off to the side of the house. As if on cue, Blake appeared to see his guests into the house.

Tracy peered down at her thrift store clothes, then to her truck that was held together by glue and a little duct tape, or at least that's what her father used to say when he was teasing her. Before she could ponder why Blake needed her services, the man who had driven the BMW into the garage reappeared in a jeep with a flood lamp on top and squealed to a stop in front of them.

"Climb in," he yelled above the motor. Tracy rushed to Ryan's side, where he took her arm and led her to the jeep. "Hop in the back," the guy called.

Ryan opened the door for Tracy and she jumped in. She wasn't even fully seated before the jeep jerked into motion, throwing her against Ryan, who eyed her with a twinkle of amusement. Her face warmed as she quickly scooted to her own side, trying without success to attach her seatbelt.

"Here, let me help you." Ryan reached across to buckle her in.

Tracy breathed in the scent of his aftershave, a mixture of spices that reminded her of warm Snickerdoodles. Now there was a pleasant thought. She found herself smiling at the image it conjured, but quickly quelled it when she noticed him staring.

Once again, the jeep jerked to a halt and in popped Blake, nearly pole vaulting into the jeep just in time for it to take off with another jolt to Tracy's ego as she fell sideways against Ryan.

Ryan winked at her, then to her surprise, threw an arm around her as the jeep twisted and turned down a series of roads to the field out back. They drove a good ten minutes further before they came to a large pasture. Tracy heard cattle lowing in the distance, a sound rarely heard at night. It was tinged with something frantic, something contagious, because as soon as one began lowing, more followed suit until there was an outpouring of discordant sounds crackling through the nighttime air.

"What's wrong with them?" Tracy demanded once

the vehicle had stopped and the spotlight had been placed on the animals so that she could see into the darkness. Her heart stilled at the sight of them. For there they lay, in a vast swathe as far as the eye could see, some staggering, back legs dragging. As she neared, she could see that many had crusty eyes and noses, but what clinched the deal was the smell. It nearly gagged her. She placed a rag that Blake offered over her mouth to quell the stench. It was as if she had walked into a pigsty instead of a cow pasture.

"You tell me," said Blake.

In the blue ray of the spotlight, he appeared refined, his slightly graying hair neat, his light blue denim shirt and blue jeans helping him fit into the Wyoming landscape, but the cologne giving him away as someone who was used to wealth and power.

"You see how the cattle are acting. At first I thought it was something simple—maybe a bovine flu of some kind."

Tracy shook her head. The signs were classic. Nothing could create that sickly sweet smell except the feces of an animal exposed to tansy ragwort, a plant that affected the nervous system, if left untreated.

"Do you have tansy on the property?" she asked.

"Tansy? You got to be kidding."

"They're showing classic signs of ragwort poisoning." Tracy pointed to their crusty eyes and noses, to the way some of them staggered throughout the grazing area. "The smell, especially, is a giveaway. I'm telling you, it's on the property somewhere."

Blake shoved his hands in the pockets of his jeans and

leaned, one leg forward. His eyes narrowed and she prepared for him to unleash on her. Instead, he simply nodded, then ran a hand across his chin.

"I promise you," he said, "there is not a tansy ragwort within miles of here."

"Have you checked?" She faced him, determined not to be intimidated.

He turned to the driver and the pair chuckled and shook their heads. Ryan placed a hand on her back as if to let her know that he supported her, and yet even he couldn't look her in the eye.

"It's clear you're not from here." Blake swiped at a steady stream of mosquitoes. "I don't have to go check, and you want to know why?"

She shook her head.

"Because tansy ragwort is rare here, and because I hire a crew to take care of all that. Besides, there'd need to be a whole lot of it, to have affected this many cattle."

True, Tracy had never seen so many cows affected by the noxious weed. One, maybe. Two perhaps. But a dozen or more?

"Can you do anything to save them?" Blake's expression appeared grim.

Tracy wished she had a magic cure that could turn this nightmare around, but the most she could offer was hope for the unaffected. "These cattle are too far gone, but be sure to check for weeds. Then all I can suggest for the remaining cattle is to give them fresh hay . . . have you given them hay recently?"

"See for yourself."

She had them train the spotlight over the area until she saw a half-eaten bundle of hay. She walked over and kicked at it. Then bent down for a closer inspection. But even in the shadow of the spotlight, she could see bits of tansy inside the feed.

"Mr. Fordham—"

"Yes?" His face was ashen and he appeared spent.

"Check the source of your hay. In fact, give me the name of your supplier and I'll check it out, to be safe. And in the meantime, remove these bales and get the animals that haven't been affected out of here. Until we figure out what's going on, find another supplier."

Blake scratched his head and sighed. "Follow me into the house, and I'll get that information for you." Then he walked over to the jeep, pulled out a rifle and a high-beam flashlight and handed them to the driver. "You know what to do."

Tracy blanched, knowing what would come next. This was the part of the job she would never get used to. Then Blake hopped into the driver's seat and urged Tracy into the front passenger seat with Ryan in back. As they drove through the darkness, the spotlight casting an eerie halo into the night, Tracy could hear the reports and flinched, the sound launching a sick feeling in the pit of her stomach: one, two, three. The sound seemed to go on and on, growing fainter with distance.

When they arrived at the house, two men stepped out from the garage. As soon as Blake stopped and the three of them exited the jeep, the stouter of the two men jumped in and flew off to collect the man they'd left behind while the taller, thinner man escorted them inside and acted as bodyguard. Tracy tempered her breathing. Everything about this night was proving strange.

Once inside the sprawling mansion, Blake called for his wife Joy. Soon, a willowy brunette entered the room in spandex and a tight-fitting blouse with a wide animal print belt at her waist. She greeted them as though this sort of thing happened routinely, and at any hour of the day or night. Tracy nodded her head in greeting, then peered up at the vaulted ceiling with heavy oak beams that gave it a lodge-like feel. The great room itself would have fit a half dozen houses like hers. Flanking the room was a two-story fireplace made with river rock in shades that ranged from pale-blue to pink in hue, but mostly gray. And it appeared by the glowing embers and ash that the fireplace was well used. A two-story bank of windows faced the snow-capped Rockies, the Sawtooth comprising merely a portion of the mountain chain. Tracy could imagine the place in wintertime.

To the left of the great room lay the kitchen, a massive room with multiple ovens and an island with two stoves. In one corner was a pizza oven, a wood plank hanging beside it along with red oven mitts. And over the island hung a collection of beautiful copper cookware.

Tracy tried to take it all in as Blake said, "Follow me. My office is down the hallway."

She gave a brief nod to Blake's wife, then trailed Blake down the hall with Ryan close behind. Framing each side of the hallway were awards and pictures of Blake with a number of stars and starlets, along with people who exuded power, but whose names and faces she didn't know.

"Back here." Blake pointed to a room off to the left.

Tracy was just about to follow him in, when she saw a light in the room off to her right, highlighting a wall of pictures and newspaper articles tacked to the largest corkboard she'd ever seen. She frowned and was about to turn into the adjacent room when she saw something that stopped her. The headline read, "Beloved Wyoming Woman Still Missing Twenty Years Later." But what struck her most was the grainy black-and-white photograph of a woman. The name written on a white piece of paper above it? Mabel. Wife of the resident ghost.

Seven

Tracy entered the boardroom and stood staring at the walled map, at the threaded thumb tacks that showed Mabel's movements prior to her disappearance. To the feed store in Cody. To get gas. A trip to the hair salon. All the normal mundane things that one does throughout a normal day. A list of people who'd last seen her was written on a clipboard to the right of the corkboard, hanging from a peg, checkmarks next to their names, all except one, and she had trouble reading that one.

"Can I help you locate something, Miss Barnhart?"

Tracy started at the sound of Blake's voice, heat flaming her cheeks as she turned to face him. "I'm sorry. I . . . is this the woman who lived in my house? Grayson's wife?"

Blake hesitated, as if not wanting to give too much away. At last, he gave a single nod. "They never found her body. For all we know, she could still be alive."

Tracy turned back to the board. Something about it troubled her, but she couldn't pinpoint what. Then it came to her with a snap of her fingers. "Where is Grayson in all this? He's not even mentioned in any of it. Was he ever interviewed . . . for the local papers?"

Blake merely snorted as though, once again, she had come up short. "He was a very private man. A World War I vet. A really good guy. Everyone says so. You'd be hard pressed to hear a single bad word about the guy. Plus he loved his wife."

"Doesn't that make him the prime suspect? The one least likely to have a motive?" Tracy held her chin up, refusing to back down.

"You've been watching too many of my movies, either that or reading too many mystery novels. No, I've been at this long enough to know he had nothing to do with her disappearance. Besides, since I've been here, looking into the matter--"

"And why, precisely, *are* you looking into it?" She leaned up against a conference table that stood in the middle of the room, a silver laptop at the ready.

"I make movies, Miss Barnhart."

"Tracy. Call me Tracy."

"Okay then, Tracy. Think of it like this. I get a movie, the town solves a mystery. It's a win-win." The steam seemed to have gone out of his engine, because he plopped down into a comfy recliner that appeared out of place for what was otherwise a conference room. Probably one of many. Tracy

68

had almost forgotten about Ryan, but heard his voice along with that of the bodyguard from the adjacent room.

"And what happens when you find Mabel?"

"Leave that to me." He rubbed his face, his eyes appearing bloodshot from what must have been a long day.

"So why do you think it wasn't the old man?" Tracy sidestepped him.

He scratched his brow and sighed. "Because someone wants me to stop investigating her disappearance. This incident with the cattle wasn't the first 'accident'," he said, a mysterious gleam to his eye.

"Oh?" She stood, hoping to learn more, but at that moment, Ryan entered the room with the bodyguard in tow.

"There you two are. I thought I'd been deserted. Weren't you going to–" He turned to Tracy, but his eyes moved to the corkboard and he froze, his mind apparently registering the implications. He frowned, then turned to Blake. "What the heck is this all about? Why are you looking into Mabel's death, not that that's a bad thing, mind you? It's just . . . odd, you being an outsider."

Tracy could tell he hadn't meant to say what he had, at least not like that. Suddenly, the light flickered.

"The power. We're off grid. Sometimes we use more than we produce. The backup generator will kick in soon. I like to be as self-sufficient as possible."

In the flickering shadows, the lines on Blake's face made him appear much older than he was. But just as suddenly, the generator kicked back in with a hum. Blake released a breath and leaned back in his overstuffed leather chair, a feminine touch from his wife, Joy, no doubt.

Everything about this man seemed at odds—the mansion, wanting to be off grid, a movie mogul raising cattle in the middle of Wyoming, population just over half a million people in a state the size of Germany. What more didn't they know about the man? And why such a remote location? Paparazzi, sure, but Tracy had the feeling there was more to the story than he was letting on.

"So let me say this again," Ryan said, clearly determined not to let this go.

"Ryan—" Tracy reached for his hand, not wanting to overstep their bounds.

"No." Blake steepled his fingers. "I have nothing to hide. The reason I'm so interested in this case—the reason I've come back to Wyoming, is to learn the truth about Mabel."

This time it was Tracy who wanted answers. "But why? Why Mabel? People go missing every day. Unsolved mysteries all over the U.S. Why her?"

His eyes glistened as he lay his mouth against his steepled fingers, emotion working at the base of his throat. "Because she's my grandmother. And I loved her."

* * *

Ryan felt in his pocket for the online address that the bodyguard had presented him.

Hopefully, this would lead to the ranch that had supplied the tansy-laced hay that had poisoned the cattle. Now, as Ryan stood in the middle of the large conference room, staring down at Blake in the overstuffed leather chair, he shook his head, thinking he'd heard wrong. Mabel . . . Blake's grandmother? Surely, he knew every person who'd grown up in this neck of the woods. The valley might be large, but the people were few. And yes he'd been young when Mabel disappeared, but surely he would have heard Blake's name before this, seen him at a picnic.

As if registering Ryan's confusion, Blake explained. "I changed my name when I moved to L.A. Didn't want my parents hounded. It was easier that way. Made up a life for myself with more cachet. You know, world traveler, winters in Switzerland. It was Hollywood. Everyone's an actor."

"Not to seem too personal, but how did you finance your enterprise?"

Blake laughed. "Actually, I took a job on set. Basically, a gofer. But the director saw me inspecting the cameras, noticed my interest and began teaching me things. Just a few things at first. Then more as time went on. Turns out he was a closet gay. When he developed HIV, no one would touch him. Friends that he'd known for years turned their back on him. His family wanted nothing to do with him. So I ended up taking care of him in his final years. Figured he had helped me learn the business. Besides, he was like a father to me." Sadness tinged his words, but he forced a smile.

"That still doesn't explain how you financed your business." Ryan cocked a brow.

"Ryan!" Tracy shot him a warning scowl.

"No! I'm fine talking about it." Blake steepled his hands beneath his chin. "When he died, he willed me the whole kit-

'n-caboodle. His mansion, houses in Switzerland and France. And he'd invested his fortunes wisely. I went from being a poor kid from the sticks one day to taking over his job as director the next. Eventually, I bought my own studio, and as they say, the rest is history.

Tracy pulled out one of the chairs with castors from around the conference desk and offered Ryan a seat, then sat in one herself. "That explains how you obtained your wealth, but who are you then, if not Blake Fordham?"

Blake reached over to an end table beside his chair and pulled out a pipe, which he promptly stuffed with pipe tobacco, cherry, by the smell of it. "My name's Colter. People called me Colt."

Ryan rolled the name around on his tongue, a vague memory forming of a skinny kid, tall and pale. Freckles. This man looked nothing like the Colt he knew. That boy was nervous and shy. This man was gregarious, poised.

"Why are you only searching for Mabel now?" Tracy strummed the arms of her chair with her fingers, her brow furrowed and her bright blue eyes mirroring the questions Ryan had about Mabel's disappearance.

Blake shrugged. "I was young when Gran disappeared. My parents were pretty choked up about it all. Never talked about it except in whispers, when they thought I wasn't listening. You know—that was back in the day."

"Back in the day?" Ryan tilted his head.

"When children were to be seen and not heard. We didn't question things like that. But now—"

"Now?" Tracy stood and walked over to the corkboard,

72

her eyes traversing the map that hung to one side. Yellow thread connected pins that marked the county, final sightings no doubt, on that fateful day that Mabel had gone missing.

"I don't know. It's just that I have kids of my own. Grown kids. One's about to give birth to our first grandson." Absent-mindedly, he picked at a family portrait on the tabletop next to him. In the picture were Blake and his wife and three strapping boys, an overfed golden retriever rounding out the photo. They were standing on a patio next to a pool. Everything about the photo screamed wealth, from the very paper it was printed on down to the placement of each member of the family, as though they were posed by a master photographer who sought an elegant yet casual look—like a day in the life of the Kennedys at Kennebunkport, Maine. And yet, something about the photo hinted at melancholy, if only Ryan could put his finger on it. And it wasn't just Blake's blank stare into the camera, as though he were looking at something just over the photographer's shoulder and wishing he were there, instead of on the other side of the camera. Nor was it the feeling that the three boys had just spent the day tossing footballs across the lawn and were spent. Or that their mother had corralled all four men and was patiently waiting for the photographer to snap his picture and be done. No, Ryan had the feeling, though he couldn't say why, that the entire family was . . . *lost* somehow. As though some integral part of the picture was missing.

Tracy brought Ryan around when she said, "So now that you will be grandparents, you wonder what it would be like for others . . . not to know. To never go searching."

Ryan joined his hands behind his head and leaned back in his chair, surprised at Tracy's astute observation. Apparently, Blake agreed, because he nodded, his eyes moistening slightly, or maybe it was simply a trick of the pendant lighting that hung in serpentine fashion over the length of the table, undulating above them and crisscrossing at each end.

"And it would make one heck of a movie." Ryan immediately regretted how crass that must sound. But it was true, and he could see he'd struck a nerve in Blake, because the movie mogul cringed. *Premier Director to Hollywood's A-list Stars Finds Missing Grandparent.*

"So, have you learned anything?" Tracy asked.

"That she didn't go back East to see her family. That she went into town the day prior, and everyone said she seemed fine . . . except for—"

"For what?" Ryan dropped his hands to his side and leaned forward.

"Well, it seems a few odd things had been happening back at the homestead prior to her going missing."

"Like . . . ?" Tracy turned away from the corkboard to face him.

"Well, like what happened here tonight. A couple of her cows showed signs of illness. And supposedly Gran had heard someone roaming around the place the night before. But Granddad never heard it. Said she must've been dreaming, at least that's what Margie said—"

"Margie?" Tracy leaned on the edge of the conference table.

Ryan knew Margie only too well. She wore a beehive and schoolmarm glasses and had seemed old even then. The woman had been a steel dynamo, once upon a time, her antics legendary. You didn't cross Margie unless you planned on a whipping when you got home. No, he'd been smart enough to steer clear of her early on, but he'd also known some who were not so fortunate. The woman gave new meaning to the word nosy.

"Used to work at the five and dime back in the day," Ryan explained.

"Granddad's hearing wasn't the best," Blake mused, "so there could have been something or someone roaming the place. After all, Gran had ears like a bat." He laughed at the irony.

Tracy stood and began pacing. Ryan could almost see the gears turning in her head.

"Okay." Tracy pivoted around to face Blake. "So you've decided to finally check into what happened to your grandmother. But there's one thing I don't get."

"Hmm?" He tapped his lower lip with steepled fingers.

"If you're looking into all that, why sell the place to a veterinarian from Seattle?" Tracy cocked her head in confusion. "And why wasn't your name on the deed when I purchased the place?"

Blake stood and headed toward the door, as if ending their meeting. But before he exited the room, he halted. "In response to your first question, because the valley needed a vet, and no one else wanted to move into the middle of nowhere. And besides, land prices around here are too steep for most people, especially a vet, so I gave you a good deal. As to the second question, the deed was held in a trust, for privacy reasons. Now, has Peter given you the address for the ranch where we were sold the hay?"

Ryan nodded.

"Okay then, Peter will see you out."

The hulking bodyguard magically appeared, as if he'd been waiting in the wings for just such a moment to usher them gone. But not before Ryan had caught a glimpse of the Colt he'd remembered from childhood. Funny . . . well-liked. Then why had he changed his name and moved hundreds of miles away to reinvent himself?

Eight

As Tracy peered back through the rearview mirror of her old GMC, she couldn't help but shiver at the sheer size and scope of the mansion. Lit up like an oasis amid the darkness, the sparkling waters of the fountain formed golden droplets that rained down in front of it. She glanced over at Ryan and wondered what he thought of the place. Of Blake. She had to admit she had been surprised by Blake's candor. She had expected a movie mogul to be . . . what? Arrogant? Full of himself? But Blake was just the opposite. She could see why he had gone far. Although she couldn't put her finger on it, she trusted him.

"I'll run you home," Tracy offered. She turned onto the main road. In the headlights she could see the reflection of animal eyes in the darkness. Something small. "*Tapitum lucidum.*" She hadn't realized she'd said the words aloud.

"What?" Ryan sat with his elbow out the window despite the coolness of the evening.

"*Tapitum lucidum.* It's the iridescence in a nocturnal animal's eyes."

"Well, expect to see a lot of them at night, because you're not in Kansas anymore, Dorothy."

Tracy couldn't help but laugh, even as she yawned, the day . . . the move, for that matter, catching up with her. She wished she were in bed with a comfy quilt wrapped around her, despite the springs that squealed when she sat on the bed. Or rolled over. Or slept.

Then her thoughts turned to the cattle she'd seen and her mood changed instantly. How could anyone do such a thing to innocent animals? She had become a large animal vet to save animals, not to see them put down over something so senseless.

As if Ryan had sensed her change in mood, he turned to her. "If it would help, I could stay the night." He immediately threw his hands up, palms out, to ward off any questions. "On the couch, I mean. So you wouldn't have to drive me home. Besides, I've rounded up a posse of men to help with the repairs tomorrow, starting with that porch of yours. They'll be there early in the morning."

Tracy paused, considering. She had to admit that sleeping alone in the dark farmhouse, no one for miles around if she needed help, *had* been a bit disconcerting. She'd given herself the "buck up" speech. Had told herself not to be a coward, but somehow her body hadn't aligned itself with her head. She'd tossed and turned the entire night. If she didn't get some sleep soon, she was going to fall asleep at the wheel. Besides, after what she'd witnessed tonight, she was dead set on not being alone.

"Okay," she said at last. "But the house has three bedrooms. I'm sure I can do better than the couch."

Ryan thanked her, then laid his head back against the headrest and closed his eyes for only a moment. Then, as if recalling her earlier driving and her current fatigue, he snapped to attention, rubbed his eyes and peered at the road.

Now that she had him back again, she said, "So, who do you think was responsible for the animal feed, and what do you think of this whole Mabel thing?"

"I don't know, on either count." Ryan stretched like a cat. "And what did Blake mean he needed a veterinarian? Not a personal vet, surely."

She had to admit, she hadn't thought of Blake possibly needing a personal vet. But whatever he'd meant, she planned to help any rancher who needed her. Another thought had been rolling around in her head since tonight's call. She didn't feel comfortable roaming the countryside alone. She needed an assistant, preferably a strong male assistant who could accompany her.

"Ryan . . . ."

"Hmm?" He rolled his shoulders as though releasing the day's tensions.

"I'm going to need an assistant. Preferably one who is used to . . . well, let's just say unique circumstances."

"Ah, I see." Ryan yawned. "You need someone like me. A former vet. Someone who can help you if things get out of hand or you have to go out on a difficult call."

Tracy patted the steering wheel. "Precisely."

"But none of my guys are vets–I mean veterinarians. We've all picked up some things about animals along the way. You can't help but learn a few things, working on a ranch."

"Who has been there the longest–has the most experience with the animals?"

Ryan closed an eye and bit his lip, thinking. "Besides Wyatt?" He shrugged his shoulders. "I guess Les, but he's the ranch manager. He's needed there."

"Who else?" She eyed him surreptitiously.

"Well, that would be me, I guess. But I'm starting up the search and rescue program with the dogs." He shrugged an apology.

Tracy drove the GMC down the dirt road toward home, the truck bouncing each time it hit a rut, casting both of them side to side, her thoughts still on the problem of finding someone to work with her on calls. "Hang on to your hat." The truck bucked and rolled once more.

"I'm used to these washboard roads." His voice rose and dipped along with the furrows in the road.

Suddenly, she slapped the steering wheel, the excitement of an idea forming in her head pushing all thoughts of fatigue out the window. "You say you have programs that help your vets learn a skill, right?"

"Yeah?" He bent his head slightly.

"Well, I could teach one of your vets a skill. Come down to the ranch a couple of times a week–teach whoever you choose about becoming a veterinarian's assistant. And I did an apprenticeship at a search and rescue camp, so I picked up a thing or two that might help you with your dog training."

Ryan grabbed the dash of the GMC as they ground to a halt in front of the dilapidated old farmstead, but she could see by the light in his eyes that she had his attention.

"So, you would teach one of my guys . . . for free?" he added, as if to make sure she knew they couldn't afford to pay.

"And one of your guys would accompany me . . . also for free. It's a win-win."

He stuck out his chin as though thinking. Then finally, he nodded. "Let's shake on it."

And with that, she had a new partner. Now it was just a matter of which vet he would choose.

* * *

Stepping gingerly over the broken boards on the porch and inserting the old skeleton key

into the lock, Tracy turned to Ryan who stood back, yawning. "So, who will my new partner be, do you suppose?"

"Me," Ryan said.

Tracy paused to take stock of Ryan, part of his face obscured by the moonlight. She

wondered whether he was serious. "But you just said you're starting up the search and rescue program. How can you afford the time away?" She pushed her way through the door, which hung on the rotting floorboard of the entryway.

"Well, truth is, James has always been eying my spot at the ranch, and I kind of like the idea of shaking things up a bit. So I don't end up in a rut, like that road of yours." He laughed, but she could hear the weariness in his voice. "Also, I figure I'm probably not veterinarian material, but I could shadow you, make sure you're safe, and in return I could use help teaching the dogs search and rescue."

"You're sure that will be a fair trade? I can't pay you."

Ryan nodded, then followed her into the kitchen where she turned on the drum light fixture that sent shards of illumination filtering through the room as she prepared them an evening snack.

"I hope you don't mind a ham sandwich."

He shook his head. "Not at all. And as to pay, I'm sure Wyatt will keep me on the payroll because I'll be bringing him a new instructor to train his men. Besides that, you'll be training me, which is the purpose of the program."

She put the sandwich together and handed it to him, then walked to the pale blue refrigerator with a design on the front that reminded her of something from the old George Jetson cartoons on the oldies channel. She brought out a bottle of milk and filled two glasses, then set them in front of each of their plates.

"What's this?" Ryan peered down at his sandwich.

"What's what?" Tracy shrugged, not sure what he was talking about.

He eyed the bread, a rich rye with white swirls.

"That?" she asked. "You don't eat rye bread?"

"Not since . . . well, ever."

Tracy laughed. "It's all I have at the moment, so it's that or nothing."

He lifted a brow, but took a bite, then swallowed it down with a gulp of milk. When he could talk again, he said, "Not bad. Not as good as the homemade stuff Emajean makes, but not bad."

When he was through eating, she took him upstairs, showed him his room, and then excused herself as she retired to her own bedroom. Despite the events of the day, she had trouble falling asleep, her thoughts swirling in her head. It was nearly 2:00 AM before she finally dozed off.

She awakened to the sound of motorcycles, followed shortly thereafter by hammers and saws. Quickly, she threw on a pair of torn jeans and a T-shirt with the words Vets Rule on it. She stuffed her feet into boots and ran, nearly tripping over the cat as she trundled downstairs.

When she opened the door, Ryan was already standing there wearing a toolbelt. Behind him, several guys worked on the porch, their Harley Davidsons and one lone Indian bike parked out front. Too late, Tracy realized she hadn't combed her hair. She tucked as much as she could of it behind her ears, hoping that traces of mascara weren't ringing her eyes like a raccoon.

"Meet my men." Ryan introduced them one by one. "This here's Bryce." A young black man, burley with tattoos running up his arms, came forward and shook her hand. "He's a master carpenter. If anyone can get this place fixed up, he can."

Bryce said, "How do you do?"

Then Bryce stepped back as Ryan introduced Reeves, a tall, scrawny fellow whose baggy jeans hung low on his hips.

His frizzy red hair was burnished by the sun to a coppery sheen. The man's muscles rippled beneath a white T-shirt with a picture of a motorcycle on it, against the backdrop of the Grand Tetons. Underneath, it said "Get Your Motor Running."

Bringing up the rear was a broad-shouldered Hispanic guy, early twenties, sporting a single stud earring. Ryan introduced him as Marcos.

Marcos nodded at Tracy, then turned his attention to Ryan. "Jason is training some of the guys and their dogs back at the ranch this morning. Said he was sorry he missed you, but will catch you next time."

"I'll message him later and explain the situation." Ryan then showed the men the work to be done.

For the next few hours, the foursome traipsed around the farm, clearing away debris and piling up the junk to be sold or taken to the dump. Tracy had been scraping the old paint off the south side of the farmhouse when one of Lindsay's ranch hands came running across the field, his breath coming in short gasps.

"We've got a ewe down. She's been tryin' to deliver for over an hour. Lindsay thinks it's a breech. Can you come?"

Tracy called to Ryan and asked him to take care of things while she went to check on the ewe. Then she ran to the truck and grabbed her bag. She followed the young man until she reached the farthest field where the sheep were penned. Sure enough, one was tipped on its side, a plaintive "baa" disturbing the other sheep who hovered around her, but at a safe distance. The other sheep bleated in return, as though standing vigil for the ewe.

For the next hour, Tracy worked to turn the lamb inside its mother, but each time she reached for the nose, and tried to push it away so she could grab the hoof, the hoof moved just out of reach. She was sweating and could feel all eyes upon her. This was it, her make or break moment. If she couldn't deliver a live lamb soon, she would lose it.

She paused for a moment, taking a deep breath before striking out one last time. Her face was on fire and sweat dripped onto her chin as she reached deep into the ewe's cavity, feeling for the tiny hoof. She growled, adrenaline flooding her as her arm reached its zenith. Then there! Finally, the hard hoof. She had it in her hand. When she'd nearly given up on saving either mother or lamb, the baby turned and moments later, the amniotic sac flowed onto the ground, the baby covered in lanolin. Within minutes it wobbled onto its feet, its legs buckling and bending as it endeavored to gain purchase. Soon, the baby was feeding from its mother. Tracy offered instructions on the care of the infant, promising to check in on it later. Only then did she realize how much time had elapsed. She was filthy and the men must be starved. She bade a quick farewell and made a beeline for the farmhouse. As she approached, she heard the motorcycles rev to life as one by one they rode off down the road, all except the last. Ryan was climbing onto the back of it, Bryce at the wheel.

"I left you a note in the kitchen. The guys and I are heading over to Grady's Diner. Wanna come?" he shouted over the roar of the engine.

Tracy looked down at herself, at the afterbirth and mud, then shook her head. Here these men had come all the way to help her with the farm, and she hadn't even been there to feed them. "I have to clean up. But thank your men for me and please apologize on my behalf. Tell them their meal is on me. I'll see if I can't get word to the diner."

Ryan nodded. "We've got to head to the ranch afterward. Do you have anywhere we could put the pups if we bring them with us tomorrow?"

Tracy wasn't sure where she would put them, but she would find a place. Furthermore, she planned to find a way to make it up to the men for all their hard work. For the unforeseeable future, she would still be learning the lay of the land. She knew she would make many mistakes before she was finally settled in, but in the meantime she could only promise to try her best.

"I'll figure it out. Go ahead and bring the pups."

Once he was gone, Tracy took a quick shower, then once dressed, turned her attention to finding a place for the service dogs. The perfect choice was behind the barn, but the amount of work it would take to clear the property to make it habitable seemed insurmountable. *One step at a time.*

Hands on hips, she took a deep breath, releasing the air slowly from her lungs. The smells of agriculture, of sheep and meadow, of the stream that ran on the other side of the barn, refreshed her. When she looked around at the landscape, despite the sheer size and scope of it, she no longer felt overwhelmed. In her mind, she could see it as she wanted it to be. A pristine white farmhouse—a wraparound porch painted in an understated blue slate. Flowers out front. A large area behind the barn for the dogs. And she would turn the inside of the barn into a state-of-the-art veterinary facility.

Only one way to begin. She marched out to the back of the barn and groaned. She could put some of the debris in the back of her truck to be hauled to the dump. The usable items she could sell, give the money to the men for their work on the farm. But first, she would need to organize the chaos into some semblance of order. She found a pile of old logs near the back of the barn. She could erect those in each of the corners and along the sides of the area where they would train the dogs. And she found a giant roll of fencing. That could be placed around the perimeter of the enclosure. She wanted it to be a fun place for the dogs. A place where not only could they learn the tasks of a service dog, but where they could play during their off time.

"Looks like another trip into town is in order." But for now, she had a gargantuan task ahead of her and the day was slipping past. She would have only five hours before sundown.

For the next several hours, she placed as much of the debris that would go to the dump into the back of her pickup. Anything that could be sold she muscled to the front of the barn either by dragging it, rolling it, or carrying it. To her disappointment, she had only a fourteen square foot space cleared next to the barn, but it was enough that she was able to find two shorter poles, insert them into the ground and fill the bases with concrete, then attach the wire mesh around the poles, securing the mesh to each end of the rear of the barn. Now, for something to store water and food in for the pups. She would need to call Ryan and ask him to bring the dog food. Fortunately, after a brief search, she found a horse trough that she filled with water for the rescue animals. But what could she give the pups to keep them busy while the men worked? She searched inside the barn as best she could in the waning light. And although she couldn't find anything specifically for a dog, she did find a partially deflated basketball to keep them busy. And she found a couple of old tires that she muscled into the pen for them to jump on. The tires could also be useful for training. She would need to find the dogs shelter as well. A tarp strung over the top would do the trick, she decided with a snap of her fingers. She ran to her truck and pulled out the old blue tarp she used for painting and all sorts of odd projects. A half hour later, she had a makeshift home for the dogs.

Exhausted after the long day, she made quick work of dinner, fed the cat, took a shower to wash off the grit, then fell into bed, every portion of her body aching from the day's exertions. For the first time since she'd come to Wyoming, she fell fast asleep and slept the entire night.

* * *

Ryan pulled up outside of Western Rentals, a nondescript building with a side yard filled with large rental equipment. His buddies waited in their trucks for him to rent the power washer and the sprayer so he could begin the task of cleaning and painting Tracy's farmhouse. He'd made the purchase and was about to leave when he heard a man in his late fifties, early sixties, say something about the veterinarian.

"Yeah, I'm here to look over the new practice," he told the clerk.

"Oh, the practice of that new gal . . . Tracy somebody or other?"

The man snorted, as though the idea that a woman could run the practice so far from civilization was preposterous. "Yeah, well if it's not up to standard, she'll be getting the boot." The pair laughed.

Ryan decided it was high time to mosey on over and set the man straight. He cleared his throat to get the man's attention. "Can I speak with you?" He nodded toward a shelf lined with tools so that they could talk in private.

"Do I know you?" The silver-haired man followed Ryan.

"I'm a friend of Tracy 'somebody or other'." Ryan tried to keep his cool. "I couldn't help but overhear you say you were here to look over her practice. Are you an inspector then?" Ryan introduced himself, then reached a hand out to shake.

For a moment, they stood at an impasse, then finally the man reached out his hand as well. "Hank," he said, offering nothing further.

"Well, Hank, does Tracy know you're here to inspect her practice?" Ryan gripped the man's hand, giving it an extra firm handshake.

"Not yet, but she will soon. I hope to stop by her place tomorrow afternoon."

The glee in Hank's eye put a knot in Ryan's stomach. He didn't want to be the one to have to tell her about the inspector, but he didn't want her to be broadsided either. "Just a quick question. Is that allowed—considering she hasn't even had time to get the place in order?"

Hank leaned in close enough for Ryan to smell hash browns and bacon on him as if having just left the Waffle House. And his breath smelled of stale coffee. "Actually, if she plans to operate here, her business requires an inspection as per Wyoming code."

Ryan wanted nothing more than to yank the man's shirt in a wadded up fist and thrust him into the wall of tools. He envisioned them cascading down on the man. But he didn't want to end up in jail. Especially not now, just as he was getting to know Tracy. And like her.

"Well, I happen to be headed to Tracy's place tomorrow morning," Ryan said through gritted teeth. "I'll give her a heads up."

Hank's rheumy blue eyes lit up, clearly mistaking Ryan's offer as an assist, not the warning that Ryan intended.

"Thanks, pal." Hank then pointed to his waiting purchase at the counter. "Better get to it then." He turned and limped back toward the counter.

Ryan stood rooted to the spot, watching the man, then turned to leave. What the heck would he tell Tracy, he wondered as he climbed into his pickup and started up the engine? She would be devastated. Whatever he did, he'd have to pick the right time, when they were alone. Still, the ride to the ranch dragged like the weight he was carrying.

Nine

Tracy didn't awaken until she heard a commotion of vehicles the following morning.

For a moment, her mind didn't register the sound. Then she heard multiple yips from excited puppies and recalled that Ryan's workers had promised to return early. Quickly, she dressed, grateful for last night's shower so she wouldn't have to contend with that. Then she ran downstairs and opened the front door. To her surprise, there stood all four men, each carrying one side of a large chicken coop made to look like an old-time saloon, complete with swinging doors. To the side of the enclosure, a ramp had been built for the chickens to climb into their nesting stalls. Chicken wire fenced in the rest of the coop. This time the men had brought a truck filled with supplies, adding in a half dozen chickens and a lone rooster, which squawked and created a racket that set the pups yipping as they gathered around the men's legs.

"What is this?" Tracy exclaimed.

"Your new chicken house." Bryce tipped his cap slightly with one hand. "Where do you want it?"

Tracy peered around and pointed to the side of the house opposite the barn . . . as far away from her bedroom window as possible. That way she wouldn't be able to hear the rooster at dawn . . . she hoped. She had a feeling mornings around here started much earlier than mornings in Seattle, where she'd wake up to a cup of coffee and gaze out over the moist skyline of the city that saw nearly perpetual rain.

She yelled her thanks as they maneuvered the chicken house to a spot well out of reach of the house, apparently realizing, as she did, that the morning wakeup call might not always be appreciated. The pups ran after the men, hot on their heels. She laughed as she watched the pups lunge at each other's ears, or roll in the grass, only to spring to life and gambol after the men.

Determined not to make the same mistake as before, Tracy ran inside the house, leaving the men to their business as she put together a hearty breakfast. Ryan returned twenty minutes later and knocked on the open door to announce his return. Today, he wore old jeans and a plain white t-shirt, his hair not quite dry from an early morning shower.

"We were thinking we would start the process of painting your house today," he said as he entered.

Tracy paused what she was doing, and leaned into the kitchen counter with relief. She had been stewing and fretting over how she would accomplish that. She'd never used a sprayer before and she'd only just begun the process of chipping away the old paint. At this rate, it would have taken months to get it done.

"We took the liberty of renting a power washer. Once we get the old paint off the place and let it dry a day or so, we can get her painted, if you don't mind."

"Mind?" She could think of nothing she minded less. A weight had been lifted from her at the thought that she would have that major hurtle down.

"Now for another matter."

Ryan's tone changed like the shifting winds and she once again stopped what she was doing to listen.

"You know how you were expecting the place to be in better condition?"

"Yeah, what about it?" She turned back to laying strips of bacon into a cast-iron skillet.

He scratched at his chin. "So you probably weren't expecting to have an inspection so soon?"

Tracy peered up sharply and read the apology in Ryan's green eyes. Her hands trembled slightly as she began cracking eggs into a large bowl.

"I ran into the inspector in town yesterday afternoon. He's here . . . to shut the practice down if it's not in good shape." Ryan came to stand beside her, placing a hand on her shoulder. "I'm so sorry."

She sagged against the kitchen sink, feeling the sharp corners dig into the small of her back, a low sigh, like a leaky kettle spilling from her lips.

"Can he do that?" Tracy realized too late that she

sounded like a petulant child.

"He can, apparently. He'll be by to talk to you later in the day. To take pictures." Ryan took up one side of the counter and began cracking eggs with her.

Tracy felt her world spinning. She had uprooted her entire life to come here, to try to start over. To test her mettle as a veterinarian and as a woman in a man's world, only to be cut off at the pass. Her house wasn't even painted, the sad irony not lost on her.

"What will I do?" She took a moment to let what he'd said sink in. "I mean there is no plan B."

Ryan stuttered and stammered as he cracked another egg, spilling half its contents onto the green speckled formica countertop. "See, the guys and I talked it over this morning after we arrived here, and we have an idea."

"Idea?" She heard his voice as though from a mile away, her thoughts heavy with foreboding.

"Well, we could use someone to teach us to train the dogs, like you mentioned the other day. We received a grant. It's not a lot, but it could keep you going for a while, maybe indefinitely if you're not a big spender." He smiled at that. "And we could do your home improvement projects . . . to keep your costs low and to turn the business into a viable veterinary practice."

"But what about the practice?" she demanded, her voice quavering. "The ranchers need me now!"

Ryan looked down at his feet, then back up to her. "You could work from the ranch . . . Our place has been inspected before. I'm sure it would pass a bill of health while we get yours going."

Tracy closed her eyes and sighed. All of her dreams, her plans, gone. *No, not gone, just changed.* She forced her eyes open, forced herself to face the truth. She would never get to start her practice as a large animal vet, if she didn't accept help. And yet she had never been good at asking for help. But she loved animals. Of all shapes and sizes. Maybe, just maybe, she was being offered a chance at a new beginning.

She began stirring the eggs and listened to the sizzle of the bacon in the pan, the wonderful aroma making her feel as though perhaps this was the right move for her. That maybe this is what she was meant to do. To her surprise, she knew she would miss working from this place . . . The farmhouse was like an ailing friend. It needed her. And the truth is, she needed the farm as much if not more.

"Okay," she said at last. "Let's give it a try." Then she just had to hope everything would work out.

Ten

Despite all the things that needed tending at the ranch that day, Tracy announced that she would need to go into town. The inspector wasn't due until the afternoon, according to Ryan. If training dogs was to be her calling, for now, she would need supplies. Lots of them. As she drove the rutted road toward town, then onto the paved highway, she couldn't help but think of everything that had transpired since she'd arrived at a farm she could only describe as a wreck. And yet there was something about it, the creak of the floorboards in the living room, the cascade of trees that lined the river next to the homestead, the moon over the Sawtooths that bathed her bedroom in a silvery blue glow at night. It was like something out of a children's book. It made her feel . . . well, like she belonged. She'd never really felt that in the city. And to her surprise, she now had a community of men to help her.

Hopefully, she would be of value to them as well.

She rolled down the window, breathing in the sagebrush-scented prairie. But worry soon settled over her like a fine powder of dust. She had been hired to get the farm up and running, to turn it into a state-of-the art veterinary clinic. But what if the inspector shut her down? Refused to give her farm another look once she'd managed to fix the thousands of problems she'd cataloged in her own private inspection. She didn't know, but this new kink in the works left her neck and shoulders feeling sore as she drove the final distance to town.

Ten minutes later, she pushed her doubts aside as she pulled into the hardware store. She would need something colorful to train the dogs to not only traverse a tight shute, but to circumnavigate a series of posts in serpentine fashion. She would also need to teach the dogs how to jump up, to turn off and on a light should the dog be used as a therapy dog for a disabled vet. To open refrigerator doors using a towel that it would pull with its teeth. Ryan had told her that half of the pups were to be trained for search and rescue, the other half for disabled vets with specific needs. And although that would require a lot of training to get them ready, her experience with dogs had prepared her for this.

She turned off the engine and sat in her truck, grateful for the sun's rays. Although thankful for Ryan's kind offer to let her use the ranch from which to operate her new veterinary practice, her heart remained committed to the farmhouse, to the path she'd chosen *if* she could talk Hank into giving her some wiggle room. In the meantime, she still needed to do research about the cattle at Blake's ranch. Blake had given her the name of the ranch where he'd been sold the hay. He'd ordered it online and had it shipped from Idaho. From the Circle T Ranch. While in town, she would need to ask around, see if anyone had heard of it. Surely someone would know about the hay and where it had come from.

As she exited the truck, she accidentally bumped into an older man, slightly grizzled, his gray hair haphazard from the wind. Stubble anchored his chin.

"Watch it!" he said.

Tracy scowled as she watched him limp off at a slow but steady pace. She turned in time to see a thin black woman with short straight hair and a round face. She came up to Tracy and introduced herself.

"Don't mind him," she said. "He's a mean old cuss. New around here. Doesn't seem to like much of anybody, by the looks of it." Then she held out her hand. "The name's Gladys. I work over there, at J & R Marketing."

Tracy shook the woman's hand then frowned. "I'm new around here too—the veterinarian living at Grayson's place."

"I know, honey," Gladys said. "Everyone knows. Small towns have big ears." She laughed. "Better get used to it. It drove me crazy when I first moved here."

"Where were you from?" Tracy asked, curious about the stranger.

"Chicago. Believe it or not, a little over a year ago, I was offered a job here that pays next to nothing in order to live in Cody. Saw it in pictures and just had to come. Now I'm part owner of J & R's."

Tracy peered up at the sign above the stanchion along

the broad wooden walkway then down at the horse railings. It reminded Tracy of something out of the Old West.

"Oh, then if you're new here, you probably haven't heard of the Circle T Ranch? Out of southern Idaho?" Tracy sighed, disappointed that her first query would be a bust.

"Can't say as I have," Gladys said. "But let me quick grab my briefcase from the trunk of my car, and then I can look it up on the computer in my office, if you can spare the time."

"Spare the time? Sure, thanks!" Tracy warmed to the woman instantly, surprised at her luck. Though young, Gladys had an almost motherly quality about her that no doubt helped in marketing.

Tracy waited for Gladys to gather her briefcase, then followed the woman into her place of business. Inside the spartan office, surprisingly modern furniture graced the room from a sleek glass countertop with gray high-backed chairs to bold color choices decorating the walls.

Gladys must have noticed her eyes scanning the room. "That was Stanford's doing," she said. "He's the designer of us two."

On cue, Stanford stood and held out a hand. He was tall and his dark hair gelled. His clothing reminded her of the men she'd seen at nightclubs. Tight knit pants and a blue-gray shirt. He seemed so out of place in Cody, Wyoming, what she knew of it at least, and yet, like Gladys, she liked him instantly. He had an infectious smile and if she had to guess, she bet dollars to donuts he had a great sense of humor. And as if he'd read her thoughts, he immediately launched in, dishing about Gladys and her penchant for black coffee.

"Black coffee!" he repeated as though she were his crazy aunt instead of his colleague. "I'm going across the street for the good stuff. Want me to bring you back something?"

Tracy hadn't had a decent cup of coffee since Seattle. Already, she could imagine the aroma, the taste. "I would love a mocha grande."

"That's a Grand Teton here, but sure. You got it." He threw a light jacket over his shoulder, a new-age Hans Solo. Tracy had to smile, in spite of herself.

"Okay, take a seat." Gladys slid a rolling chair nearer the computer. "And let's just take a look at this ranch of yours. Now what was the name?"

Tracy told her, and within moments a website popped up of a beautiful, sprawling ranch, the ranch house done in a pale sandstone with ambient lights that highlighted the interior. The Circle T Ranch.

Gladys wrote down the location, then tapped it in on her GPS. "That's odd," she said, frowning.

"What?"

"It's not showing a location." She pulled up a detailed map on her computer and typed in the address. Again, nothing appeared. "Curiouser and curiouser. Well, how about we type in the name of the ranch owner."

Together, they waited. Nothing. Tracy felt an odd tingling sensation run through her. "What does that mean?" she asked.

"I dunno," Gladys said, her brows knitted. She pursed her lips, then snapped her fingers as a thought occurred to her. "Let's just track down the web designer."

"You can do that?" Tracy asked, biting her lip.

"*Ve* have our *vays*," Gladys said in a faux German accent. Her fingers flew across the keyboard, moving rapidly between screens until finally she said, "This should do it."

But to Tracy's surprise, what popped up were the words "No such page" in the middle of a blank white screen. "What does that mean?"

Just then, Stanford appeared at the glass front door carrying two cups, one in each hand. Gladys ran to let him in.

"You two look a little shell shocked. Everything okay?" He tilted his head to one side as he entered and handed Tracy her Grand Teton mocha.

"We've got ourselves a dilemma." Gladys weaved her way back to her desk and to her computer screen, where she explained the problem to Stanford.

"So, you have no such ranch, no such person, and no such web designer. Do I follow?"

Tracy and Gladys nodded in unison.

Stanford tapped his ultra-white teeth with his pointer finger. "Hmm. You didn't hear this from me, but I know someone who can hack into anything. I'll have him do some digging. Are you two ladies game?"

Tracy took a sip of her mocha and felt the sweet taste slide down her throat. She didn't know what to think, but since she had no other leads, she quickly nodded, Gladys doing the same.

"Okay," Stanford said. "You may need to slip the guy a G note."

On Tracy's limited budget, she couldn't afford to be a sleuth. She would have to speak to Blake, but she felt certain that wouldn't be a problem. Just then, a shadow loomed in the window of the establishment. Tracy looked up in time to see the same man she had met in the parking lot. And she could almost swear he'd been watching her before he'd skulked away down the boardwalk. She shivered at the thought. Surely it was her imagination getting the best of her, but just in case, she would keep her phone handy and put Ryan's number on speed dial.

Eleven

After a couple of calls to Ryan, and a trip to the feed and seed store in town, Tracy had a truckload full of dog pens, one for each of the dogs, a toy for each of the animals to use in tracking, and twenty-foot leads and harnesses for each of the pups. Lastly, she had picked up mammoth sized bags of dog food, and too many bags of training treats to count. One of the young men from the store had helped her load out all of her supplies, and once finished, she offered a tip, which he declined. She thanked him and slammed the tailgate shut, then walked around to the cab and jumped in.

From her apprenticeship training dogs as a late teen, she had learned that they would need to be proficient at either air sniffing for missing humans, be able to follow ground disturbances, or trail the scent of a specific person. The dogs would also have to be sociable and willing to please, which

Ryan had assured her they were.

As she turned the ignition, she peered up at the clouds gathering in the sky. It had grown dark quite quickly, and cold as well. With the weather on the move and fall just two months away, the realization that she had so much to do made her numb with worry. As if to punctuate the point, the wind picked up, buffeting the truck as she backed out and exited the parking lot. Dry leaves scattered on the wind from what Ryan had said was a year of drought. According to Ryan, the first signs of the change of seasons would occur with the tingeing of the tree tops red.

As she drove toward the farm, she ran through a mental list of all the things she would need to do before then. But despite the growing list that left a weight on her chest the size of a boulder, she couldn't help but admire the gold-hued mountains in the distance, breathe in the scent of sagebrush that dotted the landscape in silver, the golden scrub of prairie grass. Sedges competed with the little leaf pussy toes amid the first of the wet meadow, nurtured by late summer rains. She only knew this because of Ryan. She smiled at the thought of him. He was so different from the men in her past. They had seemed without roots, either focused on an unknown future or still boys, really, none of them men. So few men seemed to know what they wanted at this age. But Ryan, well he had been tested, seemed sure of himself, confident. And yet what did she know about him, really?

By the time she reached the long driveway that led to the farmhouse, she was ready to put her thoughts to rest. As she bounced along the rutted road, she knew she would need to have gravel hauled out and laid before winter. No way could she drive through this syrupy mess come the rainy season, not in her old beater.

As the trees gave way to a clearing, Tracy gasped when she saw how much work the men had done while she was gone, especially to the front porch. She couldn't help but marvel at the transformation. She pulled into the dusty driveway and set the truck in park, then climbed out. Ryan was busy pounding away with a hammer, shoring up the floorboards in jeans and a plaid blue shirt. He had several nails in his mouth, pulling them out one by one to add to the porch decking. When he saw her, he waved and stood.

"What do you think?" he said with a smile. "Do you think it will pass muster?"

"It's amazing," she said, but not just because of the porch.

He grabbed her hand and nearly dragged her down the stairs. "Come see what the guys did with the side of the house. Besides having power washed the entire house in preparation for a new coat of paint, they had cleared the side yard of debris, much of it filling the back of an old trailer that had miraculously appeared. Already, the place looked nearly habitable. Between her cleaning the inside, and them cleaning the exterior, the place was beginning to take shape. For the first time since she'd arrived she could begin to see the farmhouse not as a run-down dump that needed to be torn down, but an actual home that would serve as a place of business also.

If the inspector doesn't shut me down.

"You like?" Ryan offered her a mischievous sideways glance.

"Very much," she all but gushed.

"If I can get the guys to help me on this porch and we can get it finished before today, we can get it painted by tomorrow." He hesitated afterward, frowning. "Then you will need to reroof. Sorry, but my guys aren't equipped to handle that."

"That's okay," Tracy said. "I spoke to a couple of roofing places while I was in town and got some estimates." She quickly named off the two.

"Go with the second roofer. You'll be happy you did."

Tracy nodded, relieved to have such sage advice. Still, she sensed that he had more to say as he toed the dusty soil with his boot. "Is there a problem?"

Ryan bit his lip, then threw up his hands as though giving in to the inevitable. "The dogs. We haven't been able to work with them at all. They need to be worked daily if we're going to have quality search and rescue dogs."

Tracy knew he was right. Just then, she heard a commotion and looked up in time to see two teenagers, one a boy–fourteen or fifteen, if she were to guess–the other, a girl, closer to twelve or thirteen, though appearing more like a young adult in a green v-neck sweater with her wiry black hair held back in a ponytail. Tracy needed a small crew if she planned to begin training the dogs while the men worked.

"These here are Bryce's kids. He brought the trailer," Ryan said by way of explanation. "Jayce and Sam, short for Samantha. Say howdy to Tracy here."

They mumbled their hellos, Sam turning around to keep an eye on the puppies in the pen out back. She was obviously smitten with the dogs. Tracy felt a smile edging her lips for the first time that day.

"You two want to help me train these pups?" she asked.

Sam turned to Jayce, her chocolate brown eyes wide. Together, they nodded in unison.

"Okay, then. We have a job to do." Tracy winked at Ryan, then gathered the pair and headed off toward the pen, but not before she'd seen him shaking his head and rolling his eyes.

For the next couple of hours, Tracy and the duo ran the dogs through their paces. At this age, it was hard to keep the pups' attention, but she looked for the leader of the bunch, the most compliant of the group, and let the others watch and learn from the most advanced of the pups, a trick she had mastered during her apprenticeship. And it was amazing how focused the others became on the actions of the one pup, the little chocolate lab. Her biggest challenge would be Ryan's pup, Parker. She'd found him facing the barn, as though recalling that day he'd become trapped in the debris. But what surprised her most was that he was whimpering and wriggling as though wanting to return to the barn. She'd even caught him digging at the dirt next to the chicken wire fence, as though trying to dig his way out. She frowned, determined to keep an eye on the little guy.

She was almost finished when Ryan appeared with an older gentleman at his side, slightly stooped, even though he could be no more than about sixty or so. He wore wire-rimmed glasses and a heavy beige jacket that dwarfed him. One look at Ryan's face and Tracy knew the identity of the visitor. Hank Warren. A shiver crept through her when she discovered she had seen him before. The cranky old man she'd met in the parking lot earlier that day–the one she'd seen skulking around J & R Marketing.

"May I help you?" Tracy asked, her heart sinking.

Hank came closer and held out a hand. Tracy reluctantly shook it. What would this mean for her practice?

"I know this is a bit of a surprise," he said. "Is there somewhere we can go and talk?"

"I'll leave you two alone then." Ryan excused himself, but before he left, he gave Tracy a pointed look to let her know that if she needed his help, he would be close by.

"Come with me." She gestured for Hank to follow her to the house.

Hurrying to keep up with her, Hank scanned the farm as though taking stock of the different components. Already, she felt possessive of the place, proud of the work she and Ryan had done with the help of the other vets. To think that she might have to give it up before she'd had a chance to fully settle in didn't sit well with her.

Fortunately, the porch no longer sagged, the rotted wood replaced with new wood. Soon, she would prime it and paint it, while the men coated the body of the house. The men had already taped most of it off in preparation of the paint, which would go on tomorrow. It gave her a sense of pride that she and the others had improved the look of the place so dramatically in such a short time. But if Hank inspected the place now, refused to give her time to get it up and running, all that may have been for nothing. The worst part of it was that she had embraced the house—wasn't sure she wanted to leave so soon if things didn't work out.

She opened the screen door with a screech. She would need to oil the hinges soon, among a huge list of to-dos. Yet, she couldn't worry about that now. Better to face one problem at a time. But first, she knew the drill. She entered the kitchen and put on a pot of coffee, pulling down two mugs.

Ten minutes later, she poured each one of them a cup of coffee, black for him, cream and sweetener for her. Then they retired to the living room, a small but cozy space with a fireplace. She would need to get more wood before winter set in. In just two months from now this area would most likely be covered in snow, from everything she had read.

"So, you're early." She took a sip of the hot coffee, relieved to have something to do with her hands. "I thought I wouldn't be getting an inspection until my practice was further along."

Hank fingered the lip of his mug, staring down at his coffee as if it held the answers to what he was about to say. "I was informed that you were recently called out to look at cattle, am I correct? May I see your paperwork?"

"That's right. But before we start, can you please show me your credentials?" she asked, hoping to buy some time.

He paused as though considering it, then reached for his clipboard, his credentials clearly displayed. Her mouth went dry. She set her coffee down on the round side table so that she wouldn't spill it, then quickly ran upstairs to dig through her filing cabinet where she kept her papers. She returned moments later, papers in hand.

Hank paused to read them over, then nodded and handed them back to her. "And yet, from what I can see, you have no operating clinic, is that correct?"

Again, Tracy nodded. She didn't know whether to laugh or cry. How could the man possibly expect her to be ready so soon when she'd been led here under false pretenses. She had thought it would simply be a matter of purchasing equipment and setting out a plaque on her barn door, not a total overhaul of the place from top to bottom. She glanced at the Tetons out her window. She'd loved the idea of working with Ryan and his men . . . and the dogs. And she was determined to be a large animal vet.

"Can you show me your equipment?"

"Equipment?" she repeated. "I have to purchase it, but that's the next thing on my list." She wondered if he'd see through the white lie. She couldn't purchase equipment until the barn was cleaned up, and that would take a small army of people to get rid of all the stuff in there.

"Okay, then, why don't you show me where the equipment will go," he said, forcing her hand.

She plopped down in the metal and plastic seat, determined not to cry. Not to make a fool of herself. She bit her lip to fight back tears. When she finally pulled herself together, she said, "The truth is, I have nowhere to put the equipment at this moment. You see, I was led to believe that the place was in good condition and that all I would need to do was to set the equipment in place. But as you can see, I

110

have a lot more work on my hands."

"Oh?" He leaned forward and set his mug on the coffee table, then turned to face her.

His eyes were a pale blue-gray, somewhat opaque, the first stages of cataracts, no doubt.

"The thing is, I would like to see this through. To turn this into a real clinic. But . . ." She held up her hand to keep him from interrupting. "I have an idea that would make us both happy."

"Oh?" His body language no longer seemed as welcoming. He sat back, as if to lend distance from her. "So what is this idea of yours?"

"Ryan, the man who introduced you to me—he and the other vets have a lodge on some property about five miles from here, as the crow flies. They trade services. He has offered for me to use his barn until I can get mine cleaned up and ready to go. In exchange, I would train some of the vets in search and rescue. That is, if Wyatt and the other vets agree to it. I will need to speak to Wyatt first."

Hank laughed at her audacity. "Well, young lady, for having just learned about the inspection, you sure have come up with a solution awfully fast!"

His eyes narrowed. She didn't know what he was thinking. Sweat dripped off her brow.

"I'll tell you what. I will need to take pictures of both your home and the barn." He stood and peered out of the window. "To be honest, I doubt that barn will ever be able to house a veterinary clinic. You might as well tear it down while you're ahead. Either build a new one, or move your practice elsewhere. Permanently."

Tracy's heart fell.

"Okay," Hank said with a weary sigh. "When do I get to inspect this lodge?"

"Ryan could probably take you there tonight, or you could go over in the morning, providing he gets the okay from Wyatt."

Hank stood and reached out his hand once more. "I've taken enough of your time for now. I will go speak with Ryan right away. You've been very helpful."

Relief flooded Tracy, but before Hank went to speak to Ryan, she wanted a chance to speak to him first. "Why don't you wait here. I'll go talk to Ryan." But before she could leave, Hank stopped her with a hand to her shoulder.

"What if you can't make a go of this practice? What then? This is a tough place for seasoned veterinarians much less . . ." He didn't finish his words.

Tracy gripped the doorframe, her nails digging into the wood because she'd had the same thought. But she hadn't expected the place to grow on her like it had. Plus, she felt an obligation to Mabel to find out what had happened to her. Maybe then the old man and his dog could move on. Then again, she wasn't sure she wanted them to. She had come to feel possessive about the pair.

"Don't worry," she said at last. "We'll figure that out when the time comes." She offered Hank a wan smile, then went in search of Ryan.

Twelve

Tracy found Ryan under the eaves out back and secured his agreement to call Wyatt about Hank coming to inspect the ranch. Then she returned to the farmhouse, promising to call Hank as soon as she had an answer from Ryan. She was relieved when Hank finally left. As if Hank's arrival hadn't added a sour note to her day, Tracy heard a vehicle in the driveway and peered through the kitchen window in time to see Blake pulling up in a F-350 Ford pickup, dark gray. *What now?* She met him at the front door.

"May I come in?" he asked.

In the light of the late afternoon, Blake seemed younger than before and a good deal more relaxed. His black hair was freshly washed and slicked back, and he was wearing a fitted blue shirt with pearl buttons, jeans, Doc Martens, and a bulky brown coat. She nodded and stood back to let him enter, the screen door squeaking as it slammed shut behind him.

"Can I get you coffee?" She was already heading toward the kitchen.

"No thanks," he said. "I just wanted to thank you for diagnosing my cows. I've shipped in other feed, and the rest of the herd is doing fine."

She breathed a sigh of relief. "Good!" She offered him a seat at the Formica table. Surprisingly, it didn't look all that worn compared to the rest of the kitchen.

"Maybe I'll take that coffee after all," he said, his eyes scanning the place.

Tracy put water into the pot and turned on the pilot light. She wondered if he was envisioning the interior of the house as it had been when he was a child.

"You've done a lot with the place for being here such a short time."

Tracy pulled two mugs from the cupboard then came over and sat at the table. "I wish I could take credit for it all, but I've had a lot of help from the vets. They have been amazing."

Blake snorted. "I could hardly get over the rotting floorboards on the porch the last time I was here."

"When was that?" Tracy's eyes wandered to the kitchen window over the sink where she could see Jayce and Sam running through their paces with the dogs. To her surprise, the dogs were picking up the first line of training quite quickly. That was the thing about kids and dogs. They could adapt.

"The day before you arrived," said Blake.

Tracy turned back to Blake and lifted her eyebrows. "I'm still confused about why you sold the place, considering you, well . . . you know."

"Considering I'm still trying to find out what happened to my grandmother?"

Tracy felt her cheeks warm. She knew it must be a difficult discussion as he clearly loved his grandmother.

"Believe me, before I sold it, we went over every piece of the land looking for clues, all except for the barn. But it has been like that forever. Grandpa, God love him, was a hoarder. Grandma wouldn't let him bring any of it into the house though. It was that Depression era mentality. He saved stuff . . . in case."

Tracy had noticed shelves of toy cars, toy fire engines, toy soldiers. If Old Man Grayson had been born in poverty, he no doubt was compensating for never having anything as a child. She'd read about the orphan trains, how children had been sent via rail to be adopted by families who could afford to feed and house them, or to farms as indentured servants to help the farmers survive. What a grim time in history.

Just then, her kettle whistled and she stood and hurried to fill their mugs with steaming liquid. "I hope you don't mind instant coffee."

"Of course not."

She gave him a quizzical look, having assumed that he was used to a higher standard of coffee.

With a tilt of his head, he smiled. "I know you look at my house and figure 'this guy must come from money,' but *this* is where I came from. We were just . . . normal, whatever that is."

Tracy understood completely. Her parents had struggled with the best of them to keep food on the table and a roof over their head, and she had appreciated them for that, knowing how hard it could be to make a living. To afford a home, especially in Seattle where home prices rivaled any of the large West Coast cities, was difficult in the best of times.

She placed one of the mugs in front of him. "Creme? Sugar?" But he merely shook his head. Still, she set the packets of sweetener on the table and pulled out a creamer for herself, hazelnut. Then she dug a spoon from the drawer and sat down next to Blake, stirring her coffee.

"Actually, the reason I'm here today is two-fold." He paused, then took a sip of his coffee before continuing. "First, I wanted to thank you for the other day." Before she could protest, he held up his hands to stop her. "But mostly, I wanted to give you this."

He pulled a check for services rendered, along with a map, from the inner pocket of his coat and laid them out on the table. Carefully, he unfolded the map. Once it was open, Tracy could see that it was actually a plat map of the farmhouse from the fifties.

"It's the original. I found it in one of the drawers. Thought you could use it, seeing as the place is yours now."

Tracy traced the lines of her property with her finger. She knew she'd purchased twenty-seven acres with the property, but seeing it in relation to the rest of the county made it appear small. Someday she would have to traverse the property lines to see how far her property ran.

"Your land goes right up to the river, here." He pointed at a blue, serpentine line. Funny, the other night, when she'd taken the back road to the vet ranch, it had followed the river. She hadn't noticed it being so curvy.

Blake must have seen her frown because he said, "The river has changed over the course of the years. More so after the Grand Teton Irrigation and Land Company built an off-channel reservoir for the valley's ag businesses, mine included."

"When was that?" Tracy rose, walked over to a cupboard and pulled out two small plates from one of the upper cupboards. Without asking, she filled them with some cookies she'd picked up at the store and then brought them over to the table and set them down in front of each of them.

"Haven't seen these in years." He snapped up one of the domed cookies, marshmallow on a round graham cracker, dipped in chocolate. "Takes me back to when I was a kid."

Tracy smiled. That's why she had bought them. They reminded her of her childhood. "So, back to the irrigation company. You say the river changed as a result of the reservoir?"

"The river doesn't have near the flow, so much of it goes out for irrigation these days."

"How long has the irrigation company been in existence?" she asked, not sure why she was so doggedly pursuing the issue. After all, it didn't influence her property now.

"It came in about a year before grandma died. Got under her craw a bit. She was afraid it would affect the groundwater

117

and the well."

"Why the groundwater?" Tracy shook her head, not following.

"Anytime you pull water out of the stream, it draws water from the outlying areas."

Just then there was a knock on the door and Ryan entered, appearing dirty and sweaty. She rose to meet him. Once again, she was getting the good end of the deal. He was out there working his tail off and she was in here talking to Blake, and yet it couldn't be helped.

"Oh, Blake. I saw your truck out front." Ryan made his way into the kitchen. "What brings you here?"

Blake rose and shook Ryan's hand. "I just wanted to thank Tracy here. I suppose I've done enough jawing for now." He nodded his head toward Tracy. "She's all yours."

Tracy's face grew warm. She walked Blake to the door, thanking him for stopping by. As he strode out to his truck, Tracy suddenly had a thought. "Wait!" she called. "Why didn't you take the stuff from the barn before I moved in?"

He laughed and looked down at his feet before peering back up at her. "What would I do with all that? No, I got everything I needed, but if you come across anything interesting when you clean the barn, let me know." It was his turn to blush. "I apologize for leaving all that with you. I know it's a lot of work."

"No worries." She waved goodbye and ran back inside to see if Ryan had any news from Wyatt.

Ryan was waiting for her, hat in hand. "I've called Wyatt, like I promised," he launched in. "We've got it all worked out.

118

Hank will inspect our ranch, make sure it's up to standard. And you can stay here and try to get the practice up and running."

Tracy collapsed into the kitchen chair, relieved. "Thank you, Ryan."

"No problem." He hesitated. "I don't mean to be crass, but are you going to have enough money to get this place operational? I mean, you have put a lot of effort into the property already. It's got to be a money pit."

She'd had the same thought. She was quickly growing to love the place, the people. But what if her finances couldn't stretch that far? Could she give up her dream and return home?

She peered out the front window at Blake's retreating truck. For some reason, she had a nagging feeling from their discussion that she was missing something. She shrugged. No point dwelling on that now. She had work to do. Then she would figure out a way to keep her home, to get the practice going. But how?

* * *

Ryan went to collect the pups after a day of hauling garbage to the dump and scraping paint off any spot that the power washer hadn't removed. Tracy would need to order gravel for the drive all the way to the main highway, a huge expense. As he walked down the rutted drive, he cringed at the thought of telling her the cost. He would save that for tomorrow. For now, he needed to get back to the ranch before

Wyatt called out his own search and rescue party for his missing crew. Ryan couldn't afford too many more days away from the ranch and its duties. Maybe tomorrow he could get Jason to keep the dogs while he painted Tracy's house. Bryce's kids could stop by too, to help Jason with the pups. Then Ryan would need one other person to go behind him and paint the trim.

That decided, he unhooked the latch to the dog run. He would have to look into something more sturdy in case one of the pups pounced on the gate enough times that it came unlatched. In the meantime, it would do. The pups saw him approaching and left Jayce and Sam's sides to come running over to the gate, tails wagging. Ryan squeezed through the gate, careful not to let them out.

"How'd it go with the pups?" he asked the pair.

Sam's cheeks had turned deep red from the afternoon sun, and wisps of mocha brown hair that had fallen loose from the plaits of her pigtails blew in the breeze. Summers could be quite hot, the warm nights stifling.

"Want to see?" Sam asked.

Before Ryan could answer, Sam took off running, Jayce chasing her. The dogs sensed that the game was afoot and tore off after them. Jayce called the squirming pups to his side while Sam tagged the nearest pup, the lightest colored of the bunch, to follow her. She ran between poles, the pup attempting to zigzag its way behind her, but soon the pup had outrun her in a beeline and was making its way back to Jayce, who rewarded the pup with a treat and a thorough head rub, despite the pup's somewhat dismal performance. It

120

would come . . . in time. Generally, in about six month's time, according to Tracy.

"See?" Sam flounced on her toes once she'd caught up with the little mutt. "He went through a couple of poles. And watch this." She turned to one of the other pups. "Sit," she commanded. The dog did a half sit. "Sit," she repeated. The dog reluctantly sat. Jayce immediately reached into the zippered bag at his waist and handed the dog a small reward.

Seeing the pair gave Ryan an idea. He'd been struggling to come up with a plan that would allow him to both train the dogs and to work with Tracy. And he had to admit, he liked working with her. Something about her made him feel . . . what? *Grounded.* Before this, he'd had too much chaos in his life, between his drug-addicted mother and Afghanistan. He'd always felt on edge as though he were waiting for the next bomb to drop. When he'd moved to the ranch after returning home from the war, he'd lost himself in his guitar and had spent much of his spare time behind a camera. Those had helped to keep his mind occupied so that he wouldn't worry. And he loved those, but he'd had a hard time letting his guard down. With Tracy, his fences were finally down. It had been a long time since he'd risked loving anything. Heck, if he couldn't even save a dog in Afghanistan, what made him think he had a right to happiness with a woman as smart and capable as Tracy?

He bent down and petted the dog closest to him, scratching behind its ears. "You two are doing a great job with these dogs. We should keep you on."

Sam let out a blat that sent the puppies scurrying around

Jayce. "Sorry." Sam bent down and cooed softly. Soon, the pups were squirming on her lap, nipping at her hair, and lunging at her back.

"When do we get paid?" asked Jayce.

"Jayce!" Sam squealed. "That's rude to ask."

"At the end of the week," Ryan told the boy.

Jayce was the quieter of the two, and much taller than his sister. The pair couldn't have been any more opposite than if they'd had different parents. Jayce was as shy as Sam was outgoing, and whereas her hair was almost a mahogany color, his was a deep chestnut brown. His skin was paler than hers too, chestnut like his hair. But what set them apart most were their eyes. Jayce's were almost golden in hue, whereas Sam's were deep brown flecked with gold.

"How about you work with them tomorrow, same time. I'll get the okay from Wyatt, but I'm sure he'll say okay. Deal?"

"Deal," Sam said, clearly used to speaking for her brother.

To Ryan's surprise, she stuck out her hand to shake on it. He stifled a laugh. He had to give it to the girl—she had chutzpah.

"Okay, then, can I get you two to round up the troops here and put them in the truck? I'll clean up after them," he said, noting the smell left behind by the pups. He didn't want to leave that to Tracy. She had enough on her plate.

For the next ten minutes, he scooped the dogs' pen and deposited the dog doo into a plastic trash bag and then tied it off. He was just about to leave when the ground began to tremble and he heard a sound like cracking just before the ground gave way. He let out a yell as his feet came out from under him and he dropped several feet before the trembling stopped and the ground engulfed him up to his hips. Tracy must have heard him from inside the farmhouse because she came at a run to see what had taken place. For a moment, all Ryan could feel was a sharp pain where he'd twisted his ankle.

"What happened?" Tracy rushed over to him, his legs buried to his hips.

Ryan tried not to moan, but the throbbing of his ankle and the pain shooting up his leg left him breathless. "You must have some pretty big gophers," he finally managed between groans.

"I don't think even Wyoming has gophers that big," Tracy countered.

Just then, some of the other men who had been helping repair the farmhouse returned from the acreage out back and hurried to where Tracy knelt beside Ryan.

"What happened to him?" Bryce yelled for one of the other men to bring him a shovel.

Tracy shrugged.

"I don't know," Ryan said. "One minute I was standing upright, the next minute the ground gave way. I twisted my ankle, but I don't think it's broken."

For the next few minutes, Bryce worked to dig Ryan out of the collapsed soil. Once he had him on sturdy ground, he peered down. "That's the darndest thing I've ever seen. It looks like a sinkhole."

Tracy bent down to take a look and whistled. Ryan

twisted around to get a better view and felt his stomach fall. This was no gopher hole. No, his leg had stopped just at the edge of a cavern . . . one that could swallow a man whole.

Thirteen

Tracy knelt down next to Ryan inside the dog enclosure. She spent the next twenty minutes bandaging his leg. While she tended to Ryan, Bryce, a clean-cut vet, with shaved lightning strikes in his short black hair, put the pups in kennels that he kept in the back of his truck, then loaded up Sam and Jayce.

"Let's get you to the truck," Tracy said, her breath coming in short bursts. "Bryce is going to take you home and Reeves said he would drive your jeep to the ranch for you."

"Thanks," Ryan said, grimacing.

"It's me who should be thanking you." She shook her head. Just her dumb luck that the ground had nearly swallowed Ryan whole. First the place had turned out to be a disaster, then Hank Warren had shown up early to inspect the place, now this. What else could possibly go wrong? Well, there was nothing she could do about it now. With a groan of determination, she put her arm around Ryan's waist and hoisted him up.

As they neared the bed of the truck, the dogs began barking. Once Tracy had Ryan situated in the passenger seat and the two teens in the rear of the cab, she thanked everyone for their help. Just as she was about to step away, she heard a whine and saw Parker, the little three-toned sheltie, the one she'd found in the barn the day after she'd first arrived. It licked her fingers in welcome.

"I think Parker remembers me." Tracy walked over and leaned in to inspect Ryan's bandage one last time. His ankle seemed a bit swollen, but she had felt the leg and had noticed no obvious breaks or tears. He would need an x-ray to be sure, but her equipment wouldn't be here until nearly the end of the month, and she had no place to put it, at any rate. Not with the barn in its current condition.

"The sheltie?" Ryan groaned. "That's one of Lindsay's pups. She donated him for the cause. The rest of them are all shelter dogs."

"One of Weber's offspring?" Tracy leaned around to examine the dog and could see the resemblance, though the white boots on the pup were on the opposite legs from the adult. Tracy turned back to Ryan.

"Yep." Ryan rested his sore leg on one of the running boards and tried to peer around at the pup in question. "Shelties make good service dogs. They're smart, easily trained, and they're loyal." He hesitated, as though he wanted to say more.

126

"What is it?" She gripped the side of the truck and once again felt a moist tongue on her hand.

Ryan rubbed his chin and frowned. "It could easily have been one of the dogs that had fallen in the hole instead of me. The pups are small enough that we'd have a devil of a time getting them out. Furthermore, if the soil around had collapsed in on itself, we would have never known the dog was even missing." His expression grew more serious. "We need to move the run, and we need to move it fast."

She had to admit, she'd had the exact same thought and had been eying the land, as she'd helped Ryan to the truck. The run was too close to the river. That was the only explanation she could come up with for the ground to collapse as it had. Perhaps water had eroded the soil beneath the pen, and yet the river didn't seem all that high. In fact, it was more like a trickle. But maybe it swelled in the wintertime. It would take further investigation to know the cause. She would have to add that to her to-do list, she realized with a sigh. She definitely had her work cut out for her, between the situation at Blake's and this new wrinkle. Fortunately, Bryce had offered to drive Ryan back to the ranch and the other men had packed up and were ready to go. Tracy turned to take a last look at the farmhouse. Although it still needed a paint job, the farm was starting to appear lived-in, instead of the dilapidated mess she'd come upon when she'd first arrived. Still, it had a long way to go.

Ryan squeezed her hand. "It'll be okay," he said, nodding toward the house. "I'll be in good shape by tomorrow. Then we'll come paint that house of yours." He winked.

Tracy couldn't help but laugh, even though she felt bone-weary, her day only half behind her. "Just don't push yourself . . . if your ankle is still bothering you tomorrow."

"Okay, Mom," he said, then squeezed her hand one more time as the engine fired. "I'll leave the pups home when I paint," he yelled above the engine. "Jason can train them . . . until we get the new pen put up."

Tracy dipped her head in thanks just as Bryce lifted his cap from the dash and tipped it toward Tracy. Then he put it on and they were off, the men hooting and hollering as they set out for home. Tracy just shook her head. Now for the big task of the day. She still needed to tape off around the doors and the remaining windows so that the house would be ready for tomorrow's paint. But first, she would cook herself some dinner and sit down at her laptop to pour over topography maps of the area and to call down to Stanford to see if his "hacker" had found anything on the "ghost ranch," as she'd come to think of it. The fictitious ranch where Blake had ordered his hay. With a yawn, she sliced up some apples, then dipped them in peanut butter. She threw in a roll with lunchmeat and lettuce for good measure. Not the best dinner, but it would do in a pinch. Then she sat down to her laptop.

An hour later, she realized she'd become so absorbed in the material she'd read that she hadn't yet taped around the windows and doors out front. Fortunately, that was all the men had left her to do. She owed them bigtime.

She ran downstairs to the kitchen, then grabbed the blue masking tape from the stack that sat on the counter. Thank goodness, she'd thought to buy so many rolls. Then she switched on the porch light. The evening was already beginning to cool, so she threw on a red and black plaid fleece-lined flannel jacket that McDuffy had left behind.

As she ripped off strips of tape to go around the windows, she thought about what she had read. According to the literature she'd found online, karst formations ran under parts of the Bighorn Basin, which was composed of sedimentary rock. Sinkholes could be either naturally caused, as when bedrock such as gypsum or dolomite dissolved to form underground caverns, or it could be man made, caused by lowering groundwater to unsafe levels. This could occur from any number of reasons, from what she'd read. The likeliest being that the water had been diverted for agriculture or man-made dams or ponds used for industry, like mining. Or oil. This semi-arid region with all its sage and tumbleweed, was home to 1.4 billion barrels of petroleum. Who knew?

Tracy held the roll of painter's tape in her mouth and ripped off another strip while moths flitted around the outdoor light, the bulb hissing and humming as the moths bounced off it, often to their deaths. She put up the last of the tape when, suddenly, she heard a sound behind her like the scraping of feet on gravel, but try as she might, she couldn't see anyone . . . or anything.

"Who's there?" she called.

The silence was deafening, only accentuating the sound of the light hissing. She heard a soft whistling in the trees that bordered her property, which lay due east of the arid Bighorn Basin and at the foot of the mountains that led to Yellowstone Park.

For several moments, she stood there listening. She was about to turn back to her task when she heard it again. But this time there was an added click of a dog's nails. The sounds seemed closer this time, but still she could see nothing. She wrapped the plaid jacket tighter around her, having all but forgotten the taping for now.

"Mr. Grayson?" Her words came out a mere quiver of anxiety.

Her heart pounded in her chest as she heard what sounded like the tap of a cane coming up the steps of the porch. And she could have sworn that she felt a drop in temperature just in front of her.

"Is that you?" She heard a dog's whine from somewhere in the distance. "What do you want?" The skin on her flesh crawled, making her feel cold, suddenly.

But no one answered, only the silence prevailed, punctuated by the sound of a coyote in the distance, of an owl in one of the trees further south. The screen door opened, as though tossed back by the wind, and with a languid screech of the hinges, the front door squealed open. Tracy released the breath she'd been holding.

"What do you want?" she whispered. "Do you want me to follow you . . . inside?"

She could scarcely make her feet move forward. As she did, she could swear she felt the press of fur and an animal jolt past her. Fearfully, she entered, drawn in by the sound of footsteps on the old floorboards. Even as she followed, her instincts were to run the other way, but she would not, *could not*, be intimidated. Besides, if it *was* Old Man Grayson, all had thought him harmless.

The footsteps moved toward the kitchen, and then through the kitchen and up the stairs, the click of nails trailing the sound of a cane tapping its way toward the top. Tracy paused, peering upward, every ounce of her body on alert. She hadn't realized the death grip she had on the banister rail until she heard a pause, as though whoever was at the top of the landing was waiting for her to join him.

She took a deep breath and forced her feet upward, each step measured. It seemed as though hours had passed rather than minutes before she finally reached the top. The sound of the steps began to move down the hallway, away from her room, thank heavens. If Old Man Grayson had entered her room, she didn't know if she'd ever be able to sleep there again. Instead, he continued down to the sewing room. She followed, standing at the doorway, afraid to enter. For several seconds no one moved, not the ghost of the man nor his dog. Definitely not her.

"This is silly," she whispered under her breath. "There are no such things as ghosts." And a week ago, she would have believed that. Now, she wasn't so sure. "Do you want me in there?"

Nothing.

"Why?" she asked. "What do you want me to know?"

For a moment, silence reigned. Then something fell off the bookshelf, crashing to the floor and bursting open. A large sewing basket. Tracy couldn't move. All she could do was stand there, her scalp prickling with fear. Then she felt a chill move slowly past her and heard the tapping of the cane followed by the clicking of nails as man and dog traversed the hallway and down the stairs. Moments later, she heard the front door bang shut. She walked over to the window and there, in the moonlight, she could just make out a ghostly blue silhouette. A silhouette of a man. And his dog.

Fourteen

Tracy knelt down on the weathered pine floor of the
sewing room, the boards creaking beneath her weight. If she
hadn't seen Old Man Grayson and his dog with her own eyes
and heard them with her own ears, she would have chalked
what had happened up to coincidence, nothing more. But as
she leaned over the fallen sewing basket, its contents spilling
onto the floor, she took stock of each item. She bit her lip,
thinking. What had McDuffy Grayson wanted her to find in
Mabel's sewing basket? Nothing about it seemed unusual or
out of place. The basket contained all the ordinary things
one would find in a sewing basket: a strawberry pincushion
with scores of pins, some of them pearled on the end, a tape
measure, a gilded rose embroidery scissors with a heron
engraved on one handle, and finally, numerous spools of
thread as well as silver thimbles, most of them engraved.

Below all these, in a pull-out tray, lay material that smelled musty with age and patterns that reflected the styles of the fifties and sixties. Slowly, she inspected each item, none of them unique or unexpected. Disappointed, she gathered up the bits and bobs and placed them back inside the hand-sewn sewing basket that stretched around an ordinary wicker basket and was padded with plain old batting.

She was about to set the basket back on the shelf when her fingers touched the under surface of the lid and she heard a crinkling sound, like tissue paper. Probably just another pattern. Still, she ran her fingers along the lining of the material between that and the batting. Again, nothing. She removed her fingers, this time fingering the space between the batting and the basket. She felt a quiver of excitement as her hands touched something solid, something made of paper, and very old paper, if she were to guess. Carefully, she slipped the folded sheet of paper out bit by bit until finally, she held it in her hand. She whistled. The paper was indeed old. In the interior design world, they would have described it as antique linen. So as not to risk tearing the paper, she sat it onto the sewing table and unfolded it slowly. Once she had it open, she stared at the image. For a minute, she didn't know what she was seeing. Then it came to her in a flash. This was a map of oil deposits in the area. Why on earth would someone like Mabel hide a map that showed the location of oil deposits within the Bighorn Basin? It made no sense.

Frowning, she carefully refolded the paper and tucked it in the inner pocket of the jacket she was wearing, then she returned downstairs to begin taping the front window

and door in preparation for tomorrow's painting of the
farmhouse. She would have to talk to Ryan about the map.
Maybe he would know why a mild-mannered farm wife was
hiding maps of the valley's oil deposits.

As Tracy set about finishing up for the day and preparing
for bed, she realized she hadn't yet contacted Stanford to see
if he had learned anything new about the hay and the ranch
that had supposedly sold feed to Blake for his cattle. She
yawned and stretched. Maybe tomorrow she would check her
email. With a weary sigh, she went to her room and dressed
in her pajamas, crawled into bed and turned out the light.
But as she lay there, staring at the moon out her window, she
couldn't get the image of Mabel out of her mind, and of the
old man and his dog. In the short time she had been here,
they were beginning to become part of her, as though by
caring for the farm, she had taken up their care and wellbeing
as well. She nearly laughed at the thought. A young vet caring
for three ghosts!

"Better get some sleep." She punched her pillow until
she'd made a perfect hollow for her head. She nestled into it,
exhausted and relieved to finally be able to lie down after such
a busy day. But once again, sleep was hard to come by.

* * *

Ryan's leg stiffened as he exited the jeep the following
morning. Even though he'd had the pup only a short time,
already it felt strange not to have the sheltie in tow. The dog
had quickly glommed onto him and had slept at the foot of

his bunk last night. He had hoped to have more help painting the house, but it looked like it was going to be just him and Tracy today. The rest of the men had chores to catch up on at the ranch. He'd had a devil of a time talking Wyatt into letting him go today. They needed all hands on deck to get the barn ready for winter. Besides, what had happened at Blake's place had unnerved Wyatt, so much so that he'd had the men go through every bale of hay and inspect it closely for ragweed. When Ryan had told Wyatt about the fictitious ranch and website, Wyatt had pored over the internet himself, trying to find out who was behind the tainted hay. Something like this affected them all, because if one of them could be sabotaged, any of them could be, and that hadn't sat well with Wyatt. If it hadn't been for Tracy's work as a large animal vet, and her offer of help with the dogs, Ryan felt certain Wyatt would have stopped him from coming today. And yet, Ryan would have come anyway. He wanted to see Tracy. Something about her stirred the warrior within him, made him want to protect her.

He peered up at the porch, listening for signs of life on the farm, but the house seemed still. No smoke coming from the chimney to warm the farmhouse in the chill of the morning. Just one lone rooster crowing. He ran a quick inspection of the place. Tracy would have a hard time keeping up with the homestead on her own. And although he should have run the other way at the sight of all this hard work, something made him stay, made him long to put roots up alongside her. To make this place his own. But that was wishful thinking, and he was getting way ahead of himself.

Maybe it was because he'd never had a real home. His mother drifted from place to place, man to man. He snorted. His whole life he'd felt like a drifter, an outsider. What would it be like to live somewhere permanent? To have a place to call his own . . . *their* own. But what if Tracy only thought of him as a friend and nothing more? Or worse, someone to fix up the farm and then move him along?

Just then, Boots the cat came sauntering over to rub up against his legs. He had never been much of a cat person, but for some reason he liked Boots. This cat wasn't like the other cats he'd known, the ones that reached out with claws when you least expected it and sliced at your clothing. No, this cat was more like a dog. Friendly, and inquisitive. If he was up prowling for mice this early, chances were he'd been let out, so it was a safe bet that Tracy was already up and moving. He marched up the steps and knocked.

"Coming!" Tracy called.

He waited as footsteps neared the door and the curtain rustled slightly so that she could get a good look at the person on her doorstep before answering.

"Oh, Ryan, come in!" she said, a piece of dried toast in one hand, a bite taken out of it. She chewed and swallowed before speaking further. "You're not going to believe what happened last night." She ushered him in and shut out the cold morning air, but the interior wasn't much warmer than the outside.

Ryan spied the wood stove and noticed that she had collected firewood and placed it in a log bin next to the stove. "Do you mind if I start us a fire?" He rubbed his hands together to stay warm. It's then he noticed that she was wearing a stocking cap, Old Man Grayson's plaid wool jacket, and that her nose was a shade of Rudolph red that brought a smile to his face. Even her breath billowed clouds of hot steam into the air on this unusually cold summer morning. Pundits would have chalked it up to global warming, and he had to say, he was beginning to wonder about the climate changes that melted glaciers while bringing cool air to the valley earlier than normal.

"I would be delighted if you started a fire," she said through frozen lips. She took another bite of toast. "Breakfast?" She held up the half-eaten toast. "I could put on an omelet. Just hope you don't think that's all I can cook."

"How will I know unless you invite me to dinner sometime?" he said with a half-smile.

Tracy flushed, her cheeks now matching the color of her nose. "You're officially invited. Do you like lasagna?"

"Lasagna, pizza, ravioli, whatever you want to fix me, I'm your man."

Tracy laughed. "Okay then. But in the meantime, I'll get the omelet going while you get us some heat." Again, she blushed.

"So what were you going to tell me?" he called to her in the kitchen from his place at the hearth. "By the way, do you have any newspaper I can crumple to get the fire going?"

"In the magazine rack, by the couch." She poked her head out of the kitchen, her face having suddenly paled. "I saw them," she said, pursing her lips.

He grabbed a small stack of papers, careful not to use the

most current one, and crumpled them up, setting them inside the wood stove. "Saw who?"

"Old Man Grayson and his dog."

Ryan stopped what he was doing to take stock of her, to see if she was merely joking, but one look at her face, at her furrowed brows and the sound of her quavering voice told him she was telling the truth. "Where?"

"Here," she said, a little too loud. "They came inside the house."

He stood. "Inside the house? What for?"

"I didn't know, but they seemed to want me to follow them, so I did."

Ryan recalled his own experience with the ghost. He'd always wondered if someone had spiked his drink that night before going into the military. But he'd been given a drug test upon entry and the test had come back clean. Whatever he'd seen that night had nothing to do with drugs, and he wasn't the type to hallucinate. Heck, he'd been through some of the toughest challenges on earth in Afghanistan and had never had a similar experience. Oh, there had been the odd thing or two that he'd heard from fellow combat veterans. About feeling the air change when a person died, feeling them rise, as if moving through the vet and out the other side. It had happened to him once, and it had unnerved the heck out of him. He had told no one, afraid they would think he'd gone nuts, but others had told him of similar experiences, mostly over a jug of whiskey during R & R, what there was of it.

"So what happened?" Ryan asked, the wood stove all but forgotten.

"I followed them to the sewing room. And you're not going to believe it," she said, out of breath now.

"Believe what?"

"The old guy knocked the sewing basket off the shelf, dumped the contents onto the floor. Then I could hear him and the dog walk across the hall and down the stairs. I went to the window and Ryan . . ."

Gooseflesh played up Ryan's back. Without thinking, he rubbed his arms, wishing he'd had the fire going already.

"I could *see* them." Her voice was trembling now and she looked as if she could run out of the house, get into her truck and never look back. "They were silhouetted in light."

Ryan needed to busy his hands. He reached for a log, and laid it on top of the crumpled paper. When he had the entire box stacked the way he wanted it, he lit the paper and blew on it. Then he shut the glass door and watched it light up the room in a warm glow. He turned back to discover Tracy had returned to whisking eggs for the omelet. She poured the mixture into an oiled cast iron frying pan. Then she took vegetables out of the refrigerator and began chopping them on a weathered wooden cutting board. He walked over to where she stood and began helping her.

"So why do you think the old guy knocked the sewing basket to the floor?" He couldn't imagine what could be inside a sewing basket that would be of much interest.

"Well, that's what I wondered. I mean, all I found were ordinary sewing things, right?" She threw the chopped veggies onto the egg and overlaid it with sausage and mozzarella. "I was putting the basket away when I felt a piece of paper

140

tucked up inside the lid." She reached into her jacket, to a large inside pocket, and withdrew a folded piece of paper, yellowed with age.

"What's that?" He halted what he was doing to inspect the faded paper.

"A map!"

"Of what?" He frowned, running his fingers over the frayed edges in order to get a better look at it.

"Of the oil fields in the valley. Why do you suppose someone like Mabel would hide a map of oil deposits?"

For several minutes, he stared at the map, all the while shaking his head. "Got me. Maybe we should run this by Blake later today, but first we need to get this house painted, once we warm up."

She poured Ryan a cup of instant coffee as she waited for the omelet to finish cooking, her thoughts clearly still on the map. Had the map had anything to do with Mabel's disappearance, Ryan wondered? But how? Ryan could think of no connection between the map and Mabel, much less her disappearance. Frustrated, he watched Tracy as she brought two plates down from the cupboard.

"So, it's just you and me painting today?" Quickly, she divided the omelet in half and placed one half on each plate. She handed Ryan a plate and a fork. "Here."

They meandered over to the Formica table. "Don't see too many of these still around," he said with a laugh.

"Nor the Felix the Cat clock." She pointed to the wall clock with the swishing tail. "I feel like I'm in a time warp back to the sixties. But didn't you say Grayson and his wife have been gone only twenty years?"

Again, he laughed as he scratched at his neck. "Yeah, well, they never believed in keeping up with the times. Thought it was a waste to spend money."

"So how did they end up with all that junk in the barn then?" Tracy set her plate next to his.

He dug into the omelet, savoring the flavor of the cheese and sausage. He could get used to this. "Oh, you know, Grayson was into salvage. He was a collector. Tore down barns and buildings around town and kept whatever anyone threw away. Thought it was a sin to throw things out."

"Hmm."

For the next ten minutes, they ate in silence. Then they headed outdoors for a long day of work. Yet even as Ryan prepared the paint to be sprayed, he couldn't get the map off his mind. Why would Mabel hide it in her sewing kit, and what did it signify? He shrugged, not sure. Maybe Wyatt would have a suggestion. He would make it a point to talk to him tonight. But first, he had a house to paint.

Fifteen

The day was passing quickly and although Ryan had finished painting the front and sides of the farmhouse, Tracy had only finished half of the trim, if even that. After a long morning of painting, Tracy stood in front of the mirror as she washed up before lunch. Drips of paint dotted her hair, and her cheeks were smudged where she had tried to wipe at the sweat running down her face only to leave fine streaks of white paint behind. Still, she would take this over the way the farmhouse had looked before today. With a gray washcloth she scrubbed her cheeks until they stung and glowed a bright red, but at least her face was clean and paint free. For the most part.

She smiled, as they sat down for lunch, surprised at how quickly the house was taking shape, and feeling fortunate to have received so much help from the men. While Ryan had sprayed the body of the house, she had worked behind him, doing the trim in the front of the house first, so the place looked much better. When she'd finished that, she'd painted the front porch the slate blue she had envisioned when she'd tried to visualize what the place would look like when completed. She dug into her cooked cheese sandwich, then sipped on tomato soup. Tomorrow, she would plant the front garden. Then she would need to add a walkway. But that would have to wait for another day.

After lunch, she set out to finish the trim while Ryan painted the last of the house. By the time they were done painting, the sun was nearly setting. Weary, she marched inside, Ryan promising to catch up with her once he had the sprayer cleaned.

Upstairs, she once again washed up. She picked at the latex on her hands and arms until she had removed the bulk of it. Her hair was another subject altogether. It would take days, if not weeks, to get all the paint out. Afterward, she took a brief shower then met Ryan out front via the unpainted back porch.

"What do you think?" he said, nodding toward the farmhouse.

"I can't thank you enough." Tracy flushed with warmth, suddenly feeling awkward. Ryan was so unlike the men she'd known in Seattle. There, she had dated professionals, men who owned businesses or ran them. Ryan liked to work with his hands and she appreciated that about him. He wasn't afraid to get his hands dirty. To work hard. They had that in common.

"Hey, I've been thinking," Ryan said. "I want you to meet Wyatt and the others. It's high time you get to know everybody. Maybe while you're there, you can check on one of our mares. She's about ready to foal. Could be any day now."

"I'll take a look at your horse, but what about the lasagna?" She wished she hadn't offered today, of all days, to fix him such a difficult meal.

"Do you really feel like making lasagna?" he asked, both of them sunburned and tired.

She sagged in on herself. "No." She laughed at the absurdity of it, looking back.

"We could save it for another night," Ryan said. "Why don't you hop in my jeep and I'll run you to the ranch. I can take you home later. I'm sure our cook, Emajean, can rustle you up something."

Tracy peered down at the bulky blue sweater she'd worn after the shower, and jeans, split at the knee. If she'd planned on making a good impression, she'd picked the wrong outfit, but she was too tired to protest.

"Sure. Why not?"

* * *

Nearly twenty minutes later, they pulled up to the ranch house that fronted the large log cabin, a beautiful garden both out front and on the side of the house courtesy of Emajean's green thumb. A huge red barn stood off to the side, separated by the largest old oak tree, a swing hanging off one particularly large limb. Ryan honked to let Wyatt know he and Kate had company.

"Wait until you meet Kate and Emajean. You're going to love them."

Ryan, who had bathed at Tracy's house and put on fresh clothes from Old Man Grayson's closet, felt tired but happy at the thought of introducing Tracy to Wyatt and the rest of the gang. He opened the door to his jeep. In the past year he'd come to think of Wyatt and Kate like family. Kate had taken him under her wing, become the mother he had always wanted, his own mother trapped in an abusive relationship with a druggie. Every time he thought she had changed, something would happen to send her back to square one. Always before, he had tried to help her, hoping that one day she would get clean, but he knew now that he had to put on his own life vest before he could help her with hers. Kate and Wyatt had been his life vest. And whether Tracy knew it or not, she was quickly becoming Ryan's as well.

He honked again just before stepping around to help Tracy out of the jeep. The first one out on the porch was Emajean, a fifty-something Lakota woman. Her long black hair had begun to gray over the past few years and was thrown back into a loose braid. She wore jeans, boots, and a flannel shirt. Behind her came Kate with curly auburn hair and a light smattering of freckles on her nose. She had adopted a dress similar to Emajean's, only she wore a loose-fitted peasant blouse, white that set off her tan from working all summer in the hot Wyoming sun.

Kate leaned through the opened screen door and yelled,

146

"Wyatt! Get out here. There's someone you should meet."

Ryan could see by Tracy's hesitance that meeting them all at once was a bit overwhelming, so he took her hand and gave it a squeeze, then winked at her. "Trust me," he said, under his breath. "You'll love them. Just wait and see."

"You missed dinner." Emajean greeted Tracy then maneuvered her away from Ryan and into the house, Kate and Ryan bringing up the rear.

Wyatt was coming down the hallway only to halt in surprise. "So who have we here?" He gave Ryan a firm pat on the back and smiled, a knowing expression reaching his lips, a glint in his eyes.

Ryan made quick introductions, but before he could say much about Tracy, Emajean was already rummaging through the refrigerator, pulling out leftover pot roast from the evening meal along with potatoes, carrots, and onions. She then dug some rolls out of a bag and set out a plate of sweet butter. Lastly, she warmed up some green beans on the stove and set the whole mess onto the table.

"You're family, Ryan," Emajean said. "Quit staring and go get your lady some plates and glasses. And you, Wyatt, set the table."

"Me?" Wyatt rolled his eyes, but he did as ordered.

Everyone knew who ran the show when it came to the kitchen, Ryan included. Before they were completely seated and ready to eat, Wyatt pulled a warm pie from off the stove, peach from the looks of it, and dished them each a plate.

"So, we finally get to meet the woman who has kept our farmhand distracted these past few days," Wyatt said with a wink.

"Don't let him tease you," Kate told Tracy, even though it was clear by her smile she enjoyed his teasing.

Ryan smelled the aroma of the warm food, his stomach rumbling after a hard day's work. He was so tired he could keel over. Nothing a good plate of food couldn't fix, though.

For the next half hour or more the threesome plied both Ryan and Tracy with questions. Finally, during a lull in the conversation, Ryan downed some sweet tea then patted his full belly, letting out a large sigh of contentment. Then he nodded to where Tracy kept the map she'd brought with her.

"I've got something to show you," he told Wyatt.

Tracy carefully pulled the map from an inner pocket and held it out to Wyatt.

Wyatt reached for his reading glasses and placed them on the end of his nose. "Let's take it over to the lamp for a better look."

They all retired to the living room only after Tracy and the others offered to help Emajean in the kitchen, but she would have none of it. "Go! Go!" she urged. Rarely did she ever allow anyone into her domain, but Ryan's mother would have had his hide if he didn't ask.

Seated around the coffee table, Ryan explained what had happened, leaving out the part about the ghosts. "What do you make of it? Why would Mabel have a map of oil deposits in this part of Wyoming?"

With a furrowed brow, Wyatt inspected the map for several minutes, then removed his reading glasses. "Let's take this piece by piece. Prior to Mabel's disappearance, she hid this map."

Before Ryan could answer, Wyatt pulled out his laptop and began perusing online, checking into the oil deposits first. He once again put on his reading glasses and leaned in for closer inspection of the screen. "Look at this map." He pointed to one on the topography of the basin. "Did you know this entire area is riddled with karst formations?"

"What's that?" Ryan had only recently heard about them.

"Wherever you have limestone, gypsum, or marble, which are more porous than normal stone, you get sinkholes, apparently."

"Sinkholes. Like the one on my property and the ones I read about online?" Tracy dipped her head at Ryan as if to say *my thoughts exactly*.

He could see her point, after what had happened the other day.

"Didn't you say you fell into a sinkhole?" Wyatt asked, setting the laptop aside.

"Sure did." Ryan ran his hands through his sandy hair. "Do sinkholes occur more often close to water?"

Kate and Emajean eyed each other warily at the tone of the conversation.

Just then, Emajean came in with a tray filled with decaf coffee. "Thought you all could use a little something while you talk."

"Thanks!" Wyatt reached for a mug from the tray and took a sip then pointed at an article on his laptop. "Actually, the water helps buoy up the land above it, according to this article. It's when the water table is lowered for some reason

149

that the holes form and sinkholes appear."

"The water from the river is especially low right now," Tracy chimed in. "Do you think any of this had to do with Mabel's disappearance?"

Wyatt warmed his hands on his mug. "Dunno."

A lull in the conversation gave Ryan pause to think. Could there be a connection between Blake's current troubles, now that he had returned to town, and him looking into his grandmother's disappearance? He quickly explained the situation to Wyatt who whistled at the news.

"I don't know, but I think we had all better be on alert. Clearly something's up, but what and why? That's the three million dollar question." Wyatt sat his mug down on the coffee table and leaned back, arms folded behind his head. "I'm going to tell the men to be extra careful for a while and to keep an eye on the animals' feed. And Ryan—"

"Yes?"

"Are any of these dogs you're training going to be guard dogs? We could use one on the ranch."

"Ditto." Tracy's cheeks flamed red at the admission that as a woman living so far out, in unknown territory, she needed a guard dog.

Truthfully, Ryan hadn't planned on training guard dogs, but at least a couple of the dogs could be trained to protect, now that he thought about it. In the meantime, the men needed a good veterinarian who could help in a pinch, someone who truly cared about the welfare of the animals, their health and happiness. Tracy had proven she had the right stuff when she'd risked life and limb to help him rescue the sheltie, the other day.

"Okay, we're on it, right, Trace?" he said, giving her hand a squeeze.

"You got it," she agreed. "But Ryan?"

"Yes?"

He could see the worry in her eyes. "I've trained search and rescue dogs, and medical aid dogs, but I've never trained guard dogs."

Ryan sighed. "Me neither."

Wyatt stood. "Well, how about you pick out two of your most trusted dogs. Then tomorrow we'll get Jason down your way to begin their training. You might want to build a pen farther away from the river though."

"Will do." Ryan pulled Tracy to her feet. "Oh, by the way, should I call Hank, ask him to come by tomorrow?"

"The inspector?" Wyatt paused, frowning. "Sure."

Ryan and Tracy were just about to leave when Wyatt stopped them. "Before you go, could I get you to check in on our pregnant mare? She's about to foal any time now. I wouldn't be surprised to see her go into labor tonight."

151

Sixteen

Even before Tracy entered the barn with both Wyatt
and Ryan by her side, she could hear the mare blowing
and snorting, a sure sign she was in pain. And Tracy could
smell the alfalfa, along with the metallic fear of a pregnant
mother in stress. Horses in the neighboring stalls gave nervous
nickers, heads up, ears back. Quite literally, they worried for
other members of their herd, not unlike the worry exhibited
in humans. Tell that to the more staid members of the
community and they would laugh her out of town, and yet it
was true. She had witnessed it on numerous occasions. A baby
kicking up its heels in delight when reunited with its mother.
A mother stomping and snorting for days at a lost or dying
colt. It was the same the world over. And yet some would deny
animals their "humanness." Those qualities that were shared.
Still, she had a job to do, and a mare to assist because it was

obvious from the sounds that the mother was already in labor. And true to her expectations, she saw the brown and white mare lying inside the stall on matted straw, her eyes wild, her pale tongue licking at the air as if searching for comfort where there was none.

"Steady, girl." Tracy gently probbed the mare's side to try and locate the direction of the foal inside the mother's uterus. "Ryan, could you get my medical bag? We need to deliver this foal and I think it may be too big to make it into the world on its own. I'm going to need your help."

Ryan was out the door before she could finish and returned moments later, her black leather bag in hand. He laid it down beside her. She clicked it open and immediately began laying out the instruments she would require from her foal kit; several towels, some disinfectant, sterile gloves, a thermometer to test the temperature of both foal and mare, scissors, and tail wrap to keep the mare's tail clean. Lastly, she had brought string to tie off the foal's umbilical cord and cotton swabs to clean the area once they were done.

"Where can I wash up?" She pulled her disinfectant soap from the bag to avoid passing any germs to the foal or mother.

"Over here." Wyatt hurried her out the door and to the sink that flanked the southern wall of the barn.

She quickly scrubbed, then Wyatt handed her clean towels. Afterward, she put on an obstetrical sleeve, the mare's frantic snorts ticking off the minutes as they raced back to the stall. Fortunately, Ryan had thought to restrain the mare with a halter.

"Okay, girl." Tracy wrapped the tail then lifted it and

inserted her gloved hand into the uterus. She felt around. Although the foal was in the right position, her guess had been correct. The baby was too large to deliver without help. She would need both the men if she had any hope of delivering the foal vaginally. She removed her arm from the uterus and looked around for more rope. "The mare is about to have a dystocic delivery."

"In English!" Wyatt bent down to inspect the mare more closely.

"That means the foal is too big to deliver by herself." She quickly took the temperature of both mother and foal. "I'm going to need your help. Both of you," she added when Ryan returned with a rope. "It appears the head is coming first, but I'm afraid it may get stuck in the cervix. We have a short time to get the rope around the neck and behind the leg. We want to be careful not to cut off her oxygen for too long."

"Do you want me to do it?" Ryan asked, wiping sweat from his brow.

"My hands are shorter, but they're also smaller, so I may have a better chance of getting past the cervix."

Tracy wished she had thought to bring her vaginal speculum. And it was much too late to send someone to retrieve it. Just then, the mare let out an especially loud snort and began to push, her eyes wild with fear as she rocked in an attempt to move the foal. Sure enough, that did the trick because Tracy could see the nose. But just as quickly it disappeared into the womb.

"Let's give her a chance for another push. If we can get the head through the cervix, I think I can get the rope around her shoulders. We have less than forty minutes to get the colt out or risk asphyxiation."

For breathtaking moments, they waited. Finally, the mare let loose another loud snort and began once again to push, spasms wracking her body, her lips lined with drool and foam.

"Come on, baby." Wyatt rubbed behind the pregnant mother's ears. "You can do it."

"The foal's coming," both Tracy and Ryan said in unison.

The wet and soggy head appeared encased in a layer of white lanolin, a perfect white diamond on its forehead. But the birthing went no further. It was easy to see that the foal would be a beauty if they could only get him out of the confined space of the womb.

"Let's see if mama can do it on her own." Tracy still held out hope that the young mother might be able to pull off a miracle, but it was not to be.

For another agonizing half an hour, they waited until Tracy could wait no longer. The mother was getting tired and the foal's head was lolling, its eyes dulled over time as the cervix bit down on its neck.

"Okay, men, it's up to us. Can you make a lasso, Ryan?"

But before she could even finish her words, Ryan handed her one. The foal's tongue was beginning to turn blue. She knew she had to act fast. Reaching in with her fingers, she stretched the lip of the cervix, hoping to gain enough traction to squeeze her hand along with the rope through to the body of the foal. It was too late now to do a cesarean delivery. She ran her tongue along her lips to moisten them. "From my bag, I want you to put as much of this vaseline as you can around the cervix. Hurry!" she yelled. But there was no need because Ryan sprang into action.

Quickly he lathered the cervix with vaseline, which allowed her to slowly push the cervix wider and wider until finally she was able to slip through with the rope. Now, for her arm. But before she could insert her arm in as far as she needed, the cervix clamped down, sending waves of pain shooting through Tracy's hand and shoulder. She had only moments. She bit down hard on her lip, drawing blood as the cervix finally released enough to allow her to shove her arm deeper into the cavity, the pain returning seconds later. Still, she was in. With one hand she felt around for the colt's leg. After several agonizing moments, she found it. Now to take the lasso and guide it past the hoof to the foreleg.

"Keep the mare still!" Tracy said through clamped teeth.

"You got it." Wyatt put pressure on the young mare's head, all the while stroking her neck and crooning in gentle words, telling the mama that it would be okay.

Tracy slowly guided the rope up the foal's leg only to have it kick at the last minute. Again, she guided the rope up until at last she was able to cinch it tight. She would have one heck of a bruise on her arm come morning, but she had no choice.

"Ryan. I want you to grab my legs and pull."

"What?" he said, clearly confused.

"Just do it!" she shouted.

Ryan reached down and grabbed her legs and began pulling. Pain shot through her arm as the foal's shoulder held steady at the cervix. "Release!" she called as the cervix bit down again. She counted the seconds off until the cervix relaxed again and yelled, "Now! Pull!"

Once again he yanked Tracy's feet which helped to wedge the shoulders of the foal further out of the cervix. Tracy feared she might pass out before the final pull. Still, she held on, praying that this next time would be the one that would save both mother and offspring. She ticked off the excruciating moments, as the cervix closed up around her arm. At last the cervix relaxed again and she yelled. "Now! Do it!"

This time the foal came out, placenta and all, and with it her arm. Tracy lay back on the straw, panting, the pain in her arm turning to a raw and aching throb. Although she hated what her arm would look like tomorrow, relief flooded her. She had managed to save both colt and mare. For now, that was enough.

Seventeen

By the time everything was cleaned up, it was nearly three in the morning. Kate, who had checked in from time to time to see how the delivery was going, appeared now in her pajamas and robe. Tracy closed the clasp of her medical bag after receiving a promise that someone would watch over the mare and colt for the rest of the evening. Now that the adrenaline had worn off, Tracy's eyes felt heavy and her arm ached. She would need to take something for the pain soon.

"Why don't you come inside," Kate offered. "We'll get you a bath, and then something to eat and drink. Afterwards, you can get some rest in the guest room. It's too late to be wandering the backroads."

Both Wyatt and Ryan concurred. Much as Tracy hated to admit it, it would be nice to have people around for one night instead of rambling around in the old farmhouse alone.

Unsteady on her feet, she nevertheless followed them into the house. Although she had taken to the old farmstead and longed to stay there, she couldn't imagine living out in the countryside alone. Instead she imagined a family: husband, wife, children. But what frightened her most was that when she imagined a husband, the man standing beside her was Ryan. She breathed in the scent of the night air, the lingering scent of sage, the agricultural smells that she preferred over city air, the smell of diesel and fumes.

Now, as Kate ushered her down a hallway to a bathroom complete with fresh towels and a pair of clean pajamas that Kate had laid out for her, Tracy realized she had always been a student of human and animal behavior. Because of that, she knew Ryan bore a deep wound no doubt brought on by the war, and yet she felt certain it ran even deeper than that. She hoped that one day he would open up to her about his past. For now, her eyelids grew heavy and her body ached from head to toe while her arm throbbed.

Forty-five minutes later, she rested her weary head on a clean pillow. She didn't awaken until the sun was high overhead, its rays coming through the lace curtains at an angle. It took several moments to realize the buzzing she'd heard in her dream was coming from her cellphone. She looked at the red numbers of the digital clock on the nightstand. 12:03. How could she have slept so late? She jumped to her feet and fumbled for the phone, knocking it onto the floor then diving for it before the caller hung up.

"Hello?" she said with a yawn.

"We got it," the person on the other end of the line said.

159

"At least part of it."

For a moment, Tracy didn't register the voice. Then it came to her in a rush. Gladys. "What did you find?"

"Stanford was able to track down the website for the ranch."

"Ranch?" Tracy yawned again.

"Where the tainted hay was sold? We've pinpointed it to Wyoming."

Tracy rubbed her head, trying to wrap her mind around what Gladys had said. "If the website is from Wyoming, then there must be an address, but the ranch was supposed to be from out of state."

"That's the thing," Gladys said. "If the place was legit, why go to all this trouble to hide it? And how did tansy ragwort end up in the feed? This is Wyoming. It doesn't grow here, for the most part. So how did it end up in the hay? None of this makes sense, unless someone was trying to sabotage this guy."

"But why?" That was the question. It's true that Blake had connections to hundreds of people from every walk of life: agents, directors, performers, businesspeople, and untold people in politics. But this seemed so . . . personal. The sabotage hadn't been aimed at Blake himself, rather it seemed a warning of some sort. But from whom, and why? Tracy's thoughts drifted back to the corkboard she'd seen. It's clear he had done a lot of investigation on the disappearance of his grandmother. Could that be the connection? Tracy heard a knock, Kate's voice drifting through the bedroom door.

"You missed breakfast, Tracy, but lunch is ready if you

are."

"I'll be out in a minute," Tracy called.

She listened to Kate's retreating footsteps before returning to her phone call. "So do you have an address?"

"Not yet," Gladys said with a sigh. "But if anyone can find it, Stanford can. In the meantime, hang in there."

Tracy thanked Gladys and hung up the phone. She would call Blake later and tell him what she had learned. In the meantime, she'd been a poor guest. She quickly dressed and ran her hands through her hair to try to tame it before going out to face everyone. That's when she noticed the bruises running up and down her arm in a profusion of color. To avoid comments, she changed into a long-sleeved shirt and headed downstairs. When she arrived in the living room, Ryan was waiting for her with a plastic lunchbox and a thermos.

"I want you to see what Jason has made for the pups," he said, steering her toward the back door.

Tracy tried not to grimace at his touch, merely moving to the other side so that her sore arm was far out of reach. Then she said a hurried goodbye to Kate and Emajean while Ryan explained that Wyatt was in the barn, looking in on the mare and colt. "Shouldn't I go check on them?" Tracy asked, moving instinctively toward the barn.

Ryan grabbed her good elbow and steered her toward the bunkhouse out back. "The inspector is with Wyatt. Hank arrived at eleven-thirty this morning," Ryan said, sniffing. "Wyatt doesn't like him. Neither do the men. There's something odd about him."

When Tracy peered up at Ryan, he halted and she drew in a deep breath of the cool mountain air. It held a hint of fall to come, of the sweet smell of rotting leaves. "What do you mean?"

Ryan shrugged. "He just seems too . . . nosy."

"Nosy? Aren't all inspectors nosy?"

Ryan put his arm around her shoulder and she flinched.

"Sorry, I'm still sore from the other night." She rolled her sleeve up to show him the bruises.

"Oh, yikes!" He carried her lunchbox for her, then steered her once again toward the bunkhouse. "I'll be more careful. Do you want Emajean to take a look at it? She knows all sorts of Lakota herbal remedies."

"Maybe later," Tracy said. "So what about Hank?"

"Oh, right. He's asking a lot of questions, and the men have caught him snooping through the bunkhouse this morning when he thought they were gone. What worries me most is he's been asking about you."

"Me? Why would he do that?" she asked, confused. "What could he possibly be looking for?"

Once again Ryan shrugged, all his former calm gone. Clearly, whatever had happened had them all spooked. Just then, Wyatt's new blue heeler, Tag, came galloping down the gravel driveway and plopped himself in front of them so that they were forced to stop and give the dog a good ear rubbing before being allowed to move on. As the dog rose to his feet and loped ahead, he peered back at them, tongue lolling, to be sure they were following his lead. Tracy couldn't help but laugh at his antics.

"We're not sure what Hank is looking for," he said, now that they were once moving again. "They're worried that if he knows about the dog training, he may decide to inspect that aspect of the business as well, and we can't afford to have him shut us down."

"I don't understand the problem. Why would he shut you down?" Tracy said.

"In order to train search and rescue dogs, we have to be certified trainers. We're not."

"I was," she said, "but my certification isn't good in Wyoming."

"And there's the problem," Ryan said. "Because neither of us is fully certified. I can't wait for that. It takes two years to train these pups, and we need to get started now, with the limited equipment we have, not in six months when we have kennels ready and all the right equipment."

"So you want to bring the dogs to my place . . . until things blow over?" Tracy added.

"For now, the guys would feel more comfortable at your place. Hank seems way too interested in the dogs and what we're doing with them. Whereas I think he's done with your place, once he gives the okay for you to operate out of our barn."

Tracy stopped, frowning. The blue heeler noticed and ran back to nip at her heels. "Okay, okay," she said and began walking. "But why would he be interested in anything but the barn for the large animal equipment?"

Ryan shrugged as he led her toward a fenced area that was full of colorful equipment that he'd recently purchased

163

for the pups. "I'm not sure, but until we know what's up, we're going to post a couple of guards around the place."

Tracy mulled over what he'd said as she took stock of the rainbow shaped equipment Ryan had pointed out. They would be used to teach the dogs to get comfortable climbing mounds of rubble should there be an earthquake or to locate bodies after a fire. Only three of the dogs would be search and rescue dogs. The others would become service dogs for former vets with PTSD or with a disability, all except for the one watchdog Wyatt had requested for the ranch.

Ryan broke into her thoughts with the words, "If you're okay with it, Jason and the guys will load up a few trucks with the equipment and take it to your place, but we're going to need a safer spot than behind the barn." He put his injured foot up on the bottom rung of the wooden fence.

With Ryan's help, Tracy climbed up to get a better look at the equipment. It was more than they needed, really, but she wasn't going to protest. "For now, we could divide up the pen out back, where Lindsay is keeping the sheep, until we find something more permanent. At least that way we can keep the pups confined until we get through basic training. But Ryan?"

"Yeah?"

"The men will need to know CPR and First Aid in order to work with the pups."

Already, the pups were in the pen, taking turns running through the motions with Jason, a rusty-haired guy in army fatigues. Tracy had to admit, he was good at what he did. He had picked the smartest, most attentive of dogs, an older dog he had brought for just this purpose of training the younger ones. He began putting it through its paces, making certain that the men held their leashed pups on the grass so that they could watch what the older, more experienced dog was doing, could see the rewards she was earning and hopefully mimic the other dog's behavior.

"Most of the guys already have that training from the service," Ryan said, whistling to Jason to let him know he was there.

"They'll need a refresher course," Tracy reminded him. "Not only that, they will need Hazmat training, backcountry survival—"

"I can teach them that." As if in concurrence, Tag yipped and smiled up at them, as though asking if he could join in the training. "We'll see, boy," Ryan answered.

"And Jason and I can teach them navigation," Tracy added, "while I keep up with any medical needs they may have."

"So we have a plan."

Jason handed over the lead dog to one of the other men and came running toward the fence. "What do ya think?" he said, barely working up a sweat.

But even as Tracy took stock of the fit young man, she couldn't help but worry about Ryan's assessment of the inspector. Why the undue interest in the dogs? And why did the men—*all of them*, according to Ryan—sense something odd about Hank?

Eighteen

Time to enlist the help of Gladys and Stanford . . . again.
Tracy punched in the number Gladys had given her and
listened to the rings. Tracy heard a distracted "Hello."

"Gladys, is that you?"

Just then, Kate walked up the steps of the porch outside
of the white clapboard ranch house. Kate paused at the
mention of the name Gladys, her green eyes questioning.
Tracy finished her call and hung up.

"Was that Gladys, from J & R Marketing?"

"You know her?" Tracy asked.

Kate laughed. "I would say so. I used to own part of J
& R Marketing. In fact the R stands for Roberts, my maiden
name." Kate dipped her head toward a bench seat under a
huge oak tree out front. Tracy trailed her to the oak, taking
a seat beneath its spreading branches. To the side of the

wrought-iron bench seat was a small garden complete with a bird bath and a red and yellow hummingbird feeder. "My husband designed this for me after our wedding as an apology for never getting a honeymoon. We had too much to do here to leave."

"So, why did you give up your business?" Tracy drank in the scent of yellow honeysuckle and watched a hooded warbler flit in and out of the oak tree, its lyrical melody belying its small size.

Kate reached her arms out to the land around her. "This place takes a good deal of our time. I couldn't ask Wyatt and Emajean to take care of the place all by themselves when I have spare hands to help. Besides," she added, the sun shining through her auburn hair, "I love it here. I wake up to the sound of roosters crowing, to cattle lowing, to birds chattering in the trees. I was born in New York . . . and don't get me wrong, there are all sorts of wonderful cultural places to see or concerts to attend. But I never felt at home until–"

"You moved here?" Tracy broke in with a knowing smile. She, too, had been raised among skyscrapers and heavy traffic. But she hadn't decompressed until she'd found the farmhouse, had begun to make it hers. It's as though she had been searching for something she didn't even know she wanted until she'd landed here, among the wide-open spaces, the huge cerulean skylines layered with the occasional fluffy cloud, or clouds that scuttled along the horizon like floating wisps of cotton.

Kate nodded. "When I arrived here, I finally found 'home'. Oh, I tried to convince myself that I was a city girl, that I could go back and be just fine, but in the end the draw was too much. So, though Wyoming may not like me, I like it and I'm staying."

She must have realized how that sounded, because her cheeks flushed. In that moment, Tracy could see the Irish heritage in Kate, the somewhat pinched nose, the slight freckles. She tried to imagine her among Gladys and Stanford. What an odd trio, and yet Tracy felt certain they had made a dynamic team.

"But on to another subject," Kate said, frowning suddenly. "Wyatt said that Blake is having problems with his cattle's feed. Have you learned anything new?"

Tracy hesitated, unsure how much to tell Kate, but in the end caution gave way to trust because Ryan thought so highly of Kate and Wyatt. "A friend of Gladys and Stanford was able to trace the website where they purchased the feed back to Wyoming. We know that much, at least."

"Phew!" Kate leaned back in her seat, elbows out, fingers entwined as she cradled the back of her head. "That's not very comforting. I think Gladys and Stanford are in the wrong business. They should be detectives, between this and the earlier—"

"You've had problems before?"

"A couple years back, before Wyatt and I were married. Someone tried to shut the business down, but that's a long story. All I know is that you could find no better pair than those two. I'll have to call down there and thank them for helping you."

The wind began a slow howl, the breeze lifting Tracy's

hair. And yet the chatter of the hummingbirds as they buzzed past made the day feel lazy, despite the worries that, like the wind, swirled around her in an eddy.

No longer able to sit and worry over the previous days' events, she stood to pace. Just then she saw Ryan come around the corner, Wyatt's dog, Tag, close on his heels. "The guys are packed up," he called. "You ready?"

She nodded, then turned to say goodbye to Kate. "I hope we can be friends." She reached out to shake Kate's hand, but Kate wrapped her in a bearhug.

"That's how we do things down here," she said. "You're part of the family now. Anything you need, you just ask."

Tracy thanked her and was about to turn when Kate stopped her.

"Oh, and Tracy?"

"Yeah?"

"No matter what you hear about Ryan, he's a really good guy and he deserves a second chance, okay?"

Kate paused, her eyes riveting, but before Tracy could answer Kate, Ryan came at a run, waving his hands and motioning toward the jeep. "We need to get going!" he called.

Tracy wondered what the woman had meant by her cryptic statement. But she had no time to ask as Ryan whisked her away to the waiting vehicle.

* * *

Almost the entire ride to the farmhouse, Tracy had sat quietly, as though deep in thought. Normally, she was chatty,

169

but then again, Ryan hadn't known her long. Maybe that's how she stewed, by lapsing into silence. He frowned, tapping the steering wheel of his truck with his thumb to the beat of an unheard rhythm. Still, it made him uneasy. When his mother had been angry, she yelled, or worse, backhanded him. He'd taken to flinching on more than one occasion, never knowing which side of her he would see, or who she would bring home among her string of men. He'd learned not to react when she told him to call one or the other of them dad. Instead, he would sit in abject silence and force a smile, then ride out the rocky relationship until the next one came along. As a result, he'd promised himself he would never be like her, that when he grew up, had a family, it would stick. And yet what if he *was* like her? What if he had some gene that kept him constantly on the run? He fumbled with the radio only to hear static, finally turning it off.

"What were you and Kate talking about back there?" he asked, hoping to get a conversation going, but to his surprise Tracy fidgeted.

"Did something happen . . . between you and Kate?"

"No." She gazed out the window.

He could tell by the way she faced stoically to the side that she was trying to avoid telling him something, but what? Ryan rolled down the window, needing air, the August weather creating an unwelcome warmth that only furthered his discomfort. He thought of his past, of how he'd been in trouble with the law on more than one occasion. Wyatt had come to his rescue all those years ago. Had suggested the Marines. Part of Ryan had hated the constant monitoring, being told when and how to do everything, from what time to get up in the morning to what time to go to sleep. The other part of him needed the structure missing in his daily life. Somehow, he'd never been able to reconcile those two sides of his life in and out of the military.

Until he'd come to live on Wyatt's ranch.

Once there, he'd seen the value of a good work ethic, of caring about something bigger than yourself.

"If there's anything you want to ask me . . . anything at all, I would be happy to talk about it." He lifted a brow, but either she was mad at him for something or had decided not to talk because she merely shrugged. Just when he'd been ready to give up, she turned to him.

"Kate asked me to give you a second chance," she said, puzzling her brow. "Second chance for what?"

The cab of the truck grew thick with tension. Ryan searched for the knob to the air conditioner and switched on the fan. "I guess I did say anything," he said, squirming. "Fair enough." He knew that whatever he had to say, he had only minutes before the turnoff to her place, where the other vets would be ahead of them, ready to set up the pen for this morning's training, any opportunity they had to speak gone.

"Well?" she asked, her hand strumming the armrest.

"My home life wasn't the best growing up."

Ryan felt feverish, imagining her life. A good home, a nice family. What would her family think of him? He, who had come from nothing. Single mom, no place to call home—just one rented apartment after the other. Not even a father, just two half-sisters and a half-brother that he rarely saw.

"My mother was . . . ." He couldn't bring himself to say "a druggie," but that was the truth of it. "Let's just say she had problems. I pretty much had to raise myself. I got into some trouble as a teen. Fortunately, Wyatt took an interest. Helped me get my head on straight. Steered me toward the Marines. It helped teach me discipline. I didn't like everything about it, and I saw things that I wish I could forget. It's taken me a long time to let go of that, and most of it I never will. You don't forget."

To Ryan's surprise, instead of turning away, Tracy reached for his hand, entwining her fingers with his. His heart beat frantically in his chest. He had so much he wanted to say, to tell her. So much he wanted to know about her too. But before he could say anything further, the Lombardy poplars and maple gave way to the clearing around her house, the other vets already there and unloading equipment. Any further discussion would have to wait.

172

Nineteen

Boots was waiting on the front steps of the porch with Sam and Jayce at his side, the cat's angry mewls suggesting he hadn't been pleased by Tracy's absence. In the meantime, the vets were already hauling the metal equipment out of the bed of a 350 Ford Diesel.

Marcos called over to Tracy. "Where do you want this?"

Tracy led Sam, Jayce, and Marcos to the pen out back. She hoped Lindsay wouldn't be angry at her for taking up half of the pen with the dogs. Hopefully, she could get the men to build her another pen soon.

Just then, she heard a clatter at the rear of the house. She'd been so busy these past few days that she'd forgotten today was the day that the roofers were supposed to arrive until she saw a dumpster parked next to the house and a semi riding the waves of ruts and dust to bring the roofers the shingles. She apologized to the dog handlers, then pointed toward the pen out back. Avoiding the potholes, she ran down the driveway to show the roofers where to park, the cat following her, all the while meowing his displeasure. Fortunately, Ryan took charge of the other men as well as the two teens. And while the vets spent the next half hour setting up, Tracy spoke to the foreman, a middle-aged man with sandy hair. Already, the men had ladders and were using a shovel-like shingle and nail remover to dislodge the shingles from the roof. They must have been working all morning.

By the time Tracy had the cat fed, the vets had the dogs' equipment in place and she was able to begin work with them. Unfortunately, the racket from the workers on the roof had the pups in such a frenzy that they refused to listen to commands. She ran her hands through her hair. Odds were that she should call the whole thing off. Instead Tracy and Jason used the noise as an opportunity to teach the pups to get used to strange sounds. According to Tracy's instructions, each of the men stayed with their dogs, keeping the animal's attention focused on the trainer by showing the dog the treat, then placing it in a fisted hand and holding it low to turn the pups attention away from the sounds and toward the trainer. When Tracy had first learned this technique, she had been surprised how readily it worked, even with dogs as young as these.

For the next hour, they worked with the pups, stopping and starting, seeking to garner their attention despite the granular whisk of shingles being tossed from the roof into piles around the farmhouse.

Between the mare she'd delivered, the treks into town to speak with Gladys and Stanford, and the dogs, she'd forgotten her promise to begin planting out front of the house so that the place could begin to look like a real home. Now, seeing the chewed-up foliage on all four sides of the farmhouse, she was thankful she hadn't purchased the plants she would need to begin landscaping her garden.

"The farm is starting to take shape." Ryan came to stand beside her as she monitored the pups, offering encouragement when one of the more unruly ones ran circles around the poor trainer.

"Once the roof is on, I'm going to run into town and order some plants for the garden. Want to come with?" she said, surprising herself at her forwardness.

"Sure," he said without hesitation. Then he bit his lip, as though chewing on an idea. "Do you have a computer?"

"A laptop. Why?"

He ran his thumb beneath his lip. "I have an idea. Do you mind if I use it?"

Tracy waved down Jason telling him she would be back in a bit, then together with Ryan, she lumbered off toward the house, Boots darting in and out of the remaining junk that had yet to be cleared.

Despite the dozens of shingles scattered around the property, the farmhouse no longer appeared the derelict, almost sinister looking mess she'd found when she'd first arrived in Wyoming.

Once inside, Tracy fed the cat, then grabbed a pain killer for her arm that still throbbed from last night's delivery of the foal. She downed it with a glass of water. Then she ran upstairs and grabbed the laptop from her room, brought it down to the living room and fired it up. She peered over Ryan's shoulder as he maneuvered through one site after another.

"What are you looking for?" Tracy asked, curious.

"I want to learn more about these sinkholes and what they have to do with oil and the water table, especially if we're going to be putting the dogs through their paces at your place, for the foreseeable future, that is. Don't want them being swallowed up whole."

Tracy watched as he searched for the oil reserves and their locations. Salt Creek produced the most oil at 4.5 million gallons, while Elk Basin, Grass Creek Field, Lance Creek, and the Big Muddy made up the rest.

"Do they use water to drill, do you suppose?" Tracy recalled her earlier reading about decreased water tables creating sinkholes like the one Ryan had fallen into the other day. She had assumed from her reading that the sinkholes had something to do with the agricultural use of water. But what if drilling for oil was the cause instead?

"Of course," he said without hesitation. "But whether it uses enough water to create sinkholes seems unlikely."

"Hmm." She seated herself on the arm of the chair beside him. "But what happens when the oil is displaced? I mean, what keeps the ground from sinking?"

"Let's just check and see." Pacified after his morning meal, Boots climbed up in Ryan's lap and began rubbing his face on the keyboard. "Looks like someone needs attention."

Ryan scooted the cat aside so that he could type in the words "oil and sinkholes."

Tracy saw the words "Texas sinkholes" pop up and felt a shiver up her spine. Not only could drilling oil cause sinkholes, like the massive ones that had occurred in Texas, but it had been known to cause increasing seismic activity as the drilling expanded. Tracy blew out a breath and leaned back. "Well, that's sobering."

"Sure is," Ryan concurred.

"Do you think Mabel knew about the connection between the oil deposits and the sinkholes?"

Ryan shrugged. "Anything's possible."

"What oil companies drill around here?" Tracy was suddenly aware of Ryan's close proximity, the smell of his aftershave and some unnamed scent that was unique to Ryan.

"The main one is Marloxx."

"I think that's the company Lindsay's husband, Gabe, works for."

Ryan peered up at her with a frown. "Isn't she the one who put up the fencing out back for the sheep?"

Where even now, the dogs were training. A surge of foreboding shot through Tracy. "Yeah, she's the one."

"That's odd," Ryan said, scratching behind one ear. "When the men leave with the dogs, let's run over to Blake's place and see what he knows about all this."

It would be dark by the time they arrived and that would mean putting off the garden for another day, but Tracy was eager to learn what Blake knew about Mabel's connection to the oil company.

* * *

Tracy and Ryan quickly wrapped up the dog training
and sent the vets home. In the meantime, the roofers had
finished and had taken off in the late afternoon. As the day
gave way to nighttime, Tracy gave up any notion of ordering
plants, and instead set out in her old truck for Blake's estate
with Ryan beside her. But even before they pulled to a stop
in front of the mansion, next to the fountain, two of Blake's
bodyguards were running toward Tracy's vehicle. For all the
trappings of wealth and power, Tracy couldn't get over the
feeling that the estate felt more like a compound. Ryan must
have felt the same because he exchanged a nervous glance
with her as both men ran to the truck doors, opening them
one after the other. Reluctantly, Tracy stepped down, Ryan
following suit. Was this merely a courtesy since she'd called
ahead to tell Blake she was coming, or had he ordered the
bodyguards to monitor her and Ryan? She didn't know. She
just knew that this week had left her feeling tired and out of
sorts.

Once again, the inside of the estate glowed from within,
reminding her of something from a more temperate climate,
a more tropical region. Maybe the tall palm trees added to the
illusion, or perhaps it was the hibiscus gracing either side of
the portico. Whatever the reason, Tracy felt as though she was
walking onto a movie set rather than an estate in Wyoming.
Blake met them at the front door of the large manor house
and urged them in, while Joy welcomed them with a brief
hug. Today she was dressed completely in white, her tanned

skin offsetting her blonde hair, a large turquoise and silver squash blossom embracing her neck, while a matching bracelet adorned her wrist. Blake, on the other hand, was dressed in jeans and a blue cotton shirt, open at the neck, the only jewelry on him a Rolex watch.

"Come in. Sit." Blake ushered them to a buttery leather sofa with a soft white sheepskin rug and a huge round mahogany and glass coffee table. He stepped behind an open bar and began pulling out bottles of liquor. "What can I get you?"

"Nothing for me," Ryan said, his jaw set as he peered down at the floor.

"You?" Blake asked, turning toward Tracy.

"Just a Shirley Temple, if you have it."

Blake laughed, but enthusiastically set to work preparing her drink, pouring himself a scotch on the rocks and a martini for Joy. "So—" He brought each of them a drink, setting a Vanilla Coconut Water and a glass filled with ice in front of Ryan. "Before we get started talking about the cattle, I want to show you something—something I'm planning. To bring in tourists to the valley."

Tracy and Ryan exchanged glances. She wondered what Blake had in mind, or how his fellow Wyomingites might feel about the supposed changes.

With an expression of almost childlike glee, Blake clicked a small remote that sat atop the glass table, and suddenly a hologram appeared on the table top in 3D. He pressed another button and it began to rotate.

Tracy gasped while Ryan simply whistled at the sight.

For there, atop the table, was an amusement park with a nature theme, all things western. Buffalo, bears, elk, mountain goats, wolves, literally a plethora of Old West themes, from cattle roping, bareback riding, and log rides that barreled down mountainsides with waterfalls cascading over a ledge, flora and fauna built into the fun ride. Even a miniature geyser graced the landscape. Tracy ran her hand through the hologram and felt a falling sensation as she grasped for something solid in the ghost-like image. She didn't know what she'd expected—that it would feel cool somehow, like early morning fog, or that some piece of it might be solid. But whatever she had anticipated, it hadn't materialized and she found herself giggling instead.

"How does it work?" Ryan leaned forward and inspected the hologram from all angles.

"Smoke and mirrors, my friend," Blake said with a laugh. "Smoke and mirrors. But it's a good selling tool, is it not?"

Tracy had to give him that. Both times she had come here, she'd been met with surprises, from the sickened cattle to the corkboard filled with information about Mabel. Now this. But since her thoughts had returned to the cattle, she decided to broach the subject.

"That hologram is amazing," Tracy had to admit. "But I want to talk to you about the cattle. We've been able to trace the website to Wyoming."

Blake took a seat opposite them, his dark brows coming together as he swirled his scotch on the rocks with a plastic stir stick, a horseshoe shape at the end. "The ranch was supposed to have been from out of state. From Southern Idaho, if

I recall. The hay was shipped in. And like I said before, Wyoming isn't known for tansy ragwort."

"I'm sure that's what you were led to believe," Tracy said, laying out her points like dots on a map. "But the fact remains that the website was definitely from here, so it stands to reason that the hay was also from here, though where the tansy came from is anyone's guess. Unfortunately, no physical address could be found for the website, except for the fictitious one."

Blake swilled his drink. "You're sure about the address? Has anyone tried to locate it?"

"We've checked into it. The address literally doesn't exist."

Blake reached over to Joy and grasped her hand. That simple gesture spoke volumes, Joy's set lips followed by an unending sigh making it clear to Tracy, at least, that they had been down this road before and that no matter what happened, she was with him.

"We were wondering if you had found anything more?"

Blake shook his head. "We learned something about my grandmother though."

"Oh?" Tracy leaned forward, nearly spilling her drink in the process. "And what's that?"

Joy squeezed Blake's hand for encouragement. Blake poked the button on his remote control and the hologram collapsed in on itself, disappearing beyond the glass just as readily as it had first appeared.

"The day she went missing, she stopped in at the newspaper office in town."

"The newspaper office?" Ryan said. "Why there?"

181

"She'd been searching for an article, apparently."

Outside the two-story window, the moon shone bright in the sky, its rays cascading onto the slate patio to outline a large fountain with a pineapple finial, the blue-lit mountains behind it.

"What article?" Tracy asked, the landscape lending a solitude to the estate despite its enormous size and grandeur.

Blake tapped the side of his glass with his fingernails. "That was nearly twenty years ago. No one knows."

"Then how did you find out that she went there?" Ryan asked, mirroring Tracy's thoughts precisely.

"An old friend of hers ran into her in town." Blake set his drink onto the table, and folded his hands behind his head, elbows out. "Asked where Mabel was headed."

A friend would remember a detail like that from the day the other friend went missing. "But why didn't she tell the police?" Tracy asked.

"That's the rub. She did. The police checked into it but didn't think it worth investigating, apparently, because it never showed up in any police records."

"That's odd." Ryan shifted in his seat. "Does this woman recall the officer she spoke with?"

"She called down to the precinct. Couldn't remember which officer. In any case, unless he was young at the time, he's probably long since retired or moved on."

For a moment, they all sat in silence. Then Ryan nudged Tracy, reminding her why they had come. "We've done a little digging of our own . . . about Mabel."

"Oh?" Blake asked, as Joy peered up at him, the

admiration she felt for him reflected in the soft glow of her crystal blue eyes.

"Turns out she kept a map hidden in her sewing basket . . . a map of the oil deposits in the area. Do you know why she would be interested in oil deposits?"

Blake tilted his head and threw up his hands. "I have no idea. That doesn't sound like my grandmother. She never cared much for local politics. She was too busy cooking, canning, and working in her garden to be bothered with anything like that."

"Well, for some reason she took enough interest in the oil deposits that she hid a map in her sewing basket." Tracy plucked the maraschino cherry off the top of her Shirley Temple and ate it. "I wonder if that's why she went to the newspaper that day. Maybe there was something in the paper that she wanted to investigate."

Ryan drummed a rhythm on his leg. "Why go to all that trouble if she had the newspaper at home?"

"Maybe she wanted to speak to the person who wrote the article, to see if they knew anything else."

"Or to add to the story," Tracy said, which was followed up with stone silence.

Finally, Joy spoke up. "What if she knew something . . . something that could have caused problems for certain people who were working in the area at that time? Maybe someone didn't want her to go public with what she knew."

Blake set his glass down so hard that they all jumped. Then he stood, running his hands through his hair. "This is my *grandmother* you're talking about. A woman who baked, raised kids, kept us all in line, not someone out of a Who Dunnit. What could she possibly know that anyone would care about . . . care enough to . . . ." He couldn't finish the sentence.

Joy stood and rushed over to him, placing an arm around his shoulder. Tracy saw it as her cue to leave. She signaled to Ryan and as one, they rose to their feet and thanked the pair.

"We've taken enough of your time," Tracy said. But on further introspection, she added, "Did she ever mention sinkholes on the property?"

"Sinkholes?" Blake brushed away the idea with the back of his hand. "What sinkholes?"

"Behind the barn. Ryan fell into one. The area is known for its karst formations, apparently. Sinkholes are more prevalent in that type of topography." Tracy peered out at the midnight blue sky, at the rugged outline of the Tetons to the West. "They're also common in areas where oil is drilled, Marloxx oil, to be precise."

Tracy could tell by the set of Blake's jaw that they had overstayed their welcome. "We'll show ourselves out," she said. Then she and Ryan headed for the door.

Just as she was about to turn the knob, Blake said, "Wait! I have something to show you."

Twenty

A half an hour later, Tracy pulled into the driveway of her farmhouse, relieved when she was indoors and settled. Once again, it was too late for Ryan to be driving the backroads, and the comfort of having him in the house, especially after the two late-night visits from Old Man Grayson and his dog, made it especially nice to have him here. Although she found the ghostly pair to be benevolent, overall, she had still found herself quaking in her slippers each time they'd made an appearance. And after tonight, she was through with surprises.

"What did you think of that last thing that Blake showed us?" Ryan asked, seeming as eager to stay as she was to have him there.

"Around every corner, we hit a dead end, only to find a new lead at the last minute."

Tracy busied herself making hot cocoa on the stove. Comfort food, or in this case, drink—a guilty pleasure she'd enjoyed when her folks were away and she'd gone to stay at her grandparents' place. Her mother would have never allowed it, not this late at night, but her grandmother had permitted sugared cereal in the morning and hot cocoa before bed. The milk in the cocoa had helped her sleep.

"Speaking of which," Ryan said, taking a seat in the living room, nearest the kitchen entrance, "if we have the date of Mabel's disappearance, we should be able to go through the newspaper's archives to find out what was written on that day and by whom."

"I wonder why Blake didn't do that already?" Tracy called as she readied the mugs and waited for the stove to heat the cocoa. To update the kitchen, she would need a microwave, but that was for another day.

"My question as well. Maybe he just learned the information and hasn't had a chance to pursue it."

"Could be," she said, "or could be he didn't like what he learned."

From her vantage point at the stove, Tracy regarded Ryan, who lay his head back on the doilied headrest and closed his eyes, the scene decidedly domestic. Everything about the place made her feel as if she'd returned to a simpler time, if there ever was such a thing. She turned back to the stove and blew a lock of hair from her forehead, the tumult of the day draining her of all energy. A light snoring caused her to turn. Against the backdrop of lamplight, she paused, relishing the thought of Ryan here, his dimpled cheek, his sandy hair, his work-worn hands. And yet his twitches and jerks attested to the fact that he was wrestling with something. Quietly, she continued on, pouring the hot cocoa into two mugs once the milk was fully heated. Pulling the chair from the kitchen table out carefully so as not to wake him, she sat and sipped from one of the mugs, saving his mug back for later.

There was so much she wanted to know about Ryan. He had hinted at a past that she sensed embarrassed him, and yet who was she to judge—she, who had shown such poor judgment on her first foray into adulthood that she had run her horse over a cliff, all because she thought she knew better than her friends and her parents. Or worse, because she didn't want to lose the hour she had gained by going around the snowfield. Guilt pressed down on her and she cupped her head in her hands, hoping to quell the tremor that welled up inside of her every time she recalled that horrible episode in her life.

She had been so caught up in her own grief, that she didn't realize that Ryan was reliving some painful event until she heard him thrash and cry out a single word, "Herc," followed by a shout, "No!" She jumped to her feet, nearly spilling the hot cocoa and rushed to his side.

"What is it?" She knelt down beside him, his arm nearly catching her in the chin as he thrashed in his sleep. Suddenly, Ryan awoke, but he appeared disoriented, his eyes scanning the room in hurried motions as though he were back in Afghanistan and had only now realized that something wasn't right.

"What?" Ryan shook his head, his panic bleeding out, leaving him with a confused expression that melted Tracy's heart.

"It's okay. You were dreaming. Want to talk about it?" She cupped his hand in hers. Embarrassed, Ryan looked away, but she cradled his chin and brought it around to her. "It helps to talk." She felt like a fraud, saying that. Who had she talked to after the accident? No one. Instead, she had simply picked up and moved as many miles away from that memory as possible.

"Sorry, sometimes I feel like I'm back in Afghanistan—when I sleep. I wake up in sweats." He breathed heavily as if to relieve the memory seated on his chest.

"You yelled the name Herc. Who was that?" Tracy caught a glimmer of pain in his eyes at the mention of what she assumed was a person.

For several moments, Ryan didn't answer, simply peered down at his folded hands. "It was my dog . . . he belonged to *all* of us, my entire platoon."

"What happened to him?" Tracy patiently waited until he was ready to speak.

"In Afghanistan, we weren't allowed to keep a dog. The brass worried that it might alert the enemy of our whereabouts. It was for our safety."

But even as Ryan spoke, Tracy knew there was more to the story. "Then why did you have a dog?"

Ryan bent down, his folded hands entwined against his forehead as if to lock the memory securely inside his brain. But a grimace of anguish played at his mouth, the memory refusing to stay put.

"He adopted us . . . the entire team, but me especially. He didn't give us away to the enemy," he said, his words filled with torment. "Instead, he warned us with a low growl anytime the enemy was close. He saved more lives than I can ever repay him for and we just abandoned him."

At that, Ryan fisted his hands, tears falling as he struggled to quell the emotion building in him. Tracy grabbed his wrists. "Why did you abandon him, Ryan? I don't understand."

"Don't you see?" Ryan said, tears replaced with anger that burnished his cheeks. "Anyone caught with a dog would be court-martialed, so when the commander found out, we had to disown Herc. We had to say it was a stray."

Tracy felt the heaviness of Ryan's emotion as if it were her own. "So what happened to the dog?"

Ryan once again dissolved into a puddle of anguish. "It was my responsibility to take him out and shoot him, after dark. I was supposed to drive him out into the desert, far enough away from camp that it wouldn't draw fire. I drove for miles, through dangerous country, to an area that was safe from insurgents."

"Then what happened?" Tracy whispered, scarcely able to breathe, realizing that his demons might be as fierce as her own.

"I . . . I couldn't do it. I shot into the air and then threw Herc the biggest piece of meat I could sneak out of the camp. Afterwards, I filled a bowl of water and left. Left my best friend to die out in the desert. I'm such a coward." He

189

pounded his forehead with his fist.

"No you're not," Tracy assured him, forcing him to look her in the eye. "You are *decent*. You did the only thing you could in a bad situation. You had no choice, but at least you gave him a chance at life."

"Don't you see?" Ryan said, his watery blue eyes filled with pain. "I left my best friend to die, after all he did for me and the guys. He may have been just a dog, but to us he was a hero. You don't *do* that to heroes."

Tracy turned away, her eyes filling with tears, because she had felt much the same when the helicopter had hovered overhead, the sound filling her nighttime with dread. The loud whir-whir of the rotors, the surreal sound echoing off the canyon, her friends unable to look her in the eye. It was not just one death that day. It had been the death of a lifetime of friendships. Of childhood outings, picnics, ball games. Over in an instant. Because no one could face that day without overwhelming grief.

"You may not believe me, but I do understand . . . more than you'll ever know." Her voice choked with emotion.

Ryan cocked his head, his tears abating slightly. "I mustered out that week. I never saw him again."

"So you don't know what happened to him?"

He shook his head on a sigh. "But I keep his picture under my pillow. To remember." His smile grew watery. "No man left behind, right?"

Tracy closed her eyes to give herself time to rein in her emotion. If only her horse Jedi were still alive. What lengths would she go to rescue him, if she'd had the chance? A calm settled over her because she knew the answer. She would do anything to save him. Right then and there, she determined to find Herc, to bring him home to Ryan. Maybe then she could finally resolve the guilt she felt over Jedi's death.

Twenty-One

Tracy rose the next day to greet the morning sun, hoping to get in some time on her laptop before the real work began. Fortunately, she had set up a small table she'd found downstairs in front of the upstairs bedroom window so she could gaze out over the Tetons as she worked. A rosy sky against a backdrop of deep blue hinted at a warm day.

Although she knew it was a longshot, she had heard of G.I.s bringing a dog home from overseas. But then again, those G.I.s had known where to locate the dog. She tapped the keys of her laptop and brought up a map of Afghanistan. She had only vague directions from the little she'd been able to glean from Ryan. She knew he had taken the dog twenty miles north of his base camp in Kandahar. The nearest small town was Hauz Qala. But then again, the dog could have traveled in any direction. Her best bet would be to contact Operation Pup Rescue, an organization that helped bring G.I.s' dogs home from Afghanistan and other foreign locations, but when she typed in the URL and saw the cost of the mission, she whistled and fell back in her chair, defeated. How would she ever get the three-thousand dollars it would take to bring him home? And that's *if* they could find him. If they had to do a search operation, that would cost money too. How much money, she couldn't say.

One step at a time.

Tracy closed her eyes, thinking. It was doubtful that Ryan's dog, Herc, would have had help from the Afghanis, as dogs there were considered to be more of a nuisance than a pet, believed to be unclean, according to the literature she had read. As such, they lived outside, on their own, often in stray packs. Frustrated, she opened her eyes, aware that this would be like finding something of value in that barn of hers. But then she recalled Ryan's anguish from the night before and her resolve returned. If finding Herc could make his life even marginally better, she was determined to make it happen. But she didn't want him to know until she was certain she could find the dog and bring him home. No use getting his hopes up for nothing.

"So, Herc, what do you say we bring you home?"

Then she clicked onto the website and began the process of finding Herc and reuniting him with Ryan. He deserved that after all he had done for his country.

* * *

From the adjoining room, Ryan could hear Tracy tapping on her keyboard. He squinted at the dial of the clock that sat on a nightstand next to his bed. He would need to get glasses one of these days. It was either 5:30 or 6:30. Definitely the latter, on closer inspection. What could Tracy possibly be doing on the computer this early in the morning?

He rose from the bed and padded barefoot to the next room, the door slightly ajar, Tracy's back to him, facing the screen. He knocked softly on the door and saw her jump, then slam the lid to her laptop down as though he'd caught her doing something that she didn't want him to know about. His heart sank at the thought she might have a boyfriend back home, or worse yet, maybe she was on one of those apps like Match.com. Just his luck!

"Can I talk to you?" he asked.

"Sure," she said, pointing to a spot on the bed.

He hesitated, unsure whether he wanted to sit down on her bed, a place fraught with contradictions, considering how he felt about her. His confusion over her odd reaction to being caught at the computer only heightened his anxiety. But as he looked around, he realized it was the only place available, so he sat on the far edge of the bed, keeping as much distance as possible between him and her.

"What's up?" she asked, her tone unnaturally cheery.

"I just wanted to apologize . . . about last night. I didn't mean to get emotional. It's just that—"

"No need for apology," she said, and this time he read the sincerity in her voice. "It's normal to become attached to an animal, especially in a place like Afghanistan. I, of all people,

194

should understand attachments to animals."

Ryan had to laugh, because of course a veterinarian would understand his love and commitment to a pet. That's why Tracy was perfect for him, but then he recalled the wide-eyed look she'd just given him and his enthusiasm waned.

"Truth is, I've put some feelers out to the guys about my dog. Friends from my old division. Got an email from one of my buddies, a guy named Rick. Said he'd keep an eye out."

He peered down at his nails, ragged from chewing them to the nubs everytime he recalled either the dog or some of the firefights. One especially bad memory that haunted his dreams involved an old Afghani farmer, who looked like any other, his face craggy from years in the sun, his skin dark against his Pashtun clothing—a white *burqa* and *tsadar*, a loose fitting robe and turban. What he hadn't warranted was that the man was wearing a suicide vest. Even now, the memory had him trembling so badly that Tracy rushed from her seat in front of the computer to comfort him.

"I'm so sorry," he mumbled, unable to quell the tremors. To his surprise and relief, she wrapped her arms around him and held him tight.

"It's going to be okay," she said, rocking him slightly.

"How do you know? How do you know anything?" he said, suddenly angry, though he couldn't say why. It's just that this was *his* pain. *He* had been the one to go through hell and back. How could she possibly understand?

But despite his anger, she continued to rock him, continued to offer comforting words. "You're not alone in this, Ryan."

His eyes wandered over to the laptop. Maybe he'd been wrong about her intentions. Maybe he was just imagining things that weren't there, too used to constantly being on guard, vigilant. Afraid.

Afraid of what?

But he knew the answer. Afraid that no one would love him after what he'd done. Yes, it was for the country. Yes, it was for his brothers in arms. But it had still been murder. He had walked through a village that had just been strafed with gunfire after learning of a high-level target in the location. What he hadn't expected, hadn't been ready for, was that sometimes women and children got caught in the crossfire. *His* crossfire. Even now, tears burned the back of his eyes and clawed at his throat. Here he was, just trying to form a relationship with a woman he admired and already she was seeing a side of him that he'd vowed to hide. If he wasn't careful, he might lose her before the relationship could even begin.

To his surprise, Tracy stroked the side of his cheek with her hand then reached up and kissed him, hesitantly at first, then more fiercely. Suddenly, all the pain of the past few days was swept aside in a landslide of emotions. Yet even as he tasted her soft, sensuous lips, he knew the fear and loathing would return. Only this time, he didn't know if he would be able to hold on yet again. It was always like that. One step forward, two steps back. Into hell.

Twenty-Two

Once again, the roofers arrived bright and early, ahead
of the pups. In the meantime, Tracy had gone online and
ordered a host of plants for the garden she intended for
the landscaping. One important tool a veterinarian needed
was organization, and she had stayed up late into the
night mapping out her garden on a landscaping app she'd
downloaded onto her computer. Lastly, she had ordered a
load of soil and mulch to till into the hard and barren soil
that surrounded her house. With that last bit done, the outside
would finally be finished. Now, she set about preparing
a brunch to feed the troops, as it were. She wished she'd
purchased more food when she went to town, but at least
Ryan knew of a stand nearby that sold vegetables, fruit, and
eggs, and had driven out this morning, returning with enough
to get her by until she could go to the store. And she still had a

pound of bacon and a few loaves of bread that she'd had the foresight to purchase.

As she diced, chopped, and cooked up the morning meal, she fought the urge to duck each time the roofers pounded nails into the roof or threw shingles down. They sounded like a herd of elephants dancing on her rooftop. She smiled at the imagery.

Before she'd finished preparing the morning meal, the dogs' arrival was announced with a volley of engines idling and pups barking excitedly for the upcoming training. It would be a long day of work. Because of that, she and Ryan had once again decided to put off going into town until tomorrow. And, until she could fashion a table out of some wood she had found, the men would have to take their plates and find a seat wherever possible. A few sat out on the porch, while a couple of the guys sat in chairs in the living room. Sam and Jayce made their way to the kitchen table, puppies at their side.

When everyone was finished eating, Tracy turned to Ryan. "Would you mind getting things started with the pups? I'll be right out."

"Sure," Ryan said. "But first, why don't we have the men clean up the dishes?"

Tracy held up her hands. "No way," she insisted. "Your men have already done so much for me and I'm very appreciative. I'm not saddling them with the dishes."

Apparently, she'd said it with enough conviction that he backed away. "Okay, whatever you say."

For a moment she thought he might kiss her, but as

though deciding better of it, he left, much to her dismay. Because, like it or not, Ryan was growing on her. She'd never felt like this before about anyone—this sense of belonging. Maybe it was their shared pain over the loss of an animal, a loss that each of them blamed themselves for. Or maybe it was simple chemistry. She watched him open the screen door and step out onto the porch, calling all the men together. In that moment, it was easy to see he was a natural born leader. She forced her attention to cleaning up the dishes as quickly as possible.

A half hour later, after she'd washed and dried all the dishes, she ran upstairs. In the wee hours of dawn, she had not only initiated the process of finding Ryan's dog with Operation Pup Rescue, she had contacted the local newspaper to see if they could retrieve all newspapers leading up to the week of Mabel's disappearance. She knew it was a longshot that the archives even went back that far, but it was one she was willing to take. Now that her chores were done, she decided to take a quick scan of her inbox to see if anything had shown up.

She raced up the stairs, two by two, only pausing when she arrived on the top landing. Her computer overlooked the back pen where Ryan and the other men were working with the dogs. Today they were focusing on hunting for a missing person. In this case, the pups were each given a chance to sniff a piece of their handler's clothing. Then the clothing would be hidden somewhere on the compound with a treat inside the pocket. At first, the dogs seemed confused, but little by little a few of them were picking up the idea. Those would be the missing persons dogs that would end up in search and rescue. The others would be taught to turn on and off lights, to open doors, to sense their handler's stress, and to get help by touching their paw to a button that alerted authorities or medical personnel that the handler was in trouble. In effect, those would be given to veterans with PTSD or who suffered medical problems. Her throat tightened with emotion at the thought that these animals, who had been rescued themselves, would become rescue animals for others. Only one would become a guard dog, but which one?

Just then, the hammering suddenly stopped as the roofers took time out for lunch. Tracy tore her eyes away from the scene below, then returned to her computer and opened her email. A tendril of excitement raced through her when she saw that, indeed, she had answers to both the missing dog and to the archived newspapers. First things first—she opened the one from the newspaper. Fortunately, the dates had been archived, but with shortened staff, it would take time to get those articles and it would cost thirty dollars per article. In her mind, she pictured dollars flying out the window and blowing in the breeze. Money would have been tight under normal circumstances, but with her search for Ryan's dog, the barn still needing wood, paint, and a roof, and now landscaping, this only shrank her budget further. For a moment, she closed her eyes, giving herself time to breathe. If she allowed herself to view the entire picture at once, she feared a tidal wave of panic would overwhelm her—send her packing. But if she took it one step at a time, the work was doable, so for now, she thought only of the newspaper costs, eschewing all others.

She would pop off an email to Blake to see if he could recoup the cost. That would save at least some of her budget.

Next, she opened the email response from Operation Pup Rescue. The woman who answered her couldn't have been more kind, going so far as to speak of "our babies" and "our heroes" needing to be reunited. But then came the follow-up that torpedoed Tracy's heart. "It's possible to find a dog that's currently missing, but highly expensive. It could cost ten thousand or more to locate the dog and bring him home. I'm not trying to discourage you," the woman added, "just apprise you of the realities we face." She didn't have to add what Tracy already knew, the unspoken "*if* the dog is even alive." This could all be a wild goose chase.

Tracy leaned back in her chair and rubbed her eyes with the back of her hand. For all the world she felt like crying, yet she was determined not to give in to her sense of failure. She had faced bigger hurdles than this and aced them. Yet as she checked the balance in her bank account and tallied up the cost of the roof along with all the other materials she had put on credit, a weight settled on her chest. How would she ever climb out from under this mountain of debt? All the money she had saved, which was supposed to have lasted a year, was nearly depleted and she had yet to buy a single piece of equipment for the large animal hospital. Any hope of bringing Ryan's dog home had vanished before she'd managed to get the project underway. She would just have to thank the woman from the puppy rescue service and explain that ten thousand dollars was way over her head.

She sent an email to the woman thanking her and was

surprised by how quickly she received an answer. "Don't give up," the message read. "If you have a picture or a description of your dog, we can put it on our website and ask for donations. It's worth a try."

Tracy knew that a picture would speak louder than words, if only she could get her hands on one of Herc. Her fingers hovered over the keyboard. Last night, hadn't Ryan said he kept a picture of his dog under his pillow at night as atonement, so that he wouldn't forget his pal, his hero?

"Hmm . . . ."

Tracy stood and made her way into Ryan's room. Once there, she picked up the pillow and frowned. She did a quick search of the crack between the mattress and headboard. Still nothing. She was about to walk away, disappointed, but then she ran her fingers inside the pillowcase and they caught on something ragged, the edge of a photo perhaps? She lifted it out and smiled. There stood Herc and Ryan, the dog leaning into him. She peered down at the sweet face peering back at her, a little black and white mongrel with floppy ears and what she thought of as a sensitive nature. How could anyone walk away from that face? She would quickly scan the picture into her computer and then send the copy to the rescue facility. Maybe someone would find it in their heart to help the little guy, and in doing so help Ryan. All she could do was hope and pray.

She was about to leave the room when she looked down at the dogs below to see how they were faring with Ryan at the helm. But what she saw made her breathing quicken, for staring back at her from below was Ryan. And the expression he wore made it clear he wasn't happy that she had gone into his room. She wanted to be able to explain to him, but she couldn't. Not yet. She didn't want to get his hopes up only to be dashed. Now she needed to find a way to mollify him . . . until she could tell him the truth.

* * *

Kate heard her cell phone ring and hurried to answer it, all the while keeping an eye on Hank Warren. Something about him made her flesh crawl, but she didn't know why. She just knew that her intuition had never steered her wrong.

"Oh, Kate, I'm glad I caught you. This is Tracy. I have a dilemma that I want to run by you."

Kate read the hesitancy in Tracy's voice. "Shoot," she said, watching as Hank exited the barn, his eyes scanning the perimeter as though searching for something.

"Has Ryan ever told you about the dog he found in Afghanistan?"

Before Kate answered, she leaned closer to the window, parting the curtains slightly so she could get a better look at Hank. She could swear he had something shiny in his hand, but what? She turned her attention back to the phone. "Not me, but he's spoken to Wyatt about his dog. That's been a sticking point with Ryan. A lot of guilt to carry."

"I'm trying to locate Herc," Tracy said in a rush, "to bring him home to Ryan."

Kate fell against the sofa arm, needing to sit. This was no ordinary rescue mission Tracy was proposing. It would take a miracle to find an animal in a war-torn country half a world away.

Tracy must have sensed Kate's uncertainty because she paused, as though afraid to continue. "It's just that . . . I know I'm chasing windmills here, but I also know how much this would mean to him."

"Tracy," Kate said, careful how she worded what she was about to say, "I know you want to help Ryan, but you're asking the impossible. Have you thought of just getting him another dog?"

"He's got another dog, a whole slew of them, but the only way he'll ever get over the guilt he feels will be to find Herc and rescue him."

Kate rubbed her forehead, reading the frustration in Tracy's voice. A list of all the obstacles ran through her very logical mind, but then she thought of everything she had accomplished in helping Wyatt save his ranch. Now, the ranch was even prospering and expanding. She could have given up—recognized her quixotic quest for what it was . . . impossible. But she hadn't. She had stood her ground and, in the end, she was happier than she'd ever been.

"Okay, whatever you need, I'm behind you one-hundred percent. In fact, I'll pitch in five hundred dollars and set up a GoFundMe account. That's how we helped save the ranch. You okay with that?"

"Am I ever!" Tracy breathed. "Just one problem. I needed a photo of the dog, and Ryan caught me snooping in his bedroom. I don't think he's very happy about it. Should I tell him what I'm doing?"

"Oh no! Whatever you do, you can't tell Ryan. Not until the dog is on American soil. If something happened that we couldn't find the dog, or worse, if the dog is dead, it would devastate him. He's been through enough already."

Tracy concurred. "What do I do then?"

Kate wracked her brain. She knew what secrets could do to a budding relationship. She had found out the hard way. But in this instance, she felt certain Wyatt would agree. Better to say nothing until they had found the dog and were assured he was on his way home.

"Just tell Ryan you were tidying up." Kate peered out the window and realized that Hank was gone. She didn't like it when he was off her radar. She added her best wishes to Tracy, then hung up the phone and walked to the back of the house. Once there, she caught him digging near the edge of the property with a small trowel. That must have been what he'd hidden in the palm of his hand. What on earth was that man up to, she wondered with a shiver of unease? She needed to talk to Wyatt . . . soon.

Twenty-Three

Too many years in the military had led to Ryan always peering over his shoulder, waiting for the next bomb to drop, the next sneak attack. As he stood staring up at the second-story window where he'd last seen Tracy only ten minutes earlier, he felt his hackles rise. But why? Tracy had never given him reason to distrust her . . . until now. He whistled to the dog and his handler, Bryce, putting them through their paces. Bryce's dog, Hoagie, was definitely cut out for search and rescue. The retriever had an eagerness about her that kept her on the hunt, whereas Jackson's dog, KC, had a highly tuned loyalty to his owner. He would make a great dog for a vet with PTSD.

"I'm going to run KC to the house to have Tracy look at his paw." Jackson lifted the dog's foreleg for Ryan's inspection.

From what Ryan could see, the dog had some pitch and

pine needles on the bottom of his paw, and he was limping slightly. Ryan reached over and ran a finger along the pad of his foot. The dog flinched. He must have picked the pitch and needles up at the ranch. Tracy would know what to do. Before he could send Jackson to the farmhouse, Tracy came bounding out, her hair in a ponytail, and wearing only a light jacket, unsuitable for the upcoming winters in Wyoming. The day had turned out balmier than expected and the wind had come up, rain on the horizon, rare for early July, which was typically dry. Despite his anger about Tracy going through his room, the air smelled alive with possibility.

"We've got a man down," Ryan said, trying to lighten the mood. He knew Tracy had seen him watching her from below his window. He also recognized the worry written in the crease of her brow. It's the expression he'd seen on countless of his men's faces when they'd done something stupid but without malice. He decided to talk to her. Later.

"I'll go get my bag. I have a high-tech solution for the pitch. Butter and some scissors to remove the excess matted hair."

She left in a flash. If she'd been one of his recruits, he would have had full confidence in her. He shook his head and went back to work, certain he was overthinking things. She was probably just tidying up his room. And as far as the laptop went, she could have been searching for anything. Looking up treatments for a boil, for all he knew. He whistled for the next dog and handler to run an obstacle course, then to pull at the towel wrapped around the handle of a drawer from an old dresser he'd found in the barn. The dog was then expected to run back through the obstacle course. The puppies were still way too young to really get it, but by watching an older, more experienced lead dog put through its paces, the pups would learn the routine, eventually.

Funny how quickly he'd found himself in the lead position again. He had to say, it felt good. Part of his angst upon returning home was having none of the responsibility he'd had as a sergeant. The responsibility had given him an anchor. Now, having responsibility thrust upon him again, he found he liked it. And although he hadn't had much experience training dogs, with the help of Jason and Tracy, he was quickly picking up everything he needed to know. Anything else, he had learned from reading online. He wondered how he would feel, giving over his position to Tracy, once she returned from treating the dog. But when she was finished giving first aid to the pup, the two of them fell into a perfect rhythm beside each other just as they had when working on the house. Soon Tracy, along with Sam and Jayce, had half the dogs paired off to hunt lost articles of clothing that would one day be people, while Ryan and Jason taught the other dogs the basics of turning off and on lightswitches, using the lead dog as guide. One of the men had even managed to wrestle an old and rusty refrigerator into the pen so that the dogs could practice opening and closing the door. Most were still too young to open it, yet he couldn't help but laugh at their determination. It didn't hurt that they had added a glob of peanut butter to the towel to help motivate the dogs.

Tracy and Ryan met back after two more hours of

rigorous training. If they got a good start, they could make it to town to pick up the landscaping supplies she'd ordered, as well as some other miscellaneous needs, and then stop at the newspaper to pick up copies of the newspaper printed the week that Mabel went missing. Tracy was panting and breathing hard from all the exertion.

"Who had the better workout, you or the dogs?" Ryan asked with a smile.

"Who do you think?"

They waited for the others to leave, then followed in Tracy's truck, continuing on well past the ranch as they headed toward town. Once there, they made their way toward the *Cody Sentinel*, one of the few larger, more modern buildings in town, a large brick building edged in sandstone. Inside, they spoke with a woman at the front counter who called for assistance from an elderly gentleman named Ned Farthing who reminded Tracy of her uncle, a man in his upper sixties with gray hair, a large girth, and a genteel smile.

"What can I do you for?" he asked, leaning over the counter.

Tracy explained about Mabel and her disappearance.

"I remember Mabel. Nice lady. Too bad about what happened." He marched around the counter and nodded his head toward a hallway where he led them to a back room, small with a window that overlooked an alleyway. "Take a seat," he said, pointing to two chairs. "So let me get this straight. You want a copy of every newspaper that came out the week prior to her death?"

Tracy nodded.

He put on glasses so that he could read the computer, then looked at her over the half-lenses. "Did it ever occur to you that she could have been looking for something farther back?"

Tracy turned to Ryan, trying to hide her disappointment because Ned was right. They could be chasing a ghost.

"Do you mind telling me what she was looking for?" Ned asked, pulling his glasses off and twirling them.

Tracy explained about the oil, then the agricultural angle, if water had indeed been depleted for crops, leaving the ground beneath ripe for sinkholes.

"Okay, then. I'll keep an eye out for any articles on the subjects while I'm at it, but I have to tell you, it's highly unlikely you'll find what you're looking for."

"Still, it's worth a shot." Ryan grasped Tracy's hand in his and gave it a squeeze.

"Okay, then," Ned said, turning his attention to the computer screen. "Instead of copies I can email the attachments to you. But, if you want to come back in an hour, I should be able to let you know what I've found."

Tracy gave Ned her email address, then she and Ryan stood and turned to leave. Before they could exit the door, Ned called out to them.

"Why do you want to know about sinkholes?" he asked, his eyes narrowed in grandfatherly concern.

Tracy glanced at Ryan who gave his silent assent for her to speak to the man. "We think Mabel may have had some interest in oil wells and drilling in the area, and that it may have led to her death, but we don't know why. We found a sinkhole on her property and think maybe she connected the oil drilling with the sinkholes somehow."

"That so?" Ned said, scooting his chair away from his desk and placing his hands across his expanding belly.

"She hid a map in her sewing kit. Of oil sites in and around Cody. We're not sure what she found, but we're hoping to find out."

"In an article from that time period?" Ned asked.

Tracy nodded while Ned merely said, "Hmm." When nothing more seemed forthcoming, she thanked him and they left, making their way toward the local nursery for plants. Any purchases she made would need to be hardy to survive the Wyoming winters, according to Ryan. Luckily, she had checked into that before making her online order.

An hour later, she had a truck bed filled with salvia, roses, Shasta daisies, balloon flowers, and silver carpet, as well as bags of garden soil. Plus she'd purchased some stone pavers for the walkway. Once the flowers were planted and the pavers laid, the place would look like a real home. She smiled, content. For the first time since she'd arrived, she admitted to herself how much she wanted for this to work out, for her to find enough work here that she could stay. Here, no one was judging her. Back in Seattle, at first she had felt shunned, eventually isolated. She no longer sought out new friendships. Instead, she had begun keeping to herself more and more, only communicating with people while at work. It was safer that way, the pity in her former friends' eyes gutting her.

But now . . . now she was making new connections. New friends. Friends who didn't know about that one fateful day when everything had changed.

"You're awfully quiet over there," Ryan said. "Anything you want to share?"

She shook her head while offering a wan smile. She rolled down the window. Even though it was mid summer and too warm to be leaving the window down, she loved the fresh air blowing in, the agricultural smells that were at once indescribable and delicious. Back in Seattle, she had loved the smell of freshly mown lawns, of fir trees. Here, much of the expanse was wide open. Dry. Among the many smells she couldn't name, she detected the scent of sage, that and cattle, Wyoming's largest agricultural industry, according to Ryan.

"Just thinking about the farm," Tracy said, not yet ready to explain her past and the effect it had on her. "The homestead is starting to take shape." Now, all but the planting was done. If lucky, she would have a couple of months or more before the cold weather set in. She'd never lived in an especially chilly climate and wasn't sure how she would manage driving in deep snow. That was another thing she would have to talk to Ryan about before the weather began changing.

"Well, here we are," he said, as she pulled up into the parking lot of the newspaper once more. "Let's go see what's what."

Together, they climbed out of the truck and headed indoors. Ryan held the door to the newspaper office open for her. For a moment she paused, unused to such gallantry. Then she hurried inside, feeling the temperature cool slightly from the air conditioning that hummed in the corner. Tracy stepped to the counter and gave her name to an elderly woman, who hadn't been there during their first visit.

The woman put on the glasses that hung on a seed pearl chain around her neck and peered at her screen. "Oh, right. Ned was expecting you. He had to leave, but he told me to tell you he sent the attachments you requested to the email address you gave him."

Tracy thanked her and turned to leave. She was almost to the door when the woman called out to her.

"Oh, wait. He left you a package." The woman walked to a metal filing cabinet and opened a drawer, pulling out a small manila envelope. "Here," she said, handing it to Tracy.

Once again, Tracy thanked her and they left. "What do you suppose this is?" Tracy felt the contours of the envelope as she climbed into her truck.

"Open it up," Ryan said, brows knitted in curiosity.

Tracy tore at one end, the contents falling to the floor of her truck. She leaned down to retrieve what had fallen. What she found, nestled in the palm of her hand, was a thumb drive. She looked to Ryan, who merely shrugged.

"Only one way to find out what's on it," he said as she placed it back inside the small envelope, the interior encased in bubble wrap. "Let's get this home and we'll open it up on your computer."

* * *

Hank Warren pulled away from the curb, shaded by an old elm that wept leaves onto his windshield, then drove in

213

the direction opposite of Tracy so that he wouldn't be seen. He punched Derrick's number into his phone. Seconds later, Derrick came up on the speakerphone.

"You've heard something?" Derrick asked, not bothering with the usual greetings.

"First off, I've managed to get soil samples of both Miss Barnhardt's land and the Vet ranch to see if it contains any limestone."

"Good. Bring that to me and I'll get it tested."

"Next," Hank continued, "Tracy and Ryan just left the newspaper with an envelope. They were asking for copies of newspapers from the week before Mabel died, according to the old lady who runs the desk."

Derrick whistled. Hank guessed he was either in a meeting or at lunch by the sound of the background noise.

"Did you order copies so we can see what they've found?"

Hank had thought about it, but in the end decided it would seem too suspicious to order copies of the same newspapers as Tracy and Ryan.

Derrick must have guessed what he was thinking because he said, "I'll take care of it."

"Okay." Hank was relieved when Derrick hung up the phone. Hank turned on his blinker at the light and made a hurried U-ey so he could return to the ranch before anyone grew suspicious. Lately, Kate had taken to watching him. He turned on his air conditioner, feeling warm suddenly.

As he made his way out of Cody, he peered down at his phone just as the number flashed off. But what set his heart racing was the location beneath the phone number. He slammed on the brakes and pulled to the side of the road. It wasn't possible. Derrick was supposed to be part of the larger consortium. A mucky muck. He *couldn't* be in Wyoming.

Twenty-Four

Tracy's heart dropped the minute she saw the farmhouse. Spray-painted graffiti marred the pretty white paint. She'd been so wrapped up in the thought of viewing what was on the thumb drive the moment she arrived at the farmhouse that she hadn't expected this new gut punch. After all their hard work. She read the words and tried not to blow a fuse, or worse, cry.

Tracy Barnhardt, go home! It was written in bold red paint and underneath the words was a red skull and crossbones.

As if to shield her from what she'd just witnessed, Ryan pulled her to his chest and cradled her. "It's okay, Tracy," he said.

She fisted her hands against his chest, wishing away the graffiti, the hateful words. Who wanted her gone and why?

"Quick, Tracy," Ryan said, lifting her chin. "Do you have

any leftover paint thinner?"

His words seemed to be coming to her through a thick haze, the tears she'd promised not to shed hovering on her eyelashes, precluding any further anger on her part. She shook her head to clear the cobwebs. "Paint thinner?"

"That will take off the graffiti. Plus, I'll need gloves and a mask too, if you have them. Oh, and steel wool in case I can't get it all off with the paint thinner."

Suddenly, her brain caught up with his words and she nodded. "I'm a vet. I always keep a stack of gloves and masks. And I have nearly a full can left of the paint thinner. I bought extra since I didn't know how much we would need and didn't want to run short."

She went to grab the paint thinner from inside her utility room. While Ryan poured it into an old coffee can, she pulled the plants she'd bought at the nursery from the back of the pickup and placed them beneath a stand of trees to keep them cool. Then, for the next several hours, they scrubbed the graffiti off the wall, layer by layer. Her arms ached by the time she was finished. Though exhausted and more than just a little disheartened, she made dinner afterward, the thumb drive forgotten for the moment.

Now, as they sat down to eat, her cooking skills no doubt in question after yet another simple meal—this time hamburgers and macaroni—they discussed the following day. With Ryan, she fell into such an easy rhythm, as though they were an old married couple instead of simple acquaintances. She'd never experienced that with a man. It felt . . . *wonderful*. And yet she also detected a spark of anticipation any time she was around him, the sheer manliness of his smell after a day on the farm. For a brief moment, their hands touched. Then he leaned in and kissed her for a second time, causing a slow pulse at the base of her throat. When she finally came up for air, a shiver of delight raced through her. She wanted more, much more.

* * *

It had taken all of Ryan's reserves to pull back, to keep from sweeping Tracy up into his arms and carrying her up to the bedroom upstairs with the pink chenille bedspread. What stopped him was the memory of one of his mother's many boyfriends doing just that. When *Ryan* made love to Tracy, he wanted it to be for keeps. To remember that moment for a lifetime. He ran his fingers down her cheek, running his thumb along her bottom lip, wishing he could lean in as he had moments earlier, but he was afraid of what he might do. Afraid he wouldn't be able to hold himself back. Reluctantly, he squeezed her hand one last time, then decided it was better that he finish his dinner. But before he did, he noticed the tilt of her head, the way she looked at him as though wishing for more, but just as afraid about where it might lead as he was at this minute.

When they were finished eating, Tracy urged Ryan to leave the dishes for later so that they could take a look at what was on the thumb drive. His pulse shot up at the thought of being alone with her in her bedroom, as his mind reeled back to that moment in the truck, when he'd taken Tracy into his arms. It had stirred something in him. It stirred something in him now as he followed her to the upstairs bedroom where she kept her computer.

Ryan relinquished the thoughts as he handed the thumb drive to Tracy and watched as she loaded it onto her computer. For one brief moment, her email inbox came up on the blue screen and his eyes caught the word Afghanistan. He frowned as he ran the scenarios through his head about why she might be reaching out to someone in Afghanistan. The truth is, he knew nothing about her . . . not really. And yet he hesitated to ask her, fearing he might appear nosy or controlling.

"Okay, here we go," she said, her eyes riveted to the screen.

What appeared next was a series of articles cut and pasted from different time periods, the first one starting in May of the year Mabel had died. The newsman had gone to a lot of extra work to get this information. It must have intrigued him as much as it had Ryan and Tracy.

"It cites two sinkholes in Wink, Texas, both due to oil drilling. One in 1980; the other twenty-two years later." Ryan whistled at the revelation. He watched as Tracy scrolled further and found an article about the gypsum rich soil in Laramie.

Tracy swiveled in her chair. "There!" She pointed to a spot on the screen. "Karst formations!"

"I've lived here all my life and I had never heard of karst formations until the other day." Ryan pulled a second chair out and took a seat next to her. He couldn't help but feel her closeness, smell the sweet scent of her hair.

"They're formed out of gypsum, dolomite, or limestone," Tracy read. "All water soluble."

"So they're more susceptible to sinkholes."

"And caves," she added, tapping a pencil onto the counter.

"Do you think that the sinkhole out back could have been caused by oil drilling, rather than karst formations, and that's why Mabel had the map?"

She shrugged. "It stands to reason. Sinkholes have occurred in other areas across the country where oil has been drilled in soil that's too porous."

"So you think maybe someone didn't want Mabel looking too closely at the data? But why her? What could she have possibly done to be more than a minor nuisance to a company the size of Maarlox?" Ryan asked.

His thoughts swiveled back to the email about Afghanistan. Had Tracy been checking up on him and his time in the military? But why? Or maybe she was just trying to learn more about it so they would have something to talk about, and yet no other woman he had ever known had ever shown any real interest in his time in Afghanistan. Years inside the country had made him suspicious of anyone not under his command. There were still things he was forbidden from speaking about with so many peoples' lives at stake in that faraway land. Moles could be anywhere, even here he realized, though he knew he was being paranoid. And yet he couldn't wrap his head around her sudden interest in Afghanistan.

"I know what you mean about Mabel and Maarlox." Tracy scrolled down further. "I don't understand it either. Mabel wouldn't have harmed a fly, according to Blake. She was just a sweet old lady."

Ryan trained his thoughts back to the task at hand. "There has to be more to it—something we're not understanding."

Tracy concurred.

The day was getting late, any concerns about Afghanistan abated, for now. He was overthinking, as usual. Besides, all evening, as he'd sat near Tracy, feeling the heat of her body next to his, he'd wanted to wrap her in his arms, to kiss her, to let loose the feelings that he'd had bottled inside him from the moment he'd met her. He'd never felt so keenly about anyone as her. His skin prickled at the memory of her lips on his, the sweet smell of her breath like roses, an aroma both inviting and intoxicating but not overpowering. As if she felt it too, she leaned in and he wrapped her in an embrace, her lips eager to meet his.

For several minutes, he forgot everything. Forgot that he had promised Wyatt he would be back at the ranch this evening to help him with the livestock. Forgot that he was supposed to be up early to begin working the dogs again. Forgot that they would need to mend the fencing before winter hit. His heart pounded, his lips seeking more, wanting more. He ached with longing. But then, just like that, he recalled the picture he'd seen in her inbox. Afghanistan. He pulled away, his body betraying his brain. Why had she been in his bedroom? What had she been searching for?

221

Twenty-Five

Tracy stared out the window of her bedroom at the darkness enveloping the valley in a midnight blue halo, the mountain range silhouetted against the fading light. The sheep had long since settled down in the straw bedding tossed in one corner of the pasture, their bleats silenced for the evening. Ryan had been reluctant to leave Tracy alone after the graffiti incident. Who knew what the trespassers would do next? But Wyatt had called, needing him back at the ranch. She'd urged Ryan to go, promising him that she would be okay. Still, he'd gone to her pickup and retrieved her .22 caliber handgun for her.

"Keep this by your side at all times. And Tracy?" he'd said. "If you hear anything, you call me. I'll be over as quickly as I can, but that should hold them off for a while, at least."

Despite his words and his calm demeanor, no doubt part

of his military training, his body language spoke volumes. Well, she couldn't worry about the unknown. Instead, she tasted her lips, which still carried his scent. When he'd kissed her, for the first time in her life she'd felt whole, as though she'd been missing a limb all this time and could finally walk again. She didn't know what she would have done had he stayed longer. Probably something she would have regretted. No, it was better this way—to put some distance between him and her until she could sort things out.

After he left, she scaled the stairs to her bedroom. She plopped down in the chair at her computer desk and paused before opening her email. For the past couple of days, she'd watched for any word from Operation Pup Rescue. But so far, nothing.

She thought back to the only other time she'd ever had a steady boyfriend. Erik was young, handsome, but two years ahead of her. He'd gone away to college, promising her that he would remain true, despite the distance, but it hadn't worked out that way. Finally, she had ended it. Then, after the accident with her horse, she'd withdrawn . . . from everyone. If it hadn't been for her mentor encouraging her to re-engage in life, she might have drowned in self-pity.

Before she could dwell any further on the mishap, she opened her inbox and quickly scanned it. She read the newspapers Ned had sent but saw nothing of interest. She was about to close out of her email when she noticed an email from Operation Pup Rescue. Her fingers tingled as she clicked on it and watched the email appear.

"Hi, Tracy," it said. "Thanks for your continued interest

223

in our program. You said the dog you are seeking was last seen close to a town near Kandahar, correct? We can continue to search, but we will need $600 for the initial search and there are no guarantees that we will find the dog. But if you want to proceed, go to our website and provide the names of both the dog and the G.I. Include the unit and location at the time the dog went missing. Also, if you could provide a date when the dog was last seen, that would be great. We take VISA, MC, AME or Paypal. These preliminary charges are for the initial search only, not for actually retrieving the dog and bringing him home. That could run in the thousands. A lot of paperwork is involved—all of it costs money, unfortunately. Once the dog is actually transferred, shots are required as well as a two week quarantine period to be sure the animal has no known illness or disease. We will keep you apprised of costs as we go. If you are still interested after all this, go ahead and make your payment and we can begin."

Tracy whipped an email back to the woman thanking her and assuring her that she wanted to move full speed ahead. Afterward, she brought up the website and filled out the application. Now she would have to sit back and wait, but at least she would have something to occupy her thoughts, other than to dwell on the earlier graffiti. She wondered why the spray painting had targeted her specifically. Did it have anything to do with their trip to the newspaper? She gave an involuntary shiver. She refused to let her thoughts go there or she would never get any sleep tonight. Instead, she reread the email one last time, hoping against hope that she'd done the right thing. Then she turned off her computer for the night and prepared for bed.

She had only been in bed for a short time when she heard a dog howling and the sheep bleating. What on earth? Fortunately, Ryan had suggested she add flood lights on both sides of the house, front and back. She ran downstairs and turned them on. What she saw chilled her. There, looking back at her, were two eyes that glowed in the dark. The animal appeared almost wolf-like, possibly half-wolf, half-dog. And it was intent on attacking the sheep. Still in her pajamas, she slipped on her robe, grabbed the .22, going over in her head what Ryan had said to her before he left. "I'm supposed to call him," she murmured.

Okay then. She dialed his number, hands shaking, and waited. Nothing. She left a brief message, then set the phone down and rushed out the back door and down the steps. She would need both hands, should she use her gun.

Careful to aim just above the wolf's head, she shot the gun off. For a second, the wolf paused as if considering whether to run or stand its ground. Fortunately for her, the beast paused for only a moment, then turned and loped away. That's when Tracy realized the wolf was not a male, who were generally larger, stockier, but most of all fluffier. No, this was a smaller, hungry she-wolf with markings more attributable to a dog. And if the she-wolf didn't find food elsewhere, she would be back. Tracy decided to talk to Ryan in the morning, see if he knew anything about the half-wolf, half dog.

Could be just as dangerous as a full-blooded wolf.

Tracy had read of too many incidents from people who

had bought them as pets thinking that they could be tamed only to discover that, given the right circumstances, the feral animal's instincts would kick in and they could become vicious. Despite the late hour, she decided to text Ryan. She wasn't surprised when he didn't text back. Probably still asleep.

She turned to go, when she caught a movement out of the corner of her eye. *Just my imagination.* For a moment, she stood there watching, then pivoted on her foot and hurried inside the house. She turned off the floodlights . . . for now.

When she entered her bedroom, she peered out her window one last time. What she saw both frightened her and filled her with wonder, for there, circling the paddock, was none other than Old Man Grayson's sheepdog, herding the sheep back toward the straw, then waiting for them to settle into a semblance of order and calm. Once he finally had the sheep settled, he lay down on his belly, tongue lolling in the moonlight. Tracy knew it was the ghost dog and not a real one, as it nearly glowed beneath the clear night sky. In awe and disbelief, Tracy rubbed the goosebumps on her arms. For what seemed like forever, she stood there, then sank into the chair next to her computer, her eyelids slowly drooping.

Hours later, she awoke, stiff and tired. She peered through the window at the ghost dog guarding the sheep. For some reason it gave her a measure of comfort to know he was there. Gratefully, she flopped into bed and was asleep again in moments.

When she awoke the next morning, the sun waxed high overhead and the Shetland sheepdog was gone. It saddened her to think that he was no longer there, but no matter. She had a full day ahead of her. She dressed quickly, then marched downstairs only to discover she'd left her cell phone on the kitchen counter the night before. Quickly, she plugged it in and read the message Ryan had sent. *I'll be right over*. She frowned, then glanced at the time the text had been sent. Three-thirty in the morning.

"Hmm," she muttered. "So where is he?"

She ambled into the living room, only to discover him sound asleep on the couch, jacket draping off of him onto the floor. With a quiet chuckle so as not to wake him, she tiptoed over to him and pulled the jacket to his chest. She smiled as he groaned a sleepy "thanks." Seconds later, he was out. As quietly as possible, she headed outdoors. It was high time she made this place a home.

* * *

Ryan awoke and found Tracy missing. He searched in the kitchen, then upstairs, but her bed was already made and the curtains drawn. That's when he heard a metallic scraping toward the front of the house and hurried down the stairs. He drew back the drapes and peered out the window, only to see her bent over what was now a beautiful flower bed out front. In jeans and boots, and sporting a wide brim hat and gardening gloves, she looked every bit the farmer. Something clicked when he saw her and he smiled tenderly to see her so focused on her task.

"C'mon, Boots." He peered down at the black and white

cat with its wide greenish-gold eyes. "Let's go see Mama."

The kitty meowed and darted toward the entrance. Ryan quickly put on his boots and headed toward the door. He no sooner had the door open then the cat darted past him, brushing the hem of his pants.

The cat ran straight to Tracy who said, "Now who have we here?" As Ryan shut the screen door, Tracy peered up, sweat dotting her forehead. "Hey there, sleepyhead." She fanned her face with her hat. "I thought you were going to sleep the day away."

"I couldn't help it. Some damsel in distress called me and had me driving in the middle of the night to come save her, but it appears she saved herself, this time around."

Tracy laughed as she poked her spade into the soft soil that she'd roughed up for planting. "Had ourselves a half-wolf, half-dog here last night. A she-wolf."

Ryan whistled.

"Know whose wolf-dog it is?" She squinted from the sun that stood just over the rooftop.

Ryan frowned, thinking. He would have known if anyone around here had a half-dog, half-wolf. "We do have the Wind River Indian Reservation south of Cody. Arapaho and Shoshone, mostly. They see wolves as kin, sort of like guides that aid them when needed. I suppose it's possible that one of them has a half-dog, half-wolf, but I don't know what would bring them this far north to your place."

"Is there anyone we could ask?" Tracy stretched her neck and back, then plunged her shovel once more into the ground to make a hole for a waiting delphinium.

228

"Don't you think it's a little late to be planting all this?" he asked, noting the wide stretch of flowers that now dotted the front of the house.

"It's never too late," she said with a Cheshire cat grin. "Besides, I chose perennials. Take a look at the farmhouse. It's really starting to take shape."

Ryan walked over to stand beside her, then took a couple of steps back to regard the garden and house together. He had to admit, the change from before *was* impressive. Compared to what the place looked like when she'd first arrived, it was absolutely amazing. Plus, they had managed to scrub off the graffiti, and he had touched up the spot with paint so that it was all but invisible. The farmhouse had a new roof and an almost completely rebuilt porch. Now, with the added shrubbery and flowers, the homestead looked incredible, but something was still missing. He couldn't put his finger on it, when suddenly he snapped his fingers.

"You need a cobblestone walkway up to the house. That way you won't track in dirt."

Tracy concurred with a nod of her head. "I bought some pavers. We could even add a border of stones around the flowers. I'll call and order them."

"I suppose that means more work for me," Ryan said, lifting one brow.

And yet he was invested in seeing the place restored to its former glory. He pictured it in his mind's eye. Pictured her and him in gray rockers on the front porch drinking coffee on a summer morning, the first time he'd ever envisioned himself with someone permanently. He grinned as he tucked his thumbs into his belt loops. Or maybe they could bring a glass of wine out onto the porch in the early evening. Not that he drank much wine . . . not after the many men that had moved through his mother's life, many of them with drinking problems or drug addictions. He dreaded the time when he would have to introduce Tracy to his mother. Tracy was so wholesome and stable, something he desperately needed in his life after Afghanistan. *And* his childhood.

"I guess I've imposed once too often," Tracy said with a grin, her green eyes dancing.

"Forget it. We'll get the place fixed just the way you like." He winked and was pleased to see her blush. He reached over and kissed her softly on the lips, pulling her chin to him so that he could delve more deeply in the feel and taste of her. She moaned in response.

He reveled in the moment, eager to draw her closer, but before he could take things any further, he heard a contingent of vehicles coming up the road. The first to arrive was Kate who rode alongside Wyatt, at the wheel of his four-wheel drive, Emajean in the rear seat, a giant cooler at her side. Most of the other men had followed up in a series of vehicles that came to a stop in various locations around the dirt driveway. Tracy would need to get that graveled before winter set in if she planned to avoid getting stuck in the mud and snow that was sure to come.

"What brings you all here?" Ryan asked when they began pouring out of their vehicles.

"We wanted to see what was keeping you and my men so busy these days." Wyatt flashed Ryan a pointed look with just a hint of mirth. Then he turned toward Tracy. "Oh, I see."

Once again, Tracy flushed a deep crimson. Kate elbowed Wyatt and said, "Where are your manners?"

Wyatt coughed into his fist. "We thought you could use a little break, considering how busy you must be, getting this place in shape. It was rundown years ago, even before Mabel and McDuffy Grayson died. Once Mabel was gone, I'm afraid Grayson wasn't very good at keeping it up. He was getting on in years. Walked with a cane at the end."

"I've heard."

At that moment, Emajean came to stand beside them dressed in jeans, a plain blue t-shirt, and wearing a plaid blue flannel shirt over it.

"Just the person I was hoping to speak to," Ryan said. "Tracy here had a visitor last night."

To a man, every one of them stopped talking to find out what had happened.

"We heard about the graffiti from Ryan." Wyatt lowered his cowboy hat to hang down beside him. "Anything else happen?"

Ryan peered at Tracy who gave him a nod of her head in encouragement. "This time she had a non-human visitor. A wolf."

"A she-wolf—half-wolf, half-dog," Tracy amended.

Emajean's brown eyes sparked with recognition.

"You know whose animal it is?" Ryan asked the Lakota woman who often visited the Wind River Reservation. Although not technically her people, the Shoshone were Plains Indians who had blood ties through marriage with the

Paiutes. Ironically, the Shoshone had been resettled to the same reservation with their sworn enemies, the Arapaho. The Lakota and Cheyenne had a close bond with the Arapaho, but they too fought with the Shoshone. Most of Emajean's friends were Arapaho.

"The only person I know with a half-wolf is Kima."

Tracy frowned. "Kima?"

"It means butterfly in Shoshone," Emajean explained. "But why she would be on your property that late at night is anyone's guess. If she came here, it was for a good reason."

"You've got to admit—" Kate gave a harried glance to Wyatt who seemed lost in thought, "—it's a little strange to be scouting the property so late at night."

"The Shoshone view time differently than westerners, as do the Lakota. Time is merely a construct. We lived by the seasons, followed the herds, the buffalo and elk, knew when to forage chokecherries, pine nuts, and plums. We sometimes traveled at night."

"But why do you suppose she was here?" Tracy asked. "What could she possibly want?"

Wyatt fiddled with the brim of his hat. "Well, technically, we don't know if Kima *was* here. The wolf could have become loose somehow."

In the silence that followed, Ryan knew by Tracy's expression that she was pondering that possibility. "I've got an idea," he said. "Let's go see if there are any footprints out by the pen."

A murmur arose among the vets. Ryan grabbed Tracy's hand, but not before he noticed Wyatt's raised brow. Once again, Kate nudged Wyatt and smiled at Ryan as if to say "ignore him." Ryan grinned at Kate. By the time he and Tracy reached the pen, the sheep must have scented them as only a few remaining stragglers were pushing off their knees to stand. The lead girl was already bleating and heading their way.

Ryan pointed to some tracks seen entering the pen.

"That was me, I'm afraid." Tracy peered down at what were clearly her tracks determined by size and shape.

Ryan opened the pen. "Stay here," he told the others. All except Tracy, who he pulled into the pen with him. Within moments, they were surrounded by hungry sheep. "I'll get your hay in a minute," he told them and listened to their plaintive bleats in response. Together, he and Tracy walked all the way to the back of the pen. "Nothing," he said in disgust.

"Wait!" Tracy motioned to the wolf tracks. It appeared as though the wolf had jumped the fence in one particular location because the wolf tracks were deep there. "Look!" Tracy cried, pointing to a spot on the other side of the fence.

Sure enough, the wolf had leapt from the point opposite the fence. Ryan's hackles rose when he saw another set of tracks beside the wolf tracks. Human ones. Tracy leaned into him.

"Do you think that was Kima?" she asked.

"Only one way to find out," he said. Then to the others, he yelled, "I think we have our culprit." Time to pay a visit to the reservation.

Twenty-Six

Hank had hoped to do a little snooping while inspecting the ranch, but every time he turned around he saw his shadow, Bryce, following him. He soon decided he was getting nowhere, so headed off in his Ford 350. He growled as he put the truck in reverse and spun out onto the gravel drive toward the main road.

This was supposed to be an easy job. After all, how hard would it be to scare off a young twenty-something year-old veterinarian? He squinted into the sunlight flashing off his windshield. He needed to make a housecall. The Company wasn't going to be happy about this. The vets had rallied around the new veterinarian, helping her at every turn. If she ever learned the truth about what had happened to Mabel, The Company's whole operation would be at stake.

He drove the seven miles to speak with the head of

operations. He would know what to do. They needed a new plan of attack. But whatever path they chose, it couldn't be too obvious. People were already becoming suspicious of him. Couldn't have that.

He pulled down the long dirt drive. Already he could see who he'd come to talk to standing off in the distance. By the end of the day, he would have his answer. One way or the other, Tracy Barnhardt had to go.

* * *

As Tracy watched from the passenger seat of the Jeep, Ryan at the wheel, she couldn't get over the sheer isolation of the landscape surrounding the Wind River Reservation, the sheer scale of it. Except for Crowheart Butte, a mesa that rose out of the earth like a cauldron, and the teeth-like Wind River Mountains, the area surrounding the reservation was 2.2 million square miles of flatland as far as the eye could see. A series of white clouds scudded across the indigo blue sky, but despite the beauty and desolation, she could almost feel the oppressive heat settle over her, as if the very air itself contained some form of threat. She knew that Emajean felt it too, because she had ceased talking the closer they came to the reservation, and occasionally, she sighed. Tracy would have given anything to read her thoughts.

"I feel bad for leaving Wyatt and the others back at the farm after they came all that way to see me," Tracy intoned.

Ryan placed an arm over her shoulder and peered down at her. "This sort of thing happens all the time at the ranch. People come and go. You go with the flow. There'll be another time to visit."

They drove on, passing a single car. It was the only one they'd seen for miles, an old blue and white Ford Fairlane, a young man with a ponytail driving, an elderly man in the passenger seat.

They drove another five miles down the road, when Emajean said, "Stop at the cemetery."

"The cemetery?" Tracy and Ryan spoke in unison, to which all three gave a nervous laugh.

"Sacajawea's gravesite is there," she said, pointing. "Or at least her people believe it is. Some say she died in childbirth; some say she left her husband and married a Comanche and only returned much later, dying at the age of 100."

"What do you think?" The hot wind whipped at Tracy's hair through the open window.

Emajean shrugged. "Who's to say? But I hope she's here beside her ancestors."

Once again a shroud of sadness left a pall on Tracy and the others, as they peered out the window. "There!" Tracy said, seeing a cemetery ahead.

"No, not that one," Emajean assured her. "A little farther."

Ryan followed her directions and soon they came to a stop beside a burial site festooned with white crosses and a myriad of American flags, bright silk flowers and articles left for the dead to take with them into the afterlife. But what gave Tracy pause was the many toys left for young infants and children who had died before ever reaching adulthood.

With no time to react, the Lakota woman leaped out of

the jeep and rushed ahead. Tracy trailed her, Ryan at her side. They finally came to a stop in front of a large bronze statue of a woman studying a sand dollar. Sacajawea.

"They say she was a captive, stolen from her family in Idaho and taken to North Dakota where she was sold into marriage to Charbonneau, a Quebec trapper."

Like everyone else, Tracy had read about Sacajawea while a child, in school. But what Emajean did next had Tracy puzzling her brow. From her shirt pocket, Emajean pulled out a carefully beaded barrette and laid it gently on the gravesite. Then, in her Lakota tongue, she closed her eyes and said what Tracy could only presume was a prayer for the deceased woman. Soon, she opened her eyes and thanked the spirits in English.

To Tracy's questioning expression, she said, "We honor our spirits. The Cheyenne are our sisters, and so Sacajawea is an honorary sister as well."

Tracy wondered what Emajean had prayed for but wasn't certain it was appropriate to ask, so she stood in silence as Emajean turned to the four directions, giving thanks to each of the directions: North, East, West, and South.

Then, in a quiet voice that competed with the soughing of the wind, she said, "I asked the gods to bless us, to watch over us today as we embark on this dangerous journey."

Gooseflesh rose on Tracy's arms to think that they might be in danger by coming to the reservation. But why? What made this place so menacing? Ryan asked the question that she dared not.

"Drug addiction and alcoholism are rampant here,"

Emajean explained, "just as they are on the Lakota Reservation. So is gang violence. The police force does nothing to stop it. And although alcohol isn't allowed on the reservation, the whites sell it just beyond the border. They don't care if our people die. Just that they get their money."

Here, a flash of anger directed at both Tracy and Ryan slipped past in a flurry of emotion. Tracy felt a pinprick of guilt and turned to Ryan, who must have felt it too because he squeezed her hand in reluctant agreement of Emajean's assessment of whites.

"Neither the Arapaho nor the Shoshone will be glad to see two white people," Emajean continued. "You are only here because I am with you. But I must warn you," she added, her brown eyes deadly serious and her expression dour, "don't ask too many questions and keep your cell phone off."

That last part sent Tracy's stomach plummeting. What on earth was she doing here? She had walked into the situation blind. Why hadn't she asked more questions? Her worry indicator rising, Tracy trudged back to the jeep beside Ryan and Emajean. For the next half hour, Ryan drove through the reservation. Soon they began to see clapboard houses strewn about haphazardly here and there with long stretches in between most houses. Dogs roamed everywhere, at least one dog per person, it would seem. Tracy was just about to ask how much further before they reached their destination when Emajean pointed down a long dusty driveway with a disheveled trailer at its end along with others that veered off onto dirt-filled paths—appliances or cars in various states of decay surrounding them.

"We'll be meeting with Wise Raven, an Arapaho elder. You are not to hug him ever, or speak to him until I introduce you. His daughter, Nancy, will be with him."

Tracy exchanged a quick glance with Ryan, who nodded his assent. He had been unusually quiet since they'd entered the reservation. But whether it was because he was a male in unknown territory, or because he had caught wind of the danger the reservation held, she wasn't sure.

Upon entry of the trailer, the first thing Tracy observed was Wise Raven's height when he stood from his noonday meal at the table. She felt small by comparison. The smell of fried food permeated the room and left her feeling queasy in the warm trailer, heated by the sun. Long white braids draped down either side of Wise Raven's chest and he wore a cream-colored vest and jeans, with a plaid red shirt and a beaded choker around his neck. But what she noticed most was the kind eyes behind the silver-framed glasses.

After a lengthy exchange that held hints of ceremony, his daughter Nancy translating to the elder, Emajean finally launched into the reason for her visit. For several moments, Wise Raven and Nancy spoke in their native tongue. Seconds later, a dark-skinned man in his thirties appeared from one of the back rooms. The elder gave him instructions and then the younger man left. Emajean translated, saying that Wise Raven had agreed to ask the Shoshone woman and her half-wolf to come meet with them, but he offered no promises.

For the next hour and a half, Tracy and the others waited as Wise Raven spoke of his people's history, about caring for mother earth created by *Be He Teiht*, and all the wildlife that sprang from the earth. He spoke of the sundance, outlawed by whites in order to prevent them from practicing their religion in favor of the white religions.

Entranced by the spell he'd woven, Tracy had nearly given up on the notion that she would ever meet Kima and the she-wolf when finally she heard a knock at the door. Nancy opened it, and there on the landing was a young woman with high cheekbones and arching eyebrows that had been plucked and tweezed into narrow strips. She had on jeans and a t-shirt with a picture of a gray wolf peering from beneath a dream catcher. Warily, she entered the trailer, her she-wolf bringing up the rear. Under normal circumstances, the Shoshone woman might not have entered an Arapaho home, according to Emajean, but few would bother a woman harboring a wolf.

When Tracy saw it, her stomach lurched and her skin grew cold and clammy. It was like nothing she had ever seen before, its head lower than its back and hindquarters. Nearly pure black, with only hints of silver at the tips of some of its hair, the eyes gave her pause and she stepped back, for they were gold with flecks of green and held a menace that she'd never seen in an animal before. Instinctively, she grabbed Ryan's hand and he pulled her to his side as if to protect her.

"This is Esa," Kima said, nodding toward the wolf. As if in unspoken agreement, the wolf sat but seemed to be on guard all the same.

Nancy, who looked nothing like her tall barrel-chested father, was shorter and carried more weight, her face round, hiding the higher cheekbones of the Arapaho. "Esa is the name for 'wolf'. He is considered the creator god in Shoshone and Bannock cultures. His brother is the Coyote, the foolish one. Esa is highly revered."

As a result of their reverence for wolves, Nancy seemed nonplussed by its presence despite the fact that the wolf's hackles were raised and its eyes watched intently, as though determining where to strike first should the need arise. Tracy turned her attention to Kima, refusing to allow fear to consume her.

Once introductions were done, Emajean turned to Kima. "Were you or your wolf at Tracy's homestead last night?"

Kima's brown eyes danced, her expression giving away nothing. Finally, she nodded.

"Why?" Tracy asked only to receive a silent warning from Emajean to stay quiet.

"Mabel was my grandma's friend. She used to bring food and used clothing to the women of my tribe. Back in the 70's and 80's, oil companies were stealing oil from my people, paying us some of the royalties, hiding the rest. Mabel was helping my grandma find out about the money they stole."

"And you think that had something to do with Mabel's death?" Tracy received another scathing warning from Emajean.

Kima paused, having said too much already, no doubt. Finally, she nodded. "Sorry about the sheep," she added. "I didn't know there were sheep in the pen or I wouldn't have brought Esa."

"For security?" Tracy said.

"Tracy!" Ryan hissed. "Emajean asked you to be quiet."

Once again, Kima nodded.

Despite Ryan's anger, Tracy pressed on, determined to have answers before the well went dry. "Why would anyone care about what happened almost forty years ago?"

This time it was the elder who spoke out in curt, clipped, Arapaho.

Kima's eyes widened, fear appearing to make her mouth go dry and her words garbled as she hurried to speak before they were all kicked out of the elder's home. "Because of what happened to Mabel. My friend Sparrowhawk saw you at *The Sentinel*. Word is getting around that you are asking about Mabel. You could be in danger."

It was clear she had said too much because she spoke to the elder in quick words that sounded formal and clipped, and he responded in kind. Then she turned to leave.

"Wait!" Tracy called.

Emajean grabbed her sleeve and shook it. "You are speaking out of turn," the Lakota woman said through clenched teeth.

"I have to ask!" Tracy moved toward Kima, her wolf standing at attention now. "Do you know if Mabel ever found out anything about the missing oil money?"

Silence prevailed, tension coursing between them. Finally, Kima shook her head. "I don't know."

Before she could leave, Tracy reached out a hand and heard a low rumble from the wolf, then quickly dropped her hand to her side. "Is your grandmother alive?"

"No." Kima lowered her eyes to avoid Tracy and her

many probing questions.

"Could you ask around, see if anyone knows if either your grandmother or Mabel traced the missing money?"

"We are done!" Emajean bowed apologetically to the elder and his daughter.

Kima swallowed hard, her eyes on the floor. She gave one quick nod, then she was gone. Tracy watched the retreating figures as Emajean and Ryan hustled her toward the door, all the while offering their deepest apologies to the pair. Tracy knew she was in trouble and that she hadn't heard the last about disobeying Emajean. Still, as she said her goodbyes and walked out the front door, she saw the retreating forms of Kima and her she-wolf and prayed that they would remain safe.

Twenty-Seven

By the time Tracy had returned to the farmhouse and
had set to work doing chores, she had formulated a plan to
keep Kima safe, but that could only happen if she could keep
an eye on her . . . *with* Ryan's help. Already, he had called
to the ranch and had ordered a guard placed on Tracy's
homestead round the clock, then had returned to catch up
on things there, but only after assurances from Tracy that she
would keep the gun close at hand and call him if anything
happened in the interim.

Tracy knew how much it had cost him and Wyatt . . . and
Kate, to offer their services when all hands were needed at
the ranch. Furthermore, while she'd been at the reservation,
searching for Kima and the wolf, Wyatt, Kate, and all the
men had graded the path to the house and laid the pavers
that she had purchased. As she peered out the window of

her living room, the floodlights casting shadows over her new garden and cobblestone walkway, her eyes moistened to see how beautiful the place looked. She wished she could make it up to all of the vets somehow. The only way she could repay Ryan was to bring his dog home. As for Wyatt and Kate, the only aid she could offer them now was to train both the dogs and a veterinary assistant who might eventually become a technician. One who could live on the ranch and help with the animals' needs. And she had just the person in mind. She quickly finished her chores, brought in the mail she had picked up on her way back from the reservation, then made the call to Emajean. She doubted the woman would help her after all her missteps earlier in the day but she had to try.

Kate answered the phone and seemed confused when Tracy asked for Emajean. Moments later, the woman answered the phone. Tracy quickly apologized for her earlier behavior, then explained what she wanted to do.

"You want Kima to train with you?" Normally laconic, tonight Emajean's words were even more clipped than usual, still angry with Tracy, no doubt.

Tracy pressed forward, spelling out her reasoning to the wary woman.

"Even if she agreed," Emajean said at last, "how would I get her here? If I start showing up on the reservation too often, people will wonder. Besides, she would need her father's permission."

"Her father?"

"The Shoshone live in a patriarchal society. Men make the decisions."

Now Tracy understood Emajean's hesitancy. What father would let her daughter be trained by a woman from outside the community? A white woman at that. She racked her brain to come up with an idea that would appease both Kima's father and Kima herself. She had a hunch that Kima would enjoy being a veterinarian. Clearly, she liked animals. Absentmindedly, Tracy flipped through the mail and noticed something official. She tore it open and smiled when she saw a check fall out of it for nearly fifteen hundred dollars. Her tax return. She had forgotten all about it. Suddenly an idea formed and she plopped down into the chair next to the kitchen table.

"What if Kima were to earn $500 a month plus room and board and the $500 goes to her father. In exchange, she'll have a career that she can use on the reservation sometime down the road. In the meantime, she could help you at the ranch during her practicum. It would be a win-win."

Emajean, who moments earlier had sounded hesitant, now began to show a modicum of enthusiasm. "Okay. Let me think. I have to plan this just right. I will have one of the Shoshone women approach her father and talk to him on your behalf. And we will need to speak to Kima herself." Emajean let loose a loud sigh at the enormity of the task, but persevered. "Let me take care of this, and Tracy . . . ?"

"Yeah?"

"Don't get your hopes up, okay?"

For a moment, Tracy didn't respond. "All right," she said at last. "I'll leave it up to you. But Emajean?"

"Eh?"

"Really try, okay? I think Kima's life may depend on it."

A pause ensued, when at last Emajean said something in Lakota. Then the phone went dead.

*　*　*

"Where is Hank now?" Ryan asked Kate as he finished checking on the horse stalls.

Not one of the horses had fresh water or hay. That was so unlike Bryce whose daily task it was to feed and water the animals. And on the very day that Hank was inspecting the place. Ryan's blood was pumping as he forked hay into the hay nets in each of the stalls.

"I asked Bryce to keep an eye on Hank, but one of the water lines broke in the back forty and he's been digging out all day. He just got in and cleaned up," Kate said as she busied herself filling the wall troughs. She paused, chewing on her lip. "He thinks someone tampered with the water lines."

Ryan stopped what he was doing. "Why does he think that?"

"He found a spot that looked as if it had been recently dug up. That's where he found his leak. Said it was too clean a break for normal wear and tear."

Angrier than before, Ryan thrust hay into the net of the mare who'd foaled not long ago. None of the day had gone according to plan. Wyatt and Kate had planned to surprise Tracy with a picnic followed by the men building her a walkway. They had even brought a couple loads of gravel to get the driveway started. Then Ryan, Tracy and Emajean had

247

gone in search of Kima and her wolf, Esa, while everyone else had stayed to get the work done. No telling what Hank had been up to in the meantime.

Just then, Ryan heard a scraping sound near the door of the barn and put his head out of the stall to see who had entered. There stood none other than Hank himself, the man looking none the worse for wear. Well, he would when Ryan was finished with him.

Ryan kept his fists tightly at his side as he tossed his pitchfork aside and rushed at Hank, a paunchy man with skin so ashen it was as though he'd never seen daylight in his life. That should have been the first giveaway that he wasn't a real inspector. Those men moved from site to site. This guy looked as if he'd spent his whole life pushing a pencil.

"What the heck have you been up to?" Ryan shouted. "Did you mess with our water pipes?"

Kate came rushing out of the stall just as Wyatt came running from nearby. Hank threw his hands up and stepped back. "I don't want any trouble."

"You should'a thought of that before you went traipsing around our property," Ryan said, raising a fist. "Where were you, you—?"

"Ryan!" Wyatt shouted.

Kate rushed to Ryan's side. Everything in him longed to punch the man. What inspector sabotaged a man's livelihood, especially the livelihoods of vets? His chest heaved and his fist stayed raised, but he didn't want to jeopardize his place at the ranch. He'd done that one other time and Wyatt had ended up with a gunshot wound through his leg. It had been an accident, and yet it was a reminder of what unchecked anger could do. Breathing heavily, he dropped his fist to his side.

"Well, what do you have to say for yourself?" he growled through gritted teeth.

"You can't pin that on me," Hank said, nervously licking his lips. "Probably just old pipes. Besides, I went to town. Had a friend I needed to meet. I just got back."

"Funny how the pipes broke while we were all away so that Bryce didn't have time to feed and water the animals. While you were supposed to be inspecting the barn. And you couldn't be bothered to call one of us and let us know there was a problem."

Hank just stood there, a slow smirk lighting up his face.

"I suppose you took pictures of the empty bins," Ryan hissed.

The smirk crept to Hank's eyes. He flashed Ryan an "I gotcha!" grin.

Ryan's chest heaved as dust played against the hanging lights inside the barn, the swish of the horses' tails counting down the minutes as the animals munched hay and lapped at the fresh water they'd been given. It acted like a ticking clock as they all waited to hear what Hank had to say for himself, but he remained silent, his smile saying it all.

"Well, if you want to do us a real favor," Ryan growled, his fists clenched, "get back in that truck of yours and get lost, y'hear?"

For a second, the man just stood there. Then he kicked the dust at his feet, sending it flying into the air. "I don't need this!" Hank hissed.

Wyatt stepped aside to let the man leave, while Ryan lunged one last time, only to find that Kate had grabbed his arm and was holding tight.

"You can't afford trouble with the law, Ryan," she urged.

Still, his stomach roiled and his chest ached to take the man down a peg. None of his fellow vets would ever let an animal go hungry or thirsty and get away with it. Hank had set the whole thing up. Ryan hadn't allowed animals to go hungry in his platoon, with his men, and he wouldn't allow it here, with Wyatt's animals. He raised his chin into the air and closed his eyes, providing precious seconds to cool down. If he wanted a life with Tracy, he would have to learn to control his anger, and yet the role of husband and father had never been modeled for him. What did he know about domestic life? He opened his eyes.

Wyatt came and stood next to him. "Let me give you a little advice, son," he said. "People like that aren't worth your time. Tracy's worth it. You're worth it. But him . . . ?" He pointed over his shoulder. "He's a piece of—"

"Wyatt!" Kate interceded. "I think you've given him enough advice for one night," she said with a sly grin. Then she took his hand and led him out of the barn.

Ryan quickly finished up. Wyatt was the closest thing he'd ever had to a father. He'd taught him what a real man looked like. Ryan had seen the love and respect that Kate and Wyatt had for each other. It gave him hope. An ache, unlike anything he'd ever experienced before, welled up inside him. If only Tracy thought as much of him as he thought of her. Someday soon, he planned to declare his feelings for her. He just prayed he wouldn't be rejected by her the way he'd been rejected by his bio dad.

Twenty-Eight

Ryan hadn't been able to come by the following day. Instead, Bryce had been put in charge of protecting Tracy. She tried to hide her disappointment when the young vet with tattoos running up his arm and chest showed up early in the morning with a knock on her front door.

"Come in," she said, gently shoving Boots aside with her foot.

Once inside, Bryce informed her about the run-in with Hank the day before. "He's been kicked off the ranch. Ryan's afraid he may show up here, so he wants to make sure I secure the perimeter and add more security lights around the place. He said you have a toolbox, so I didn't bring one."

Tracy grabbed the toolbox she kept handy in the kitchen. She handed it to him. "You think Hank might come here?"

Bryce plopped down in one of the chairs, then opened

the toolbox and rummaged through it to see what all she had. "Dunno, but we want to take precautions, just in case."

Tracy mulled that over. "So Ryan doesn't think he's a real inspector?"

"That's what he says." Bryce frowned as he reached for a wrench. "This should do."

"How are the pups?"

"Jason and my kids have them today. They've them hunting for missing persons. Use socks coated with a scent. Hides them around the property. The pups aren't real good at finding them yet, all except for the sheltie."

"Parker?"

"That's the one. He seems to have a knack for it. He may be our only real search and rescue dog of the bunch. But there's plenty of need there for vets with PTSD. Dogs like that can cost a veteran from 20,000 to 60,000 dollars, depending on the training." He closed the toolbox and stood. "We'll use grant money for the training, but other than that, the dogs will be free to the vets. It's only fair after everything we've been through."

Tracy agreed wholeheartedly. She thought about Ryan's dog, Herc. It had been nearly two days since she had first received a response from Operation Pup Rescue. Every morning, once during the day and each evening, she checked her inbox. Nothing. She knew she shouldn't expect anything this soon, but she couldn't get over the disappointment when her inbox turned up empty. She would give anything to be able to offer Ryan this one special gift.

Today, Tracy planned to begin tackling the barn while

she waited to hear from Emajean about Kima. Where to begin. "Hey," she said, as Bryce prepared to head outdoors and begin adding more lights, "is there anything in the barn that you or the guys could use over at the ranch?"

"I could take a look."

For the next hour, they rummaged through the barn, but Tracy hadn't put even a small dent in the large number of items there before Bryce left to add more security lights to the place. Fortunately, he had agreed to take a neon beer sign, a tooled leather saddle, an antique tractor, which they would have to dig out from beneath the pile of stored junk, and a few odds and ends items. Then Tracy went through the stuff closest to the barn door. She pulled out one of two antique sewing machines and dragged it toward the house. It would make good decoration, if nothing else. One by one, she pulled out the drawers and lifted off the ornate wooden hood. Fortunately, the sewing machine was on wheels so she wheeled it to the front of the house. She would ask Bryce to help her lift it up the steps, onto the porch, and into the living room. In the meantime, she brought in the four drawers, two at a time. She was just about to stack the last one atop the other one when it slipped and tumbled to the floor. Boots yowled and hissed, back arched.

"Oh, for the love of—"

Buttons lay scattered about, vintage buttons in all shapes and sizes. Tracy bent over one especially bright gold button emblazoned with an eagle and surrounded by stars. She knelt down when she recognized it as a Civil War button from the Yankee side. Some of the remaining buttons were bakelite, while others were made from seashells. She even discovered Victorian shoe buckles. From beneath the pile of sewing paraphernalia, Tracy discovered a corner of an envelope. On the front of the envelope was an address, but not just any address. She felt sure the name on the front of the envelope belonged to Kima's Grandmother. Tracy was so excited that she nearly slipped on the pile of buttons.

"Boots! It's a letter from Mabel to Kima's grandmother," Tracy cried, grateful that Bryce wasn't within earshot to hear her talking to a cat.

Careful to avoid tearing the yellowed and lined paper, she gently opened the envelope. Goosebumps played at her back when she realized the letter had been written in Mabel's hand. But why hadn't Mabel sent it to her friend? Tracy turned it over and saw that the stamp had never been validated. She frowned, then squinted to see it better. Unlike today's kids, who relied on technology, Mabel had clearly been trained in perfect cursive, her curls even with the stripes lining the page. Tracy quickly read what was written and then watched the letter flutter to the floor as she ran to make a phone call. She tapped her foot impatiently as the phone rang on and on.

Finally, Kate picked up with a harried, "What?"

"Oh, Kate, sorry to bother you but I need Emajean, right away."

Kate seemed out of breath, not herself. "Oh, sorry, Tracy. I didn't realize it was you. Some things have gone missing around the ranch, and we've been hunting high and low."

"Things?"

"Papers . . . about the ranch, the finances. Where we get our funding, that sort of thing. Even our plat that details the layout of the ranch. I'm worried, Tracy."

Tracy heard the fear in Kate's voice and forced herself to stay calm. "Do you think Hank would have taken them?"

"That's as good a guess as any. He was here by himself yesterday. Bryce had a crisis to handle and was called away, so he couldn't keep an eye on him. And Tracy?" She paused.

"Yes?" Tracy wasn't sure she wanted to hear what Kate had to say for fear of what it might mean to her and her farmhouse, or for the ranch.

"I never trusted the guy. He was too slick, always poking his nose into things. I don't know . . ."

Tracy had to concur. She felt a chill as she peered out the front window onto the porch at the freshly laid gravel and garden, to the trees beyond. Could Hank be out there even now? And how was he tied into all this with Blake, Mabel, and Grayson, and possibly even Kima, if he was at all? Maybe there was no connection, but the timing of his arrival seemed awfully strange. Could Hank work for the oil company if what Tracy was beginning to suspect was true? Maybe he was here to do damage control. Tracy almost forgot why she had called.

"I promise to keep an eye out for Hank and call you the minute I see him, and hopefully, you'll do the same."

Kate readily agreed. "Oh, did you still want to talk to Emajean? She's here now. I'll put her on."

Tracy thanked Kate and listened with impatience to the rustle as Emajean situated herself before answering the phone. Finally, she picked up.

"Emajean!" Tracy said without introduction. "We've got to get Kima here and we have to get her here now."

"Why?" Emajean asked, followed by a muffled response to someone at the ranch.

"Because I found a letter warning Kima's grandmother to be careful, that someone had been asking too many questions and that Mabel had been threatened. Now we've been doing the same thing by including Kima in all this. I worry she might be at risk. And I've been threatened too. "

"Who by?" Emajean asked.

"I don't know. But Emajean?'"

"Yes?" Emajean said.

Tracy's frayed nerves made her hands tremble. "Mabel's letter was dated the day before her disappearance."

* * *

Ryan gassed up the tractor and had just got it running, when he saw Emajean hurry toward him across the grassy expanse of the back acre behind the house. She was waving and calling to him, her long braids swinging, a sterling silver dreamcatcher at her neck. The woman was the most stoic person he knew, so to see her panicked meant something must be seriously haywire. He quickly turned off the engine and hopped down off the seat.

"What's wrong?" he asked, loping toward her.

"We have to get Kima and we have to get her now," Emajean said. "I just talked to Tracy—"

He stopped walking. "Tracy? What does Tracy have to do with this?"

"There's no time to waste. Get in the jeep and I will tell you on the way."

Normally, her Lakota dialect was a bit stilted with its many clicks, and the way the words seemed almost sing-song, as if a rolling cadence set to music. But now, her words were nearly indecipherable as she strung them together in rapid-fire succession. He threw his hands in the air.

"You're not making sense, Emajean. Does Wyatt know you're doing this?"

"Kate does," she glowered, hands on hips in challenge.

"Okay, okay." He closed his eyes and breathed deeply of the agricultural smells—corn, hay, alfalfa. When he had himself centered again, he took Emajean's arm and led her to the jeep. "Hop in."

Once he had her situated and they were on the road, she began to explain.

"So let me get this straight. Because of some old letter from twenty-odd years ago, you think Kima's life is in danger *now*?" He turned left onto the road that led to the highway. On either side of the roadway, houses dotted the rugged high desert filled with sagebrush and the white-flowered bitterroot, Indian paintbrush, and the Badland mules-ears that mirrored miniature sunflowers when in bloom. The pungent odor of sage filled the cab as he drove.

"Mabel found something—warned Kima's grandmother that she was in danger, then disappeared a day later."

"But again," Ryan said, wishing he'd taken his patience

pill, "that was twenty years ago. What does that have to do with today?" But then he thought of the graffiti on Tracy's siding and the cut water main and realized she was probably right. He turned on his blinker, signaling a turn onto the highway that would take them to the reservation.

"Just listen, Ryan. A bunch of important papers are missing. Wyatt and Kate think that Hank guy took them."

Ryan's resolve slipped as he tapped the steering wheel with his thumbs. Nothing made sense. Why would Hank need papers from their ranch, if he was after Tracy. Emajean was talking in circles. Then again, maybe he simply wanted to put Tracy out of business so that she would return home. But why? What was on that property that had stirred up a twenty-year-old secret?

"I called down to the reservation. Talked to Kima's grandfather. He said that someone had been calling, wanting to talk to Kima. Said he knew she'd been up by Tracy's place with Esa. Some white guy. He knew we had been down there talking to her too. Said if she didn't keep her mouth shut, he couldn't guarantee her safety."

"You think it was Hank?" Ryan asked, still feeling like he was missing something.

"Coulda been. But Ryan–?"

"Yeah?" Ryan pulled down the visor to avoid the worst of the mid-morning glare. Although the sun hung lower on the horizon this time of day, it was still warm and blinding.

"Kima's grandpa gave her all the letters, the ones from Mabel. Thought she might find something in there. Then he sent her to stay with an aunt. Safer that way. So white men don't call asking questions. Making threats."

"But you want *us* to protect Kima?"

For a brief moment, Emajean folded her hands in her lap and peered down at them as though needing her own patience pill. Then in a carefully controlled voice, she said, "You're a former GI, aren't you?"

The question astounded him, and he nearly ran them off the road as he yawed toward the berm. Finally, he got his bearings and said, "We're vets, Emajean, not GIs."

She sat there in silence, once again thinking. Then in a quiet tone, she said, "Same difference, no?"

"So?" He drummed the steering wheel, still not understanding her meaning.

"As a former GI, your motto is to serve and protect, yes?"

He shrugged and rolled down his window, immediately blasted with a blistering heat despite the fact that it was not yet noon.

"Well, Kima needs protection," she said, staring out the windshield. "Trust me on this one, Ryan. Too many of our women disappear as it is. Please help me find Kima."

Emajean, who never cried, stared straight ahead, a hint of moisture in her burnt sienna eyes. Ryan groaned inwardly. "Okay. We'll find her, but we can't guarantee that her father will let us take her."

But it was enough that Emajean smiled.

Twenty-Nine

Tracy finished her morning rounds. She fed the chickens
and the cat first, checking on the sheep to make sure no
wolves had encroached during the night, then she watered her
newly planted garden. When she'd finished that, she decided
to head upstairs and see if there was anything new in her
inbox. She knew it was too soon to expect anything, but it
wouldn't hurt to look. That way she could keep her mind off
Kima and Esa.

Boots, who seemed to recognize her moods and who
had quickly become her sidekick, followed her into the house
and up the stairs. Deftly, he jumped onto the bed and began
parading up and down the foot of the bed as Tracy drew up a
seat in front of the computer and tapped on her inbox. To her
disappointment, she found nothing on Herc. She didn't want
to come across as a pest, so she let it be for now. If she didn't

hear anything by the end of the week, she would try emailing the dog rescue organization again.

In the meantime, she looked through her other emails, most of them advertisements, when her eyes alighted on something from Ned at the newspaper. "Take a look at this article," the email read. Tracy opened the attachment. It was about the missing oil money from the reservation. To her surprise, the article was dated 2014. It talked about a bank in Lander, Wyoming. Tracy blinked rapidly, not sure she'd read it right. According to the article, armored trucks had arrived on the scene with men in helmets and uniforms, who had surrounded the bank carrying semi-automatic weapons. But what surprised Tracy most and caused her to whistle, bringing Boots in closer with a rumbling purr, was the fact that the money was being deposited on behalf of the federal government—delivering millions to the Wind River Reservation in lost revenue from unpaid oil and mineral claims. Once again, Tracy whistled. So Mabel had been onto something. Good for her. But what had happened to her in the process? Tracy couldn't help but feel that the letter and the disappearance were no coincidence.

Tracy was about to close down her inbox when another email popped up. It was from Gladys and Stanford. "Tracy," the email read, "I found out something about your Circle T Ranch, but I think we should talk about it in person. I'll be here all week."

Tracy wondered if she should call Emajean first, before she left the ranch. She hadn't heard back from her since talking to her this morning. In the end, she decided to go see

Gladys and Stanford. Ever since she'd read the faded letter from Mabel to Kima's grandmother, she'd felt edgy. She found herself peering over her shoulder despite the fact that Ryan had given her a bodyguard. She traipsed outside and flagged Bryce down, telling him she would be back in a few hours. Fortunately, he didn't mind watching the place alone.

"I was used to standing guard by myself when I was in Iraq," he said. "And when I finish installing the lights, I'll go over the barn again and itemize some of the junk. Then I'll give Wyatt a call to see if he wants any of it. I'm sure he could use some of the stuff I found out there."

Tracy thanked him, then drove the GMC to town. The sun was at its zenith by the time she arrived at J & R Marketing. Gladys was just finishing up with a man in jeans, cowboy boots, and a big Stetson hat. He tipped his hat to Tracy as he sauntered out.

"Who was that?" Tracy asked once the man had left.

Gladys tapped the eraser end of her pencil on the counter. "Get a load of this. That's J. D. Beringer."

"Beringer, like the rifle?"

Stanford sauntered over with something akin to a swagger, a snide smile on his lips. "Not spelled the same, but he definitely puts it out there, eh ladies?" he added, one eyebrow cocked. "Can you say ma-*chis*-mo?"

Tracy couldn't help but laugh. On anyone else, Stanford's words would have sounded snide, but on Stanford it came across as nothing more than sarcastic humor. She doubted he had a mean bone in his body.

"What does he do?" Tracy asked. The trio watched the

man's retreating figure through the blinds on the window.

"He's in oil," Gladys said, letting that sink in before she continued. "And do you want to know how I found Circle T Ranch?"

"You found it?" Tracy's voice rose, eager to learn more.

"Did I ever. And guess who it traces back to." Gladys pursed her lips, waiting.

"Quit the suspense, sister." Stanford pushed his way between Tracy and Gladys. He nodded toward the man who even now was crossing the street in a bowlegged walk that made him seem even more macho than what Stanford had alluded to.

"You don't say." Tracy leaned in, determined to get a better look at the man. "And he's one of your clients?"

"He is. But not for oil. He really does have a ranch, but it's not called Circle T."

"No?"

For a couple of seconds, neither of the pair spoke. Finally, Stanford said, "Well, if you're not going to tell her, I will. It's the J. D. Beringer Ranch, duh!"

"He raises thoroughbred horses out of Jackson. Wanna see something?" Gladys wriggled her finger and walked over to her computer screen. With a few taps on the keyboard, she pulled up the ranch.

Tracy whistled when she saw the place. It backed up to the Tetons, at the base of Yellowstone. The land was green and lush with a river running through it. The main house was a log cabin, and the interior consisted of a combination of Native American rugs and baskets, and rugged western furniture, the heads of deer, elk, antelope, and buffalo lining the walls.

"He markets his thoroughbreds online."

"Then why would he be selling hay? Does he grow it?"

"Not that I know," Gladys said.

Stanford, whose lean body draped over Gladys as he too peered at the screen, stood up straight and gestured to the screen. "He could have purchased the hay anywhere and sabotaged it. He wouldn't want it traced back to his ranch, after all. The man's not stupid."

"But why Blake, and how did J. D. even know Blake was back in town, or that he would be investigating his grandmother's death?"

"Beats me," Gladys said, hands splayed on the keyboard.

"Well, I know how he *could* have found out," Stanford said in that affected way of his, with one eyebrow cocked.

"Oh?" Gladys said. "Enlighten us."

Stanford held up a finger while saying, "Watch and learn, ladies. Watch and learn."

Gladys merely rolled her eyes causing Tracy to laugh at Stanford's antics. Moments later, he'd pulled up footage on Blake's return to Wyoming. Tracy had to admit that Blake had quite the press entourage. His arrival had made the local news, Blake being somewhat of a hometown celebrity. She listened to the news interview, where invariably the newscaster brought up the disappearance of Blake's grandmother from all those years ago. Tracy's heart stilled as she heard him say, "I'm researching the disappearance and hope to make it into a made-for-TV movie."

For a moment, everyone sat in stunned silence, gazing at each other to discern what the other was thinking. At long last, they all spoke at once, followed by nervous laughter.

"You first," Gladys said.

"Well, that explains a lot," Tracy said. "But I still don't understand why Blake sold the house to me if he was still investigating her disappearance."

Stanford sat on the counter, arms folded as he stared down at his perfectly manicured nails. "I'm sure he scoured the place before he sold it to you. From everything I've heard, the place was rotting away."

It amazed Tracy how much everybody knew about her farm and her business. But what amazed her more is that the location had never been vandalized . . . until the other day, that is. Had Blake used someone close by to watch over the place? And what had prompted the vandalism now? Her arrival, but why?

"So back to this J. D. guy. You think he's the one who sabotaged Blake, or do you think someone set it up to look that way?"

Stanford entwined his fingers, then stretched his arms out and cracked his knuckles before answering. "Well, if it quacks like a duck . . . Just saying."

Tracy would need to do more research. "I think you guys are in the wrong business. You should be private investigators."

"You want us to keep looking?" Gladys asked, clearly as interested in the outcome of the investigation as Tracy herself.

Tracy nodded. "But I'm going to have to start paying

you." She didn't know where all the money was going to come from. She needed veterinary jobs, real jobs. But clearly, Hank wasn't going to allow her to practice anytime soon. That is, if he *was* a real inspector. She would need to check on that as well. In the meantime, she needed to put out her shingle, and she needed to start right away. So far, she had only earned money from the call to Blake's ranch the other day and her work on Lindsay's ewe. Other than that, she had nothing, and money seemed to be pouring out like water over a falls. She needed to dam up the outpouring of cash before she was left high and dry.

"I'd better get back to the farm," she said, turning to leave. "And thank you guys. I can see why Kate loves you two."

"She does, doesn't she?" said Stanford, once again admiring his nails.

"We'll call you when we find something," Gladys assured her.

Tracy said a hasty goodbye and then hoofed it to her truck. But before she went to hop in, she could see that someone had left a calling card on her windshield. She opened the note and read the contents, then dropped it as if it had caught fire. Because burned into her memory were the words in bold-faced type.

Before leaving your driveway, always test your brakes. It followed up with a smiley face and a "have a good day."

* * *

Ryan had spent half the day driving around the reservation searching for Kima and Esa with Emajean by his side. Though the Arapaho and Shoshone were normally hesitant with strangers, the fact that Emajean had met many of those from the reservation during the powwows helped ease the way to ask about Kima and her half-wolf. But as Ryan drove down the streets of Wind River, heat beating down on the windshield of his jeep, he couldn't get over the sheer desolateness of the place, the land arid with only the occasional scrub tree to offset the barren expanse of rolling hills. The reservation had a reputation for gang violence, five to seven times the national average, depending on the year. That set his nerves on edge and had him scouring each location for potential ambush. He was about to call it quits and head back home empty-handed when Emajean yelled "stop" as they neared the high school with its signature giant tom-tom atop the entrance.

"There, over there! That's her. Pull into the parking lot."

Ryan eased the jeep onto the tarmac. He didn't relish having a half-wolf in the back of his jeep, even if it was for a good cause, and he still wasn't sure the idea wasn't half baked. Just living on the rez put these kids in danger much of their lives, what with the high crime rate and violence.

Kima was walking with a couple of friends, one a round-faced girl with wide cheekbones and eyeliner that swished up at the corner of her narrow brown eyes. The other was a skinny teenage boy, with stringy hair and all angles, hunched over at the shoulders. The wolf walked in front of them, head down scouting the lay of the land. Ryan wondered how Esa would react around dogs, which seemed to loiter at nearly every corner of town, most of them thin and scroungy as though they hadn't had a good meal in some time.

Ryan waited in the truck while Emajean jumped out to do the talking. It surprised him when she started speaking to the young girl in the Uto-Aztecan Shoshone language rather than English or her own, which she used on occasion back at the ranch. As she spoke, she gestured with her hands, the movements reminding him of sign language, her hands probably filling in the gaps of those Shoshone words she didn't know. Whatever she had said to Kima, the message seemed to have rung through because the girl's face changed from one of languid indifference to instant alarm, her eyes scanning the distance as though searching for danger.

Emajean pointed toward the back of the jeep, urging Kima to get in. Kima glanced at her peers, her eyes wary, their eyes matching hers. Ryan worried she would bolt. He tapped his thumbs on the steering wheel, waiting. "Tell her either to get in or we'll follow her to her father's house."

Emajean translated. After a short pause, Kima climbed in, her wolf jumping in beside her in the back seat. Ryan put the jeep in gear then drove through Fort Washakie to a trailer house far on the outskirts of the Shoshone section of the reservation. On the porch lay mounds of clothing, which Kima explained was used to help the poor in Wind River. The neighbors viewed Ryan with suspicion when he walked to the front steps. Chills ran the length of his backbone despite the heat. He wiped his brow, relieved when Kima opened her front door and bade them enter.

As Emajean had explained on the way to the reservation, there were protocols to be upheld when they spoke with Native American officials like Kima's father. Ryan stood back, hands at his sides, while Emajean went through the greeting rituals. Within a half hour, they were on the road, heading back, Kima and Esa in the rear of the jeep.

"How did you get Kima's father to agree to allow us to take her?" Ryan asked once they were off the reservation.

"He already knew she may be in danger. He didn't want her to end up like his mother. Dead. I told him that Kima would learn a skill and that Tracy and the vets would protect her until things blew over."

Ryan steered north, eager to close the distance between the reservation and Cody. "And he was okay with that?"

Emajean shrugged. "I made a vow to *Tam Apo*–that's the Shoshone name for The Great Spirit–that I would keep Kima and the wolf safe."

"So where are you going to put the pair, once we get back to the ranch? In the spare room with you?"

Emajean chuckled. "Of course not. We're taking her to Tracy's place."

Ryan slammed on his brakes. "Tracy? Why Tracy?"

Emajean cocked her head at him, clearly surprised by his reaction. "Why? Does that bother you?"

He hated to admit it, but after all the work he had invested in the farmstead and the feelings he was starting to have for Tracy, he had come to think of the farmstead as theirs, his and Tracy's. He had hoped to give their relationship time to grow without the interference of a teen and her wolf.

Even as he thought it, he knew he sounded petty, but he wanted a chance to explore his feelings for Tracy within the confines of their small unit of three: Ryan, Tracy, and Boots. Now he would have to widen that view. As he once again pressed on the accelerator, he peered at the pair through the rear-view mirror, at the girl and her wolf. He breathed a sigh of frustration. Why hadn't Tracy told him of her plan? Tension settled on his shoulders as he slowly watched the reservation recede into the distance.

* * *

Emajean sent word that she and Ryan had found Kima and Esa, but her words had seemed stilted, hesitant. There was something she wasn't saying, and Tracy had a feeling that that *something* had to do with Ryan.

As Tracy pondered the call, she ran upstairs with Boots at her side and began cleaning out the third bedroom, her thoughts returning to the ominous message she had received on the windshield of her truck. On the way home from her trek to see Gladys and Stanford, she had tapped her brakes over and over, worried they wouldn't grip. But each time, they worked just fine. Still, she'd been a wreck by the time she arrived at the farmhouse. What would Ryan think when she told him about the threat?

Well, she couldn't worry about that now. She needed to get Kima's room ready for the girl's arrival. Tracy hadn't aired out the third bedroom as she had hers and Ryan's rooms, so she struggled with the window latch, old paint crusted over it.

Then she tugged at the window itself, which had nearly stuck to the jamb, it had been so long since it had last been opened. When she finally managed to get it to budge, she breathed in the stale air of late summer. Although summer was still in full swing, fall would round the corner in no time. Already, many of the plants Tracy had purchased for the garden were starting to hint at yellows and oranges and reds that would soon offset the green. Still, she wasn't ready for fall. Summer had seemed especially short, what with traveling, cleaning, painting, and planting. She had never spent a winter in a place like Wyoming, which natives had assured her would be cold and snowy. Heck, she didn't even know how to drive in snow or put snow chains on her truck. Come to think of it, she would need to buy snow tires and chains soon, before the weather caught her unaware.

Next, she set about cleaning the bedding and reordering the room so that it didn't look quite so old-fashioned. But then again, what did she know about a young teenage Shoshone's fashion sense? She covered the bed in a star quilt and brought cut flowers from the garden to adorn the dresser with its blue willow pitcher and basin, which she washed and filled with fresh water. She finished off the look with a dusty rocking chair she'd found in the barn that she cleaned up and oiled so that it shined and smelled of fresh lemons. By the time she was done, the room seemed inviting. Now, viewing it anew, she wondered why she hadn't taken the same time and care with her own room and Ryan's as she had this one. One last touch. She added a welcome sign that she wrote in calligraphy from a class she had taken in college. All in all, her effort wasn't half bad.

She was whistling as she headed off to her room to check her emails before heading downstairs to prepare dinner. She had decided on spaghetti with garlic bread and a salad. Maybe Ryan and Emajean could stay. And thankfully, Bryce was still wandering around the place somewhere. When she'd told him about the threat, he'd gone into full bodyguard mode, checking her truck's brake lines, searching the perimeters to make sure someone hadn't boobytrapped the place when he wasn't looking. It made her smile, knowing that he had her back. That Ryan had her back too.

She quickly pulled up her email, her heart racing as she saw one from the dog rescue. Without hesitation, she opened the email, her eyes scanning the lines, her eyebrows coming together in a frown.

"Word has it that the American troops may be pulling out of Afghanistan soon. If that happens, we have only a short window of time to find your dog and get him out before the fighting between the Afghani and Taliban begins. From our sources, some are saying the Afghani army can hold them off for a while; others are saying it's a lost cause. Please advise us what you would like us to do. We can continue the search, but it will be hazardous and costly. I give it two weeks to a month, if that, before we learn about the pullout. I have spoken to a man who is part of the Afghani network inside Kabul. If anyone can find the dog, he can. But as you can guess, there are more pressing matters than getting a dog out, so it will be expensive. Probably seven thousand dollars or more. Maybe as much as ten thousand. Your call. Sorry to be the bearer of bad news."

Tracy sat back and rubbed her eyes, tired suddenly. Where would she possibly get that kind of money? She peered through the window down at the barn. Was anything in there worth that much? Or maybe she could hold an auction. Still, that was a lot of money to come up with, and she didn't have much time. She thought about just calling the whole thing off, but decided to think about it first. Maybe she could better answer the email after she'd slept on it overnight. Reluctantly, she closed out her email. For now, she had a dinner to prepare.

Thirty

Though Emajean appeared keen to return to the ranch, the smell of spaghetti and garlic bread swayed her to allow Ryan to stay awhile longer for the evening meal. Even so, he seemed edgy, unsettled. Tracy figured he'd eventually get around to what was bothering him. In the meantime, she had her own issues, what with the threat placed on her pickup and this new hiccup, should the troops pull out of Afghanistan. Gathering up two potholders, she pulled out the garlic bread from the oven and sat it on the stove next to the pot of spaghetti.

As soon as she opened the window to cool the kitchen, which felt stuffy this late in the day, Bryce smelled the food and came running. He offered to set the picnic table he'd discovered inside the barn and had placed out front. She smiled, grateful to have him here to help with the dinner, and grateful to have the others here to help pave the way with Kima. Tracy hadn't been around young teens since her stint as a camp counselor for one summer following high school. But what she did recall is that they could sometimes be moody.

"Can you help carry the food to the picnic table outdoors?" she asked Ryan.

He reached in without question and grabbed the bowl of spaghetti and a pair of serving tongs. Tracy handed the salad and dressing to Emajean to carry out.

"Could you get the garlic bread, Kima?"

Kima stood frozen for a moment, then grabbed the plate of garlic bread and followed them, Esa at her side. The golden-yellow eyes of the beast seemed to press against Tracy's back, causing her hackles to rise. The enormity of the undertaking she'd tasked for herself by bringing a young Shoshone with a half-wolf into their lives sent a wave of nausea coursing through her, but she forced herself to remain calm as she grabbed the pitcher of lemonade. By the time she arrived on the front lawn, Bryce was setting the picnic table with forks and napkins.

"Where'd you get the picnic table?" Ryan set the spaghetti down onto the middle of the table.

"Bryce found it in the barn," Tracy explained.

"I helped carry it out," Bryce said.

"He has been a great asset," Tracy added.

"Oh?" Ryan lifted a brow.

Was that a hint of jealousy she detected? Tracy couldn't say why, but it gave her a small thrill. She couldn't help but think back to the other day, when he had kissed her, the passion that he'd ignited in that small gesture.

Once they were seated and the meal served, Bryce was the first to bring up the subject about the less-than-veiled threat about her brakes.

"Let me see the message," Ryan said, his dinner forgotten.

Tracy hurried to her truck, parked no more than a stone's throw away from where they ate. She opened the passenger side door and pulled the bright note from her glove compartment, then walked it back to where Ryan sat straddling the bench. He opened it and read it, then whistled, lips pursed.

"So what should I do?"

"We put a guard on your truck, for one thing, check the brakes before you go anywhere for another."

"I can't have someone with me at all times when I'm at the farmhouse *and* when I go to town. You'd have no one left to run the ranch if you did."

Ryan puzzled over her words. "What would you suggest?"

"You teach me how to test my own brakes."

Tracy had almost forgotten about Kima and Esa until she noticed Kima filling up a plate and setting it down for the dog. They would need to purchase food for the wolf, but how could Tracy possibly come up with enough wild meat to keep the animal satisfied?

As if he read her thoughts, Ryan said, "Tomorrow, I'll bring over some venison and elk we have in the storehouse.

For now, spaghetti will have to suffice."

That and the garlic bread would have to make do for the night. Not the best meal for a wolf, but she supposed it wouldn't hurt the animal for one evening.

When the wolf was through eating, to everyone's surprise, it came over and laid down beside Ryan. Without thinking, he brushed the wolf's fur with his hand and said, "God I miss Herc. I think about him every day." With that, he jumped to his feet and made an excuse about needing more napkins.

Tracy peered down at the stack of napkins still on the table. Silence prevailed as each of them delved into their own private thoughts. Tracy reread the email from the rescue site over in her mind, her thoughts stumbling over the ten thousand dollars. She'd seen the tears forming in Ryan's eyes at the mention of Herc–heard the quaver in his voice. From what she'd witnessed so far, he didn't go in for displays of emotion, and especially not in front of other people. She decided to go after him. Maybe talking about it would help.

"Excuse me. Keep on eating. I'll be right back," she said, then hurried in after him.

To her surprise, Ryan wasn't anywhere on the bottom floor. She noticed Boots at the top of the stairs and climbed up to where he waited on the landing. That's when she noticed Ryan's room partially open. She walked over to his door, the floorboards creaking and saw that he was standing next to the window, staring out at the waning light that crested the mountains. His hands were in his pockets, his head back as though trying to stifle some unspent emotion and having trouble corralling it into its pen where it belonged.

"Ryan?" Tracy said. "Are you okay?"

He hurriedly brushed at his eyes and nodded, but she could see by the way he worked his jaw that he was still thinking about Herc, about his responsibility to the dog. For a moment she stood there undecided. Go to him, or give him his privacy? In the end, she decided to take him in her arms. For several minutes, neither spoke, they just rocked in each other's arms, the motion calming.

"I love you, Tracy," he murmured.

Tracy pulled back, frightened by the depth of his emotion. He didn't know her, not the real her—the one that made mistakes. The one who had let her horse down in a way that still kept her up at night. She'd never meant to cause harm—to anyone or anything and especially not to her horse.

Ryan sensed her hesitation and immediately apologized. "I'm just kicking myself," he said. "And you . . . well, you've made me feel . . . valued, I suppose. Sorry. I'm not making a lot of sense."

"No, you are, Ryan," Tracy said, snatching his hands up into hers. "I totally get it, but let's take it one day at a time, okay?" If only he knew how much she got it. Once again she thought about her quest to find Herc. *Ten thousand dollars*. How could she possibly raise that much money? But she knew Ryan would never feel whole again until he brought his dog safely home. She had failed one animal, but she wouldn't fail this one. Right then and there she determined, no matter the cost, she would find Ryan's dog and bring him home.

After the meal was over, and once everyone was gone

except Bryce, who would stay one more night before trading off with another vet, Tracy showed Kima to her room. For a second, Tracy had witnessed a glimmer of a smile from the girl when she entered the room and saw all the feminine touches Tracy had added to make the place feel more like a home. She gave the girl a blanket for the wolf-dog to sleep on.

"I'll make him a bed tomorrow," Tracy promised. "And Kima?"

The young teen bent down and hugged Esa as though needing the security of the one familiar in her life, the wolf.

"I'm glad you came. And I promise to train you how to become a veterinarian. After all, if you can handle a wolf, you can handle anything." Tracy pointed to a bookshelf she had painted white and placed on the wall next to her bed. "I left some of my old veterinary books, if you want to have a look at them. Or if you want to read before bed, I found some books in the barn. They're old, meant for teens in the 60s, not 2021, but maybe you'll like them anyway." Tracy shrugged, not at all certain Kima would, but at least she had tried to make the teen feel at home. Then she said a hasty goodnight and shut the door.

Afterward, she made a beeline to her room and to her computer. She sat down in the chair facing it and closed her eyes, willing herself to find a way to come up with both the money for the dog's return and means to get Herc home. Before all of Afghanistan collapsed.

With that, she typed in the words, "Find Herc and bring him home."

280

Abas sat with Herc by his side, scouting for information
on the computer about the coming withdrawal. As an
interpreter for the U.S. mountain unit, it had been his job to
gather information and to help the U.S. servicemen interpret
it, make sense of not only the things being said, but not being
said. Like any other language, both Pashto and Dari had their
nuances that an American might not understand. It was his
job not only to translate, but to decipher the true meaning
behind the spoken or written word. Dari was the official
language of the government, the Persian language. It gave
him insight into what the Afghani government was thinking
and planning. But Pashto was just as widely spoken as well.
The dog licked his hand as he typed.

Absentmindedly, Abas rubbed the dog's ears. He would
miss Herc, if Abas could ever get to the States. Worry edged
his thoughts. If Afghanistan fell, the interpreters would be
some of the first to die. The realization that he had only
weeks if not days to find a way out of Afghanistan sent a chill
down his spine that left him weak in the knees. It didn't help
that he was so exhausted that he could easily curl up and
sleep for a week. But there was no time for that. He sighed,
knowing he had no good options and his time was running
out. He decided to check his email, see if anyone else had any
news.

He saw a message from one of the men from the
mountain unit—Rick Langston. He was the one who had
asked Abas to find the dog, had given him approximate

coordinates. In a time of war and strife, it had seemed a huge hurdle and a foolish one at that. Dogs didn't have the same appeal that they had in the West. Here, in Kabul, they ran wild, roamed the night, snapping and snarling at passersby. In his culture, they were considered *haraam*, forbidden. And they *definitely* were not allowed inside the house. He'd had to overcome his inherent fear and distrust of dogs to bring Herc indoors. His wife had been adamantly against such a morally abhorrent breach of etiquette, but Rick had promised to get them and their children out if Afghanistan fell and the Taliban took over. That had been enough to silence her. Still, they'd had to make accommodations that, even now, found her scowling at him for going against the teachings of Islam. But the fear of what would happen to both her and the children should Afghanistan fall to the Taliban had spared Herc.

"It's not a certainty, but we're pretty sure the entire American force in Afghanistan will be leaving soon. Money is filtering in from the Brits to get Herc to England before it falls. There's a former marine there who rescues animals left behind. I am trying to secure you and your family's transport out should that happen. So far, things are up in the air. Americans will go first, but I'm sure that translators will be second to leave. Hang tight. I'm working on the logistics at my end. Rick."

Abas fell back in his seat, his heart thrumming in his chest. Fear crested over him like a wave. So many uncertainties. But one thing he knew. The Afghani government was corrupt. He felt certain the first plane out would be that of the Afghani leader along with all the money he had hoarded over the months and years he'd been in office. And without further backing, the Afghan army would simply fold up into the night and disappear without a trace. To do otherwise would be a fool's mission. No, the drumbeat had begun. He had learned to read the sound of it many eons past. It was time to pack, to leave. But to where, and how? He knew Rick meant well, but Abas had to find his own way out . . . in case. He would send his wife and children out first. Then he would leave once he knew they were safe. Herc . . . well, Herc would have to fend for himself in the streets, just like all the other wild dogs.

Thirty-One

Before heading downstairs, Tracy checked in on Kima who was still asleep, her wolf at her feet. Tracy tapped on the partially opened door. If Kima was to become a veterinarian, she would need to be able to rise at all hours of the day or night. If not, she would have to find another career. The will and desire would have to come from her.

Kima sat up, rubbing her eyes. "What time is it?" she murmured through sleepy lids, her voice groggy.

"It's 8:00 AM."

Kima frowned while Esa, who had been lying on her side on the blanket Tracy had provided, stirred and came to rest on her paws.

"I would like you to help me fix breakfast, then I'm going to have you go through the barn with me. We need to sell some of the stuff out there."

"Why?" she said, stretching.

As if on cue, Esa rose to her feet and padded over to Kima, but her focus was trained on Tracy, who couldn't help but shiver at the sight of those feral golden eyes. Something about them gave Tracy the feeling that she was being hunted, that given half a chance, the wolf would strike. Last night, after she'd said goodnight to Kima, she had gone to her room and googled wolves. What she read had disturbed her. Owners of wolves, almost to a man, had said that they'd raised wolves for years, only to have a wolf turn on them. Most were lucky and got by with only a scratch. Some were less fortunate. Tracy's throat tightened at the memory of those stories.

"I need to sell some of the stuff from the barn so I can make some money. I'll explain it more over breakfast," she said, then she made a quick exit from the room.

Even as she walked through the hall and down the stairs, her back prickled with the sensation of being watched. And she had to consider Boots, too. What if Esa saw him as prey?

Fortunately, over breakfast of ham and eggs with hash browns and toast, Tracy was able to talk Kima into keeping Esa in the pen Tracy had designed for the dogs until they could figure out what to do with her.

"So how did you come by the wolf?" Tracy asked, despite Emajean's warning that, like the Lakota, the Shoshone weren't very wordy, so not to pry too much.

"*Dogo* found her. Esa's mother had been trapped. She died, so we kept the cub."

"*Dogo?*"

"That's the Shoshone word for Grandfather," Kima explained.

"Do you ever worry that she'll . . . ?" Tracy left the sentence dangling as she sipped on coffee laced with peppermint mocha creamer and sweetener.

"Attack me?" Kima finished for her.

Tracy nodded as she bit into a slice of buttermilk toast with marmalade jam.

"We believe in *Appi*, our creator," Kima said, her accent heavily laden with the clicks of the Shoshone language. "Wolf and Coyote are the two opposing forces. Wolf created both people and the solar system, whereas Coyote is a trickster, out to deceive mankind, to create disorder, much as we are seeing now."

And it was true. Every newspaper came with a new tragedy of some sort.

"My father—he is Christian, but he also believes in the old ways."

"And you?" Tracy asked, setting her mug down in front of her.

"I feel the same. Esa has helped me many times. She protects me."

Tracy reached for another slice of bacon and offered one to Kima as well. She had a feeling the girl had needed protection on the reservation, if the crime rates were as high as Emajean had quoted.

When they were done eating, Tracy quickly washed dishes, while Kima dried. Then they headed out to the barn. Tracy's heart sank as she opened the door and once again saw the mountain of work ahead of her.

"I need to get this stuff sold. I was thinking about an auction," Tracy sighed, certain she would never get it set up in time before the bad weather set in.

"Have you thought of selling some of the stuff on Craigslist?" Kima said.

Tracy found that she had a hard time reading Kima, her emotions held in constant check. She had yet to see any real enthusiasm in the girl, nor any anger. Just a quiet solitude about her and a reticence of strangers, Tracy included.

"How hard would it be to set up?"

"I could do it for you," Kima offered.

"I need to sell the most expensive items first." Tracy peered around, unsure where to start. She picked up a few things, but each time she did, Kima shook her head. "Not enough money?"

"No. Look for anything Harley Davidson or Indian Motors. That brings the real money." Kima began poking around, moving oil cans and grass clippers, toolboxes and old rolls of wire.

Tracy set aside the shovels and hoes for work around the farm. She pointed to an old rustic table that had seen more than its fair share of use. "How about that?"

"How much you lookin' to get?"

"Thousands," Tracy admitted.

"That won't bring much more than a hundred or so."

"How do you know so much about old junk?" Tracy asked, dust and cobwebs settling over her clothing.

"Brothers," Kima said simply.

Mice had clearly made a mess of anything that could be eaten or used for their nests. Tracy grabbed them each a pair of gloves and 3M respirators to keep out the dust.

"So what do we have that *is* worth anything?" Tracy lifted and discarded one thing after another according to the shake of Kima's head.

"There!" Kima said finally.

Tracy looked to where Kima was pointing and gasped. An old green Studebaker covered in dust. It probably hadn't been run in almost twenty years and would need work to get it to operate, but the interior looked okay, and from what Tracy could see of it, which wasn't much, it didn't have any dents or dings.

"How much do you think I could get for something like that?" Tracy asked, pulling things aside as best she could.

"Maybe five, six thousand."

Tracy leaned back against the antique table. Six thousand dollars could go a long way toward retrieving the dog. And time was of the essence. But first they had to figure out how to get the car out so they could snap a picture of it in order to attain a true estimate of its cost. The door was too narrow to get it from this direction. But they could get it from the wide front doors of the barn, *if* they could unlock the rusted bolt.

"Wait here," Tracy said. "I'll go get Bryce." But before she could head out back, where Bryce had set up a spot on top of the old shed so he could view things from a distance, Ryan's jeep came rumbling down the driveway with Ryan at the wheel. "Talk about the perfect person," she said, when he came to a stop and jumped out of the jeep.

"Uh-oh," he said with a laugh. "That sounds like work, to me."

"It is. We need to haul an old Studebaker out of the barn."

"What are you going to do with the Studebaker?" he asked, tucking his hands in the pocket of his jeans.

"We're going to sell it," she said.

Just then, Bryce, who must have seen Ryan arrive, rounded the corner of the farmhouse. He waved to Ryan and asked to speak with him privately. Tracy frowned as she watched the pair saunter off, behind the house. What had Bryce found, and why hadn't he said anything to her?

In the meantime, Tracy had discovered the rusted lock on the barn's large double doors closest to the vehicle, behind a mountain of weeds and brush growing up in front of the doors. She and Kima had begun clearing the brush, but it was slow going. Fortunately, Tracy had found a pair of bolt cutters but so far hadn't had any luck prying off the lock. She waited for Ryan to return to give him a turn at the lock. Five minutes later, he came sauntering around the corner of the barn.

"I have a job for you," she said, sheepishly holding up the bolt cutters.

"Here." Ryan reached for the tool. He made quick work of removing the lock, which he tossed aside into the weeds. Next, they pulled back the giant doors with a rusty squeal. Ryan and Tracy pushed with all their might to get the rollers to budge. When at last they had the doors open, the inner coolness of the barn blew past them, the pungent smell of ancient motor oil released in a plume of stale air.

There it sat. The Studebaker. It alone could provide enough money to begin the search for Herc. Tracy had already put the first installment for the search on her Visa card. Soon she would be expected to pay more. Now she would have some way of paying for at least a portion of the upcoming bill.

For the next half hour, Tracy and Kima moved as much of the pile closest to the door onto the gravel driveway . . . what there was of it. Once that was done, Tracy, Ryan, and Bryce pushed, while Kima steered the old Studebaker until they finally had it out in the sunlight for the first time in years. The wide whitewall tires were flat, and the rims rusted, but all in all the interior and exterior were both in good shape.

Ryan whistled at the sight.

"So what do you think I can get for the old girl?" she asked the two men. "Kima thinks it should sell between $5000 and $6000."

Ryan and Bryce conferred. "I would put $6000 on it to start with. The buyer can always talk you down."

"You heard him," Tracy told Kima. "My computer's upstairs." For the first time since Kima had arrived there, she smiled. "Thank goodness Kima offered to set up the Craigslist account," Tracy said, once she was gone. "One less thing for me to do. Do you think I'll get any takers?"

"The question is how many takers will you get?" Ryan amended. "But why the sudden urge to sell?"

Tracy peered around the musty interior of the barn. She still had mountains of stuff to sift through, but it felt good to make this small dent in the pile and to finally have some means of making money, even if it would go for the dog, not food or the mortgage. Fortunately, she had saved up enough to make the downpayment and the first six months payment, so she was okay there. But eventually, she would have to quit going in the red and actually make some gains.

"If you haven't noticed by now, I have no income and bills to pay." She dug around some more, hoping to find something of value.

For the next twenty minutes or more, Tracy continued making a pile. Some of the junk she would simply haul to Goodwill or sell for scrap metal. Some would go in a dumpster that she would need to rent. Already, she was filthy by the time Kima came running toward her with Tracy's cell phone in her hand.

"I hope you didn't mind, your cell phone rang and I answered it. A woman named Lindsay needs you to come quick. Says one of her sheep was mauled by a wolf."

A frisson of fear ran through Tracy as she grabbed the phone and ran to the pen to see if Esa had escaped. She was out of breath by the time she reached the wolf only to discover it safely inside the pen, chewing on one of the puppy's toys. Kima struggled to keep up.

"It wasn't Esa, I swear," she said.

Ryan, who had brought up the rear, took one look at the wolf and said, "Good to know. I have venison for her. Hang on a sec." Then he ran back to his truck and threw what he had in the cage.

While Ryan fed Esa, Tracy wrote down directions from Lindsay, then the trio ran for Ryan's jeep, Ryan yelling over to

Bryce that they would be back in a bit.

"C'mon, Kima." Tracy placed her medical bag in the back of his jeep. "Get ready to learn how to become a veterinarian."

Thirty-Two

As they bounced along the rutted road toward the
Lindsay farm, Tracy held onto the door handle to keep from
being bucked off the bench seat of Ryan's jeep. She felt better
knowing that Bryce was back at the ranch, holding down the
fort. Without him there to keep an eye on things, she didn't
know what might happen. They had taken Ryan's jeep,
not wanting to risk anything, in case someone had actually
tampered with the brakes on her GMC, though that seemed
unlikely with Bryce guarding the farm. Ryan winked at Tracy
from the driver's seat, Kima in between them. Tracy's face
flushed with warmth. She knew he wasn't thrilled about her
taking on a teen, especially now that they were growing closer,
but she refused to hang back and do nothing if the girl's life
might be in danger.

"Look!" Ryan pointed.

There, in the distance, sat a farmhouse atop a knoll, a wooden barn attached to the siding of the stone structure.

"It's from the late 1800s," Ryan explained. "You don't see those kinds of stones these days. Comes in all colors."

And, indeed, as they neared, the house seemed almost whimsical, the stone changing color depending on the sun, from pink to green and even to gray-blue. The roof tile was done in a sage green with corbels supporting the two upside-down, v-shaped overhangs. Pens jutted off to the side where the sheep were housed.

From the entrance of the stone barn, Tracy saw Lindsay waving frantically. She sported a blue, Levi shirt, white vest and jeans, her long gray hair running in waves down her back. As the jeep came to a halt and Tracy jumped out, she could see a man peering through the window of the house, his expression wary.

"Over here!" Lindsay said, taking off at a trot. "We think a wolf got ahold of one of the sheep. Left a tuft of hair and some prints."

She pointed to a spot of barbed wire. Tracy had to admit the hair did look like wolf's hair and Kima confirmed the tracks that ran alongside the fence were that of a wolf.

"See here?" the teen explained to both women, her fingers tracing the tracks. "Too big to be a coyote, which are smaller than most dogs. And the pads on a mountain lion are more rounded."

Tracy cocked her head, surprised that the girl knew so much about wildlife.

"I hunt with my father and grandfather sometimes,"

Kima explained. "That's how I found Esa."

"Esa?" Lindsay said, just as Ryan caught up to the three women.

"Her wolf," Tracy explained.

Lindsay bristled, her outward friendliness transformed to a sudden chill.

"Don't worry, she's in a pen," Tracy said, to which both Ryan and Kima confirmed with a nod of their heads.

"Oh, okay," Lindsay said, warming slightly.

"So where is the ewe?" Tracy didn't have long to wait for the answer because she heard a bleating sound, both plaintive and frightened.

"Over here," Lindsay said, opening the gate to the pen. Over a hillock, Tracy found the ewe lying in the grass, her neck torn and bleeding. She could clean the wound and suture it, but whether the ewe would live, only time would tell. Fortunately, the wolf must have been startled into leaving the wounded sheep, because it hadn't managed to bite deeply enough to do real damage. Still, trauma was often just as bad as the actual injury to domestic animals. Tracy showed Kima how to administer a tranquilizer to prevent the ewe from bucking. When the animal was calm, she taught the girl how to provide lavage by spraying the laceration down with Wound Coat. Then she taught her how to debride the wound.

"See here?" Tracy said, handing her a scalpel and tissue forceps. "You want to remove any damaged tissue before we suture it."

Though awkward at first, Kima got the knack of it fairly quickly. Finally, Tracy showed her how to do the suturing then allowed her a hand at the process.

"You sew it up just like you would a quilt," Tracy explained.

"More like our deerskin dresses," Kima said, her words clipped.

Tracy was surprised at how quickly the girl caught on. And although Kima didn't respond with enthusiasm to Tracy's praise for a job well done, she did glow with an inner light when she was finished.

Now that the worst of the damage was treated, Tracy felt around the hind quarters, explaining to Kima as she went. "Wolves often grab the back of the animal to pull it down, then go for the jugular." Sure enough, she found teeth marks along the haunches where the wolf had dug in to yank down its prey. Although fairly deep, those hadn't done any permanent damage to the tendons. Tracy sprayed more of the medicated solution onto the ewe's haunches, the ewe kicking slightly despite the mild tranquilizer.

Once that was done, she peered up at the sky, dark clouds gathering, shuttering the sun. "Okay, we need to get the ewe inside before it rains. We need an area to keep her clean and separate from the other sheep while she heals."

"I've already got a spot set up in the barn," Lindsay said.

With Ryan's help, as well as that of Kima and Lindsay, they managed to roll the ewe onto a tarp and drag her out of the pen and over to the barn. By the time they had her loaded onto clean straw, her eyes were rolling and her tongue lolling as she made several unsuccessful attempts to turn onto her stomach from her side.

"You'll want to keep an eye on her." Tracy wiped up at the sink inside the barn, Kima doing the same.

"Let me run inside and get my checkbook," Lindsay said as Tracy made out the billing for her and Kima's work.

While they waited, Tracy peered around inside the barn. In a tack room off to the side, Lindsay kept a work desk. Behind it, the wall was lined with photographs. Tracy stood in the doorway, gazing at the pictures. A chill raced down her spine as she saw Lindsay's husband standing next to a man whose hat identified him as an oilman from Texas and someone else. Someone Tracy thought she recognized. Tracy walked through the doorway to get a better look and saw the name of the company beneath the picture. Maarlox Oil.

"Can I help you with anything?" Lindsay said, returning with her checkbook.

Tracy started, then turned to see Lindsay frowning at her for the intrusion into her workspace.

"No, sorry. I thought I saw a familiar face, that's all. My mistake." Then she backed out of the office. But she hadn't made a mistake. She *did* know that face, and she didn't like where her thoughts were taking her.

* * *

Before Ryan even had time to park the jeep in front of Tracy's farmhouse, he received an urgent message from Wyatt. The text had read simply, "Get here quick. We've got a problem." Ryan had tried to call back, but no one answered, so he texted: "On my way."

He could see that Tracy had something she wanted to

297

talk to him about, that something seemed to be worrying her, but it would have to wait until after he figured out what was going on at the ranch.

The engine idling, he turned to Tracy and said, "I have to go. But Bryce will be here if you need him." He read the frustration in the set of her jaw, but he'd been neglecting the ranch far too long, and he knew he couldn't do it much longer. When he saw her downturned lips, he added, "I'll be back as quickly as I can. I promise."

As soon as Tracy and Kima exited the jeep, he revved the engine and put it in reverse, flying toward the main road. The sky was overcast, rain on the horizon. He could smell it in the air. By the time he reached the gravel driveway that led to the ranch, the skies burst open and a torrent of rain unleashed its fury on the surrounding hillside. Ryan turned his windshield wipers to high speed, the rhythmic sound only counting down the seconds as he waited to learn what had gone wrong. He had a feeling it had something to do with Hank.

It didn't take long to realize that his hunch was correct. Through the rain-soaked windshield, Ryan saw Wyatt dressed in a slicker and hat, mud nearly to the top of his boots. When Ryan stopped the jeep and jumped out, he heard some of the other men calling at the top of their lungs. Just then, a flash of lightning crackled across the sky in root-like fashion.

"Quick!" Wyatt yelled. "Someone let the horses out of the barn!"

But before the added words "watch out" were fully out of his mouth, a frightened quarter horse came galloping around the corner of the barn, rearing up on its hind legs and then

298

slashing at the mud-soaked earth where Ryan stood, sending him crashing to the ground. Then it was gone. Ryan fingered his head, felt the warmth of blood as it cascaded down his face and chin.

Wyatt ran over to him and tore off his shirt, balling it in his fist to stave the blood flow. "Kate! Emajean!" he called.

Despite what had just happened, Ryan felt surprisingly calm, as though it were someone else, not him, who lay bleeding on the ground.

"Quick, we need to get him sewn up. Take a look at this, would you, Emajean?" Wyatt yelled as she ran to kneel beside him in the mud.

Emajean inspected his forehead. "I would feel a whole lot better if a doctor checked him over," she said, frowning. "A leg wound I can sew up, but a head wound can be more tricky."

Kate, who had just arrived on the scene said, "It'll take too long for a doctor to get here."

For a moment, they all stared at each other, while Ryan felt himself slipping in and out of consciousness.

Emajean shook her head. Despite her stoic nature, she seemed particularly bothered by the gash to Ryan's forehead. She bit her lip over and over, then snapped her fingers. "Why not call Tracy? I'm sure she's dealt with animals with a head injury before."

"Emajean, I love you," Wyatt said, giving her a grateful hug.

"I'll go make the call," Kate yelled, but she was already running toward the house.

Thirty-Three

Tracy hung up the phone, grabbed her raincoat and dashed out the door, almost forgetting Kima and her wolf. She yelled to Bryce, who had ignored the rain and was behind the barn, shoring up the hole that Ryan had fallen into.

"I need to get to the ranch. Ryan is hurt," she called over the wind and rain. "Have you seen Kima?"

Bryce gave a loud whistle toward the back of the house and the girl came running. Bryce pointed toward Tracy, who was already in the truck and had the motor running. She revved it to urge Kima to hurry. By the time Kima reached the truck, her chest was heaving and water dripped down her face and neck.

"What happened?" Kima's eyes darted to the pen out back where even now the wolf was seen pacing despite the rain, stopping only to stare at the girl before it continued on.

"Ryan's hurt. I'll need your help . . . and your silence."

Kima paused for only a moment, then nodded.

"Your wolf will be safe with Bryce."

Reluctance clouded Kima's expression, but she acquiesced willingly. The girl clearly liked these forays, after her first attempt at becoming a veterinarian. Tracy had to admit, she was a natural.

Through the driving rain, Tracy pushed her truck hard, hoping it could hold up under the strain. Up ahead, a semi was turning. She pressed down on the brakes and, with a sickening dread, felt them give.

"Oh no!" she cried, pumping them.

"What's wrong?" Kima said, her eyes registering an alarm.

Tracy's heart hammered in her chest as she tried over and over again to slow the truck. *How?* She hadn't thought to check the brakes, she was in such a hurry when they left.

"The brakes have been cut. We're going to crash! Get ready!"

Kima let out a short scream and shut her eyes as they braced for impact. The GMC reeled in slow motion, as the truck barrelled toward the back of the semi. Tracy held tight to the steering wheel just as they were about to hit the rear end of the semi.

"Help us, God," she whispered.

Then, as she fought back her panic while awaiting the inevitable screech of metal on metal, the semi lurched forward and turned, giving her a hair's width to swerve around it. Her hands were shaking, and Kima was screaming, but she had no time to dwell on that now. Somehow, she had to stop the truck before it was too late. She saw the ranch looming in the distance, but it was a downhill slide, the rain making the road slick. If only she could make it to the driveway without hitting anything, she could try using the handbrake to slow the truck down enough for it to turn onto the gravel. She didn't know how she would slow it after that except to keep her foot off the gas pedal and hope that the truck stopped in time to keep from hitting anything.

"Hang on!" she urged Kima, who was crying softly now.

As Tracy closed in on the turn, windshield wipers slapping at the rain, she kept her foot off the gas and cranked on the parking brakes while turning the steering wheel.

"C'mon, c'mon," she urged the old truck.

Two of the wheels nearly came off the ground, as the truck leaped and bounced onto the muddy road, still going too fast for her taste, but at least the truck was upright. *For now.*

"Please, baby. Slow down," she urged the truck, every nerve ending on fire. For several moments, her prayers went unanswered. Then finally, the gravel did its job and the truck coasted the rest of the way, coming to a stop well before they reached the ranch house.

Tracy's entire body was quaking as she and Kima stepped out of the truck. Through the mud and rain, she ran over to where Ryan lay on the ground beneath the old oak tree in a vain attempt to keep him dry. Emajean held Wyatt's shirt to Ryan's head. Blood filled the shirt and ran down Ryan's shoulder and chest, where he appeared pale but awake.

"What just happened?" Kate demanded, pointing at the truck.

"The brakes were tampered with," Tracy said. "I'll tell you about it later. After we get Ryan stabilized."

Kate let out a gasp. "I'm glad you two are okay," she said, with a sigh of relief. "We brought clean towels and fresh water for Ryan. Also some iodine."

"Let me take a look at him." Tracy donned gloves and handed a pair to Kima. The girl leaned in, inspecting the wound along with Tracy.

A huge knot had formed on Ryan's head, and at least a three-inch gap ran down his forehead where the horse had kicked him. Tracy said a silent prayer, thankful that he was alive. Still, they would have to watch for a concussion, but first she needed to stop the bleeding. She had Kima use antiseptic on the wound, explaining as she went about the need for applied pressure on an open head wound. She knew Ryan should probably get an MRI, but they had no time to get help this far out. He needed to be cleaned and sutured now.

"It's just like what you did with the sheep," she told Kima as she deadened the area before she began suturing. "Only you make your sutures shallow because of the skull and you want to take care not to cause any puckering that will leave a lasting scar. Can I get someone to hold an umbrella over him?" Tracy asked. "I need him to be dry if I'm going to be able to suture him properly."

Kate ran inside and was back in moments. She flipped open the umbrella and held it over them, thunder rumbling in the distance. Fortunately, the lightning had veered off and only the rain remained.

Once the area was fully numbed and his forehead dried, Tracy began slowly drawing the suturing material through the skin, using her smooth forceps to help pull it through. Despite the fact that her hands still shook from her ordeal getting here, it didn't take long before she'd tied off the last suture and the bleeding had stopped.

"Let's get him inside," she said, when she was finished.

Wyatt, along with several other men standing nearby, lifted Ryan and hauled him carefully across the front border to the house, up the stairs and through the screen door. When Ryan was safely inside, Tracy turned to Kate and explained what had happened to her brakes.

"Oh, my!" Kate said, still harried after her own ordeal. "Let me get one of the men to take a look at them. I'm sure we can get your brakes fixed before you leave for home. And Tracy," she added, squeezing Tracy's shoulder, "thanks for coming so quickly."

Tracy fought back the raw emotion in her throat. "Ryan's not out of the woods yet, not by a longshot. Make sure he stays awake tonight. He needs round the clock care."

Kate bit her lip and frowned. "Why don't you stay the night? I'm sure Ryan would love having you here. That would give one of our men time to go over your truck thoroughly."

Tracy glanced at Kima, who only shrugged. Tracy had a feeling she was used to being passed around. "Bryce can feed Esa."

"Okay," Kima said.

Although the girl had a shy way about her, she also had a

resilience born of necessity. Tracy had learned from Emajean that she had no mother, her mother having died when she was ten years old. For whatever reason, over these past twenty-four hours Tracy had come to feel almost motherly toward her, and she had a sneaking suspicion that Kima felt the same.

"We can put you up in the guest bedroom, if you don't mind bunking together," Kate quickly added.

As they headed toward the house, Tracy said, "So what happened to Ryan?"

Kate stopped walking, her blue eyes pensive and her brown hair slightly mussed, as though lifted by the wind. "Someone freed the horses."

Tracy shot a glance toward Kima. "All of them?"

"All of them. We've spent the entire evening rounding them up. Ryan didn't know what he was walking into."

Tracy thought about that. Who would release all of the horses, knowing the havoc it would cause? Especially with the driving wind and rain they'd had, not to mention the lightning. She had a sneaking suspicion. Should she tell Kate?

"Yesterday, when I was out at the Mitchell ranch, I was treating a ewe with a wolf bite."

"Oh?" Kate's eyes drifted toward the ranch house, as though she were wishing Wyatt was in on this. "And?"

"I noticed an office . . . inside the barn. I didn't mean to poke, but I saw a photograph of Gabe . . . and two other men."

"Who?" Kate asked, all ears now.

Tracy glanced at the house. "I don't know who one of the men was—just that he was a Texas oilman."

"And the other?"

Tracy paused. "The second man was Hank."

Kate gasped. "Are you sure?"

Tracy nodded. "Dead sure."

But why? Why was the inspector in a photograph with two other men in a location not far from here? As if the thought had just occurred to Kate as well, she let loose a long slow whistle that sent a chill through Tracy. Something was wrong with this picture. But what?

Thirty-Four

Blake examined the corkboard filled with notes and suppositions as he answered the call he'd been waiting for most of his life. Late last night, he'd received an email from an unknown person. The only thing it said was, "I know what happened to Mabel." Blake responded to the email–urged the person, who went by the tag "Night Owl," to call him in the morning.

He took a deep breath before pressing the screen. "Hello?" No answer. "Are you there?" Still no answer. He bit his lip in frustration. "Who is this?" he shouted. "If you have something, I want to know. I promise, nothing will happen to you. I just want to know what happened to my grandmother."

He heard a dial tone and threw down his cell phone. The jerk had hung up on him. He fell back into his chair next to the computer desk, all the while looking at the map with its many pins, every one a potential lead. He closed his eyes and rubbed his face. He hadn't slept well last night, his mind playing over the many possible scenarios of this call, none of which had actually happened. Now, in retrospect, today's outcome seemed far worse.

Suddenly, the phone rang again and he rushed to answer it. "Don't hang up!" he pleaded.

"Why would I hang up?" his wife, Joy, said, clearly confused.

"Oh, sorry, I was expecting another call."

"Well, thank you very much," she said, a slight pique to her voice. "So, you want to tell me what's going on? I saw the bathroom light last night, and when you were sleeping, you were tossing and turning. It doesn't take a detective to know something's wrong."

He picked up a pencil that he kept atop his desk to scribble notes onto a memo pad, when a thought came to him. He tapped the ink blotter. Little unconnected pencil points dotted the blotter when he was through.

"Well, are you going to spit it out?"

"All right," he said, not sure if he had anything to tell, under the circumstances. "I received an email last night from someone going by the username Night Owl. Said they knew what happened to Mabel. I gave the person my number but the caller hung up on me. Now what?"

"You stupid man," Joy said, teasing. "Go online and look up the caller's number."

He had to admit, he did feel stupid when she put it like that.

"I'll be home in a bit. In the meantime, don't do anything funny, okay?" she said.

"Got it!" he agreed.

When she hung up, he turned to his computer and punched in the number then waited for the name to appear. To his surprise, the name that came up was no one he knew or recalled his parents or grandparents ever having known. So who exactly was this person?

He decided to dial Tracy to see if she had found anything. Maybe the caller and the person who had sabotaged his hay were one in the same.

*　*　*

Despite the fact that Tracy's brakes had been fixed and one of the guys at the ranch had checked her truck over with a fine-toothed comb, the drive home had been harrowing. She couldn't get over the fact that someone was so determined to keep a decades old mystery a secret that they were willing to kill for it. Now, as she turned into her driveway and made the final trek toward home, she hoped that things would go well today. But before she could even pull up in front of her house and turn off the ignition, she saw Bryce seated on the front porch holding a towel filled with ice to the back of his head.

"What now?" Tracy cried, hopping out with Kima right behind her.

Tracy and Bryce quickly swapped stories.

"Someone hit me over the head from behind when I went to feed Esa. When I woke up, the wolf was gone. I went looking for her, but she must have followed the river because I lost her prints in the underbrush."

Tracy's eyes strayed to where the pen door stood open and her heart sank. "This is one of those times I wish one of the pups was a fully trained tracking dog." So far, she'd had little time to train the dogs the way she'd hoped.

Kima ran to the pen and stood there, as if willing her wolf back into the cage. For several minutes she called to Esa, whistling occasionally, but the wolf was nowhere to be seen. Tracy just prayed that Esa didn't attack any of the local livestock and wind up having one of the ranchers shoot her. Tracy would never forgive herself if anything happened to the wolf, and she had a feeling that Kima wouldn't forgive her either.

Before she could formulate a plan of attack, her phone rang. Blake's number appeared. "Blake, what is it?" Tracy stepped to one side so she wouldn't be heard.

"Have you learned anything about the hay?"

Tracy told him what she had gleaned from Gladys and Stanford as well as what the newspaper reporter had given her from his old files. In turn, he told her what had happened on the phone.

"I looked up the person's number. It was from a woman. A Mildred Shumann. Have you ever heard of her?"

"Can't say as I have but I'll ask around. If anyone can find out about her, Gladys and Stanford can."

"Maybe I should put them on the payroll."

"Maybe you should," Tracy agreed. She decided to bring him up to speed about the horses being let loose, Ryan's accident, Bryce's attack, and her brakes being sabotaged. "All in all, it's been a tough day."

"It certainly sounds like it, and Tracy . . ."

"Yes?" she said.

"I didn't mean to get you involved in all of this. I know you're taking a lot of heat for something you had nothing to do with."

"You couldn't have known." She scanned the perimeter for either the wolf or the assailant, but all seemed calm, despite the day's peril.

"Still, I'm sorry to put you through this. I hope I can repay you in some way." His voice sounded tired, defeated.

"We'll get to the bottom of this." But even as she spoke, she didn't know how, or if she *could* accomplish it.

They said their goodbyes, then she hung up. But before she could do anything further, she received another call. Who now?

* * *

From the moment Stanford had shown Gladys what he'd found, she couldn't wait to call Tracy, but customers had come in by the droves this morning and she'd had no time to do anything but take calls and sit with clients, going over their marketing strategies. When they'd finally had time to breathe, Gladys once again had Stanford show her what he'd discovered. The minute she saw the computer screen, she'd experienced an inner chill, as though a northern draft had breezed through the room and cooled it by a good fifteen

311

degrees. Without thinking, she grabbed her sweater and shrugged into it.

"Hey, girl," Stanford said, twirling a rubber band around his finger as he talked. "Don't go all soft on me now."

"Make me a cup of coffee," Gladys pleaded.

But Stanford wouldn't stand for that. Instead, he jumped up from his chair and said, "I'll do you one better. I'll get you a Grand Teton mocha."

Before she could protest that he needn't go to all that trouble, he was out the door and across the street. Leave it to Stanford to have struck up a conversation with a complete stranger before he'd ever made it into the Cody Cafè.

She turned back to the computer screen. How Stanford had found such an obscure article from over twenty years ago, she didn't know. It was a geological map of the Bighorn Basin. What she found most interesting was the location of oil on the map. One ranch stood out among the rest. It had originally belonged to William Carter who owned the Carter Cattle Ranch. His 1879 cattle drive from Oregon to the Bighorn Basin had led to one section of the Basin being named the Oregon Basin. But what really interested Gladys was that in 1895, Buffalo Bill had purchased it and renamed it the TE Ranch. Over time, it became one of the many oil fields in Wyoming. But when she saw the amount of oil and gas available from the existing fields and the net worth of that gas and oil, she whistled.

"Why the whistle?" Stanford asked, pushing the door open with his backside.

"Guess how much money is tied up in the Oregon Basin

Fields." She sat back in the chair and steepled her fingers, trying not to appear smug.

"I don't know." He handed her the Grand Teton and set his coffee on the desk. "Enlighten me."

"Twenty-six *billion* dollars." She let that roll around for a while.

"Say what?" He plopped down in his chair and rolled over to the computer screen.

Gladys turned back to the screen and pointed out what she'd just read.

"Okay," said Stanford, gesturing eloquently with his hands. "Enough to kill for?"

"Maybe." Gladys frowned, not ready to make that leap just yet.

Stanford lifted a brow. "Didn't Tracy say that drilling may have caused sinkholes in some parts of the country?"

"She did."

"And that *she* has a sinkhole in her backyard?"

Gladys didn't bother to answer, merely nodded while pursing her lips.

"Curious and curiouser," Stanford said, bobbing his head slightly. "Me thinks something is rotten in Denmark."

"Me thinks you readeth too much," Gladys countered.

"Okay, so far we've got zilch. Just conjecture and a few small leads. Now what, Sherlock?" It was his turn to appear smug.

"So what if Mabel found out about these sinkholes and was going to go public with it? True, that field is way south of Tracy's property, but look at how many more are in the area.

313

There are at least 134 oil fields in the Bighorn Basin. If even one was at stake, they were all at stake."

"But again," Stanford said with an exaggerated sigh, "how are you going to pinpoint exactly who felt threatened?"

This is where Gladys had him. She smiled, wriggling her brows. "We find out which oil field is closest to her property and take it from there. Then we go back into the archives and find out who operated that field, and voila!"

Stanford rolled his eyes, clearly unimpressed.

"Well? Do you have a better idea?"

Stanford did a mock scowl, then they set to work. When Gladys finally thought they had something, she made the call she'd wanted to make all morning.

Thirty-Five

"Okay, we have it," Gladys said, without even introducing herself.

Eager to see if she could locate any wolf tracks or find the man who had mugged Bryce, Tracy scouted the perimeter of the house as she listened to Gladys on the phone. She had been sure to grab her .22 first.

"What do you have?" Tracy replied, her thoughts still on Ryan's injury and the missing wolf, not to mention Bryce.

"Okay, so you know how you said Mabel had a map of the oil fields in the Bighorn Basin?"

"Yes." Tracy knelt down to inspect the spot next to the pen where Bryce had encountered the intruder. It was easy to see that there'd been an altercation. The soil held no single set of tracks, but a multitude as Bryce tried to fight off the offender but failed. Tracy hadn't noticed that Kima had trailed her until the girl pointed out a set of paw prints that continued toward the river. Another set, this time human, ran off toward what must have been a waiting vehicle, the tires having dug into the loose soil as the perpetrator peeled away, leaving the wolf to roam freely. But why had he let the wolf go? What was the point in that?

"Are you still there?" Gladys asked.

Tracy quickly explained what had happened.

Gladys tsked. "Oh, girl, do be careful."

"So, what have you learned?" Tracy asked. Part of her hoped she'd spot the wolf, while the other half hoped she wouldn't, knowing that a wolf could be unpredictable, even a half wolf.

"Well, first off, oil is big money with a capital M."

"Tell me something I don't know." Tracy laughed, glad to ease some of the tension of the day.

"We're talking in the billions of dollars here in the basin. So I got to thinking about what you said about the sinkholes and the karst formations. So what if Mabel discovered that the oil was creating sinkholes?"

"I'm listening," Tracy said, having forgotten about her earlier worries.

"So I did a little digging and found out which company drilled closest to Mabel and Grayson's property."

Gladys paused for effect, straining Tracy's already frayed nerves.

"Well?" Tracy demanded. "What did you find?"

"It's Maarlox."

Tracy tried not to let her impatience show. "I already

know about Maarlox, remember?"

"Yes, but guess who runs it?" Gladys said, her voice filled with intrigue.

Tracy could hear the other woman tapping her pencil on the table and felt her nerves snap. "Who?"

"J. D. Beringer. The guy you ran into at our office the other day."

If Tracy'd had a chair, she would have plopped down into it. Still, something didn't make sense. Something that Tracy couldn't put her finger on. Suddenly, it came to her when she visualized the old, torn and faded map.

"Okay, this J. D. Beringer guy wasn't that old. He couldn't have possibly been running Maarlox back in the day. He would have been in his early twenties, tops, if even that."

Gladys sighed. "I hadn't thought of that. But maybe the company still has something at stake if word got out."

Tracy marched over to a fallen log and sat on it, head back, thinking. Something about this still didn't make sense. "If this was a big deal, why haven't we heard of other sinkholes? Surely where there's one, there's another, and yet in twenty years we haven't heard of any, have we?"

"Hang on a sec," Gladys said. "I'm at my computer. Let me type in the question."

Tracy could hear Stanford in the background lending suggestions and Gladys chiding him for touching the keyboard.

"So far we're only finding natural reasons for sinkholes. It says here, Anchor Dam was built in '44 but kept draining into sinkholes because of two areas containing dolomite.

317

Apparently, the water came from Owl Creek, but never went back into the creek because it disappeared into the substrate below. Owl Creek itself is known for sinkholes, but again they're natural sinkholes. Maybe Mabel's is just a natural sinkhole, so why kill for it?"

"That's it?" Tracy dug at the dirt with the toe of her boot, wondering where Kima had gone.

"I found another sinkhole in the Laramie Basin, but same thing there. Totally natural. I'm afraid you may be right. We've got nothing."

"Thanks for checking though. By the way, did Blake ever contact you? He said he might like to hire you since you're such good investigators."

"Some investigators we are," Gladys mumbled.

"Don't worry. We'll figure this out one of these days."

"Maybe we should stick to marketing," Gladys said with a snort.

"Well, if I hear anything, I'll let you know." Tracy thanked Gladys then hung up.

She stretched her aching back then started toward the house. Bryce was where she had left him, nursing a sore head and shoulders, but otherwise he seemed all right. She frowned when she couldn't find Kima. *Now where has that girl run off to?*

* * *

When Ryan awoke, he wasn't sure of the time or day. Only Emajean seemed to be around. He could hear her humming in the kitchen in a near monotone. Detecting no

318

one else, he called out to her. Moments later, she appeared as if by magic on silent feet.

"The dead have arisen," she said, drawing back the curtains.

The light from the window blinded him and he shielded his eyes with his hands. As he waited for his eyes to adjust, he squinted. "What day is this?"

"We kept you up for twenty-four hours to make sure you didn't have a concussion. Then we let you sleep the night away. It's nearly noon." Normally, this would have been an admonishment, but today she smiled in relief that he had pulled through without a concussion.

"Noon of which day?" His brain felt fuzzy still, as if the words went through him, circled around and then came out the other side of him without ever landing inside his thick skull.

"You were kicked in the head by one of the quarter horses, day before yesterday." She ordered him to sit, whereupon she pulled up his pillow and ordered him to lie back. "I'll bring you breakfast. I saved some from this morning."

He knew it would cost her to have to microwave his food. She believed in serving food fresh, but it couldn't be helped today. Ryan felt his forehead, counted the stitches. "Yikes! Ten stitches." He drew a blank where the memory should be of the doctor who'd helped him.

"If you're wondering, Tracy stitched you up."

"Tracy?" he said, unable to contain his surprise.

"That's right," she answered, then she left.

319

Ryan sat pondering that for a moment. Tracy had raced clear across the valley to come stitch him up? Grateful didn't begin to describe the feeling he had for her, knowing that it could cost her her license if anyone found out. One thing for certain, he wasn't about to be the one to squeal on her. If anything, it raised his esteem for the lady.

While Emajean readied his meal, he dressed in jeans and a fresh t-shirt. Emajean must have put them there, his dirtied and bloodied clothes gone. Knowing Emajean, they were already washed and folded, and sitting in his bedroom, waiting for him to put them away. He had just sat down on the edge of the bed and was pulling his feet up onto the quilt when Emajean reappeared with a tray full of food, which she laid across him once he got settled.

"So what happened? Fill me in."

"What do you want to know about first—the accident or what's going on over at Tracy's place?"

He'd meant the accident, but his antenna shot up with the mention of Tracy. "Why, what happened to Tracy?"

"Believe it or not, someone hit Bryce over the head and freed the wolf."

Ryan tried to jump to his feet, but Emajean was too quick for him. She shoved him back down against the pillow, righting the tray that he'd almost knocked over in his haste.

"If you promise to stay put, I'll tell you the rest." She gave him the stink eye, then continued. "Tracy called us yesterday morning to fill us in. By the way, someone cut her brakes that same evening the horses got loose."

"What?" Once again, Ryan shot up only to be shoved

320

back onto the pillow.

"Quit squirming," Emajean chided, sliding the plate back into position. "Eat!" she ordered. She waited until his mouth was full before she continued.

"Go on," he said through a bite of egg.

"Hold your horses!" Emajean said.

When he dutifully remained silent, she pressed on.

"Seems like we've got someone who wants the entire operation shut down and Tracy gone. We're still not sure why."

Ryan could see the wheels turning in Emajean's brain and wondered what she had in mind.

She bent low, as though in confidence and said, "I think it's because the purification ceremony wasn't performed for Mabel when she died, so her spirit isn't at rest. And the spirits of her husband and dog can't rest until she does. That's why all these bad things are happening."

Ryan stopped chewing and swallowed, gulping his food down with a swig of milk. "So you've heard the legend?"

"About Grayson's ghost?"

He nodded.

She shrugged, once again leaning in. "I saw Grayson and his dog, when I was out walking one evening."

She said it so matter-of-factly that he didn't know how to respond.

"He's sad. He misses his wife. He can't move on until her body is found and the purification ceremony is performed."

"But she's not Lakota," Ryan reminded her.

"You don't have to be Lakota to do what's right."

Ryan rubbed his chin. One of his buddies in Afghanistan had lived in China for a year while his father taught at the university there. He had regaled Ryan and his fellow soldiers with stories that at the time seemed outlandish. The one that stuck most in his mind was of a woman giving birth. For a month following birth, the woman wasn't allowed to visit friends or family for fear of bringing mice to the person's doorstep. As though the mice could somehow scent the afterbirth. He had laughed at the time, but seeing Emajean's set jaw, and recalling that night that he too had seen Grayson and his dog at the cemetery, he wasn't sure what to think. Maybe some of the native beliefs *did* have some basis in fact, however obscure to Westerners.

"Do you think we'll ever learn what happened to Mabel?" Ryan asked.

Emajean gave one quick nod. "I have prayed to *Wakan Tankan. Mitakuye Oyasin*. We *will* find her."

Thirty-Six

Tracy searched for Kima and Esa for nearly an hour, then finally gave up and trudged toward home. Bryce had insisted that she let him do the searching while Tracy stayed behind to guard the farm. After all, the intruder could still be out there, watching. Waiting. Yet, as she explained to him, she was no safer at the farmhouse than outside. Case in point, the lump on his forehead. Reluctantly, he acquiesced. Now, every ounce of her muscles ached as she climbed the bank next to the river's edge and sauntered toward the house. The sun would set in half an hour and Tracy had yet to eat dinner, her stomach rumbling as proof. To her surprise, Kima and Bryce were seated on the porch swing waiting for her.

"There you are, Kima!" Tracy chided. "Where have you been?"

"Looking for Esa," she said in that dry, Shoshone way of

hers.

Weary, Tracy took a seat on the porch steps and lay her head against the newel post. It amazed her. The girl never appeared ruffled, even when she'd lost her wolf. "Did you find Esa?" Tracy asked, already knowing the answer. She had passed the empty pen on her way in.

"No. I lost her tracks down by the river. She must have crossed over further downstream, but it was getting too late to search."

Tracy's thoughts exactly. It's a wonder she had missed the girl on her return home, considering they had probably taken nearly the same path in the woods down by the river. As for the wolf, if it attacked a cow or a sheep, as the one had at Lindsay's house, a rancher would be within his rights to shoot. The only protection Esa would have would be inside Yellowstone, where wolves had been reintroduced, much to the dismay of ranchers and farmers alike.

"We can search tomorrow."

Kima shook her head stoically. "If Esa wants to return, she will. It is up to her. Did you know that we have a legend about the wolf?"

Tracy leaned forward. "Oh?"

"It is said that Wolf can bring back the dead." Her eyes drifted eastward to where the cemetery was located. "But Coyote made fun of Wolf, said that the dead should remain dead. So when Coyote's son died, Wolf refused to revive his son. From that day forward, Wolf never again raised the dead."

"But you believe he can help locate the dead so that the

person can be given a proper burial?" Tracy held her breath as she awaited the girl's answer.

Kima merely blinked. "I do . . . so the people waiting on the other side can rejoin the deceased. Rest easy, knowing that their loved one is safe."

A chill ran down Tracy's spine, the wind howling in unison. Tracy could have sworn she heard a wolf howl in the far distance. Wherever Esa was, Tracy hoped she was all right. If only she could make it to Yellowstone where she would be protected. Anywhere else . . . Tracy shook her head, unwilling to go there.

* * *

Mildred Shumann sat at her desk, staring at her computer monitor. She'd been going over the books for hours, but her mind kept unspooling, like a bobbin on her sewing machine that she rarely used anymore. All her grandchildren had grown up and now they preferred store bought clothing. Her thoughts turned to Mabel and Blake. Mabel never got to see her grandkids grow old. To see them trade in skinned knees and a bicycle for their first hot rod. Never got to see them go to their first prom. Get married.

Mildred glanced at the photograph she kept beside her computer of her granddaughter's first beau, all dressed up. Gone were the corsages of her days, replaced by gowns fit for the red carpet. Her granddaughter was no exception when it came to that. She was, in a word, beautiful, but the thought still haunted her that she got to be there for her granddaughter's graduation. Mabel had not. Despite the years that had passed, moist tears formed at the crevices of her eyes when she realized she could have done something. Been a true friend to Mabel. Warned her. But of what? What did she really know about anything, even now?

Mildred's eyes drifted to the phone. She had called him . . . Blake. Had planned to say something, but in the end had chickened out. What if she was right? What if there had been more to Mabel's disappearance than just a woman who'd taken off to parts unknown? Mildred clucked, knowing that Mabel would no more do that than Mildred herself. No, they were both family people—women who loved their kids and grandkids.

She pulled open her desk drawer and lifted out her organizer filled with paper clips and rubber bands. Beneath the organizer sat the email she had printed out and saved. It had been addressed to her boss, not her, but had somehow inadvertently ended up in her inbox, the message no doubt CC'd from another email meant for her.

She read the contents of the message. It didn't say who it was about, but she'd had the uncanny feeling they had been talking about Mabel even then. It said simply, "She knows too much." But knew too much about what? At the time, Mabel had been going on about sinkholes and oil drilling. About water being pumped for agriculture. About karst formations and gypsum, how the water tables kept the gypsum from caving in. About money disappearing. Oil money owed to the Indians. Had it just been an older woman with extra time on her hands filling her days with something that interested her?

Or had she become an activist who might have opened a can of worms that someone wanted to keep sealed?

Part of her wanted to just keep going, as Mildred always had, forget the past. It did no good to dwell. But when she was being especially uncharitable to herself she knew she was a coward, afraid that she too might be targeted by men with axes to grind. She licked her lips, her fingers hovering over the keyboard. Then she took one last look at her granddaughter's picture. Was it wrong to want to be around to watch her grow, become a mother, a grandmother, should Mildred be so lucky? No, it wasn't wrong. It was smart. She shrugged off the tension that had settled in her neck and upper back. For the first time in days, she felt a weight lift from her shoulders. She'd been right to hang up. Had been right to go on with her life. Had been right to choose her family over a ghost from her past. Even so, she said a quick prayer of remembrance for her friend. And she prayed for Mabel's family that they always remain safe and happy.

Thirty-Seven

Several days had passed since Ryan's accident. Although he had called Tracy daily, he still seemed tired and weak. Since then, Tracy had been out on three calls, all of which would help pay her mortgage . . . for now. It had given her a chance to show Kima the ropes. Today, as she drove into the driveway after a surprise C-section she'd performed at one of the neighboring farms, she idled the engine and turned to Kima.

"I'm going to run over to the ranch to check on Ryan. His stitches aren't due out for a couple of days."

Bryce had been replaced with Jason, who had brought a pair of dogs with him for training.

"Maybe you could help Jason with the dogs."

Kima brightened at that. She had met Jason only briefly before they'd left for the C-section, but they'd gotten on well, almost too well. Tracy had seen the sparks between them, and although Kima was nearing her eighteenth birthday, she had several months to go. Whereas Jason was twenty-three. Not a huge age difference, Tracy conceded, but enough to cause problems should they become chummy too quickly.

"You'll look after things?" Tracy said, eyeing Kima carefully, hoping she got the underlying message.

Kima nodded slowly. "I'll be careful," she said, but the gleam in her eyes was hardly convincing.

Against Tracy's better judgment, she left Kima to help with the dogs. In three months time, Tracy would have no say whatsoever. Like any caregiver—albeit temporary—she would just have to hope and pray that Kima could be trusted to make the right decisions.

She thanked Kima for her help with the lamb, then put the truck in reverse and circled around to the driveway, which she'd had graveled the other day. Now, instead of dipping into ruts, her wheels spewed tiny pellets of rock behind her, her tires crunching into gravel as she drove the length of the driveway. Ever since the day her brakes had been tampered with, she'd been fastidious about checking them before she went anywhere.

As she turned onto the main road, she noticed the seasons changing. Fall was just around the corner, and thankfully everyone's hard work had paid off. Her dilapidated farmhouse thrilled her every time she returned home and saw how beautiful it all looked, now that it had been painted and the weathered boards replaced. She would have to tackle the barn next, but at least now she had a place to live that she could be proud of.

The tires hummed as she crossed the valley, the dry ground suddenly springing to life after the deluge they'd had the other day. Everywhere she looked, newly minted green fields stretched as far as the eye could see and the area's first snow in the alpine reaches gave a powder-sugar dusting to the mountaintops that would soon dissolve until the real cold set in, which Kima had assured her would be in no more than a month or so.

At the sight of the ranch, Tracy felt her heart swell. She hadn't realized how much she'd missed Ryan until she saw the ranch and knew he was just moments away. As she neared, she saw Kate on the porch waving, a bowl of something green in her hands.

Kate set the bowl aside, with what appeared to contain green beans, as Tracy exited the truck. "Did you see all the sunflowers on your drive in?"

"Sure did. They were stunning," Tracy said as she ran up the steps and gave her new friend a hug.

"This is my favorite time of year." Kate's cheeks were rosy from exertion and the afternoon heat mixed with just a hint of coolness as summer edged toward fall. "Cold's coming in early this year, according to Wyatt. Says it's due to climate change."

And it's true, the giant oak out front had the beginnings of color, while a dogwood that had been recently planted to the left of the property had leaves that Kate assured her would become jewel tones come fall: red, yellow, green, orange, and even a lovely shade of pink. To top it off, shiny red beads would lace the lower edges of the tree, attracting a whole flock of northern flickers to the edible fruit.

"How's Ryan doing?" Tracy asked, changing the subject.

"See for yourself. He's been dying to get out to your place but I wouldn't let him drive. Not until that bump on his head is cleared up. Maybe you can give us your professional opinion."

"That was the plan," Tracy said with a laugh.

Ryan must have heard them because he came barreling out the screen door and scooped her up in his arms then twirled her around. Without thinking, she kissed him, the kiss mutual with just a hint of cinnamon on his breath. She'd all but forgotten Kate until she heard a clearing of the throat.

"Thanks for coming," he said, his voice husky with emotion.

"Hey, how many times have you been there for me?" Tracy said in return.

He took her hand and squeezed it. In that moment, she felt as if she'd come home, as though in his arms she was where she was meant to be, with the person she was meant to be with.

"Do you mind if I steal Trace away from you for a bit?" Ryan asked, throwing his arm around Tracy.

Kate laughed, but nodded for them to be on their way as she finished snapping beans on the porch. Ryan winked at her to which she said, "You old charmer. Go charm that girl of yours."

A grin lit up his face as he once again grabbed Tracy's hand and began ushering her down the porch.

"What is all this about?" she said.

"You'll see. I've been working on a project."

"What kind of project?" she asked as he propelled her down the dirt road toward the log cabin out back.

"Patience. All will be revealed soon."

The afternoon was alive with birds as the cattle quietly chewed on hay and grass, all the while watching Tracy and Ryan's progress with a disinterested amusement that bordered on entertainment. All the cares of the past few days fell away as Ryan led her to a building off to one side of the drive.

"What is this?" she asked.

"Our foundry. We built it out of old wood we've collected from other torn-down barns. Kate's brother, Craig, runs it. He's pretty darn good at it too. You should see some of his projects. His work is used in lodges, museums, you name it."

He opened the door, and immediately Tracy was assailed with the odors of burned metal and the dank smell of oiled wood. Her eyes took a moment to adjust to the darkened interior, but as dark became light, she saw forms popping out at her from every corner of the space. An egret with part of its copper feathers soldered on, while other feathers remained on the deeply gouged wooden countertop. A giant pair of handcrafted doors stood to one side bearing horses, their manes flowing as they galloped across the imaginary landscape. But possibly her favorite was of a buffalo mounted on several layers of fine mahogany, its mane done in winding strips of soldered wire of every color: silver, copper, even the pale gold armature wire that gave its mane a filigree overlay.

"Those are all Craig's," Ryan explained, introducing him

to Kate's brother.

Tracy took Craig's outstretched hand as he came over to introduce himself. He wasn't much taller than Tracy, his hand nearly black from working with solder and high heat. His hair was nearly the same color, with recent specks of gray filling in at the sides.

"You do amazing work, Craig," Tracy gushed.

Ryan held up his hands. "Don't expect my work to look anything like Craig's. My metal casting isn't nearly as good as his."

"You do metal casting?" Why had he never mentioned it before?

"I wanted to surprise you, to make something for the garden. It's not finished yet."

Craig ducked his head and motioned toward a countertop workspace. "Before you get the idea that Ryan doesn't know what he's doing, take a look at this."

He weaved his way over to the far wall, Tracy following, Ryan not far behind. And there, beside the workbench, stood a dog that looked like the one she'd seen late at night when she'd thought she was dreaming. A sheltie built life-size from an assortment of bits and baubles from leftover equipment. How Ryan had managed to put it all together to resemble a dog was beyond her. But as she glanced further, it dawned on her why he had chosen a dog for his composition. In the fine detail she could see that it was an ode to the dog he'd left behind, and it was true. Despite the fact that it resembled a sheltie, the tag on the dog's collar read Herc. She fought back the tightness in her throat. How could she ever find Herc before the U.S. pulled out of Afghanistan? It was a fool's errand to even try.

"You don't like it," Ryan said, brows knitted together in confusion.

"No, no!" She threw up her hands in protest. "It's not that. It's just the name on the collar." She bit her lip, recognizing Ryan's emotion in his rapid blinking.

Craig could see that they wanted to be alone, so he quickly excused himself as he went to retrieve some materials from the barn.

Tracy took Ryan's hands in hers. "Ryan, it wasn't your fault. You know that." She bent down so that he would look her in the eye. Slowly, he lifted his head, his eyes meeting hers.

"I was a coward!" He snatched his hands away from hers and ran them through his hair. "I should have told my commanding officer he was mine. I should have told him that the dog saved our lives." He began pacing, becoming more and more agitated as he did. "I should have at least stood up for Herc. I mean, what kind of guy leaves a dog behind after he saved our lives? I wouldn't be here today if it weren't for that dog. Then we just send him off through the desert without food or water, except for the little I gave him, and hope he makes it on his own? Heck, most grown men would have a hard time surviving alone in that desert."

"Ryan," Tracy said, taking a seat next to the workbench, "we *all* do something we regret in our lives. Something we should have done, shouldn't have done . . ." She couldn't finish the sentence. "But you've got to believe that things work out, eventually. Maybe not the way we plan them. And maybe

334

we can only pay it forward. I don't know. I just know that most of us would be stuck forever if we didn't try to forgive ourselves."

He stopped pacing, his face bearing the strain of his remorse.

"None of us is perfect," she added.

She stood to face him. In that moment, a spark of understanding passed between them and she leaned in just as he leaned down to kiss her. It was the balm that she needed for the remorse that *she* felt over the loss of her horse. She'd thought that putting distance between the past and the present might change things, but it hadn't. Now, in the arms of a man she'd known only a short time, she'd found solace, peace. For the moment, anyway. She pulled away, the lingering scent of him still on her lips. She'd never felt so instantly connected with anyone the way she had Ryan. It's as if he'd reached into her soul and recognized the real her. Loved her for what she was, rather than for what she wasn't. And she wasn't perfect. She would never be perfect. Furthermore, she was tired of trying.

"Thank you for that," Ryan said, running his hand along her cheek. "I've had a hard time letting go."

Oh, how she understood his plight.

"Can you stay long?" he asked.

"For a bit. Then I need to get back to the farm and check on Kima and Jason."

"Oh? Did you ever find the wolf?"

Tracy shook her head. "If one of the ranchers finds her, she'll be culled. We've tried looking for her but my tracking skills aren't that well honed."

"And wolves are notoriously wary of people, for good reason." Ryan grabbed her hand and led her out of the foundry.

He walked her down a dirt road that led alongside the large log cabin, a burbling stream on the other side, a small kingfisher flicking in and out of the weeds and brush, cottonwood and aspen. Dry leaves were already beginning to swirl around them, fall just a month away, the sweet smell of rotted apples and the moist, earthy smell of algae and fish lending a sense of ease, as though the world had slowed its rotation.

Once they were far enough back that no one could see them, Ryan removed his jacket and laid it on the embankment so they could sit. He eased her back onto the jacket.

"I know it's too early," he said, his eyes scanning hers, "but I want to be with you. For the first time in years, I don't feel lonely anymore. I feel like I have a place with you. I know that sounds stupid."

He peered down, as though afraid to face her, but she cupped his chin and drew him to her. "It isn't stupid, and I feel the same."

He blinked rapidly, then let out a whoop and kissed her. Tracy couldn't help but laugh, the sound mirroring the burbling stream. The next half hour she spent wrapped in Ryan's arms, completely at peace.

She was still reeling by the time she reached the farm with promises from Ryan that he would be by the next day, even if he had to get someone to drive him over. Darkness had just settled over the valley, the moon riding high in the sky. It would soon be a harvest moon. It glowed with a golden hue and loomed larger than normal. The lingering year-round snow on the mountaintops glistened silver in the dusk while an elk bugled in the distance. Tracy breathed in the cool air. Though leaves hadn't yet littered the ground to give off their sweet, earthy scent, the smells of sage and agriculture filled her to the brim with happiness. She wanted to twirl, content for the first time in a long time.

Inside the farmhouse, a warm glow filtered through the windowpanes and she could imagine a Christmas tree bedecked in twinkling lights, a garland of popcorn and cranberries draping the circumference, and bright gold and white bulbs. She planned to drape a cedar garland with holly leaves along the porch railing, maybe put up lights. She hugged herself, hoping she never awoke from the dream she'd created for her life.

Though reluctant to forgo this magical moment, the coolness of the evening finally drove her inside. She opened the door and called Kima's name.

"We're up here," Kima yelled. "In my bedroom."

Kima and Jason upstairs, alone? Tracy's daydream fell to the wayside, as she hurried up the stairs, angry at herself for leaving the pair by themselves so long without supervision. Why were they in Kima's bedroom? She didn't have long to find out as the door stood wide open and Jason and Kima lay on the floor on their stomachs, side by side, going through an old photo album Kima had found.

"Where did you get that?" Tracy asked, kneeling down

beside the pair.

"I found it under some old clothes in the bureau. Look at this."

Kima pointed to a photograph of Mabel and Old Man Grayson. At the time, they were middle-aged, Mabel's hair curled tight against her scalp while Grayson was no longer old and stooped, but a tall man with straight dark hair and thick black-framed glasses. Beside them stood another dog, a different dog. They must not have had the sheltie yet. But what really caught Tracy's eye was a young man in uniform next to a woman in sixties clothing, bell bottoms and a brown and red bohemian blouse.

"Who is the man in uniform?" Tracy asked, frowning. Something about him seemed familiar, but she couldn't place him.

Kima turned the photograph over. "Says it was Amos Grayson and that he had enlisted in the army, headed for Nam."

"Nam." Blake's father? She would have to ask. "And who is the woman?"

Kima turned the photo over again. "His wife, Amy."

Tracy took the photograph from Kima and studied it closely. When she squinted, she could detect Blake in the set of the man's eyes, in height and stature, though if this *was* Blake's father, instead of McDuffy Grayson, he had a wider cheekbone structure and a receding hairline. Next she studied the woman and saw something she hadn't noticed on first inspection. A slight roundness in her midsection. Amy was pregnant. With Blake? And did Amos return home safely?

Another question for Blake.

For the next half hour, they poured over the photographs. Then Jason took his leave, ready to guard the place while they slept. Tracy hoped he'd been able to nod off for a while in the afternoon. She would make sure he got to sleep all day tomorrow to make up for any lost rest.

Tracy stood, stretching her back. "I had better get to bed so I can give him some relief in the morning. See you tomorrow."

Kima smiled. Tracy shut the door behind her and traipsed into her bedroom. Before she climbed in bed, she opened her laptop and checked her email. Her heart stuttered in her chest when she read the headline. "We've found your dog." Tracy quickly clicked into the email and scanned the message. "We've found Herc, but we don't know if we can get him out before the pullout of the troops, which is set to happen in two days time, August 24th. If we don't get him out before that time, it will be next to impossible to retrieve him. In the meantime, please be patient. We are doing our best."

Tracy's emotions ran from high to low in a matter of minutes. They were so close. They had Herc, but could they get him out before the withdrawal? It had been rumored that the ousted president of Afghanistan had fled via helicopter on the 18th . . . and had emptied the treasury when he left, leaving the Afghan troops with nothing to sustain them. If that was true, then Afghanistan stood no chance of standing once the Taliban arrived.

Two days!

Though she needed rest, she knew there would be little

shut-eye now.

Thirty-Eight

Tracy rubbed her eyes, weary from a night of little sleep. She made quick work of bacon, eggs, and toast for the trio, then urged Jason to get some rest. Unfortunately, the way things stood, she would need Kima here, guarding the farm while she went to visit Blake and to tell him what she had learned. Tracy showed Kima the gun she kept, should she need it, then set off for Blake's estate, only after she had checked her brakes to make sure they were working.

The trip over was uneventful whereas the magnificent spread never failed to amaze her. Still, she would take her farm over this sprawling mansion any day. It had a coziness that the mansion did not.

Even before she had stepped out of her truck, one of Blake's men came running toward her to escort her inside. She supposed it was a matter of course for someone of

Blake's stature in Hollywood. Perhaps he feared paparazzi or prying fans. Whatever the reason for such tight security, she found it stifling and knew she wouldn't breathe fully until she left the estate.

Inside the great room, Blake was seated in front of a giant monitor where he was reviewing one of his latest movies. Beside him, a woman who he introduced as his assistant, took notes of changes that would need to be made before the movie could go to the big screen. He scrubbed his hands through his hair, clearly frustrated at the intrusion to his busy day. At last, he clicked pause so that he could give her his full attention.

"Have you found anything?" Blake asked with a harried sigh.

"Before we talk about Mabel, who is Amos?"

Blake cocked a brow and leaned back. "Amos? How do you know about him?"

"Is he your father?" she asked, to which he merely chuckled.

For a second, he took stock of her as if deciding how much to tell her. Finally, he bent forward and steepled his hands beneath his chin.

"Amos was my uncle, my father's brother. He looks a lot like my father. In fact, most people said they could have been twins, only my father was slightly taller than Amos."

"Oh," she said, disappointed. "We found a photo of him and Amy."

"Ah!" Blake said, nodding. "And?"

"He was in the army and Amy . . . well, Amy appeared

342

pregnant."

"And that interests you, why?" Blake couldn't hide the amusement in his voice.

"I just thought that perhaps Amos was your father—"

"And Amy was pregnant with me? No." He shook his head. "Amos was a war hero, got shot down in Nam, when he was being medevaced out. Never made it home to see his child."

Tracy didn't know why that information shocked her, but it did. She didn't know what to say. "And your father?"

Blake scratched the back of his head, his expression wary. "My dad was given a Section 8."

"Translation?"

"It means he was mentally unfit, had a breakdown after Amos died. Took him years to recover. But he was a good dad, a decent man. He helped Amy all he could. Felt guilty because he lived and Amos died."

Tracy licked her lips. So much tragedy for one family. She didn't know what to say except to give her condolences and tell him how sorry she was to hear all that. "If you felt the way you did about your dad, why did you change your name when you went to Hollywood?"

Blake turned to his assistant. "Will you excuse us, Janice?" Then he turned back to Tracy. "Why don't you sit." He scooted over to offer her a seat, then faced her. Once Janice had left the room, he said, "There was a lot of bad blood between my dad and some of the men around here. In their mind, you don't leave the military for any reason, except in a body bag. It's just the way it is."

343

"So they couldn't see past his affliction?"

He shrugged and shook his head.

"And as his child, you were affected by that."

"Pretty much. I was called names. You know. Kids can be cruel."

"Why did you come back then?"

He stood and began pacing, pausing only to stare out of the floor-to-ceiling windows that looked out over the valley and to the mountains beyond, their peaks smattered in snow.

"I've told you before, I'm getting to the age where I could be a grandparent soon, and it didn't sit well not knowing what happened to my grandmother. She was a nice woman. You would have liked her."

Tracy had a feeling she *would* have liked Mabel, had she met her then.

He turned back to her. "The thing about Mabel though, when she caught hold of something, she worried it to the bone. Wouldn't let go. And I think this thing with the oil and sinkholes might have ruffled some very powerful feathers. That and the money owed the Wind River Reservation."

"I did some research and oil's a multi-billion dollar industry here in the valley."

Blake chewed his upper lip, frowning.

"And you want to know whose feathers she ruffled."

Blake nodded, his lips pursed.

"Well, we have a few suspects." She shrugged off her jacket in the stifling heat of the fireplace. "But I'm not sure who will pan out this late in the game."

"Oh? And who is that?" He took a seat in a designer

344

chair opposite her.

"Hank, for one. I found a picture of him at the Lindsay place, standing side-by-side with Lindsay's husband, Gabe, who is in the oil industry as well as ranching."

"Who else?" he asked, tapping his toe on the Brazilian pecan porcelain tile.

"Gladys and Stanford found the man who heads Maarlox. He also is tied to the website where you purchased your hay."

Blake whistled. "Glad I was seated for that one."

She told him about J. D. Beringer, but if Blake knew him, he was holding his cards close to his chest. "And as you know, someone left me a calling card outside J & R Marketing. Warned me to check my brakes from now on. I should have taken him more seriously because I could have ended up in a ditch or dead."

Blake merely shook his head.

Then she told him about Bryce being hit over the head and the wolf being released. "They also let the horses loose at Wyatt's ranch and Ryan was injured. I stitched him up, though you didn't hear it from me."

"Whoa!" he said, breathing deeply. "Do you think we should contact the police? It seems like whoever is involved wants our silence."

"And to let what happened to Mabel go. I think for now, they're simply firing across the bow in warning, but next time we might not be so lucky."

Blake seemed to mull that one over for a while. Then he said, "I didn't mean to involve you in all this. I had no idea it would ever get this far."

"Yeah, well, like it or not, we're all involved. Short of leaving the state, I don't see any way around it. In the meantime, I think we should sit tight. Keep a watch on both our places."

"Do you want me to send one of my men over until all of this blows over?"

Tracy thought about it for a moment. She couldn't keep asking Wyatt to lend her his men. They were needed at the ranch. "I would appreciate that," she said finally, then put on her jacket and stood. She shook his hand and he thanked her for coming. Then he walked her to the door.

As she drove away, she saw that Blake was standing at the open doorway long after, watching her truck recede down the driveway. She hoped she hadn't made a mistake in having him wait before calling the police. It's just that she needed time to grow her practice. And she would never be able to do that if she was called into controversy shortly after her arrival. Better to wait, and to hope that whoever felt threatened would eventually give up their fool's quest. Yet, as long as Blake continued to pursue what happened to his grandmother, there would be no peace. She thought of her own grandmother—of the two of them baking cookies together, or Tracy chattering to her as the older woman ironed. She smiled, remembering. No, she loved her grandmother. She would no more give up on her own grandmother than Blake could on his. In the end, love is love, and how many people would go to the ends of the earth for the ones they loved? Now, more than ever, she understood that, because whether she liked it or not, she was feeling true pangs of tenderness for Ryan. It was too early to say what might happen in the future. For now, it was just wonderful knowing that he was there and that he cared for her.

* * *

Abas kissed the image of his wife and children, then tucked it into the small bag he'd set aside for clothing and important documents. All the rest would be left behind. The news had been spread far and wide that people were lining up at the airport, hoping to be allowed aboard one of the planes leaving for the United States. If he was to survive, he would need to be on one of those planes. He swiveled his head, taking one last look at the only home he'd ever known, a small room downstairs and the two bedrooms upstairs. Everything he owned was here, all except what he'd put in his case and what his wife and children had been able to smuggle out—a portion of their savings and pictures of their ancestors. Only one thing left to do.

He bent down to the dog he'd been tasked to keep. Herc. Though Afghanis didn't view dogs the way Americans did, in this moment, he could almost understand their love for them because Herc was the only living tie to his past, but the dog too would soon be gone. Would disappear into the ever panicking crowd of people to fend for himself among the other dogs that roamed the streets. He said a quick prayer to Allah, and made a mental apology to Rick for going back on his word. Abas simply could wait no longer for Rick to arrive.

If he wanted to save himself, he had to sacrifice the dog and his friendship with Rick, even if it meant that he would no longer receive the meager funds that the GI had sent him to keep the dog safe.

He bent down, sighing heavily. From this point forward, his life would change forever. No longer would he enjoy the safety of Americans. Once the Taliban arrived, Afghanis like himself would wear a target on their back. Oh, the Taliban had made promises to the Americans not to retaliate, but pacts were often broken in times of war and he knew this time might be no exception. A zebra didn't change its stripes nor was it likely the Taliban would honor their agreement. And although he might hope otherwise, experience had taught him well.

"Goodbye, my friend. I must release you now. Pray to Allah that you find shelter and food. Safety." Yet, as he spoke, he knew he was saying it as much for himself as for Herc.

The dog's tongue lolled, and although one might take it for a smile, Abas had come to recognize the animal's nature and saw the tension in the squint of his eyes. The dog knew he was being set free to the whims of nature and a war-torn country. How a dog could comprehend this, Abas didn't know. But dogs were smarter than he'd given them credit for in the past.

Abas bent down and did something he'd never done before. He hugged the dog as he would a man and patted his head, looking into the big beast's trusting eyes. "You and me, our futures are unwritten. Pray Allah we both survive and thrive."

Then, with moist eyes, he opened the door. Herc looked up at him for one last, lingering time that told of his sorrow. A goodbye. Abas's jaw quivered. They were both being thrust into a world of unknowns. Finally, the dog walked slowly toward the open door and together they plunged into the melee of a world upended.

Thirty-Nine

When Tracy arrived home, Kima was in the fenced area out back putting the young dogs through their paces. She had a command of animals that Tracy had never witnessed before. She had the dogs sitting, following scents, even climbing up, over, and around obstacles.

"How did you learn that?" Tracy asked, amazed.

Kima shrugged. "Dogs," she said simply. "They're everywhere on our reservation. When I cut school, I would go out back and train the dogs. They like it, as long as you don't beat them. Not that I would." Again, she shrugged.

Tracy wondered at the statement but thought better of asking. "Maybe we should have you training the dogs," she said, only half in jest.

"Okay," Kima said, the slightest smile alighting her face.

Tracy had come to learn that Kima didn't smile much.

She wasn't sure if it simply wasn't in her nature or something to do with her heritage, but she felt it impolite to ask.

"Okay, then. I'm going inside to fix lunch. I'll call you when it's ready."

She went indoors, but decided to check her email first. In only two days, the evacuation in Afghanistan would begin. Two days to get the dog out. But when she sat in front of her computer and opened her emails, her heart sank.

"So sorry to bring bad news, but Herc is gone. The house where he was being kept has been evacuated. We don't know yet whether the dog went with the owner or was set free. We have someone searching for him now, but I have to be honest, Tracy. The odds are not good that we will be able to find him and rescue him before the country falls into Taliban hands. I'm so sorry."

Tracy fell back in her seat, warm tears stinging her eyes. She didn't know why the news had hit her so hard, but it had. Ryan would never get his dog back, would always carry that guilt just as she did. Now, she would never be able to redeem herself. The die was cast and she had lost.

* * *

Ryan set about welding pieces of the pooch he'd begun designing for Tracy's front yard. When he pictured her home, he imagined himself in it, husband and wife. It was the image he'd set out for himself in the years since he'd left home—had gone off to war. Forever wishing for something solid, stable. Something he could trust. Whenever he thought of Tracy, he

knew she was *the one*–the one he'd been waiting for his entire
life. Someone who wouldn't let him down the way his mother
had countless times with all her drug-addled boyfriends.

He peered through his welder's helmet, heard the sparks,
the smell of burning metal. It was like his life. He'd been
through fire, had all the scars to prove it, and had somehow
transformed like this dog he'd named Herc so that he would
never forget the mutt he'd left behind. As the torch sizzled
and popped, his thoughts flashed back to that moment, the
firefight, the dog barking just moments before the rockets
were launched. It bought his men precious seconds to
scramble away from camp, to save themselves. If not for Herc,
everyone in the entire platoon might have perished that night.

Until too late, he didn't realize his whole body was
trembling, or that he had broken into a profuse sweat, unable
to breathe. He switched the arc welder off and yanked off
the helmet, gulping in great bursts of air. Craig saw him and
came running. He guided him to a metal chair beside the
workbench and urged him to sit.

"Flashback?" he said, used to this sort of thing by now,
having had many himself.

Ryan closed his eyes, could only nod, his chest burning
and in need of oxygen. Craig grabbed a paper bag and made
him open his eyes, then told him to breathe into it. After
several moments, Ryan's breathing returned to normal and he
set the bag down.

"You were having a panic attack," Craig said. "Been
there, done that."

He laughed, making light of it, but Ryan knew Craig

was only trying to help him save face. Ryan attempted a weak smile.

"You're back," Craig said.

Like Ryan, Craig knew the despair that could engulf a vet. Anything could trigger it. Often, it came on so fast, so hot and heavy, that all Ryan could do was to hang on for dear life. Hope he could maintain a grip on his sanity. Fortunately, Craig had been there to help him. *This time.* Next time Ryan might not be so lucky. What if it happened while he'd been driving? He'd had a few episodes like that, but always he'd been able to steer over to the side of the road and cut the engine until he could get a grip. But who knew how long his luck would hold out?

"You okay, bud?"

Ryan shook his head, still too traumatized to speak.

"How about you sit a spell, then I'll get us something to eat while you clear your head. That alright with you?"

Ryan nodded, grateful to his friend for being there when he'd needed him. That's what made this place so special. They all helped each other when things went haywire. While Craig left to pick up lunch from Emajean's kitchen, Ryan once again thought of Tracy. Who was he kidding? She got a whiff of one too many of these episodes and she'd be running for the hills. And wait until she got a load of his mother and all *her* baggage. He snorted, his chest still painful from the earlier lack of oxygen. He wanted so badly for Tracy to love him, to want to stick by him. Why couldn't he be normal like other guys? He buried his face in his hands and balled his fists. But he knew the answer. Because other men didn't watch their friends die in far off lands, see limbs blown off and carry the what-ifs around like body bags.

* * *

Gladys watched Stanford peer through the slats of the office blinds, staring out at the passersby as he did most slow days, and today was an especially boring day. So far, he'd done nothing but sip on his latte, making comments about nearly every person who passed by on the boardwalk.

"Don't you have anything to do, like clean out the bathrooms or something?"

Stanford turned and grimaced at Gladys at the idea of him "mucking out stalls," as he called it, an odious job apparently by the sour expression on his face.

"Well, someone has to do it," she said with a lifted brow.

"Well, that someone is not going to be me, missy." He lifted both brows and nodded in a touché meant to sting. He turned back to the slats, head bobbing back and forth to get a better look at the parade of people marching past. "That woman wears her heels too high. How much you wanna bet she has bunions by the time she's forty."

"Oh, please." And yet Gladys wore sensible shoes—always had, always would. No ankle breakers for her.

"Ooh!" Stanford said, snickering. "Lady Chatterley has a lover."

"What are you talking about?" Gladys stood and walked over to the blinds to see for herself.

There, in full view, was a man and woman in a tight embrace, kissing. Gladys elbowed Stanford. "Step away from

354

the window," she said, not even bothering to hide the disdain in her voice. But just as she pulled on his sleeve, she caught sight of someone off to the right, a little. J. D. Beringer, the man who ran Maarlox. But what drew her attention most was the man next to him. The man he was speaking to was unusually large. He reminded Gladys of a wrestler and even wore a silver loop in his ear. The pair were deep in conversation.

Before she could utter the words to Stanford, he leaned in and said, "Who do you suppose the big bald dude is? He reminds me of a bouncer I once met. Kinda scary looking, don't you think?"

"A bouncer?" Gladys said, her eyes glued to the pair. "What were you doing with a bouncer?"

"Don't ask," Stanford answered, one eyebrow lifted.

The guy gave her the willies. Why was J. D. meeting with a man like that, and what did it have to do with Mabel? She didn't know, but she planned to find out.

Forty

The phone rang and rang. Tracy raced to pick it up
before the caller on the other end of the line could hang up.
*Who knows? It could be another house call, another job to help pay
the mortgage.* She answered the phone only to discover a man
wanting to look at the Studebaker. For a moment, his words
didn't register, she'd been so caught up with all her recent
dilemmas. Esa was still missing. And somewhere out there
was a man—or woman—willing to kill to silence the past. Worse
still, she had sunk all of her money into finding Ryan's dog,
Herc, only to learn that the dog was gone, along with her
money—$3000 so far and counting. At least if she sold the
Studebaker, she could recoup some of her losses. One bright
point in her day, Ryan was on the mend and had called to
say he was coming over with a surprise. She had a feeling she
knew what it was, but she would let him keep his surprise, for

now.

"This is Ollie and my wife, Freda," the caller said. "We live just a couple of miles north of you. Can we come take a look at the Studebaker?"

"Of course," she said.

Twenty minutes later, a man with scraggly white hair and a large paunch pulled up with a flatbed and a wench, ready to haul the car away, his wife at his side. For the first time in days, Tracy felt the weight of her worries melt away. If she could sell the car, she would be back in business.

For the next half hour, the man examined the vehicle from every angle, going so far as to inspect the glove compartment. "I belong to the local car club," he explained. "I'm looking for a new project."

His wife had come along for the ride. "Don't let him fool you, he has projects all over the place. His barn looks a lot like Grayson's."

Tracy chuckled. "Seems to be a trend."

Finally, the negotiating began in earnest. Eventually, they struck a deal at $5500. Not ideal, but perhaps since the Operation Pup Rescue team hadn't been able to locate Herc, the costs would at least stay at the $3000 mark that she'd already put into the search. Plus the $135 donation that the center had received on Herc's behalf. And then there was the GoFundMe account, which was up to $650. At least that was something. Still, she moaned inwardly at all the costs going out since she'd arrived. The thought depressed her. Here she had hoped to do something that she could be proud of, and it had backfired. Tracy just had to accept that she had

357

done what she could for Herc and Ryan. Determined not to keep beating herself up over it, she motioned to Ollie, who had climbed into his truck and was backing toward the Studebaker.

He inched his flatbed toward the vehicle until Tracy called, "There. Stop!" She stood to the side as her neighbor loaded the Studebaker onto the back of the flatbed. Freda came to stand beside her and they watched as the wench hummed.

"Did you hear the news?" Freda's eyes were trained on the Studebaker and she gave her husband directions by signaling with her hands.

"News?" Tracy frowned, still kept out of the loop of most of the valley's rumor mill.

"Yeah, Lindsay and her husband, Gabe, finally found that wolf. Shot it last night. That's one less wolf to bother the sheep."

Stunned, Tracy opened her mouth but couldn't put words to her feelings. Before she could speak, Freda yelled to her husband, who had just finished loading, to wait up. "It was good meeting you."

Ollie came over and handed Tracy a check. Then they jumped into the cab and yelled their goodbyes, all the while waving farewell.

Kima heard the commotion and exited the house onto the porch. How could Tracy tell Kima that her wolf may have been put down? The Mitchells wouldn't have cared whether it was Kima's wolf that had killed their sheep. Any wolf would have sufficed. And yet Tracy couldn't be certain it *was* Kima's wolf, Esa, that had been killed. She decided to wait. Maybe, just maybe, Esa would return on her own. Tracy knew it was a longshot, but she had to hold out hope.

She walked up onto the porch just as Ryan's pup scurried out of the house, Jason trailing behind him. Before he could stop Parker, the dog had sprinted toward the barn. Jason went galloping after, his words floating through the warm summer breeze.

"Darned dog. He's obsessed with that barn."

* * *

Ryan couldn't wait to bring Tracy his finished project. Even Craig had been impressed by how well the sheltie had turned out. With the help of Craig, Ryan had put it in the back of his cab, careful to lock his truck up as he stopped in town to buy some bags of cement and bolts to hold the sculpture in place. The last time he had been to Tracy's house, he'd found a perfect spot for the statue in the middle of her garden. It would be both a tribute to Herc, and a tribute to Old Man Grayson and his dog.

He entered the hardware store and purchased his supplies. He'd done some heavy thinking about Tracy and him since last night. The flashback had really thrown him, but he had talked to Craig who had offered him sound advice.

"Look, Ryan," he'd said over sandwiches and cookies, "this Tracy might be more resilient than you give her credit for. She knows you're a veteran—that you've been in Afghanistan. I mean, think about it. Anyone who deals with

359

large animals like she does is no shrinking violet. She knows the score. Don't you think she would have bailed before now if she was going to?"

Ryan thought it over, and he supposed he could give her that, that she might not bail just because of his flashbacks, but what about his family, if you could call it that? A mother who did drugs, who brought all sorts of unsavory characters into his life. And he had half-brothers and half-sisters. That was a lot more baggage than most women wanted to take on. He tried to explain it to Craig.

"At least give her a chance, man. You're counting her out before she's even allowed to decide for herself."

So, Ryan had packed up his sculpture and had decided to make it official. He was going to lay his cards on the table, let her know what she was getting herself into by being with him and then straight out ask her if she wanted to marry him. It had taken real courage to get this far. Yet as he paid for the items, then drove the cart out to load his supplies in the truck, his courage began to flag.

Frustrated and unsure of himself, he came around the front of the jeep. He was just about to climb in when he saw a folded piece of paper beneath his wiper blades and lifted it off. Darned people, always trying to sell this or that. He opened the paper and read, his eyes widening and his heart picking up the pace as he lingered on the words, "What do you really know about the new veterinarian?" A newsline attached read: "Woman brought up on charges for reckless endangerment resulting in death." Ryan's skin crawled at the words. Death of what, or of whom? Why hadn't Tracy told him any of this? What *did* he know about her, truly?

His jeep loaded, he climbed into the cab and started it up, then put it in reverse. Which way should he go? To Tracy's or back to the ranch? He put in the clutch and headed north.

* * *

Gabe felt history repeating itself. Why did Blake have to move back to town? Furthermore, why did that busy-body vet keep poking her nose into things that were none of her concern? He tamped out his pipe into the wastebasket beside his desk, wondering what to do next. For years, he had managed to put the past behind him, to keep moving forward with one eye over his shoulder. He plopped down into his desk chair and swiveled around to face the pasture. So much of his life had been spent in oil. Now, that was behind him. Retirement had been everything he'd imagined and more. More time to pursue the things that interested him. Farming, hunting, fishing. More time with his wife and grandchildren. He'd had it all. How many people could say that about their lives? He watched the sheep frolicking out his window, a quiet settling over him.

"You okay in there, honey?" his wife said, bringing him lunch as she did every day at this time.

"Yeah." He took stock of his wife, Lindsay. The bloom of youth had faded, but she still had a spark that lit her from within. He reached for his sandwich. He hadn't always been the best husband, what with work taking up such a huge

361

chunk of his time each day. And truth be told, he hadn't realized how much he loved her until he'd had time to be with her, to appreciate what he'd seen in her when he first proposed some forty plus years ago.

"Penny for your thoughts."

For a moment, he hesitated. Then he reached for her hand and held it, gazing into her eyes and really looking at her as he hadn't in years. "I just want to let you know how much I love you," he said, stroking the side of her face.

"What's brought all this on?" she asked, her head cocked to one side in a quizzical expression.

He hesitated once more, then merely shook his head and smiled. "We've had a good life, haven't we?"

She chuckled until she realized he'd meant it as a serious question. "Of course. Why do you ask?"

"No reason," he said. "No reason at all." Then he bit down on his sandwich and chewed, his thoughts on all that he stood to lose. This was his heart and soul, this ranch, the animals, his wife. He had difficulty swallowing, his throat choked with emotion. How much longer would he have it all . . . before his life changed forever?

Forty-One

Rick walked the streets of Kabul, searching for the safehouse and Abas. For Herc. Tension settled over him just as it had Kabul and the surrounding countryside as word grew that the withdrawal was to go through. Today, people were lining up at the airport, along sewage ditches, anywhere close to where the airplanes would land and take off, hoping to be one of the lucky ones to be evacuated out. Now, as he searched in vain for Abas, turmoil engulfed him in a swirl of emotion reflected in the streets of the city: horns honking, people shouting, donkeys braying, dogs barking—all of it jangling his already frayed nerves. He had one day left to get Herc on that plane. Not to America, as he had hoped, but to the UK where a former British pilot, assigned to Afghanistan, ran a dog rescue program, funded mostly by a few kind donors.

Rick inhaled the traffic smog, the smell of embers burning as stalls sold what wares remained ahead of the onslaught. Once the Taliban arrived, who knew what would happen, but if history were any indicator, their arrival could prove disastrous, their atrocities legend.

His eyes lit up when he saw through the rush of people fleeing that he was on the right road. He counted the units until he reached Abas' house. Six doors down, on the left. But when he arrived at his destination and saw that the door swung wide open, litter already infiltrating the corners of the main room, he knew he was too late. His heart sank and for one brief moment, he gave in to pity. But wasn't he the one who always chided the men from his platoon to save the pity party for later, to just get on with things? He grabbed the doorjamb and took one brief breath of the many odors that assailed his senses. Green cardamom, turmeric, and cumin– all flavors of Afghanistan. All evidence of a home once lived in.

Refusing to give in to self-doubt, he turned and began to search the narrow alleyway. Fortunately, some houses remained occupied. One by one, he knocked on doors. Some residents were too fearful to answer, whereas others opened their doors just enough to get a look at who was knocking. The first of these slammed the door in his face when he saw that Rick was an American, but on his third try he was able to speak with a young man who was familiar with Americans and therefore agreed to speak only long enough to say that Abas had sent his family abroad and had left for the airport to stand in a miles-long line with the others fleeing the war-torn country.

"Do you know what he did with his dog, Herc?"

The rail-thin man frowned and shook his head, then pointed to a house two doors down. "Aleem was a friend of the family. Perhaps he knows." Then he closed his door to Rick with the words "*Allah hafiz*"—may God protect you.

Rick paused only a moment before pushing his way through the throng of people to the door of Abas's friend.

To Rick's surprise, just as he lifted his hand to knock, the door flung open and a man who Rick assumed was Aleem exited with a single suitcase, his wife and children at his heels.

"Who are you?" the man demanded, the whites of his eyes a halo around his pupils and his breathing labored.

"I'm looking for Abas."

"He's gone," Aleem said, attempting to push past him.

"I know," Rick said. "I'm actually trying to find his dog, Herc."

"Herc?" The words didn't seem to register. Aleem's eyes went blank, so focused was he on escape.

"Yes, the dog is gone. Did Abas take it with him?"

Aleem drew his head back as though Rick had gone crazy. "Of course not," he said, his bushy eyebrows lowering over deep-set eyes, darkened circles beneath them. "The dog can fend for itself like all the other dogs."

Rick grabbed Aleem's arm, his eyes cascading over the long white top and vest, the loose white pants and sandals. Aleem let out a stream of Afghani words that reminded Rick that he was not in America and that he was treading on dangerous territory. He let loose of the man, panting now.

"Sorry," he said. "I don't know what got into me. Where do the dogs go when they're set free?"

Aleem shrugged, the expression on his face conveying to Rick that a dog's welfare was no concern of his. "Where all dogs go, I suppose. Where they will find food and water."

"And where is that?" Rick asked, maintaining control of his anger as best he could under the circumstances.

"The market, most likely. They sometimes have running water, but the water is full of disease."

Rick didn't wait to hear more. He nodded his thanks then took off running, pushing and shoving his way through the crowd, all the while calling Herc's name. He had until morning to locate the dog. That would be the Brit's last flight in. If he couldn't find Herc by then, the dog would have to survive on his own. A lump formed at the back of his throat.

"Where are you, Herc? Where in God's name are you?"

* * *

Something must have gone wrong. Ryan had yet to arrive, even though he'd set out for Tracy's house hours ago. Then Jason had been called away. He'd made apologies, but even as he'd offered them, she knew something was wrong. That he wasn't telling her something. Then one of Blake's security men had arrived as planned and she'd taken an instant dislike to him. He stood well over six-feet tall, had broad shoulders like a wrestler, and sported a bald head. But what bothered her most was the stern set of his jaw and his cold marble brown eyes that seemed to appraise both her and Kima, only to find them lacking in more ways than one. No way could

366

she leave Kima alone with this stranger, but she needed to find out what was going on with Ryan. Why hadn't he called to say he wouldn't be coming? Furthermore, why had Jason been ordered to return to the ranch without explanation?

Although she abhorred the idea of leaving a complete stranger alone at the farm after all the work she and the others had put into it, she had to get to the bottom of what was going on with Ryan.

"We'll be back as soon as possible," she told the man who'd introduced himself as Peter Flanagan. "Hold down the fort. And if you have any problems, call me, okay?"

He muttered something unintelligible, something that came out as a growl. She sighed. She would just have to hope and pray he would take care of the place until she returned. As per her custom these past few days, she checked her brakes and was relieved when they held tight.

The ride to the ranch seemed interminable. Plus the guilt of keeping the wolf's death a secret weighed heavily on Tracy. She knew she couldn't keep quiet forever. News like that would circulate through a town this size. With a whisper of anxiety, she peered over at Kima who seemed just as troubled as Tracy over Jason's hurried departure.

"Kima, there's something I need to tell you."

As often occurred with Kima, she didn't respond. She merely waited for Tracy to speak.

"Esa? Your wolf?"

Kima's face went still, but her eyes registered alarm.

"A wolf was shot over at the Mitchell place."

Kima flinched as though she'd been physically assaulted,

but still she didn't speak.

"We don't know if it's Esa. It could be any wolf," Tracy was quick to add.

For a moment, Kima's bottom lip quivered. Finally, she said, "Most wolves live in Yellowstone. Few wolves live in the valley."

Tracy knew she was right. Except for a few stragglers, wolves had long since been hunted out by ranchers, which is why Yellowstone had decided to reintroduce the gray wolves to the park. But she also knew that a wolf had attacked one of Lindsay's ewes. That meant that at least two wolves made the valley their territory. It also meant a fifty-fifty chance that Esa was still alive.

Tracy reached for Kima's hand. The girl took it, her grip light, as was customary in her tribe and many like it, according to Emajean.

"I promise we'll get to the bottom of this. When we're done talking to Ryan, we'll go to the Lindsay farm and find out if it was Esa or another wolf, okay?"

Kima nodded, but faint tears brushed her cheeks.

Just then, the ranch came into view. Tracy took in the sprawling ranch, the barn and stables that bordered the Sawtooths, as she turned into the gravel driveway. Although it was nothing like Blake's place, she actually preferred it, the gardens, the huge log cabin out back with the koi ponds and bunkhouse. But today, as soft cotton clouds billowed above it in the cerulean sky, she felt untethered like a balloon about to float away. Why had Ryan called to say he was coming over, only to never show up without a word of explanation? She kneaded the steering wheel, determined to get to the bottom of this.

As Tracy pulled up in front of the farmhouse, Kate came rambling out on the porch, Emajean at her side. Even before Tracy stepped out of the truck, she could see that Kate had something on her mind.

"Emajean, could you take Kima into the house, give her a snack?" Kate asked, stepping aside to allow Kima and Tracy to ascend the steps.

Emajean nodded and turned to Kima, speaking in her Shoshone tongue. According to Emajean, the Lakota and the Shoshone tribes had been enemies in centuries past, but the Resettlement Act and the removal of Indian children into American Indian boarding schools had made fast friends of former enemies. The decree that the children speak only English had ensured the severance of ties from their parents and grandparents who spoke no English whatsoever. Without a shared language, the children were left with neither tribe nor country. Simply adrift in a foreign land. The genocide of a culture complete.

Emajean, who had been spared Tracy's musings, turned to Kima and in English said, "I just made an apple pie with huckleberry ice cream."

The pair clucked like two old hens as they opened the screen door and went inside, the door slamming behind them with a rusty squeal of the hinges. Once they were gone, Kate turned to Tracy, her mouth pinched, and said, "Come, sit." She pointed to the porch swing.

Uh-oh. Tracy's heart stammered in her chest. She hadn't

felt this way since she'd been called to the principal's office in high school after a classmate offered her a drag of her cigarette in the bathroom. Though she hadn't taken a drag, it had been hard to prove otherwise since the monitor found her knocking the cigarette to the ground and grinding it out with her shoe.

"What's this all about?" Tracy demanded.

Kate took a seat beside her, her expression serious but with all the usual empathy that she normally showed Tracy. As they sat there, a car drove by that looked as if it had just been through a whirlwind. It was covered in dust, half the paint long since gone, and the woman and man inside were an unsavory blend of characters that Tracy would have half-expected to see in downtown Seattle, in the skid row area. She noticed Kate watching the pair too, her eyes wary.

She turned to face Tracy. "Ryan was on his way to your house."

"I know," Tracy said, feeling small suddenly. "He was supposed to be there hours ago."

"He decided not to come," Kate explained, hesitance straining her words.

"But why?" Tracy rocked in the swing, the normally comforting swoosh now only a screech that needed oiling.

"Maybe this will explain it." Kate held out a note and a piece of the newspaper that had been clipped out of *The Seattle Times,* an apology written in her expression.

Tracy's heart sank when she saw what was written there. She closed her eyes, feeling as though she might faint. So, her past had caught up with her. But this made her out to be worse than she was, as if she were a killer rather than someone who had used poor judgment as a teen.

"This isn't what it seems," she said, her mouth suddenly dry. "It was an accident." She proceeded to tell Kate about the horse, the graduation ride, the snow. One moment of carelessness had led to a lifetime of grief.

"Oh, Tracy." Kate bent over and hugged Tracy. "I knew there had to be some easy explanation. I'm usually a good judge of character and the truth is I like you, and you're good for Ryan."

A rush of relief washed over Tracy. "But what about Ryan? How do you think he'll feel when I talk to him? And what if he doesn't believe me?"

"Well," Kate said with a glint in her green eyes, "then we'll just prove it to him." She dipped her chin. "Let's walk out to the bunkhouse and speak to him."

Tracy steeled herself for what lay ahead. Fortunately, Kate's intuition about Tracy had helped her see the truth for what it was, but would Ryan? According to Kate, he had a lot of trust issues because of his mother.

"Where are you two headed?" Wyatt asked as he stepped out onto the porch.

"To see Ryan," Kate shot back over her shoulder. "We'll be back in a while."

Wyatt just grinned, clearly used to Kate taking charge when it came to the social aspect of the men.

The sun felt warm, the earlier heat of August giving way to a respite of cooler weather that hinted at fall. The smell of ripened blackberries lent a trace of sweetness to the air and the breeze off the babbling brook that ran beside the property smelled of fish and algae, a somewhat pleasant odor.

"What do you think Ryan will do when I tell him?" Tracy fretted.

"Only one way to find out, and that's to talk to him. What do you have to lose?"

Tracy wanted to say, "A lot." She had already lost most of her friends after the terrible incident with her horse. Part of that was self-inflicted. The newspaper article and the news story that filled the nightly airwaves had sent her into hiding. Afterward, she had drowned herself in work, refusing to meet or talk with anyone, despite the many times she had been ambushed in order to keep the media grist mill going. It had taken months before the news had died down and she was no longer front page headlines. She prayed that Ryan wouldn't shut her out, not now when they were finally connecting on a deeper level. He was the first person she had allowed in, really *in*, to the sheltered world she had so carefully crafted for herself.

As they neared the bunkhouse, she could hear shouting and name calling and saw the scroungy woman and man standing at the doorway to the bunkhouse. "After all the years I've raised you. I could have kicked you out like I did your half-brother. And now you can't lend your mother a measly six hundred bucks to see me through a difficult month?"

"All your months are difficult, Ma."

Tracy heard Ryan's voice from inside the bunkhouse. The shock of learning that this was his mother—the stringy haired woman with a deep voice from smoking too many cigarettes—

brought her crashing to a halt.

"You'll just spend it on drugs or your boyfriend. That's what you do. That's what you always do. Besides, you were never there for me. Your boyfriends raised me while you were out at the bar. You're a user."

The woman shoved her way inside followed by a resounding slap. Then she turned on her heels and came rushing outside telling her boyfriend to get in the car. "We're leaving!" she growled.

Seconds later the woman started up the engine, put the car into gear and squealed in a circle, nearly running Tracy and Kate over before racing down the driveway, spitting gravel in her wake.

Ryan came to the door, holding his reddened cheek where his mother had slapped him. He prepared to slam the door shut when he registered Tracy and Kate standing there watching. His eyes widened and his mouth fell open. "Tracy!" He shook his head as if to dispel her image. "What are you doing here?" he asked, his face pale, his jaw trembling with rage and embarrassment that she'd had to witness such an ordeal.

"Are you okay?" Tracy asked.

"I'm going to leave you two alone," Kate said, "but Ryan?"

"Huh?" he said, his eyes never leaving Tracy's.

"I want you to listen to what Tracy has to say. Promise me."

His eyes darted to Kate for only a second before returning to Tracy, but he said okay.

"And Tracy?"

Tracy turned only infinitesimally, her gaze on Ryan.

"Ryan's a good man. He's had a lot to overcome, but there's one thing I know because I can see it in both your eyes." Tracy swallowed down the raw ache in her throat. "You two are perfect for each other. I know it, and every other person on this ranch knows it. You bring out the best in each other. So try to get past—" Here she made a wide sweep of her hands to encompass everything that had transpired. "—all this stuff." With that, she turned and stormed down the road.

Forty-Two

"Look," Ryan started as he stood awkwardly in front of the bunkhouse facing Tracy, Parker at his side. "Kate's intentions are good, but she has no business giving advice to me or anyone else on this property. My business is my own. I'm sorry you had to witness that," he added pointing in the direction of his mother's departing jalopy.

"It's—" Tracy tried to speak but nothing came out.

Ryan refused to be railroaded. His mother had been doing it her entire life, always playing the guilt card on him as though he owed her for having given him life and not much else. "I have nothing to say to you. Who are you, anyway? A murderer? Is that why you came all the way to Wyoming, so that no one would know about your past?"

"No, Ryan, listen."

"No, you listen," he said, taking her by the arm.

"I wanted someone who's not like her." He jutted a finger toward the road, a hot anger settling in the pit of his stomach refusing to be dislodged. "I wanted a real woman. Not someone like my mom, a liar. I thought that you . . ." He bent his head, unable to continue for fear of revealing too much emotion.

"Thought what, Ryan? What did you think?"

He gazed up at her, no longer afraid to let his tears show. She didn't deserve the right to pity him. He pitied *her*.

"I thought you were different. I thought . . . well, that maybe the farm would be *our* farm, that maybe we could be a team. But you're a user just like the rest, so long as I'm fixing up your place, right?"

"No, Ryan, you have it all wrong."

Ryan gave a snort of disgust. "You needed someone to paint the house, to fix the floorboards, to make the place liveable while your naive lackey falls into place, isn't that true?" He shook his head. "You may be pretty, and you may be from the city, but you're just like my mother and I want nothing to do with you."

Tracy grabbed his shirt. "It's not like that. It never has been. I have been so lonely for so long."

The words held a breathiness that he hadn't heard before when she spoke, a desperation that spoke of words unsaid, tears unshed.

"I didn't murder anyone," she added. "You have to believe me. I'm not that kind of person. I made a mistake. A foolish mistake, and I've paid for it for years. You don't think I haven't beaten myself up almost every night over that one mistake?"

Tears flooded her eyes as she released him, then pounded on her chest with her fist. "I've regretted that day ever since."

"Regretted what? What have you regretted?"

Her eyes appeared haunted, her expression dissolving into grief so profound that it set Ryan aback.

"I did something stupid, Ryan. Me and my friends—we were celebrating our high school graduation. We took our horses up to Gros Peak. It was supposed to be a fun outing . . . a celebration. But I was an idiot."

Here her knees buckled. To his surprise, he reached for her, wrapped her in his arms and cradled her before she collapsed completely. "What did you do?"

"I ran my horse across an ice field instead of taking the long way around," she sobbed, her hands balled in fists, tears streaming down her cheeks, her throat thick with emotion. "He fell, Ryan. Over an embankment. I couldn't save him. It was my fault!" She pounded her fists against his chest, her voice a wail. For the next twenty minutes, she poured out her grief, leaving out nothing.

"It was an accident, Tracy. We all make mistakes." And in that moment, he knew it was true. "You don't think I haven't stayed up nights replaying that day I set Herc loose in the mountains? The day I betrayed the dog that saved my life and the lives of my friends?"

"Yeah, but did everyone you ever knew or loved shun you, Ryan?" Tracy asked, her voice thick with emotion. "Did everyone act like you had some terminal disease? Refuse to be near you?" She looked into his eyes as though searching for the answer. Then she seemed to turn inward, her eyes shuttered against the pain. "After that, I shut myself off from everyone. Worse yet, I was so traumatized, I couldn't even cry." She gave a soft, self-deprecating laugh, the sound moistened by sorrow.

He could see it in her eyes, and realized that she had the same haunted expression he did when he awoke in the middle of the night and went into the bathroom to run cold water over his face in an attempt to shake the memories. But they grabbed hold of him like a lasso, pulling ever tighter around his midsection.

"So maybe we understand each other?" he said, amazed at this turn of events.

She shook her head, her face blotchy, her eyes red from the tears. His heart swelled as he drew her once again to his chest and hugged her. Maybe, just maybe, his adult life didn't have to match his childhood. Maybe his life could change for the better if he would just open the door to her . . . a little.

The door!

A catch formed in his throat as he pushed her away from him and turned. "Parker? Parker, are you there?" *Nothing.* "I left the door open." He grabbed her hand and pulled her into the bunkhouse which was empty, the men all out doing ranch chores. Frantically, they combed every square inch of the room but the dog was nowhere to be seen. Together they ran outside, calling the pup's name. "Look, over there," he called, "scramble marks beneath the fence."

"You don't suppose he's heading to my house?"

Ryan threw up his hands. "I don't know. Could be."

"Jason said he has an obsession with the barn. Just the day before, he took off for it like a racehorse. Jason barely caught him before he launched himself onto the same pile of junk."

Ryan frowned. *What is up with the dog and that barn?* Well, one thing was for certain, Parker would do great in earthquakes because he seemed taken with the huge pile of refuse.

"Get in the jeep," Ryan yelled, already racing in that direction.

"What about Kima? She's in the house with Emajean."

"We'll come back for her later. Get in!"

She jumped inside and had barely shut the door before he began peeling out. "How much you want to bet we'll find Parker inside the barn."

She shook her head. "I don't think I'll take that bet."

* * *

Every muscle in Rick's body ached after a night spent searching in vain for a dog that could be anywhere. The market had proved a bust, so he'd fanned out from there to back alleyways that stank of rotting garbage mixed with the smells of human cohabitation with the environment. Furthermore, his voice was hoarse from having called Herc's name over and over, again to no avail. He had hoped to be the one to find Herc . . . for Ryan. After all, Rick had been the one who'd mistakenly slipped and told the wrong person about the dog. At the time, he'd thought it no big deal, but when the boom landed and the dog was carted off, he knew it was his fault. He rubbed his eyes and leaned against the pale walls of a mud-brick home, one of many that climbed the hills in a warren of haphazard structures made of mud brick or concrete. Meanwhile, night was giving way to daylight that teased its arrival by lingering just below the horizon in a halo of yellow-gold. His stomach growled and his mouth felt gritty.

He would remember this day for the rest of his life. The day he'd failed Ryan. Failed Herc. So many failures, and now the Americans were leaving. He had only hours to find Herc, get him on the plane to the UK, then seek out his own means of transport out of this god-forsaken city that he both loved and hated. He'd met so many truly amazing Afghanis, kind people who loved their families just as much he loved his wife and daughter back home. Despite all that the Afghans had been through over the years of war and the ravages it wrought, most had remained optimistic, smiled easily.

And then he'd met the Taliban, some morphing into ISIS-K fighters, their incursions and the atrocities that followed chilling his blood to think that people could be that evil. Though the CIA had never directly funded the Taliban, they *had* given money to the mujahideen to fight Russian forces, and some of those fighters had later joined the Taliban. Soon, they would take over the city and his chance to flee would be gone. He pulled a piece of jerky from his backpack and chewed on it, then washed it down with water he kept in a flask. Now, to do the impossible. To find a dog and fly out of Kabul . . . before it was too late.

* * *

Gladys hadn't been able to concentrate on her job since the moment she'd seen J. D. Beringer talking to that unnamed man outside. Something about him didn't sit right with her. Stanford had done his typical teasing, which normally put her in a good mood, but moments earlier she had snapped at him and now he sat sulking behind a computer monitor, pretending she didn't exist. For the first time since they'd teamed up, they'd had a falling out, all because of her.

She rolled her chair away from the desk and tapped her pencil on a stapler to get his attention. When he still refused to take the bait, she said, "Okay, I know I've been a sourpuss today."

"You have." He refused to look up, merely sat especially erect to show her how aggrieved he felt, shoulders back, eyebrows up.

"Look, I'll get you a Teton Mocha if we can call a truce."

"With chocolate sprinkles on top?" he asked, still refusing to face her.

"With chocolate sprinkles."

That was all it took to break the tension. He turned to her, excited now. "A secret, I have," he said, waggling his eyebrows mysteriously and training his voice so that he sounded like Yoda.

"Oh?"

"That man, the one talking to J. D.?"

"What about him?"

"Found him, I have."

Gladys was so excited that she dropped her pencil, which bounced off the stapler and went flying halfway across the

381

room.

"Watch it." Stanford once again appeared aggrieved, only with mock indignation this time. "You could take out an eye with that thing."

"Just tell me," Gladys hissed in exasperation.

"I'll do you one better," he said, then turned his computer screen her way. "Look familiar?"

It was an article about the movie mogul, Blake Fordham. Off to his right, in the background stood a big man, bald. She couldn't be sure. Then she saw the earring. "That's him," she squealed. "But what's he doing with Blake?"

"That's the head of his security detail."

"Security detail? Then what's he doing with J. D.? That man is in oil. What does that have to do with Blake?"

"Me not know," Stanford said with a shrug, once again doing his Yoda voice.

"I wonder if Tracy knows anything. I think I'll give her a call."

Forty-Three

"There! Up ahead!" Tracy shouted.

Sure enough, the little sheltie's legs were flying as it raced down the road and toward the barn, just as she had suspected. And though Ryan's truck could easily outpace the dog, they didn't want to run him over. Shelties were notorious herders and they loved nothing better than to herd cars . . . and jeeps. Better to stay back, to try to call the dog before it reached the barn and found a way inside. Fortunately, she'd left the back door closed, but the front of the barn lay open after the sale of the Studebaker. The rollers to the sliding barn door were so rusted that she'd had a hard time opening it, much less closing it, and since the weather was supposed to hold, she'd left it ajar.

"Uh-oh!" Ryan said. "There he goes, straight to the sliding door in front."

He pulled to a stop in time for Tracy to see the dog scramble over a mountain of debris, picking its way carefully across the hoarded belongings until it reached the same spot it had the first time it had entered the barn.

"What do you suppose is over there, Ryan? The dog seems to have an infatuation with that spot."

"Let's go around back again. You know the drill."

"I'll get cat food and a rope . . . Oh, that's right, my rope is in my truck and that's back at the ranch."

"I probably have one in the toolbox."

He dug around in his box as Tracy raced into the house to get the cat food. But just as she opened the front door, she ran smack-dab into Peter Flanagan, Blake's security guy.

"Looking for something?" Peter asked.

The man was a solid mass of muscle and sinew. Tracy slunk around him, unable to get over the creepy vibe he gave off. Maybe Ryan could bring back one of his men and they could send this one packing. She would speak to Ryan about it once the pup was safe.

"Just getting some cat food." She pulled a can down from the cupboard and forced back the pull tag. The smell gagged her, but she fought it down. Then she pushed past Peter, who had refused to move from the doorway. So much for chivalry.

Once outside, she made a beeline for the back door to the barn. Already, Ryan was draped over the second of two treadle sewing machines, the other one inside the house. He was talking to Parker, who seemed interested in something below. The dog kept sniffing the ground and whining. And every time Ryan tried to woo the dog out, he merely stepped out of reach, refusing all help.

"Here." Tracy rubbed some of the oily fish onto the lasso portion of the rope, then held the can out dutifully, as she had before, when they'd first found the little guy trapped amid the mountain of antique objects.

"C'mon, Parker. Come out of there," Ryan coaxed, but the dog only ducked his head and moved as far back as he could in the tightly confined space. The ground beneath him trembled slightly. Ryan turned to Tracy. "Can you start removing things carefully? I'm worried this stuff is going to collapse on him before we can get him out of here."

Tracy heard her phone jingle in her back pocket, but she had no time for phone calls now. One by one, she began lifting off boxes of junk. Now if they could just get the treadle sewing machine off the pile, they would be in business. But try as she might, the machine wouldn't budge, only further causing the ground to shift and the pup to whine.

"I know, Buddy," Ryan said. "We're trying."

"What are we going to do?" Tracy knew she could never pick up the sewing machine and its ornate cherry wood base by herself. Even with Ryan's help it would be next to impossible in these tight quarters.

Just as she was about to tell Ryan that, she heard a loud groan and screamed. "Ryan! Watch out!"

The floorboards buckled slightly, giving her a jolt that sent a wave of pain pummeling her abdomen, but she held on.

"What the heck?" Ryan called. "Hang on, Tracy. Don't move anything!"

But before she could react, she heard another loud groan and a squeal of wood giving way beneath them.

"We've got to get the heck out of here!" Ryan shouted.

But just then, the floorboards rumbled yet again beneath her feet and she braced herself. She felt the air whooshing up around her as the whole barn reverberated with a loud crash—dust and debris floating skyward, settling only slowly. Shaken to her very core, Tracy felt droplets of blood where her shin had been scraped to the bone. And her shoulder ached from a box that had become dislodged when the floor gave way and hit her full force, sending her careening further.

For several seconds, she moaned as the pain came in waves. Where was Ryan?

"Ryan? Are you alright?"

For a moment, she heard no answer, then a beleaguered, "Over here. I'm okay, just knocked the wind out of me. Where's the pup?"

It took a moment for Tracy to dislodge herself enough to peer over the debris that had fallen on and next to her, but when she looked down, her heart sank to her toes because what she was looking at wasn't a floor at all. It was a huge sinkhole, and there, at the bottom, the dog lay injured but alive.

"He's hurt!" she called to Ryan. "There's a sinkhole."

"Holy—"

"What'll we do?"

Carefully, Ryan pushed a box aside so that Tracy could see him and speak to him without having to shout. He leaned over ever so slowly and peered down into the abyss that Tracy had warned him about. Like her, his breathing was labored.

"Tracy?" he said, his words slow and purposeful.

"What?" she asked, too afraid to peer over the side for fear of falling in.

"There's a body down there."

Tracy blinked rapidly, thinking she'd heard incorrectly. She turned her head to the side and leaned briefly onto her elbow. What she saw left her breathless, for indeed, there *was* a body.

"It's Mabel, isn't it?" she said, her voice trembling, as she pulled herself down slowly for fear of causing another collapse..

"That would be my guess," Ryan agreed.

* * *

Daylight had arrived and with it the hum of activity. Everywhere Rick looked, a steady stream of people flowed like a river toward the Kabul airport. People walking, on bicycles, motorcycles, cars. Traffic jams abounded with cars honking, people shouting and Rick feeling the most alone he'd ever felt, despite the crush of humanity. Like a human pinball he bounced from one person to another. He had given it all he had. Time had done what he could not. It had forced his hand. He offered up one last prayer in hopes that he could find Herc. Out of the crowd, a lone man held up a bottle of water.

"Forty dollars, forty dollars here."

For a bottle of water? Rick scoffed.

"Hey, you, American. Forty dollars for a liter of water."

Rick wanted to belt the man for preying on the misery of others, but then he saw a woman and her kids, knee deep in sewage, moving steadily toward the airport. Saw another woman by the side of the road, her eyes wandering thirstily over the proffered water.

He knew better than to do it, but he tried to extract money from his pocket as discreetly as possible. "Give her the water," he ordered. "She needs it more than I do."

The seller frowned, then shrugged. Forty dollars was forty dollars. Rick continued on, not waiting to hear the thanks from the woman and her children. That's when he saw Herc. For a second, his heart stalled and a pain gathered somewhere near the back of his throat as he lost sight of the dog. He had no more than ten minutes left to get Herc aboard the chopper and to find his ticket out of there before the airlift ended and he was on his own. Frantic now, he raced this way and that, stumbling over people, catching sight of the dog only to have him disappear again. He had almost given up hope of reconnecting when he zagged to the left and ran almost headlong into the dog.

"Herc!" He bent down and grabbed onto the dog's muzzle, laughing, crying. He knew he must look like a madman to the Afghani who saw dogs as a nuisance, if they thought anything about them at all.

The dog had lost weight. Rick felt the mutt's ribs beneath his thin coat of brown fur. Exhausted from a night of little sleep and a swarm of emotions, Rick gathered the dog up in his arms, surprised at how willingly Herc allowed it. Then he wound his way in and out of the many lines of people, searching for a spot to get above the crowd so he could locate the British helicopter . . . *if* it was still there.

He'd almost given up on the idea that he'd ever make it out of this quagmire when he heard a whirring sound and saw an American serviceman directing the steady stream of traffic. Over the whir of blades, he raised his hand, shouting to the officer to look his way.

"I'm American," he yelled. "Army."

The guy nodded and hailed him toward him. Rick could just make out the words, "You can't take a dog aboard the plane."

"I'm not," Rick yelled back. "*He's* going to take him."

He pointed toward the British helicopter where the chopper pilot was waiting to take off. Seeing the dog, the American pilot motioned them over. The serviceman scanned Rick's papers, and then gestured toward the helicopter. Rick thanked him, then bent down, running, the wind from the bird's blades tugging at his hair and clothing. Bits of dirt stung his eyes, but he pressed forward until he reached the copter and lifted the dog up. Rick handed the pilot a note he'd had tucked in his pocket for days now. A note that explained how to reunite Herc with his former army mate, Ryan.

"Take good care of Herc!" he yelled.

"What's his name?" the pilot said, pointing at his headset.

"Herc," Rick mouthed. "Herc."

The pilot nodded, hooked the dog into the designated seat, then gave Rick the thumbs up. Tears stung Rick's eyes as he quickly backed away from the helicopter blades and watched the bird lift off with Herc on board. The wind whipped at his hair, his face, his clothes, but Rick merely saluted, grateful that on this day of misery that at least one thing had gone right.

* * *

"What are you doing?" Stanford said as he stood over Gladys, their earlier snit forgotten.

"I can't get a hold of Tracy, so I'm calling Blake. What does it look like I'm doing?" Gladys wasn't sure why her hackles were up. Maybe it was her years of living in Chicago or the fact that her father had been a detective on the force, but she had learned a thing or two from him. Always trust your gut instinct, and her gut was screaming loud and clear right now. Something about Blake's security guy wasn't right.

"Answer, answer, answer," she said through gritted teeth as she listened to the phone ring over and over again.

Gladys was just about to give up when she heard, "This is Mrs. Fordham."

"Thank goodness," Gladys said on an exhale. "I need to talk to Blake Fordham. It's important."

"My husband's busy right now," she said, no doubt used to all sorts of unwanted calls from any number of sources. "If you'd like, I can take down your number."

"Just listen to me," Gladys said, not meaning to be so forthright. "Do you have a Peter Flanagan working for you, a large bald man with a hoop earring?"

A long pause ensued.

"Are you there?" Gladys asked, afraid the woman had

hung up.

"Yes," the woman said warily. "Why do you ask?"

"Because I believe he may not be who you think he is."

"Just a minute."

Gladys could hear Blake's wife calling for him, then the sound of her handing over the phone so that the words came out muffled. Heard her say, "The woman says it's important" and a belabored, "Oh, alright," from Blake.

"Yes?" he said, picking up the phone. "How may I help you?"

Gladys explained the situation and heard the strained silence that followed.

"Do you know where Peter is now?" Gladys asked, her nerves all but shredded. No wonder her father drank coffee by the gallons.

Again a pause, but finally Blake answered. "He's at Tracy Barnhart's place."

Gladys fell back in her seat as she fought the rising nausea.

"What? What?" Stanford demanded, coming to sit on her desk, arms folded in front of him.

"Give me a sec," she told him, holding up a finger.

"Call Peter. Call him back now," she ordered. "No, nix that. I'll get the sheriff over there. And Blake . . . ?

Silence.

"You probably should go nowhere near the man." And with that, she hung up.

Forty-Four

Tracy turned in time to see Peter enter the barn. "Over here," Tracy called.

"What are you two doing in here?" Peter's head swiveled around to get a better view. "Whoa! Someone was a major hoarder." He started to step toward her.

"Don't move! There's a sinkhole. Ryan's dog fell in it, but he's alive. We need to get him out before the entire floor collapses."

"Okay," the security guard said, his eyes roving around the room for anything of use.

"We had a rope, but I think it fell in the sinkhole. And–"

"Yeah?"

"There's a body. We think it's Mabel."

The heavyset man's brown eyes narrowed and Tracy could swear that something had passed through him, an almost evil glint that made her heart stall. Maybe she was right not to have trusted him, and yet he was their only hope right now. If either of them moved, the whole place could collapse. As if the thought had occurred to him at exactly the same time, she noticed a smirk as he reached for a stack of boxes, but he wasn't looking to lighten the load. He was looking to pull the stack down on top of them.

"No!" she yelled, just as another voice cried out, but it wasn't coming from Ryan. It was coming from somewhere near the open doorway.

"Touch that box and you're dead!" the man shouted.

Tracy was just able to make out a uniform and a badge. Moments later, another man came to stand beside him, and another appeared in the doorway at the back of the building.

"We've got you surrounded. Put up your hands."

She heard a rustling of movement, sensed the ground shifting slightly and felt another stab of pain as something metal gouged her wrist. From across the way, Ryan said, "It's okay, Tracy. We'll be okay, just hang on."

She peered over at him, tears in her eyes. He reached out to her but was only able to cup her fingertips. "I love you," he whispered. "And I'm sorry . . . for everything. For not believing in you."

"Me, too." She laughed, but the sound came out garbled through the tears.

From behind her she heard Peter scrambling to make his escape, but the officers blocked the exits. Still, he struggled, shoving one down while throwing a grappling hook at another, narrowly missing his head when the officer ducked.

Though Peter fought hard to grab the older officer's pistol, the younger one managed to trip him before he could take it from the older man. Once he was down, the officer cuffed him.

"We've got him!" he yelled.

He and the older man marched the security guard to the squad car while the other officer, who had entered at the rear, shouted, "Hang on! The fire department is on its way. It should be here any moment. We'll get you out of here, I promise."

Tracy lay perfectly still. Though terrified, Tracy wanted to savor this moment, tragic as it was.

"We've got a sinkhole," Ryan yelled to the officer, "and a dog in the sinkhole. Plus . . ." He looked to Tracy. "This is your story to tell."

"We think we found Mabel," Tracy called. "Mabel Grayson."

* * *

It took several hours before the fire department was able to wedge Tracy and Ryan out of the pile in the barn and to collect the dog. And Mabel. At last, the contents of the barn lay scattered about the building, a testament to another time, another life. The rest of that day, one person after another stopped in to extend their services, to bring food, and to offer advice. Kate had promised to keep Kima for the night. Tomorrow, Tracy, Ryan, and Kima would go speak to Lindsay and her husband, to tell them about Mabel and to ask about the wolf they'd shot.

When Tracy and Ryan were finally alone that night, he came up behind her as she stood on the porch and cradled her in his arms. Together, they stared up at the moon, crystalline stars dotting the night sky. He nestled his chin in the crevice of her shoulder. It was as if that place had been designed especially for him. She closed her eyes, breathing in the nighttime scents. Somewhere in the distance, a wolf howled.

She opened her eyes and turned. "Do you think that could be Esa? That she's still alive?"

"I don't know," he said, "but there's only one way to find out."

"So you'll come with me to the Mitchell's place tomorrow?" she asked, her eyes seeking out his in the moonlight.

"Of course. If you want me to."

"I do."

"But Tracy?"

"Hmm?" she said, taken by the moment.

"We still don't know for sure who killed Mabel."

It was a thought that had occurred to Tracy while waiting to be rescued. Just then she saw a faint glow appear from around the side of the house and froze. "Do you see them?" she whispered, goosebumps playing up her arms.

Ryan turned, and she felt, rather than heard, his answer as he jolted slightly.

"It's Grayson."

"And his dog."

Somehow it only seemed fitting that they would be here,

by the light of the moon, to honor Mabel, who had finally come home to rest.

* * *

Tracy awoke, sore but glad to be alive. The coroner had collected Mabel's body and planned a forensic autopsy to determine the woman's death. The autopsy was scheduled for today, while the police had taken Peter and J. D. Beringer in for questioning. First thing that morning, Tracy called Gladys and Stanford to thank them for their quick thinking. Then she called Jason to ask him to guard the farmhouse. Kima decided to stay and help him, preferring not to see the deceased wolf if indeed it was Esa.

Now, as Tracy stood at the threshold of her home, Ryan gave her a long lingering kiss, one that set her toes tingling. Reluctantly, she pulled away. There would be time for more of that, later.

"Let's go find out about that she-wolf," Ryan said, tapping her on the nose.

Twenty minutes later, the Mitchell's ranch came into view. It stood at the end of a long gravel driveway that twisted and curved past pens of sheep and cattle. The stone structure belonged in another era, when pioneers built houses to last. In the window stood Gabe, just as he had before, but this time he appeared resigned as they marched up the steps to the front door. Gabe opened it, not exactly welcoming them in as she might have expected.

The interior was decidedly more modern than the

exterior of the home, its walls white with a white-veined marble floor-to-ceiling fireplace. The sofa was of pale wheat and two cow-hide chairs faced it, a glass coffee table between the sofa and the chairs. Wooden beams framed the high ceilings in the open plan living area and kitchen. But what drew her attention most was the utter look of defeat on Gabe's face.

"Is Lindsay here?" Tracy asked.

Gabe merely shook his head.

"Oh." Disappointment caused her to reassess her approach. Might as well spit it out. "Did you hear about Mabel?"

His blue-gray eyes registered fear. "When?"

"Yesterday. In the barn. That's part of the reason I'm here, to speak to Lindsay. That and I know what happened, but I wanted to discuss it with her first. Maybe she can fill me in."

"It wasn't her fault," he pleaded, his eyes filled with grief. "You have to understand, we stood to lose everything." Gabe began pacing, all the while running his hands through his hair.

What wasn't Lindsay's fault? Tracy realized she'd forgotten to mention the dead wolf. No wonder he had no idea what she was talking about.

"If word got out that there were sinkholes, and that my oil company had caused them, we would have been ruined."

A chill crept up Tracy's neck and she could see that Ryan was also confused and alarmed.

"She just went to talk to Mabel. That's all. She didn't mean to threaten her—just to tell our side of the story. To beg her to stop poking her nose into things that could have destroyed us. Don't you see?" He quit pacing and turned to her, hands outstretched. "You have to believe me, it was an accident. Lindsay was trying to explain, but Mabel got scared, ran to the barn. My wife tried to tell Mabel that she wouldn't hurt her, but Mabel wouldn't listen. She climbed up on a stack of stuff."

"And it collapsed," Tracy finished for him, her heart notching up a beat.

"And it collapsed," he echoed. "A sinkhole. If she'd told anyone about what happened . . . we would have lost the farm, my livelihood, everything we had worked for our entire lives." His shoulders slumped in defeat as he sank into one of the brown and white cowhide chairs. "This was my grandfather's farm, passed down to my father and then to me. I couldn't be the one to lose it."

"So you told no one . . ."

He shook his head.

"And you've lived with the guilt all these years."

His face crumbled, his mouth trembling as he struggled through the sobs that he had held in for so long. He sat like that for many minutes. Finally, he lifted his head, tears streaking his cheeks. "You've got to understand. I love Lindsay. I've always loved her. If I lose her, I don't know how I'll go on."

Never had she heard such misery in a man's voice. Just then, the door opened and in walked Lindsay, her mouth falling open when she saw her husband's face. She rushed to him and fell to her knees before him, running her fingers through the edges of his raven colored hair.

"It's okay," she murmured. "We knew this day would come." Then she peered up at Tracy and Ryan, her eyes pleading. "You understand, don't you? What a person would do for love?"

Tracy shared a glance with Ryan, and in that moment, she knew that she would do the same for the man she loved. They had what they wanted, to know what had happened to Mabel. The real culprits behind bars. Sending Lindsay to jail at this late date would do no one any good now. Tracy asked to speak with Ryan privately in the kitchen.

Once they were alone, she posed the question that at its heart spoke of the trust they shared. "What do you think?" she whispered. "They're good people, decent people, and in the end it was an accident."

"But what if there are other sinkholes out there? What if another person dies because of the drilling?"

Tracy pondered what he'd said. "We should at least find out for sure that it *is* the oil causing it."

Ryan concurred.

"Okay, then." She and Ryan returned to the living room. "Ryan and I have spoken to each other. Why don't we make sure the drilling is actually what's causing the sinkholes before we do anything rash. Agreed?"

Gabe and Lindsay shared their relief in a lingering gaze. "Thank you," Lindsay said.

"I can't promise that things will turn out like you want them to, but at least we should make sure that we're doing the right thing, whatever the outcome."

Tracy was about to leave when she remembered why she'd come. "I need to ask you one thing. The wolf you shot—was it a purebred wolf, or a dog-wolf mix?"

Once again Gabe and Lindsay shared a glance. "A wolf, why do you ask?"

"Can I see it?"

Lindsay rose to her feet, giving Gabe's hand once last squeeze. "This way." She took them out the side door to the deck out back, and down the steps to the stalls. Behind the stone barn, she led them to a small shed. Beside it lay the wolf.

Tracy swayed at the sight, Ryan reaching in to shore her up. "It's not Esa," she said once she was able to catch her breath. "Kima will be so glad to hear that."

"Kima?" Lindsay asked.

"I'll explain later." For now she needed to find out what was causing those sinkholes. To finish the job that Mabel had started.

* * *

The sheriff was waiting for them on the porch when Tracy and Ryan returned to the farmhouse, an entire contingent of men sifting through the carnage of years of hoarded objects in the barn. One by one, they were pulling every single object out of the cavernous interior and categorizing it. At least it would save her having to go to all that trouble. Once she'd gone through what she wanted, she could have an estate sale for the rest. Maybe it would help pay for her futile search for Herc.

"That guard?" the sheriff said as they exited the truck. "He *was* working for the oil company."

"Which one?"

"Not Gabe's, if that's what you want to know. A consortium of oil companies that weren't thrilled that Mabel was prying into their business. They were afraid you and Blake might open up a can of worms that they wanted to keep hidden, especially after that fiasco on the reservation. Cost them millions. But the worst of it came out in the end as by now you probably know."

"You mean bilking the reservation of their share of profits for the oil deposits?"

The sheriff nodded.

"And Hank?"

"He'd been hired by the consortium to keep an eye on you and to report to Peter and J. D. Beringer, the man who owned the ranch with the tainted hay. Beringer apparently used a code name when speaking with Hank and Peter."

"Oh?" Tracy waited, scarcely breathing.

"Derrick." The sheriff laughed at the irony.

It all made sense now. She leaned against the railing, thoughts drifting to Mabel. "Have they found out if Mabel was the one in the sinkhole and how she died?"

"We did," the sheriff said. "Blake came in and offered up his DNA. It was a match. Only a grandchild would have that many DNA markers. As to her death, she died instantly, from what the coroner could ascertain. From the fall and the weight of the items that buried her."

"No foul play?" Tracy asked.

"Not that we could find," the sheriff said, removing his cap and swiping at the moisture on his brow.

Good. It would make Tracy's decision easier. It had been an accident, after all. Lindsay and Gabe had suffered enough. Just then, one of the men leading the perusal of the items in the barn yelled, "Sheriff, Miss Barnhardt, over here."

By now, the barn was nearly empty, only a few stacks remaining. Alone, this would have taken weeks, months, if not years to complete. She thanked the officer for the effort his men had put into tearing out the contents of the barn.

The spot where the sinkhole had formed was now fully visible. "Take a look," he said, "but watch your step."

He had them all kneel down next to the crater and pointed. To her amazement, this was no sinkhole. "What is it?" she asked.

"See those beams and the chisel marks, the way the shaft goes clear back into the wall that runs alongside the river?"

Ryan bent down and frowned. "He's right. Is this a mine shaft?"

"Best guess is that it was a gold mine. That's the reason the entire floor of the barn didn't give way. This area was known for mines. But after all this time, many of the shafts from back in the late 1800s were closed up, the maps of where they're located gone. I'd say you've got yourself a goldmine down there." The officer laughed at his pun.

"Do you suppose there's any gold left in there?" Tracy asked, dusting off her hands and standing.

"I doubt it," the officer said. "That's why they abandoned the mines, because they weren't producing, but I suppose anything's possible."

"So what do I do now?" she asked.

"To be safe, the shaft should be refilled and closed up for good. My bet is that the opening comes out somewhere along the riverbank, but it's probably covered up by brambles and debris."

All she could see were more dollar signs heading out instead of in. She was sinking fast. "Ryan?" she said, hoping that he had an idea.

"We have a foundation specialist in town. It'll cost a pretty penny though to seal that off."

Tracy balled her fists and sighed. The farmhouse was quickly becoming a money pit.

Just then, Kima raced in out of breath. "Kate brought me over in her pickup," she explained. "What's going on?" Kima asked, seeing the barn clear of the thousands of possessions, and a narrow shaft under the barn that could swallow someone whole if they didn't do something about it.

"We'll tell you later," Tracy said, "but for now we've learned that Esa wasn't the wolf killed."

Kima flipped a circle and said something in Shoshone, a prayer of gratitude, no doubt.

Over the course of the next half hour, Tracy gave Kima and Kate the lowdown on everything that had happened in the past twenty-four hours. When the officer was preparing to leave, she walked him out onto the farmhouse porch.

"What will they do with Mabel's body?" Tracy asked.

"That's up to Blake," the sheriff responded.

But even as he said it, she knew what needed to be done.

She waited until the sheriff had left, then called Blake.

"Mabel needs to come home," she said, surprised when Blake readily agreed. "To be placed beside Grayson and his dog."

"You're right. We can hold a ceremony . . . finally."

Tracy longed to tell Blake what she had learned, but she didn't want to jeopardize Lindsay's newfound peace, after all these years. Truth is, Mabel had been barking up the wrong tree about the sinkhole, though she had scored a ten when it came to finding out about the rez being bilked. Besides, the accident could have happened anywhere on the property during a wet spell. Tracy wished she'd had the opportunity to know Mabel. She had a feeling she would have liked her. Despite the events of the past few days, her heart was full by the time she ascended the stairs and entered the room Mabel and Grayson had once shared. She dressed for bed and had pulled back the pink and white chenille bedspread when she decided to check her email one last time. Might as well get the bad news over with.

And there it was. All it said in the headline was Herc.

Herc. Failure wore at her like a second suit. At least she had tried. Ryan couldn't fault her for that. But when she opened her email, to her surprise and amazement she read the words:

Herc is in Germany under quarantine. He will be on his way home in two week's time. He was supposed to go to England, but when the Englishman who rescues military dogs heard you were searching for Herc, he sent him to Germany for quarantine so he could be sent straight to America once he's been cleared. Herc is coming home.

Tears moistened Tracy's eyes causing the words to blur. Herc was coming home. She wanted to dance, to scream, to go tell Ryan that his dog was coming home, but she couldn't. She didn't want to spoil the surprise. Instead she said a quick prayer of thankfulness, her prayers finally answered.

Forty-Five

It had taken two weeks to set up, but the estate sale went amazingly well, netting Tracy nearly ten thousand dollars in the process. She put her feet up on a stool she had placed on the porch for just that purpose. Every ounce of her ached from lifting, hauling, sorting, and taking whatever was left to either Goodwill or the dump. Yet she couldn't rest on her laurels. Tomorrow half the town would be there for Mabel's celebration of life. Already people had streamed in to bring supplies, Lindsay and Gabe painting the cemetery fence and planting flowers around it as penance. They'd also catered the celebration and had hauled in folding chairs, while others had brought in platters of meats and cheeses, cookies and cakes to add to the mix. Still others had brought fruit and vegetable trays.

The air's crispness hinted at the coming fall, and

blackberries that bordered the river lent a sweetness to the air that reminded Tracy the seasons were changing. She would need to pull out her winter wardrobe, purchase new clothes for the harsher winters she could expect in this new climate. Still, she wouldn't trade her new home for the world.

Ryan came up behind her and laid his arm over her shoulder, reeling her into a warm embrace. The memorial would take place around noon, after which she had a surprise, courtesy of Wyatt, who had learned what Tracy had done through Kate. He offered to pick up Herc at the airport. Excitement zinged through her, and despite her exhaustion, she felt like jumping up and dancing.

"You're awfully quiet," Ryan said, leaning down and giving her a kiss.

"It's been a big day," she said, winking at Kima who she'd let in on her plans.

"What's all that about?" Ryan asked. "Nevermind," he said, thrusting his hands in the air. "It's probably girl stuff."

Kima, who rarely smiled, lit up like a Christmas tree, but all she said was, "Yep."

* * *

Though Tracy had never known Mabel, she wept as they lay her to rest beside Grayson and his dog, Weber. Blake had commissioned a headstone that told part of Mabel's story, about her death in the gold mine shaft. And Emajean had been allowed the purification ceremony to guide the trio–Mabel, Grayson, and Weber–into the afterlife at long last. On

407

this clear, sunswept day, nearly half the town, it seemed, had shown up to see Mabel off. Tracy couldn't have wished for anything more.

"Mabel was pure gold," Blake said as they interred her into the soft soil alongside the riverbank. "She would have loved knowing you all came to say goodbye to her."

Tracy had picked a spray of flowers from her garden, a variety of pink roses and baby's breath, ferns for the greenery. With it, she had placed the porcelain sheltie that she'd spotted on her first day there and Mabel's husband's cane that she'd found among his belongings to be interred along with her casket. That way she'd have a memento of her life here on earth, of the man and dog who had meant so much to her.

For his part, Ryan had brought over the sculpture of the sheltie and placed it in Tracy's garden, its dog tags a reminder of his lost dog, Herc. Today of all days, that was especially poignant.

Later, they went inside and each person honored Mabel in some way by offering up small memories that made Tracy smile through the tears. She didn't know why Mabel's life had touched her so. Just knowing that Grayson and his dog had been unable to move on without her made her come alive in Tracy's mind. Would anyone remember her in the same way? She doubted it. Still, it heartened her to know that someone like Mabel had existed.

She checked her watch. The news would start soon and Wyatt should be here any minute. She hoped the last of the guests would be gone by the time he arrived. She'd asked Wyatt to park around the left side of the house to avoid any chance of Ryan seeing him ahead of time.

"How soon is Wyatt supposed to be here?" Tracy asked
Kate as she plopped down heavily into one of the brocade
chairs next to the fireplace.

"Any minute," Kate said. "Oh, there he is now!"

She stood, but when Tracy heard Ryan shut off the water
to the kitchen sink, where he was busily cleaning up with a
woman who lived nearby–Marge somebody or other–Tracy
urged Kate to sit and act natural.

Marge came through and bid a hasty farewell–something
about a problem back home, a cow that had gone missing
from the pasture. Tracy thanked her, then hurriedly took a
seat. She'd been waiting for this moment for a very long time.

* * *

Soon, the last of Mabel's friends and loved ones had left,
all except Kate, who was seated next to Tracy in the living
room. Ryan, who'd been helping clear away the last of the
dishes in the kitchen, ambled into the small living room and
looked around with a frown, glad to finally have a chance to
rest after such a busy day.

"Where's Wyatt?" Ryan asked, peering out the large
living room window. "I had expected to see him here today.
Couldn't he make it?"

Kate shared an uneasy glance with Tracy, who casually
clicked on the evening news.

"Up next. A heartwarming story of a military dog, soon
to be reunited with his owner."

Ryan heard the words, but they didn't register.

"Have a seat next to me," Tracy said, scooting over just enough so that he could sit.

"What's up, ladies?"

Neither of the women answered.

"Would someone like to tell me what's going on?" he repeated, the heat in his cheeks cranking up a notch.

"You'll see," Kate said mysteriously.

The commercials seemed to drag on, only adding to the drama. Whatever their game, he wasn't playing. It had been a long day and he was ready to call it good. He stood, but Tracy held tight to his hand.

That's when he saw it . . . or rather him. A dog. But not just any dog.

"Is that Herc?" His skin tingled and he thought he might lose it, right then and there. "My God, that *is* Herc." And Wyatt, too. He turned to Tracy who smiled, tears lacing the tips of her eyelashes. He watched the rest of the news segment, ending with a serviceman ceremoniously giving Wyatt a flag to give to the dog's owner . . . to thank him for his service. Moisture filled Ryan's eyes. He watched until they went to commercial, then he jumped to his feet and whooped, throwing an imaginary hat into the air.

Just then, he heard footsteps coming up the porch and the scratch of nails on wood. He paused, listening. The door opened, and before he could let out a yell, Herc came leaping into his arms, knocking him to the floor, tail wagging and body flailing, his whines of homecoming bringing everyone to their feet.

"Herc! Herc!" he called. "It's you. How?"

He peered up at Wyatt.

"Don't look at me," Wyatt said. "You have that lady to thank."

He pointed to Tracy, who merely stood there, tears streaming down her cheeks.

"But I don't understand."

Then it hit him with a thunder clap. All the times she'd tried to hide the computer from him. He'd thought she was seeing someone else. Emailing someone else. Instead, despite all the work she had to do to get the farmhouse up and running, along with her practice, she had spent time and energy searching for his dog—so that he wouldn't suffer a lifetime of guilt, the sentence she had been given with the loss of her horse.

"How can I ever repay you?"

"Look at all you've done for me!" she said, holding her arms out to encompass the entire house and the surrounding landscape. "You deserve this and more."

Gently, he pulled his dog off of his lap and stood, taking her in his arms. In the pandemonium, he'd forgotten all about Wyatt. He turned to thank him, but the former vet was already outside, mounting the flag to the front stanchion of the house.

* * *

Tracy lifted her face to meet Ryan's. His coffee brown eyes said it all. She saw a love reflected that she hadn't allowed herself to acknowledge before now, believing she didn't

411

deserve it, as if by the very virtue of birth she'd been damned to live a life alone. How had she come to believe such a perverse thing as that?

The sun was setting on the horizon, basking the mountains in a hazy auburn glow that made them appear as if they were on fire. "Let's go for a walk. Take Herc. Introduce him to Mabel and Grayson . . . and Weber."

Ryan dipped his head, then shrugged his shoulders. "Why not?"

They gathered Herc's leash from Wyatt.

"We'll be back in a bit."

"We really need to get going," Wyatt said, "but congratulations, man." He patted Ryan on the back. "You've been talking about that dog forever. Now we have a new addition on the ranch," he added, "unless, of course, you plan to stay here." He let the words linger as he pulled Kate to her feet and helped her into her jacket. He paused at the front threshold, then winked.

Tracy didn't begin breathing again until she heard their motor start. She reached down and scratched Herc behind his ears. Truth is, she wanted it all–marriage, commitment, the works. She had a feeling Ryan wanted that too, though she knew it was too soon to discuss anything that personal. Yet, she felt certain that would come, in time. By then, she'd be ready.

"You want to go for a walk with us?" Tracy asked Kima, grateful when the girl said no, realizing, no doubt, that they needed time alone together.

Ten minutes later, with Ryan at her side, Tracy arrived at

the small family cemetery and came to a halt in front of the three gravesites–Mabel's, Grayson's, and his dog, Weber.

"Do you think Grayson will finally be able to rest now?"

"I think we've seen the last of him."

Ryan squeezed her hand, as if feeling the same melancholy as she did, knowing that they would never see the pair again. For several minutes, they stood silently staring at the three sites, together again for the first time in years. That's when Herc did something odd, something that had Tracy lifting her chin to Ryan in question. He laid his head down on Weber's grave and whined. And as if in response, they heard an echoing whine that sent a chill racing up Tracy's spine. A goodbye, Tracy felt certain.

Although they never saw the pair again, Tracy could almost imagine the three out for a walk at dusk, just as she, Ryan, and the dog did every evening from that day forward. Every time she pictured it, she smiled.

Epilogue

Winter had come and gone from the valley. And spring
had arrived, first with the daffodils, and later with the tulips,
which thankfully Tracy had planted in the early fall. Now
summer loomed on the horizon, and Yellowstone had finally
reopened for visitors. Tracy had long heard about the buffalo
and bison, bear and antelope. The wolves. But she had yet
to see it for herself, so on a somewhat warm day in mid-May,
Ryan packed up his truck, Kima on one side, Tracy in the
middle—one of the rare times the two dogs, Herc and Parker,
had been left behind.

As they drove the miles toward Yellowstone, Tracy could
almost imagine Chief Joseph and the Nez Perce on their flight
from Yellowstone to the Absarokas in their attempt at asylum
in Canada. In the warmth of the cab, she peered out at the
jagged, snow-capped peak and marveled that so many had

survived the long trek through harsh cold and heat.

Ryan pulled her to him and gave her shoulder a squeeze. So much had happened since she'd met him almost a year ago. Peter Flanagan had gone to prison for attempted assault, but not before Blake had fired him and had filed a restraining order, encouraging Ryan and Tracy to do the same. J. D. Beringer had been given a slap on the wrist and released. But first, he was required to pay back Blake for the loss of his cattle. They'd also been warned that if they ever so much as looked cross-eyed at any of those involved in the investigation, they would be jailed and this time the sheriff would throw away the key.

In early spring, Kima had been the one to locate the opening to the mine, covered in a thick layer of bramble. The vines and brush had been torn away during an especially heavy rain to reveal a soggy and crumbling vertical mine shaft. Then just as the spring flowers began to bloom in earnest, Tracy and Ryan had married. Tracy smiled, remembering. They'd cleared out the barn in case the weather turned bad and then set up hay bales around the perimeter. Ryan had built a stand for the country band he had formed. Along a series of tables placed end to end on the opposite side of the barn, they'd offered food and drinks, and of course a cake, which Emajean had made for the occasion, complete with Native American touches. Kima had acted as Maid of Honor.

Tracy laid her head on Ryan's shoulder, recalling that magical night when they had danced the night away, Tracy and Ryan proposing the first dance. The entire barn had been strung with lights—Kate's addition. As her gift to Tracy and Ryan, she told them her grandmother's "A Thousand Bits of Wonderful" story . . . about finding the right man. How it was like the night sky, the lights representing the stars. "Though there might be a million stars in the sky," she'd said, "when you find the right one, you've been blessed with *your* thousand bits of wonderful." And Tracy supposed she had been blessed. On top of all that, she had inherited not only Herc, but Parker, the search and rescue puppy. Because of his injuries, the dog could no longer work in search and rescue, but he had been amazing for Ryan's PTSD, just as Herc was. On top of it all, he was the grandson of Grayson's dog. That made it all the better.

The search and rescue dogs were nearly halfway through their training. Then they would go to places across the country. All except one. The park ranger at Yellowstone had asked if they would train one to scout wolf scat so they could monitor their health and movements. Tracy did it by building a platform with multiple holes drilled out. Set into the holes, she'd placed jars filled with different animal feces, the dog receiving a treat when it correctly identified wolf droppings.

As if reading her thoughts, Kima asked, "Do you think we'll ever find Esa?"

Tracy shrugged. "Who knows, maybe once the dog is through with his training we can send him on a scouting run."

Kima only nodded, her eyes on the vista of jagged peaks and fir trees as if she could somehow devine the animal's whereabouts.

Changing the subject, Ryan said, "Did Blake ever get his

amusement park approved?"

"I spoke to him yesterday. He just broke ground." The place he'd imagined all those months ago coming to life, only this time, instead of a virtual 3D hologram of his dream, he would have the real life thing. And in the end, he had scrapped the story about Mabel, preferring to remember her as she was–a wonderful woman who had loved her family.

Ryan reached down and kissed Tracy, just as thrilled as Tracy herself to be there amid the wildlife and towering mountains that caressed the sky. A canvas that needed no airbrushing. Now, as they drove through Yellowstone, past a lumbering bear, on a road bordered by bison, she really did believe she'd found what she was looking for in this man. They shared a glance filled with love and laughter.

"Look," Ryan exclaimed, as excited as if he were seeing it for the first time, "Old Faithful!"

They found a parking spot and climbed out to watch the magnificent spray amid the bubbling cauldrons of boiling water, a thin layer of snow still littering the ground. All around, bison roamed. And in the distance, a wolf howled.

"Did you hear that?" Kima said, her eyes misting at the loss of her wolf, the sound filling her with emotion.

Tracy nodded. The wolf's cry sent a shiver through her. They stood like that for a long time. Then, as they were preparing to leave, Tracy heard another howl, closer now, just at the tree-lined perimeter. "Oh my– Look, Kima!" she whispered.

And there, just at the edge of the trees, a female wolf emerged from the shadows, two cubs at her side. Something wasn't quite right about the wolf though. Tracy lifted the binoculars that she kept on a strap at her neck. Sure enough.

"Take a look!" She lifted the binoculars over her head to give to Kima.

Kima held up the binoculars, then lowered them slowly. For a long time, Kima didn't speak. Then, in a high-pitched cree, she spoke in Shoshone, ending her words with a tilt upwards as though to carry her words on the wind.

"What did you say to her?" Tracy asked, rubbing her arms of the goosebumps that played up them.

"I said, 'It is well, my sister. It is well.'"

About the Author

Author **Carol L. Craig** has published five books besides
A Walk in the Dark:

A Thousand Bits of Wonderful (Romance from the
Mending Warrior Series)
Dancing the Loom *(Fantasy* from *The Tapestry Series)*
Threading the Loom *(Fantasy* from *The Tapestry Series)*
The Vast In Between (Historical Women's Fiction)
The Great Unraveling (Historical Women's Fiction)

For over twenty years she has had the pleasure of editing a long
list of traditionally published authors for Editing Gallery, LLC.
She has been a guest speaker for Women Writing the West in
Tucson, Arizona, has given one-on-one editing sessions at the
Willamette Writers Conference. She has helped new writers get
their start. And, she has spent many happy hours with friends at
Colonyhouse, a writer's retreat in Oregon.
While at home in Oregon, she enjoys writing, reading, garden-
ing and editing as well as coffee klatches with her husband and
dog, Parker.

Be Sure To Sign Up For Her Newsletter At
www.editinggallery.com to read articles from writers, editors,
artists, filmmakers, book cover designers, interior book cover
designs, professional bloggers, as well as those in marketing.

You Can Find Carol At
www.editinggallery.com
Facebook: facebook.com/EditingGallery1
Instagram: @clcraig7
LinkedIn: https://www.linkedin.com/in/carol-craig-b33a2b263/

Acknowledgments

Thanks go to all the authors and friends who have helped guide me and make me a better writer, who have gently nudged and encouraged me. As New York bestselling author, Jane Kirkpatrick, reminded me recently, we writers have to stick together, so thank you, Jane, for being there for me. And Carmen Peone, I can't tell you how much it means that you shared your books with me and entrusted me with your review. Moreover, your genuine kindness reminds me of the good in mankind. Candy Calvert, you took time out of your busy life (and your garden!) to not only read my book, but to offer suggestions and find what my tired eyes couldn't. Evan Howard, both client and friend, you made a huge contribution to my overall growth as a writer. Thank you so much! Karen Hall, you wrote such kind words about my book. I can't thank you enough. And to an agent who will go unnamed, but who has contributed to my life in untold ways, you are a true gem.

I also want to thank the many people who have helped me over the years. Special thanks to Valerie Brooks, the den mother to all writers within her sphere, and to Patsy Hand and Chris Scofield, part of my writing circle for many years. Laine Stambaugh, former librarian for the U of O for her mounds of literature on writing and the many books she has shared with me over the years. Elaine Stek, a truly kind and caring person who is like a sister to me and a great writer in her own right.

I can't thank Amanda enough for her help in marketing

Dancing the Loom. As well as Jenna for her adorable pictures of my previous book with Koda the Fluff, or as I call him, Koda the Wonderdog. He would make the perfect advocate for my book about dogs . . . just saying!

To my real sisters, both living and passed, Anne, Barbara, Sue, and Tanya, all who have been supportive over the years and who have helped me in untold ways—bless you. And my brothers, as well, Robert and Scott. You rock! While alive, my parents supported me in my journey and I will always appreciate that. And of course, I would be remiss if I didn't include the person (and dog) who inspired this journey, my husband, Les and my dog, Parker. Lastly, to my daughter, Sara, and granddaughter, Kaylee, who keep me buoyed and make life a joy. Humor is their middle name.

Oh! And I can't forget Joe, the UPS driver, who stopped me on the street to ask what happened to Ian (a character in *A Thousand Bits of Wonderful*). What *did* happen to Ian...? Hmm....

www.ingramcontent.com/pod-product-compliance
Lightning Source LLC
Chambersburg PA
CBHW011936210726
48290CB00011BA/2719